MARK TWAIN

HUCK FINN
AND TOM SAWYER
AMONG THE INDIANS

AND OTHER UNFINISHED STORIES

THE MARK TWAIN LIBRARY

The Library offers for the first time popular editions of Mark Twain's best works just as he wanted them to be read. These moderately priced volumes, faithfully reproduced from the California scholarly editions and printed on acid-free paper, are expertly annotated and include all the original illustrations that Mark Twain commissioned and enjoyed.

"Huck waited for no particulars. He sprang away
and sped down the hill as fast as his
legs could carry him."

—THE ADVENTURES OF TOM SAWYER

Mark Twain at the Hannibal train station in June 1902.

MARK TWAIN

HUCK FINN
AND TOM SAWYER
AMONG THE INDIANS

AND OTHER UNFINISHED STORIES

Foreword and Notes by
Dahlia Armon and Walter Blair

Texts established by
Dahlia Armon, Paul Baender, Walter Blair,
William M. Gibson, and Franklin R. Rogers

A publication of the
Mark Twain Project of The Bancroft Library

University of California Press

Berkeley   Los Angeles   London

This Mark Twain Library volume reprints ten of Mark Twain's works as they were published in four volumes of the Mark Twain Papers and Works of Mark Twain: *Satires & Burlesques* (1967), ed. Franklin R. Rogers; *Hannibal, Huck & Tom* (1969), ed. Walter Blair; *Mysterious Stranger Manuscripts* (1969), ed. William M. Gibson; and *The Adventures of Tom Sawyer; Tom Sawyer Abroad; Tom Sawyer, Detective* (1980), ed. John C. Gerber, Paul Baender, and Terry Firkins. All but the first of these editions were endorsed by the Center for Editions of American Authors (CEAA) or its successor, the Committee on Scholarly Editions (CSE). The selection reprinted from *Satires & Burlesques* has been re-edited in accord with standards set by the CSE, and errors since identified in the other texts have been corrected in this reprinting and are recorded in the note on the text. An eleventh work, "Letter to William Bowen," has not yet appeared in the Papers and Works and has here been edited from the original manuscript in, and with the consent of, the Harry Ransom Humanities Research Center at the University of Texas at Austin. Newly typeset matter has been proofread in accord with CSE standards.

University of California Press
Berkeley and Los Angeles
University of California Press, Ltd.
London

Manufactured in the United States of America.
1 2 3 4 5 6 7 8 9 0

The Mark Twain Library is designed by Steve Renick.

Editorial work on this volume has been supported by grants from the National Endowment for the Humanities, an independent federal agency, to the Mark Twain Project in The Bancroft Library, University of California, Berkeley. Those grants included funding conditional on its being matched dollar for dollar, which was done by the William Randolph Hearst Foundation and other donors to The Friends of The Bancroft Library. Mark Twain's works in, and all his words quoted from unpublished sources in the annotation for, *Huck Finn and Tom Sawyer among the Indians, and Other Unfinished Stories*, are © 1938, 1942, 1967, 1969, and 1989 by Edward J. Willi and Manufacturers Hanover Trust Company as trustees of the Mark Twain Foundation, which reserves all reproduction or dramatization rights in every medium. Editorial foreword, explanatory notes, biographical directory, and note on the text are © 1989 by The Regents of the University of California.

Library of Congress Cataloging-in-Publication Data
Twain, Mark, 1835–1910.
[Short stories. Selections.]
Huck Finn and Tom Sawyer among the Indians and other unfinished stories / Mark Twain; foreword and notes by Dahlia Armon and Walter Blair; texts established by Dahlia Armon . . . [et al.].
p. cm. — (Mark Twain library)
ISBN 0-520-05090-8 (alk. paper).
ISBN 0-520-05110-6 (pbk.)
I. Armon, Dahlia. II. Blair, Walter, 1900– . III. Title. IV. Series: Twain, Mark, 1835–1910. Mark Twain Library.
PS1302.A7 1989
813'.4—dc19
88-27894
CIP

The texts reprinted in this Mark Twain Library volume,
Huck Finn and Tom Sawyer among the Indians,
and Other Unfinished Stories,
are drawn from four volumes of the Mark Twain Project's comprehensive edition of
The Mark Twain Papers and Works of Mark Twain,
and from one original manuscript at the Harry Ransom Humanities Research Center
at the University of Texas, Austin. Editorial work for this volume has
been supported by a generous donation from the

WILLIAM RANDOLPH HEARST FOUNDATION

and by matching funds from the
NATIONAL ENDOWMENT FOR THE HUMANITIES,
an independent federal agency.

Without such generous support, these editions could
not have been produced.

CONTENTS

FOREWORD

In one of his 1887 notebooks Mark Twain enunciated his fundamental literary tenet:

> If you attempt to create & build a wholly imaginary incident, adventure or situation, you will go astray, & the artificiality of the thing will be detectable. But if you found on a *fact* in your personal experience, it is an acorn, a root, & every created adornment that grows up out of it & spreads its foliage & blossoms to the sun will seem realities, not inventions. You will not be likely to go astray; your compass of fact is there to keep you on the right course. (*N&J3*, 343)

The works reprinted in this volume, all written between 1868 and 1902, demonstrate Mark Twain's reliance on what has come to be known as the Matter of Hannibal—the "realities, not inventions" of his early life in Missouri, which inspired much of his best-known work.

The three nonfiction pieces provide particularly direct evidence of Mark Twain's dependence on this "compass of fact." "Letter to William Bowen" (1870) evokes the escapades, pleasures, and occasional terrors of boyhood, recalling events that would eventually be put to use in *Tom Sawyer* (1876) and *Huckleberry Finn* (1885). "Jane Lampton Clemens" (1890) is the only one of the nonfiction pieces that Mark Twain wrote with publication in mind—although, for reasons unknown, he never did publish it. A loving biographical tribute to his mother, and a sharply focused portrait of Hannibal as a small, slave-holding community, it also affords striking insights into the mature author's values and social attitudes. The most intriguing of the factual works, however, is "Villagers of 1840–3," published here in its entirety for the first time. This extended series of notes about life in antebellum Hannibal contains over one hundred capsule biographies of the town's residents, including Mark Twain's own family. Written in 1897, forty-four years after Samuel Clemens left his boyhood home, it is a remarkable feat of memory, compelling both as a historical and a literary document. Evidently Mark Twain intended to use it as a master list of possible characters for any subsequent stories he might set in St. Petersburg or Dawson's Landing, his imaginary re-creations of Hannibal.

Of the eight stories reprinted here, only the earliest, "Boy's Manuscript" (1868), was ever completed. This diary of the school days, pastimes, and lovesick torments of a young boy is clearly the embryo of *Tom Sawyer*, which Mark Twain began writing several years later. The unfinished state of the other seven stories is in part the result of Mark Twain's characteristic method of composition. In 1906, in his autobiography, he explained: "As long as a book would write itself I was a faithful and interested amanuensis and my industry did not flag; but the minute that the book tried to shift to my head the labor of contriving its situations, inventing its adventures and conducting its conversations, I put it away and dropped it out of my mind." A work would then remain pigeonholed—*Huckleberry Finn*, for example, was twice set aside for periods of three years—until Mark Twain could approach it with renewed interest. There is no evidence, however, that he returned to any of these stories, which were no doubt among the works he called "books that refuse to be written. They stand their ground, year after year, and will not be persuaded. It isn't because the book is not there and worth being written—it is only because the right form for the story does not present itself" (AD, 30 Aug 1906, CU-MARK, in MTE, 196, 199). Nonetheless, four of the stories in this volume were already substantially developed when Mark Twain put them aside. "Huck Finn and Tom Sawyer among the Indians" (1884)—written as a sequel to *Huckleberry Finn* when its author was at the height of his creative powers—is a vivid adventure incorporating many of the classic elements of the Western novel. "Tom Sawyer's Conspiracy" (1897), another attempted sequel to *Huckleberry Finn*, is a parody of popular detective fiction that stops just pages shy of completion. "Hellfire Hotchkiss" (1897), one of Mark Twain's few works with a female protagonist (and an emancipated one at that), and "Schoolhouse Hill" (1898), an early version of his "Mysterious Stranger" fantasy, are rich in autobiographical allusion and have stretches of writing that compare favorably with his best efforts.

However fragmentary and unfinished, all of the works reprinted here illuminate each other as well as the more famous works to which they are akin, and they manage to entertain even as they provide fresh glimpses into the heart of Mark Twain's imaginative universe.

MARK TWAIN

HUCK FINN
AND TOM SAWYER
AMONG THE INDIANS

AND OTHER UNFINISHED STORIES

Boy's Manuscript

[*two manuscript pages (about 300 words) missing*]

me that put the apple there. I don't know how long I waited, but
it was very long. I didn't mind it, because I was fixing up what I
was going to say, and so it was delicious. First I thought I would
call her Dear Amy, though I was a little afraid; but soon I got
used to it and it was beautiful. Then I changed it to Sweet Amy
—which was better—and then I changed it again, to Darling
Amy—which was bliss. When I got it all fixed at last, I was going
to say, "Darling Amy, if you found an apple on the doorstep,
which I think you did find one there, it was *me* that done it, and
I hope you'll think of me sometimes, if you can—only a little"—
and I said that over ever so many times and got it all by heart so
I could say it right off without ever thinking at all. And directly
I saw a blue ribbon and a white frock—my heart began to beat
again and my head began to swim and I began to choke—it got
worse and worse the closer she came—and so, just in time I jumped
behind the lumber and she went by. I only had the strength to
sing out "Apples!" and then I shinned it through the lumber
yard and hid. How I did wish she knew my voice! And then I

got chicken-hearted and all in a tremble for fear she *did* know it. But I got easy after a while, when I came to remember that she didn't know *me,* and so perhaps she wouldn't know my voice either. When I said my prayers at night, I prayed for her. And I prayed the good God not to let the apple make her sick, and to bless her every way for the sake of Christ the Lord. And then I tried to go to sleep but I was troubled about Jimmy Riley, though she don't know him, and I said the first chance I got I would lick him again. Which I will.

Tuesday.—I played hookey yesterday morning, and stayed around about her street pretending I wasn't doing it for anything, but I was looking out sideways at her window all the time, because I was sure I knew which one it was—and when people came along I turned away and sneaked off a piece when they looked at me, because I was dead sure from the way they looked that they knew what I was up to—but I watched out, and when they had got far away I went back again. Once I saw part of a dress flutter in that window, and O, how I felt! I was so happy as long as it was in sight—and so awful miserable when it went away—and *so* happy again when it came back. I could have staid there a year. Once I was watching it so close I didn't notice, and kept getting further and further out in the street, till a man hollered "Hi!" and nearly ran over me with his wagon. I wished he had, because then I would have been crippled and they would have carried me into her house all bloody and busted up, and she would have cried, and I would have been per-fectly happy, because I would have had to stay there till I got well, which I wish I never *would* get well. But by and bye it turned out that that was the nigger chambermaid fluttering her dress at the window, and then I felt so down-hearted I wished I had never found it out. But I know which is her window now, because she came to it all of a sudden, and I thought my heart, was going to burst with happiness—but I turned my back and pretended I didn't know she was there, and I went to shouting at some boys (there wasn't any in sight,) and "showing off" all I could. But when I sort of glanced around to see if she was taking notice of me she was gone—and then I wished I hadn't been such a fool, and had looked at her when I had a chance. Maybe she thought I was cold towards her? It made me feel awful to think of it. Our torchlight procession came off last night. There was nearly eleven of us, and we had a lantern. It was splendid. It was John Wagner's uncle's lantern. I walked right alongside of John Wagner all the evening. Once he let me carry the lantern myself a little piece. Not when we were going by *her* house, but if she was where she could see us she could see easy enough that I knowed the boy that had the lantern. It was the best torchlight procession the boys ever got up—all the boys said so. I only wish I could find out what she thinks of it. I got them to go by her house four times. They didn't want to go, because it is in a back street, but I hired them with marbles. I had twenty-two commas and a white alley when I started out, but I went home dead broke. Suppose I grieved any? No. I said I didn't mind any expense when her happiness was concerned. I shouted all the time we were going by her house, and ordered the procession around lively, and so I don't make any doubt but she thinks I was the captain of it—that is, if she knows me and my voice. I expect she does. I've got acquainted with her brother Tom, and I expect he tells her about me. I'm always hanging around him, and giving him things, and following him home and waiting outside the gate for him. I gave him a fish-hook yesterday; and last night I showed him my sore toe where I stumped it—and to-day I let him take my tooth that was pulled out New-Year's to show to his mother. I hope *she* seen it. I was a-playing for that, anyway. How awful it is to meet her father and mother! They seem like kings and queens to me. And her brother Tom—I can hardly understand how it can be—but he can hug her and kiss her whenever he wants to. I wish I was her brother. But it can't be, I don't reckon.

Wednesday.—I don't take any pleasure, nights, now, but carry-

ing on with the boys out in the street before her house, and talking loud and shouting, so she can hear me and know I'm there.
And after school I go by about three times, all in a flutter and
afraid to hardly glance over, and always letting on that I am in
an awful hurry—going after the doctor or something. But about
the fourth time I only get in sight of the house, and then I weaken
—because I am afraid the people in the houses along will know
what I am about. I am all the time wishing that a wild bull or an
Injun would get after her so I could save her, but somehow it
don't happen so. It happens so in the books, but it don't seem
to happen so to me. After I go to bed, I think all the time of
big boys insulting her and me a-licking them. Here lately, sometimes I feel ever so happy, and then again, and dreadful often,
too, I feel mighty bad. *Then* I don't take any interest in anything. I don't care for apples, I don't care for molasses candy,
swinging on the gate don't do me no good, and even sliding on
the cellar door don't seem like it used to did. I just go around
hankering after something I don't know what. I've put away my
kite. I don't care for kites now. I saw the cat pull the tail off of
it without a pang. I don't seem to want to go in a-swimming, even
when Ma don't allow me to. I don't try to catch flies any more.
I don't take any interest in flies. Even when they light right where
I could nab them easy, I don't pay any attention to them. And I
don't take any interest in property. To-day I took everything out
of my pockets, and looked at them—and the very things I thought
the most of I don't think the least about now. There was a ball,
and a top, and a piece of chalk, and two fish hooks, and a buckskin string, and a long piece of twine, and two slate pencils, and
a sure-enough china, and three white alleys, and a spool cannon,
and a wooden soldier with his leg broke, and a real Barlow, and
a hunk of maple sugar, and a jewsharp, and a dead frog, and a
jaybird's egg, and a door knob, and a glass thing that's broke off
of the top of a decanter (I traded two fish-hooks and a tin injun
for it,) and a penny, and a potato-gun, and two grasshoppers
which their legs was pulled off, and a spectacle glass, and a pic-

ture of Adam and Eve without a rag. I took them all up stairs and put them away. And I know I shall never care anything about property any more. I had all that trouble accumulating a fortune, and now I am not as happy as I was when I was poor. Joe Baldwin's cat is dead, and they are expecting me to go to the funeral, but I shall not go. I don't take any interest in funerals any more. I don't wish to do anything but just go off by myself and think of *her*. I wish I was dead—that is what I wish I was. Then maybe she would be sorry.

Friday.—My mother don't understand it. And I can't tell her. She worries about me, and asks me if I'm sick, and where it hurts me—and I have to say that I ain't sick and nothing don't hurt me, but she says she knows better, because it's the measles. So she gave me ipecac, and calomel, and all that sort of stuff and made me awful sick. And I had to go to bed, and she gave me a mug of hot sage tea and a mug of hot saffron tea, and covered me up with blankets and said that that would sweat me and bring it to the surface. I suffered. But I couldn't tell her. Then she said I had bile. And so she gave me some warm salt water and I heaved up everything that was in me. But she wasn't satisfied. She said there wasn't any bile in that. So she gave me two blue mass pills, and after that a tumbler of Epsom salts to work them off—which it did work them off. I felt that what was left of me was dying, but still I couldn't tell. The measles wouldn't come to the surface and so it wasn't measles; there wasn't any bile, and so it wasn't bile. Then she said she was stumped—but there was *some thing* the matter, and so there was nothing to do but tackle it in a sort of a *general* way. I was too weak and miserable to care much. And so she put bottles of hot water to my feet, and socks full of hot ashes on my breast, and a poultice on my head. But they didn't work, and so she gave me some rhubarb to regulate my bowels, and put a mustard plaster on my back. But at last she said she was satisfied it wasn't a cold on the chest. It must be general stagnation of the blood, and then I knew what was coming. But I couldn't tell, and so, with *her* name on my lips I delivered myself up and went through the water treatment—douche, sitz, wet-sheet and shower-bath (awful,)—and came out all weak, and sick, and played out. Does *she*—ah, no, she knows nothing of it. And all the time that I lay suffering, I did so want to hear somebody only mention her name—and I hated them because they thought of everything else to please me but that. And when at last somebody *did* mention it my face and my eyes lit up so that my mother clasped her hands and said: "Thanks, O thanks, the pills are operating!"

Saturday Night.—This was a blessed day. Mrs. Johnson came to call and as she passed through the hall I saw—O, I like to jumped out of bed!—I saw the flash of a little red dress, and I knew who was in it. Mrs. Johnson is her aunt. And when they came in with Ma to see me I was perfectly happy. I was perfectly happy but I was afraid to look at her except when she was not looking at me. Ma said I had been very sick, but was looking ever so much better now. Mrs. Johnson said it was a dangerous time, because children got hold of so much fruit. Now she said Amy found an apple [I started,] on the doorstep [Oh!] last Sunday, [Oh, geeminy, the very, very one!] and ate it all up, [Bless her heart!] and it gave her the colic. [Dern that apple!] And so *she* had been sick, too, poor dear, and it was her Billy that did it— though she couldn't know that, of course. I wanted to take her in my arms and tell her all about it and ask her to forgive me, but I was afraid to even speak to her. But she had suffered for my sake, and I was happy. By and bye she came near the bed and looked at me with her big blue eyes, and never flinched. It gave me some spunk. Then she said:

"What's your name?—Eddie, or Joe?"

I said, "It ain't neither—it's Billy."

"Billy what?"

"Billy Rogers."

"Has your sister got a doll?"

"I ain't got any sister."

"It ain't a pretty name I don't think—much."

"Which?"

"Why Billy Rogers—Rogers ain't, but Billy is. Did you ever see two cats fighting?—*I* have."

"Well I reckon I have. I've *made* 'em fight. More'n a thousand times. I've fit 'em over close-lines, and in boxes, and under barrels —every way. But the most fun is to tie fire-crackers to their tails and see 'em scatter for home. Your name's Amy, ain't it?—and you're eight years old, ain't you?"

"Yes, I'll be *nine,* ten months and a half from now, and I've got two dolls, and one of 'em can cry and the other's got its head broke and all the sawdust is out of its legs—it don't make no difference, though—I've give all its dresses to the other. Is this the first time you ever been sick?"

"*No!* I've had the scarlet fever and the mumps, and the hoop'n cough, and ever so many things. H'mph! *I* don't consider it anything to be sick."

"My mother don't, either. She's been sick maybe a thousand times—and once, would you believe it, they thought she was going to die."

"They *always* think *I'm* going to die. The doctors always gives me up and has the family crying and snuffling round here. But I only think it's bully."

"Bully is naughty, my mother says, and she don't 'low Tom to say it. Who do you go to school to?"

"Peg-leg Bliven. That's what the boys calls him, cause he's got a cork leg."

"Goody! I'm going to him, too."

"Oh, *that's* bul—. I like that. When?"

"To-morrow. Will you play with me?"

"You bet!"

Then Mrs. Johnson called her and she said "Good-bye, Billy" —she called me Billy—and then she went away and left me *so* happy. And she gave me a chunk of molasses candy, and I put it next my heart, and it got warm and stuck, and it won't come off, and I can't get my shirt off, but I don't mind it. I'm only glad. But won't I be out of this and at school Monday? I should *think* so.

Thursday.—They've been plaguing us. We've been playing together three days, and to-day I asked her if she would be my little wife and she said she would, and just then Jim Riley and Bob Sawyer jumped up from behind the fence where they'd been listening, and begun to holler at the other scholars and told them all about it. So she went away crying, and I felt bad enough to cry myself. I licked Jim Riley, and Bob Sawyer licked me, and Jo Bryant licked Sawyer, and Peg-leg licked all of us. But nothing could make me happy. I was too dreadful miserable on account of seeing her cry.

Friday.—She didn't come to school this morning, and I felt awful. I couldn't study, I couldn't do anything. I got a black mark because I couldn't tell if a man had five apples and divided them equally among himself and gave the rest away, how much it was —or something like that. I didn't know how many parts of speech there was, and I didn't care. I was head of the spelling class and I spellt baker with two k's and got turned down foot. I got lathered for drawing a picture of her on the slate, though it looked more like women's hoops with a hatchet on top than it looked like her. But I didn't care for sufferings. Bill Williams bent a pin and I set down on it, but I never even squirmed. Jake Warner hit me with a spit-ball, but I never took any notice of it. The world was all dark to me. The first hour that morning was awful. Something told me she wouldn't be there. I don't know what, but *something* told me. And my heart sunk away down when I looked among all the girls and didn't find her. No matter what was going on, that first hour, I was watching the door. I wouldn't hear the teacher sometimes, and then I got scolded. I kept on hoping and hoping— and starting, a little, every time the door opened—till it was no use—she wasn't coming. And when she came in the afternoon, it was all bright again. But she passed by me and never even looked at me. I felt so bad. I tried to catch her eye, but I couldn't. She always looked the other way. At last she set up close to Jimmy

Riley and whispered to him a long, long time—five minutes, I should think. I wished that I could die right in my tracks. And I said to myself I would lick Jim Riley till he couldn't stand. Presently she looked at me—for the first time—but she didn't smile. She laid something as far as she could toward the end of the bench and motioned that it was for me. Soon as the teacher turned I rushed there and got it. It was wrote on a piece of copy-book, and so the first line wasn't hers. This is the letter:

"Time and Tide wait for no Man.

"mister william rogers i do not love you dont come about me any more i will not speak to you"

I cried all the afternoon, nearly, and I hated her. She passed by me two or three times, but I never noticed her. At recess I licked three of the boys and put my arms round May Warner's neck, and *she* saw me do it, too, and she didn't play with anybody at all. Once she came near me and said very low, *"Billy, I—I'm sorry."* But I went away and wouldn't look at her. But pretty soon I was sorry myself. I was scared, then. I jumped up and ran, but school was just taking in and she was already gone to her seat. I thought what a fool I was; and I wished it was to do over again, I wouldn't go away. She had said she was sorry—*and I wouldn't notice her.* I wished the house would fall on me. I felt so mean for treating her so when she wanted to be friendly. How I did wish I could catch her eye!—I would look a look that she would understand. But she never, never looked at me. She sat with her head down, looking sad, poor thing. She never spoke but once during the afternoon, and then it was to that hateful Jim Riley. *I* will pay him for this conduct.

Saturday.—Going home from school Friday evening, she went with the girls all around her, and though I walked on the outside, and talked loud, and ran ahead sometimes, and cavorted around, and said all sorts of funny things that made the other girls laugh, *she* wouldn't laugh, and wouldn't take any notice of me at all. At her gate I was close enough to her to touch her, and she knew it, but she wouldn't look around, but just went straight

in and straight to the door, without ever turning. And Oh, how I
felt! I said the world was a mean, sad place, and had nothing for
me to love or care for in it—and life, life was only misery. It was
then that it first came into my head to take my life. I don't know
why I wanted to do that, except that I thought it would make her
feel sorry. I liked that, but then she could only feel sorry a little
while, because she would forget it, but I would be dead for always.
I did not like that. If she would be sorry as long as I would be
dead, it would be different. But anyway, I felt so dreadful that I
said at last that it was better to die than to live. So I wrote a letter
like this:

"*Darling Amy*

"I take my pen in hand to inform you that I am in good health
and hope these fiew lines will find you injoying the same god's
blessing   I love you. I cannot live and see you hate me and talk
to that Jim riley which I will lick every time I ketch him and
have done so already   I do not wish to live any more as we must
part. I will pisen myself when I am done writing this and that is
the last you will ever see of your poor Billy forever. I enclose my
tooth which was pulled out newyears, keep it always to remember
me by, I wish it was larger. Your dyeing BILLY ROGERS."

I directed it to her and took it and put it under her father's
door. Then I looked up at her window a long time, and prayed
that she might be forgiven for what I was going to do—and then
cried and kissed the ground where she used to step out at the
door, and took a pinch of the dirt and put it next my heart where
the candy was, and started away to die. But I had forgotten to get
any poison. Something else had to be done. I went down to the
river, but it would not do, for I remembered that there was no
place there but was over my head. I went home and thought I
would jump off of the kitchen, but every time, just I had clumb
nearly to the eaves I slipped and fell, and it was plain to be seen
that it was dangerous—so I gave up that plan. I thought of hanging, and started up stairs, because I knew where there was a new
bed-cord, but I recollected my father telling me if he ever caught

me meddling with that bed-cord he would thrash me in an inch of my life—and so I had to give *that* up. So there was nothing for it but poison. I found a bottle in the closet, labeled laudanum on one side and castor oil on the other. I didn't know which it was, but I drank it all. I think it was oil. I was dreadful sick all night, and not constipated, my mother says, and this morning I had lost all interest in things, and didn't care whether I lived or died. But Oh, by nine o'clock *she* was here, and came right in—how my heart did beat and my face flush when I saw her dress go by the window!—she came right in and came right up to the bed, before Ma, and kissed me, and the tears were in her eyes, and she said, "Oh, Billy, how *could* you be so naughty!—and Bingo is going to die, too, because another dog's bit him behind and all over, and Oh, I shan't have *any*body to love!"—and she cried and cried. But I told her I was not going to die and *I* would love her, always—and then her face brightened up, and she laughed and clapped her hands and said now as Ma was gone out, we'd talk all about it. So I kissed her and she kissed me, and she promised to be my little wife and love me forever and never love anybody else; and I promised just the same to her. And then I asked her if she had any plans, and she said No, she hadn't thought of that—no doubt I could plan everything. I said I could, and it would be my place, being the husband, to always plan and direct, and look out for her, and protect her all the time. She said that was right. But I said she could make suggestions—she *ought* to say what kind of a house she would rather live in. So she said she would prefer to have a little cosy cottage, with vines running over the windows and a four-story brick attached where she could receive company and give parties—that was all. And we talked a long time about what profession I had better follow. I wished to be a pirate, but she said that would be horrid. I said there was nothing horrid about it—it was grand. She said pirates killed people. I said of course they did—what would you have a pirate do?—it's in his line. She said, But just think of the blood! I said I loved blood and carnage. She shuddered. She said, well, perhaps

it was best, and she hoped I would be great. Great! I said, where
was there ever a pirate that *wasn't* great? Look at Capt. Kydd—
look at Morgan—look at Gibbs—look at the noble Lafitte—look
at the Black Avenger of the Spanish Main!—names that 'll never
die. That pleased her, and so she said, let it be so. And then we
talked about what *she* should do. She wanted to keep a milliner
shop, because then she could have all the fine clothes she wanted;
and on Sundays, when the shop was closed, she would be a
teacher in Sunday-school. And she said I could help her teach
her class Sundays when I was in port. So it was all fixed that as
soon as ever we grow up we'll be married, and I am to be a pirate
and she's to keep a milliner shop. Oh, it is splendid. I wish we
were grown up now. Time does drag along so! But won't it be
glorious! I will be away a long time cruising, and then some Sunday morning I'll step into Sunday School with my long black
hair, and my slouch hat with a plume in it, and my long sword
and high boots and splendid belt and red satin doublet and
breeches, and my black flag with scull and cross-bones on it, and
all the children will say, "Look—look—that's Rogers the pirate!"
Oh, I wish time would move along faster.

Tuesday.—I was disgraced in school before her yesterday. These
long summer days are awful. I *couldn't* study. I couldn't think
of anything but being free and far away on the bounding billow.
I hate school, anyway. It is *so* dull. I sat looking out of the window
and listening to the buzz, buzz, buzzing of the scholars learning
their lessons, till I was drowsy and did want to be out of that
place so much. I could see idle boys playing on the hill-side, and
catching butterflies whose fathers ain't able to send them to
school, and I wondered what *I* had done that God should pick
me out more than any other boy and give me a father able to send
me to school. But *I* never could have any luck. There wasn't anything I could do to pass off the time. I caught some flies, but I got
tired of that. I couldn't see Amy, because they've moved her seat.
I got mad looking out of the window at those boys. By and bye,
my chum, Bill Bowen, he bought a louse from Archy Thompson

—he's got millions of them—bought him for a white alley and put him on the slate in front of him on the desk and begun to stir him up with a pin. He made him travel a while in one direction, and then he headed him off and made him go some other way. It was glorious fun. I wanted one, but I hadn't any white alley. Bill kept him a-moving—this way—that way—every way—and I did wish I could get a chance at him myself, and I begged for it. Well, Bill made a mark down the middle of the slate, and he says, "Now when he is on my side, *I'll* stir him up—and I'll try to keep him from getting over the line, but if he *does* get over it, then *you* can stir him up as long as he's over there."

So he kept stirring him up, and two or three times he was so near getting over the line that I was in a perfect fever; but Bill always headed him off again. But at last he got on the line and all Bill could do he couldn't turn him—he made a dead set to come over, and presently over he *did* come, head over heels, upside down, a-reaching for things and a-clawing the air with all his hands! I snatched a pin out of my jacket and begun to waltz him around, and I made him git up and git—it was splendid fun —but at last, I kept him on my side so long that Bill couldn't stand it any longer, he was so excited, and he reached out to stir him up himself. I told him to let him alone, and behave himself. He said he wouldn't. I said

"You've got to—he's on my side, now, and you haven't got any right to punch him."

He said, "I haven't, haven't I? By George he's *my* louse—I bought him for a white alley, and I'll do just as I blame please with him!"

And then I felt somebody nip me by the ear, and I saw a hand nip Bill by the ear. It was Peg-leg the schoolmaster. He had sneaked up behind, just in his natural mean way, and seen it all and heard it all, and we had been so taken up with our circus that we hadn't noticed that the buzzing was all still and the scholars watching Peg-leg and us. He took us up to his throne by the ears and thrashed us good, and Amy saw it all. I felt so mean that I sneaked away from school without speaking to her, and at night when I said my prayers I prayed that I might be taken away from school and kept at home until I was old enough to be a pirate.*

Tuesday Week.—For six whole days she has been gone to the country. The first three days, I played hookey all the time, and got licked for it as much as a dozen times. But I didn't care. I was desperate. I didn't care for anything. Last Saturday was the day for the battle between our school and Hog Davis's school (that is the boys's name for their teacher). I'm captain of a company of the littlest boys in our school. I came on the ground without any paper hat and without any wooden sword, and with my jacket on my arm. The Colonel said I was a fool—said I had kept both armies waiting for me a half an hour, and now to come looking like that—and I better not let the General see me. I said him and the General both could lump it if they didn't like it. Then he put me under arrest—under arrest of that Jim Riley—and I just licked Jim Riley and got *out* of arrest—and then I waltzed into Hog Davis's infant department and the way I made the fur fly was awful. I wished Amy could see me then. We drove the whole army over the hill and down by the slaughter house and lathered them good, and then they surrendered till next Saturday. I was made a lieutenant-colonel for desperate conduct in the field and now I am almost the youngest lieutenant-colonel we've got. I reckon I ain't no slouch. We've got thirty-two officers and fourteen men in our army, and we can take that Hog Davis crowd and do for them any time, even if they *have* got two more men than we have, and eleven more officers. But nobody knew what made me fight so—nobody but two or three, I guess. They never thought of Amy. Going home, Wart Hopkins overtook me (that's his nickname—because he's all over warts). He'd been out to the cross-roads burying a bean that he'd bloodied with a wart to make them go away and he was going home, now. I was in business with him once, and we had fell out. We had a circus and both of

---

*Every detail of the above incident is strictly true, as I have excellent reason to remember.—[M.T.

us wanted to be clown, and he wouldn't give up. He was always contrary that way. And he wanted to do the zam, and I wanted to do the zam (which the zam means the zampillerostation), and there it was again. He knocked a barrel from under me when I was a-standing on my head one night, and once when we were playing Jack the Giant-Killer I tripped his stilts up and pretty near broke him in two. We charged two pins admission for big boys and one pin for little ones—and when we came to divide up he wanted to shove off all the pins on me that hadn't any heads on. That was the kind of a boy he was—always mean. He always tied the little boys' clothes when they went in a-swimming. I was with him in the nigger-show business once, too, and he wanted to be bones all the time himself. He would sneak around and nip marbles with his toes and carry them off when the boys were playing knucks, or anything like that; and when he was playing himself he always poked or he always hunched. He always throwed his nutshells under some small boy's bench in school and let him get lammed. He used to put shoemaker's wax in the teacher's seat and then play hookey and let some other fellow catch it. I hated Wart Hopkins. But now he was in the same fix as myself, and I did want somebody to talk to *so* bad, who was in that fix. He loved Susan Hawkins and she was gone to the country too. I could see he was suffering, and he could see I was. I wanted to talk, and he wanted to talk, though we hadn't spoken for a long, long time. Both of us was full. So he said let bygones be bygones—let's make up and be good friends, because we'd ought to be, fixed as we were. I just overflowed, and took him around the neck and went to crying, and he took me around the neck and went to crying, and we were perfectly happy because we were so miserable together. And I said I would always love him and Susan, and he said he would always love me and Amy—beautiful, beautiful Amy, he called her, which made me feel good and proud; but not quite so beautiful as Susan, he said, and I said it was a lie and he said I was another and a fighting one and darsn't take it up; and I hit him and he hit me back, and then we had a fight and rolled down a gulley into the mud and gouged and bit and hit and scratched, and neither of us was whipped; and then we got out and commenced it all over again and he put a chip on his shoulder and dared me to knock it off and I did, and so we had it again, and then he went home and I went home, and Ma asked me how I got my clothes all tore off and was so ragged and bloody and bruised up, and I told her I fell down, and then she black-snaked me and I was all right. And the very next day I got a letter from Amy! Mrs. Johnson brought it to me. It said:

"mister william rogers dear billy i have took on so i am all Wore out a crying becos i Want to see you so bad the cat has got kittens but it Dont make me happy i Want to see you all the Hens lays eggs excep the old Rooster and mother and me Went to church Sunday and had hooklebeary pie for Dinner i think of you Always and love you no more from your amy at present
                                                                          Amy."

I read it over and over and over again, and kissed it, and studied out new meanings in it, and carried it to bed with me and read it again first thing in the morning. And I did feel so delicious I wanted to lay there and think of her hours and hours and never get up. But they made me. The first chance I got I wrote to her, and this is it:

"Darling Amy

"I have had lots of fights and I love you all the same. I have changed my dog which his name was Bull and now his name is Amy. I think its splendid and so does he I reckon because he always comes when I call him *Amy* though he'd come anyhow ruther than be walloped, which I *would* wallop him if he didn't. I send you my picture. The things on the lower side are the legs, the head is on the other end, the horable thing which its got in its hand is you though not so pretty by a long sight. I didn't mean to put only one eye in your face but there wasnt room. I have been thinking sometimes I'll be a pirate and sometimes I'll keep grocery on account of candy   And I would like ever so much to be a brigadire General or a deck hand on a steamboat because they have fun you know and go everywheres. But a fellow cant be everything I dont reckon. I have traded off my sunday school book and Ma's hatchet for a pup and I reckon I'm going to ketch it, maybe. Its a good pup though. It nipped a chicken yesterday and goes around raising cain all the time. I love you to destruction Amy and I can't live if you dont come back. I had the branch dammed up beautiful for water-mills, but I dont care for water mills when you are away so I traded the dam to Jo Whipple for a squirt gun though if you was here I wouldnt give a dam for a squirt gun because we could have water mills. So no more from your own true love.

> My pen is bad my ink is pale
> Roses is red the violets blue
> But my love for you shall never change.

WILLIAM T. ROGERS.

"P.S. I learnt that poetry from Sarah Mackleroy—its beautiful."

Tuesday Fortnight.—I'm thankful that I'm free. I've come to myself. I'll never love another girl again. There's no dependence in them. If I was going to hunt up a wife I would just go in amongst a crowd of girls and say

> "Eggs, cheese, butter, bread,
> Stick, stock, stone—DEAD!"

and take the one it lit on just the same as if I was choosing up for fox or baste or three-cornered cat or hide'n'whoop or anything like that. I'd get along just as well as by selecting them out and falling in love with them the way I did with—with—I can't write her name, for the tears *will* come. But she has treated me Shameful. The first thing she did when she got back from the country was to begin to object to me being a pirate—because some of her kin is down on pirates I reckon—though *she* said it was because I would be away from home so much. A likely story, indeed—if she knowed anything about pirates she'd know that they go and come just whenever they please, which other people can't. Well I'll be a pirate now, in spite of all the girls in the world. And next

she didn't want me to be a deck hand on a steamboat, or else it
was a judge she didn't want me to be, because one of them wasn't
respectable, she didn't know which—some more bosh from relations I reckon. And then she said she didn't want to keep a
milliner shop, she wanted to clerk in a toy-shop, and have an
open barouche and she'd like me to sell peanuts and papers on
the railroad so she could ride without it costing anything.

"What!" I said, "and not be a pirate at all?"

She said yes. I was disgusted. I told her so. Then she cried,
and said I didn't love her, and wouldn't do anything to please
her, and wanted to break her heart and have some other girl
when she was dead, and then I cried, too, and told her I *did* love
her, and nobody but her, and I'd do anything she wanted me to
and I was sorry, Oh, so sorry. But she shook her head, and pouted
—and I begged again, and she turned her back—and I went on
pleading and she wouldn't answer—only pouted—and at last when
I was getting mad, she slammed the jewsharp, and the tin loco-
motive and the spool cannon and everything I'd given her, on
the floor, and flourished out mad and crying like sin, and said I
was a mean, good-for-nothing thing and I might go and *be* a
pirate and welcome!—*she* never wanted to see me any more! And
I was mad and crying, too, and I said By George I *would* be a
pirate, and an awful bloody one, too, or my name warn't Bill
Rogers!

And so it's all over between us. But now that it *is* all over, I
feel mighty, mighty bad. The whole school knowed we were
engaged, and they think it strange to see us flirting with other
boys and girls, but we can't help that. I flirt with other girls, but
I don't care anything about them. And I see her lip quiver sometimes and the tears come in her eyes when she looks my way
when she's flirting with some other boy—and then I do *want* to
rush there and grab her in my arms and be friends again!

Saturday.—I am happy again, and forever, this time. I've seen
her! I've seen the girl that is my doom. I shall die if I cannot get
her. The first time I looked at her I fell in love with her. She

looked at me twice in church yesterday, and Oh how I felt! She
was with her mother and her brother. When they came out of
church I followed them, and twice she looked back and smiled,
and I would have smiled too, but there was a tall young man by
my side and I was afraid he would notice. At last she dropped a
leaf of a flower—rose geranium Ma calls it—and I could see by
the way she looked that she meant it for me, and when I stooped
to pick it up the tall young man stooped too. I got it, but I felt
awful sheepish, and I think he did, too, because he blushed. He
asked me for it, and I had to give it to him, though I'd rather
given him my bleeding heart, but I pinched off just a little piece
and kept it, and shall keep it forever. Oh, she is *so* lovely! And
she loves me. I know it. I could see it, easy. Her name's Laura
Miller. She's nineteen years old, Christmas. I never, never, never
will part with *this* one! NEVER.

Letter to William Bowen

Sunday Afternoon,
At Home, 472 Delaware Avenue,
Buffalo Feb. 6. 1870

My First, & Oldest & Dearest Friend,

My heart goes out to you just the same as ever. Your letter has stirred me to the bottom. The fountains of my great deep are broken up & I have rained reminiscences for four & twenty hours. The old life has swept before me like a panorama; the old days have trooped by in their old glory, again; the old faces have looked out of the mists of the past; old footsteps have sounded in my listening ears; old hands have clasped mine, old voices have greeted me, & the songs I loved ages & ages ago have come wailing down the centuries! Heavens what eternities have swung their hoary cycles about us since those days were new!—What Since we tore down Dick Hardy's stable; since you had the measles & I went to your house purposely to catch them; since Henry Beebe kept that envied slaughter-house, & Joe Craig sold him cats to kill in it; since old General Gaines used to say, "Whoop! Bow your neck & spread!"; since Jimmy Finn was town drunkard & we stole his dinner while he slept in the vat & fed it to the hogs in order to keep them still till we could mount them & have a ride; since Clint Levering was drowned; since we taught that one-legged nigger, Higgins, to offend Bill League's dignity by hailing him in public with his exasperating "Hello, League!"—since we used to undress & play Robin Hood ~~wi~~ in our shirt-tails, with lath swords, in the woods on Holliday's Hill on those long summer days; since we used to go in swimming above the still-house branch—& at mighty intervals wandered on vagrant ∅ fishing excursions clear up to "the Bay," & wondered what was curtained away in the great world beyond that remote point; since I jumped overboard from the ferry boat in the middle of the river that stormy day to get my hat, & swam two or three miles after it (& *got* it,) while all the town collected on the wharf & for an hour or so looked out across the angry waste of "white-caps" toward where people said Sam. Clemens was last seen before he went down; since we got up a ~~mutiny~~ rebellion against Miss Newcomb, under Ed. Stevens' leadership, (to force her to let us all go over to Miss Torry's side of the schoolroom,) & gallantly "sassed" Laura Hawkins when she came out the third time to call us in, & then afterward marched in ˌinˌ threatening & bloodthirsty array,—& meekly yielded, & took each his little thrashing, & ~~&~~ resumed his old seat entirely "reconstructed"; since we used to indulge in that very peculiar performance on that old bench outside the school-house to drive good old Bill Brown crazy while he was eating his dinner; since we used to remain at school at noon & go hungry, in order to persecute Bill Brown in all possible ways—poor old Bill, who *could* be driven to such extremity of vindictiveness as to call us "You *infernal* fools!" & chase us round & round the school-house— & yet who never had the heart to hurt us when he caught us, & who always loved us & always took our part when the big boys wanted to thrash us; since we used to lay in wait for Bill Pitts at the pump & whale him; (I saw him two or three years ago, & *I* was awful polite to his six feet two, & mentioned no reminiscences); since we used to be in Dave Garth's class in Sunday school & on week-days stole his leaf tobacco to run our miniature tobacco presses with; since Owsley shot Smar; since Ben Hawkins shot off his finger; since we accidentally burned up that poor fellow in the calaboose; since we used to shoot spool cannons¿, & cannons made of keys, while that envied & hated Henry Beebe drowned out our poor little pop-guns with his booming brazen little artillery on wheels; since Laura Hawkins was my sweetheart————————

Hold! *That* rouses me out of my dream, & brings me violently back unto this day & this generation. For behold I have at this moment the only sweetheart I ever *loved*, & bless her old heart she is lying asleep upstairs in a bed that I sleep in every night, & for four whole days she has been *Mrs. Samuel L. Clemens!*

I am thirty-four & she is twenty-four; I am young & very handsome (I make the statement with the fullest confidence, for I got it from her), & she is much the most beautiful girl I ever saw (I said that before she was anything to me, & so it is worthy of all belief) & she is the *best* girl, & the sweetest, & the gentlest, & the daintiest, & the most modest & unpretentious, & the wisest in all things she should be wise in, & the most ignorant in all matters it would not grace her to know, & she is sensible & quick, & loving & faithful, forgiving, full of charity—& her beautiful life is ordered by a religion that is all kindliness & unselfishness. Before the gentle majesty of her purity all evil things & evil ways & evil deeds stand abashed,—then surrender. Wherefore, without effort, or struggle, or spoken exorcism, all the old vices & shameful habits that have possessed me these many many years, are falling away, one by one, & departing into the darkness.

Bill, I know whereof I speak. I am too old & have moved about too much, & rubbed against too many people not to know human beings as well as we used to know "boils" from "breaks."

She is the very most perfect gem of womankind that ever I saw in my life—& I will stand by that remark till I die.

William, old boy, her father surprised us a little, the other night. We all arrived here in a night train (my little wife & I were going to board), & under pretense of taking us to the private boarding-house that had been selected for me while I was absent lecturing in New England, my new father-in-law & some old friends drove us in sleighs to the daintiest, darlingest, loveliest little palace in America—& when I said "Oh, this won't do—people who can afford to live in this sort of style won't take boarders," that same blessed father-in-law let out the secret that this was all *our* property—a present from himself. House & furniture cost $40,000 in cash, (including stable, horse & carriage), & is a most exquisite little palace (I saw no apartment in Europe so lovely as our ~~little~~ drawing-room.)

Come along, you & Mollie, just whenever you can, & pay us a visit, (giving us a little notice beforehand,) & if we don't make you comfortable nobody in the world can.

[And now ₐmyₐ princess has come down for dinner (bless me, isn't it cosy, nobody but just us two, & three servants to wait on us & respectfully call us "Mr." & "Mrs. Clemens" instead of "Sam." & "Livy!") It took me many a year to work up to where I can put on style, but now I'll do it. My book gives me an income like a small lord, & my paper is ~~not~~ a good profitable concern.

Dinner's ready. Good bye & ~~g~~ God bless you, old friend, & keep your heart fresh & your memory green for the old days that will never come again.

Yrs always

Sam. Clemens.

Tupperville-Dobbsville

Chapter 1

THE SCENE of this history is an Arkansas village, on the bank of the Mississippi; the time, a great many years ago. The houses were small and unpretentious; some few were of frame, the others of logs; a very few were whitewashed, but none were painted; nearly all the fences leaned outward or inward and were more or less dilapidated. The whole village had a lazy, tired, neglected look. The river bank was high and steep, and here and there an aged, crazy building stood on the edge with a quarter or a half of itself overhanging the water, waiting forlorn and tenantless for the next freshet to eat the rest of the ground from under it and let the stream swallow it. This was a town that was always moving westward. Twice a year, regularly, in the dead of winter and in the dead of summer, the great river called for the front row of the village's possessions, and always got it. It took the front farms, the front orchards, the front gardens; those front houses that were worth hauling away, were moved to the rear by ox-power when the danger-season approached; those that were not worth this trouble were timely deserted and left to cave into the river. If a man lived obscurely in a back street and chafed under this fate, he only needed to have patience; his back street would be the front street by and by.

Above and below the town, dense forests came flush to the bank; and twice a year they delivered their front belt of timber into the river. The village site, and the corn and cotton fields in the rear had been formerly occupied by trees as thick as they could stand, and the stumps remained in streets, yards and fields as a memento of the fact. All the houses stood upon "underpinning," which raised them two or three feet above the ground, and under each house was usually a colony of hogs, dogs, cats and other creatures, mostly of a noisy kind. The village stood on a dead level, and the houses were propped above ground to keep the main floors from being flooded by the semi-annual overflow of the river.

There were no sidewalks, no pavements, no stepping stones; therefore, on a spring day the streets were either several inches deep with dust or as many inches deep with thick black mud. People slopped through this mud on foot or horseback, the hogs wallowed in it without fear of molestation, wagons got stuck fast in it, and while the drivers lashed away with their long whips and swore with power, coatless, jeans-clad loafers stood by with hands in pockets and sleepily enjoyed this blessed interruption of the customary monotony until a dog-fight called them to higher pleasure. When the dog-fight ended they adjourned to the empty dry-goods boxes in front of the poor little stores and whittled and expectorated and discussed the fight and the merits of the dogs that had taken part in it.

One of the largest dwellings in this village of Tupperville was the home of the widow Bennett and her family. It was built of logs, and stood in the back part of the town next to the corn and cotton-fields. In the common sitting room was a mighty fire place, paved with slabs of stone shaped by nature and worn smooth by use. The oaken floor in front of it was thickly freckled, as far as the middle of the room, with black spots burned in it by coals popped out from the hickory fire-wood. There was no carpeting anywhere; but there was a spinning wheel in one corner, a bed in another, with a white counterpane, a dinner table with leaves, in another, a tall eight-day clock in the fourth corner, a dozen splint-bottom chairs scattered around, several guns resting upon deer-horns over the mantel piece, and generally a cat or a hound or two curled up on the hearth-stones asleep. This was the family sitting room; it was also the dining room and the widow Bennett's bedchamber. The rest of the house was devoted to sleeping apartments for the other members of the household. A planked passage-way, twenty feet wide, open at the sides but roofed above, extended from the back sitting room door to the log kitchen; and beyond the kitchen stood the smoke-house and three or four little dismal log cabins, otherwise the "negro quarter."

Since this house was in all ways much superior to the average of the Dobbsville residences, it will be easily perceived that the average residence was necessarily a very marvel of rudeness, nakedness, and simplicity.

Clairvoyant

WHEN I was a boy, there came to our village of Hannibal, on the Mississippi, a young Englishman named John H. Day, and went to work in the shop of old Mr. Stevens the jeweler, in Main street. He excited the usual two or three days' curiosity due to a new comer in such a place; and after that, as he seemed to prefer to keep to himself, the people bothered themselves no more about him, and he was left to his own devices. It was not difficult to give him his way in this, for he was taciturn, absorbed, and therefore uncompanionable and unattractive. As for looks, he was well enough, though there was nothing striking about him except his eyes, which, when in repose, suggested smouldering fires, and, when the man was stirred, surprised one by their exceeding brilliancy.

Mr. Day slept, cooked for himself, and ate, in the back part of the jewelry shop, and he was not seen outside the place oftener than once in twenty-four hours. He seemed to be nearly always at work, days, nights and Sundays. By and by, one noted this curious thing: he would accost a citizen, go to his house once, apparently study him an hour, then drop the acquaintanceship. You must understand that there were no castes in our society, and the jeweler's journeyman was as good as anybody and could go anywhere. At the end of a year he had in this way made and discarded the acquaintanceship of pretty much everybody. So here was a man who might be said to know all the town; and yet if any one were spoken to about him, the reply would have to be, "Well, I have met him—once—but I am not acquainted with him; I don't know him." It was odd—Mr. Day really knew everybody, after a fashion, and yet had wrought so quietly and gradually, that the town's impression was that he didn't know anybody and didn't wish to.

He seemed to have but one object in view in contriving his brief acquaintanceships; and that was, to get an opportunity to examine people's ears to see if they were threatened with deafness. He did not claim that he could cure deafness, or do anything for it at all; he only claimed that if a person had the seeds of future deafness in him he could discover the fact. The physicians said that this was nonsense; nevertheless, as Mr. Day did not charge anything for his examinations, the people were all willing to let him inspect their ears. He had no disposition to keep his theory a secret; but while his explanations of it sounded plausible to the general public, they only confirmed the physicians in their conviction that there was nothing in it. In time the irreverent came to speak of Day as the "Earbug," and he of course got the reputation of being a monomaniac—if "reputation" is not too large a word to apply to a person who was so little talked about.

By and by, I was apprenticed to the jeweler, and was placed under the tuition of his journeyman. Day was kind to me, and gentle; but during the first week or two he did not speak to me, except in the way of business, although I was with him all day and slept in the same room with him every night. I quickly grew to be fond of my silent comrade, and often staid about him, evenings, when I could have been out at play. He would work diligently at something or other until I went to bed at ten. Then, as the stillness of the night came on and I seemed to be sleeping, (which I wasn't,) he would presently tilt himself back in his chair and close his eyes —and then the strong interest of the evening began, for me. Smiles would flash across his face; then the signs of sharp mental pain;

then furies of passion. This stirring panorama of emotions would continue for hours, sometimes, and move me, excite me, exhaust me like a stage-play. Now and then he would glance at the clock, mutter the time and the day of the month, and say something like this: "People who think they know him would say the thing is incredible." Then he would take a fat note-book out of his breast pocket and write something in it. I marveled at these things, but took it out in marveling; I believed that the observing them clandestinely was dishonorable enough without gossiping about them.

One summer night, about midnight, I was watching him through my half closed lids, waiting for him to begin—for he had been reading all the evening, to my disappointment and discontent. Now he put down his book, and for a moment appeared to be doing something with his hands, I could not see what; then he settled himself back in his chair, closed his eyes peacefully, and the next moment sprang out of his seat with his face lit with horror and snatched me from the bed, stood me on my feet, and said:

"Run! don't stop to dress! young Ratcliff, the crazy one, is going to murder his mother. Don't tell anybody I said it."

Before I knew what I was about, I was flying up the deserted street in my shirt; and before I had had time to come to myself and realize what a fool I was to rush after one lunatic at the say-so of another, I had covered the two hundred yards that lay between our shop and the Ratcliff homestead, and was thundering at the ancient knocker of the side door with all my might. Then I came to myself, and felt foolish enough; I turned and looked toward the hut in a corner of the yard where young Ratcliff was kept in confinement; and sure enough, here came young Ratcliff flying across the yard in the moonlight, as naked as I was, and I saw the flash of a butcher knife which he was flourishing in his hand. I shouted "Help!" and "Murder!" and then fled away, still shouting these cries. When I got back to the shop, Day was not there; but in the course of half an hour he came in, and for the first time was talkative. He said a crowd gathered and captured the lunatic after he was inside the house and climbing the stairs toward his mother's room. He said Mrs. Ratcliff ought to know that I had saved her life, but he would take it as a great favor if I would keep carefully secret the fact of his own connection with the matter. I said I would, and it seemed to please him; and from that time forward he began to talk with me more or less every day, and I became his one intimate friend. We talked a good deal, that night, and at last I asked him why he hadn't gone to give the alarm himself instead of sending me, but he did not reply; and by and by when I ventured to ask him how he had divined that a man two hundred yards away was about to murder his mother, he was silent again; so I made up my mind that I would not push him too closely with questions thenceforward, at least until his manner should invite the venture.

Almost every day, now, my curiosity was laid on the rack. For instance, we would be sitting at work, and I would chance to mention some man or woman; whereupon Day would take up the person as a preacher would a text, and proceed in the placidest way to delineate his character in the most elaborate, searching and detailed way—and in nine cases out of ten his delineation would contain one and sometimes a couple of most absurd blunders, though otherwise perfect. I would point these out to him, but it never made any difference, he said he was right, and stuck calmly to his position. Then I would say, "Do you know this man personally?" And he would answer, in all cases, "No, not what you would call personally; I have met him once, for an hour." And when I retorted, "Why, I've known him all my life," he would simply say, as sufficient answer, "No matter; I know him as he is, you merely know him as he seems to be." On one occasion something brought up the name of G——, who had killed B——, over on the Sny, four years before, in a quarrel over some birds—the gentlemen being out shooting together at the time. Straightway Mr. Day began to paint G——'s character, according to his custom; and it was beautiful to hear him; you couldn't help saying to yourself all the time, "How true that is; how well he does it; how perfectly he knows this man, inside and out." But all at once, as usual, he spoilt it all, by remarking upon G——'s remorse on account of the homicide.

"Remorse!" I said. "What an idea that is. Why, the thing that

G—— is mainly hated for, in this town, is that he can be so perpetually and unchangeably cheerful, day in and day out, with that thing in his memory."

Day looked at me gravely and said:

"I tell you the man has never had one good, full, restful, peaceful hour in all these four years. He thinks of that crime with every breath he draws, and all his days are days of torture."

I said I didn't believe it and couldn't believe it. Day said:

"He has wanted to commit suicide, this long time."

I said that that statement would make the public laugh if they could hear it.

"No matter. He is his mother's idol, and is resolved to live while she lives; but he is also resolved to release himself when she dies. You will see; he will kill himself when she is taken away, and people will think grief for her loss moved him to it. She has been very sick for a week or two, now. If she should die, then you will see."

She did die, two or three days after that; and G—— killed himself the same night.

My days were full of interest, passed, as they were, in the presence of this fascinating and awful power. Now and then came an incident which one could smile at. One day old Mr. E——, a miserly person but of honorable reputation came into the shop and said to Mr. Day:

"Here is a bill on a broken Indiana bank which you gave me last Thursday in change. I ought to have brought it back sooner, but I was called away to Palmyra."

Day gave him a good bill for it, and E—— thanked him and went away. Then Day stood there with the bad bill in his hand, thinking, and presently said, as if to himself:

"There must be some mistake; I couldn't pay out a ten dollar bill and not remember it."

Then he did a thing which I had often seen him do before. He took a metal box out of his pocket, searched in it, put it back, and the next moment he said, in a surprised voice:

"Why, the man is a pitiful rascal."

"What has he done?" I asked.

"He has brought me a bad bill which he knew he did not get here."

I wanted to ask how he knew; but I restrained that impulse, and merely said it was a pity the shop had to lose all that money.

"It isn't lost," said Day; "he is on his way back, now, to get his bad bill again."

A minute or two later Mr. E—— bustled in, and said he had been mistaken about getting that bill in our shop, and he couldn't see how he happened to make such a—and there he stopped. Day was looking him placidly in the face, and just there E—— looked up, caught his eye, stopped speaking, turned red, re-exchanged the bills, and went away without another word, looking very crest-fallen.

I was prodigiously surprised, and said so; but Day said that if he had thought a moment he would have suspected E—— in the first place.

"He was the first man in whose parlor I sat in this town. I spent an hour or two there, talking; and he had it in his mind to forge T. R. Selmes's name to a check, for he was in money difficulties at the time."

"He—forge a check! Impossible. Did he say he was going to?"

"Nonsense—of course he didn't. But he had it in his mind to do it. I made a memorandum of it at the time."

He got out his note-book, and said:

"No, it wasn't Selmes—it was Brittingham he was going to forge it on."

Huck Finn and Tom Sawyer among the Indians

Chapter 1

THAT OTHER book which I made before, was named "Adventures of Huckleberry Finn." Maybe you remember about it. But if you don't, it don't make no difference, because it ain't got nothing to do with this one. The way it ended up, was this. Me and Tom Sawyer and the nigger Jim, that used to belong to old Miss Watson, was away down in Arkansaw at Tom's aunt Sally's and uncle Silas's. Jim warn't a slave no more, but free; because—but never mind about that: how he become to get free, and who done it, and what a power of work and danger it was, is all told about in that other book.

Well then, pretty soon it got dull there on that little plantation, and Tom he got pisoned with a notion of going amongst the Injuns for a while, to see how it would be; but about that time aunt Polly took us off up home to Missouri; and then right away after that she went away across the State, nearly to the west border, to stay a month or two months with some of her relations on a hemp farm out there, and took Tom and Sid and Mary; and I went along

because Tom wanted me to, and Jim went too, because there was
white men around our little town that was plenty mean enough and
ornery enough to steal Jim's papers from him and sell him down the
river again; but they couldn't come that if he staid with us.

Well, there's liver places than a hemp farm, there ain't no use to
deny it, and some people don't take to them. Pretty soon, sure
enough, just as I expected, Tom he begun to get in a sweat to have
something going on. Somehow, Tom Sawyer couldn't ever stand
much lazying around; though as for me, betwixt lazying around
and pie, I hadn't no choice, and wouldn't know which to take, and
just as soon have them both as not, and druther. So he rousted out
his Injun notion again, and was dead set on having us run off, some
night, and cut for the Injun country and go for adventures. He said
it was getting too dull on the hemp farm, it give him the fan-tods.

But me and Jim kind of hung fire. Plenty to eat and nothing to
do. We was very well satisfied. We hadn't ever had such comfortable times before, and we reckoned we better let it alone as long as
Providence warn't noticing; it would get busted up soon enough,
likely, without our putting in and helping. But Tom he stuck to the
thing, and pegged at us every day. Jim says:

"I doan' see de use, Mars Tom. Fur as I k'n see, people dat has
Injuns on dey han's ain' no better off den people dat ain' got no
Injuns. *Well* den: we ain' got no Injuns, we doan' need no Injuns,
en what does we want to go en hunt 'em up f'r? We's gitt'n along
jes' as well as if we had a million un um. Dey's a powful ornery lot,
anyway."

"*Who* is?"

"Why, de Injuns."

"Who says so?"

"Why, I says so."

"What do *you* know about it?"

"What does *I* know 'bout it? I knows dis much. Ef dey ketches a
body out, dey'll take en skin him same as dey would a dog. *Dat's*
what I knows 'bout 'em."

"All fol-de-rol. Who told you that?"

"Why, I hear ole Missus say so."

"Ole Missus! The widow Douglas! Much she knows about it. Has *she* ever been skinned?"

"Course not."

"Just as I expected. She don't know what she's talking about. Has she ever been amongst the Injuns?"

"No."

"Well, then, what right has she got to be blackguarding them and telling what ain't so about them?"

"Well, anyway, ole Gin'l Gaines, *he's* ben amongst 'm, anyway."

"All right, so he has. Been with them lots of times, hasn't he?"

"Yes—lots of times."

"Been with them *years*, hasn't he?"

"Yes, *sir!* Why, Mars Tom, he—"

"Very well, then. Has *he* been skinned? You answer me that."

Jim see Tom had him. He couldn't say a word. Tom Sawyer *was* the keenest boy for laying for a person and just leading him along by the nose without ever seeming to do it till he got him where he couldn't budge and then bust his arguments all to flinders *I* ever see. It warn't no use to argue with Tom Sawyer—a body never stood any show.

Jim he hem'd and haw'd, but all he could say was, that he had somehow got the notion that Injuns was powerful ornery, but he reckoned maybe—then Tom shut him off.

"You reckon maybe you've been mistaken. Well, you have. *Injuns* ornery! It's the most ignorant idea that ever—why, Jim, they're the noblest human beings that's ever been in the world. If a white man tells you a thing, do you know it's true? No, you don't; because generally it's a lie. But if an Injun tells you a thing, you can bet on it every time for the petrified fact; because you can't get an Injun to lie, he would cut his tongue out first. If you trust to a white man's honor, you better look out; but you trust to an Injun's honor, and nothing in the world can make him betray you—he would die first, and be glad to. An Injun is *all* honor. It's what they're *made* of. You ask a white man to divide his property with you—will he do it? I think I *see* him at it; but you go to an Injun, and he'll give you everything he's got in the world. It's just the difference between an

Injun and a white man. They're just all generousness and unstin-
geableness. And brave? Why, they ain't afraid of anything. If there
was just one Injun, and a whole regiment of white men against
him, they wouldn't stand the least show in the world,—not the
least. You'd see that splendid gigantic Injun come war-whooping
down on his wild charger all over paint and feathers waving his
tomahawk and letting drive with his bow faster than anybody could
count the arrows and hitting a soldier in any part of his body he
wanted to, every time, any distance, and in two minutes you'd see
him santering off with a wheelbarrow-load of scalps and the rest of
them stampeding for the United States the same as if the menag-
erie was after them. Death?—an Injun don't care shucks for death.
They prefer it. They *sing* when they're dying—sing their death-
song. You take an Injun and stick him full of arrows and splinters,
and hack him up with a hatchet, and skin him, and start a slow fire
under him, and do you reckon he minds it? No sir; he will just set
there in the hot ashes, perfectly comfortable, and *sing,* same as if he
was on salary. Would a white man? *You* know he wouldn't. And
they're the most gigantic magnificent creatures in the whole world,
and can knock a man down with a barrel of flour as far as they can
see him. They're awful strong, and fiery, and eloquent, and wear
beautiful blankets, and war paint, and moccasins, and buckskin
clothes, all over beads, and go fighting and scalping every day in the
year but Sundays, and have a noble good time, and they love
friendly white men, and just dote on them, and can't do too much
for them, and would ruther die than let any harm come to them,
and they think just as much of niggers as they do of anybody, and
the young squaws are the most beautiful be-utiful maidens that was
ever in the whole world, and they love a white hunter the minute
their eye falls on him, and from that minute nothing can ever shake
their love loose again, and they're always on the watch-out to
protect him from danger and get themselves killed in the place of
him—look at Pocahontas!—and an Injun can see as far as a telescope with the naked eye, and an enemy can't slip around anywhere, even in the dark, but he knows it; and if he sees one single
blade of grass bent down, it's all he wants, he knows which way to

go to find the enemy that done it, and he can read all kinds of trifling little signs just the same way with his eagle eye which *you* wouldn't ever see at all, and if he sees a little whiff of smoke going up in the air thirty-five miles off, he knows in a second if it's a friend's camp fire or an enemy's, just by the smell of the smoke, because they're the most giftedest people in the whole world, and the hospitablest and the happiest, and don't ever have anything to do from year's end to year's end but have a perfectly supernatural good time and piles and piles of adventures! Amongst the Injuns, life is just simply a circus, that's what it is. Anybody that knows, will tell you you can't praise it too high and you can't put it too strong."

Jim's eyes was shining, and so was mine, I reckon, and he was excited, and it was the same with both of us, as far as that was concerned. Jim drawed a long breath, and then says:

"Whoosh! Dem's de ticket for Jim! Bust ef it doan' beat all, how rotten ignornt a body kin be 'bout Injuns w'en 'e hain't had no chance to study um up. Why, Mars Tom, ef I'd a knowed what Injuns reely *is,* I pledges you my word I'd—well, you jes' count me *in,* dat's all; count me in on de Injun-country business; *I*'s ready to go, I doan' want no likelier folks aroun' me d'n what dem *Injuns* is. En Huck's ready, too—hain't it so, Huck?"

Course I warn't going to stay behind if they went, so I said I was.

Chapter 2

So we went to making preparations; and mighty private and secret, too, because Tom Sawyer wouldn't have nothing to do with a thing if there warn't no mystery about it. About three mile out in the woods, amongst the hills, there was an old tumble-down log house that used to be lived in, some time or other when people cut timber there, and we found it on a coon hunt one night, but nobody ever went there, now. So we let on it was infested with pirates and robbers, and we laid in the woods all one rainy night, perfectly still, and not showing fire or a light; and just before dawn we crept up pretty close and then sprung out, whooping and yelling, and took it by surprise, and never lost a man, Tom said, and was awful proud of it, though I couldn't see no sense in all that trouble and bother, because we could a took it in the day time just as well, there warn't nobody there. Tom called the place a cavern, though it warn't a cavern at all, it was a house, and a mighty ornery house at that.

Every day we went up to the little town that was two mile from the farm, and bought things for the outfit and to barter with the Injuns—skillets and coffee pots and tin cups, and blankets, and three sacks of flour, and bacon and sugar and coffee, and fish hooks, and pipes and tobacco, and ammunition, and pistols, and three guns, and glass beads, and all such things. And we hid them in the woods; and nights we clumb out of the window and slid down the lightning rod, and went and got the things and took them to the cavern. There was an old Mexican on the next farm below ours, and we got him to learn us how to pack a pack-mule so we could do it first rate.

And last of all, we went down fifteen or twenty mile further and bought five good mules, and saddles, because we didn't want to raise no suspicions around home, and took the mules to the cavern in the night and picketed them in the grass. There warn't no better mules in the State of Missouri, Tom said, and so did Jim.

Our idea was to have a time amongst the Injuns for a couple of months or so, but we had stuff enough to last longer than that, I reckon, because Tom allowed we ought to be fixed for accidents. Tom bought a considerable lot of little odds and ends of one kind and another which it ain't worth while to name, which he said they would come good with the Injuns.

Well, the last day that we went up to town, we laid in an almanac, and a flask or two of liquor, and struck a stranger that had a curiosity and was peddling it. It was little sticks about as long as my finger with some stuff like yellow wax on the ends, and all you had to do was to rake the yellow end on something, and the stick would catch fire and smell like all possessed, on account of part of it being brimstone. We hadn't ever heard of anything like that, before. They were the convenientest things in the world, and just the trick for us to have; so Tom bought a lot of them. The man called them lucifer matches, and said anybody could make them that had brimstone and phosphorus to do it with. So he sold Tom a passel of brimstone and phosphorus, and we allowed to make some for ourselves some time or other.

We was all ready, now. So we waited for full moon, which would be in two or three days. Tom wrote a letter to his aunt Polly to leave behind, telling her good bye, and saying rest easy and not worry, because we would be back in two or three weeks, but not telling her anything about where we was going.

And then Thursday night, when it was about eleven and everything still, we got up and dressed, and slid down the lightning rod, and shoved the letter under the front door, and slid by the nigger-quarter and give a low whistle, and Jim come gliding out and we struck for the cavern, and packed everything onto two of the mules, and put on our belts and pistols and bowie knives, and saddled up the three other mules and rode out into the big moonlight and started west.

By and by we struck level country, and a pretty smooth path, and not so much woods, and the moonlight was perfectly splendid, and so was the stillness. You couldn't hear nothing but the skreaking of the saddles. After while there was that cool and fresh feeling that tells you day is coming; and then the sun come up behind us, and made the leaves and grass and flowers shine and sparkle, on account of the dew, and the birds let go and begun to sing like everything.

So then we took to the woods, and made camp, and picketed the mules, and laid off and slept a good deal of the day. Three more nights we traveled that way, and laid up daytimes, and everything was mighty pleasant. We never run across anybody, and hardly ever see a light. After that, we judged we was so far from home that we was safe; so then we begun to travel by daylight.

The second day after that, when we was hoping to begin to see Injun signs, we struck a wagon road, and at the same time we struck an emigrant wagon with a family aboard, and it was near sundown, and they asked us to camp with them, and we done it.

There was a man about fifty-five and his wife, named Mills, and
three big sons, Buck and Bill and Sam, and a girl that said she was
seventeen, named Peggy, and her little sister Flaxy, seven year old.
They was from down in the lower end of Missouri, and said they
was bound for Oregon—going to settle there. We said we was
bound for the Injun country, and they said they was going to pass
through it and we could join company with them if we would like
to.

They was the simple-heartedest good-naturedest country folks in
the world, and didn't know anything hardly—I mean what you call
"learning." Except Peggy. She had read considerable many books,
and knowed as much as most any girl, and was just as pretty as ever
she could be, and live. But she warn't no prettier than she was
good, and all the tribe doted on her. Why they took as much care of
her as if she was made out of sugar or gold or something. When
she'd come to the camp fire, any of her brothers would get up in a
minute and give her the best place. I reckon you don't see that kind
of brothers pretty often. She didn't have to saddle her own mule,
the way she'd have to do in most society, they always done it for
her. Her and her mother never had anything to do but cook, that is
all; the brothers got the wood, they built the fires, they skinned the
game; and whenever they had time they helped her wash up the
things. It ain't often you see a brother kiss his own sister; fact is, I
don't know as I'd ever seen such a thing before; but they done it. I
know, because I see them do it myself; and not just once, but plenty
of times. Tom see it, too, and so did Jim. And they never said a cross
word to her, not one. They called her "dear." Plenty of times they
called her that; and right before company, too; they didn't care;
they never thought nothing of it. And she didn't, either. They'd say
"Peggy dear," to her, just in the naturalest off-handedest way, it
didn't make no difference who was around; and it took me two or
three days to get so I could keep from blushing, I was so ashamed
for them, though I knowed it warn't the least harm, because they
was right out of the woods and didn't know no better. But I don't
wish to seem to be picking flaws in them, and abusing them,
because I don't. They was the splendidest people in the world; and

after you got that fact stowed in your mind solid, you was very well satisfied, and perfectly willing to overlook their manners; because nobody can't be perfect, anyway.

We all got to be uncommon friendly together; it warn't any trouble at all. We traveled with them, and camped with them every night. Buck and Bill and Sam was wonderful with a lasso, or a gun, or a pistol, or horseback riding, and they learned us all these things so that we got to be powerful good at them, specially Tom; and though he couldn't throw a lasso as far as a man could, he could throw it about as true. And he could cave in a squirrel's or a wild turkey's or a prairie chicken's head any fair distance; and could send both loads from his pistol through your hat on a full gallop, at twenty yards, if you wanted him to. There warn't ever any better people than the Millses; but Peggy she was the cap-sheaf of the lot, of course; so gentle, she was, and so sweet, and whenever you'd done any little thing for her it made you feel so kind of all over comfortable and blessed to see her smile. If you ever felt cut, about anything, she never asked about the rights of it, or who done it, but just went to work and never rested till she had coaxed the smart all out and made you forget all about it. And she was that kind of a girl that if you ever made a mistake and happened to say something that hurt her, the minute you saw by her face what you had done, you wanted to get down on your knees in the dirt, you felt so mean and sorry. You couldn't ever get tired looking at her, all day long, she was so dear and pretty; and mornings it warn't ever sun-up to me till she come out.

One day, about a couple of weeks after we had left the United States behind, and was ever so far away out on the Great Plains, we struck the Platte river and went into camp in a nice grassy place a couple of hours before sun-down, and there we run across a camp of Injuns, the first ones we had been close enough to, yet, to get acquainted with. Tom was powerful glad.

Chapter 3

I T W A S just the place for a camp; the likeliest we had found yet. Big stream of water, and considerable many trees along it. The rest of the country, as far as you could see, any which-way you looked, clear to where the sky touched the earth, was just long levels and low waves—like what I reckon the ocean would be, if the ocean was made out of grass. Away off, miles and miles, was one tree standing by itself, and away off the other way was another, and here and yonder another and another scattered around; and the air was so clear you would think they was close by, but it warn't so, most of them was miles away.

Old Mills said he would stop there and rest up the animals. I happened to be looking at Peggy, just then, because I mostly always happened to be looking at her when she was around, and her cheeks turned faint red and beautiful, like a nigger's does when he puts a candle in his mouth to surprise a child; she never said nothing, but pretty soon she got to singing low to herself and looking happy. I didn't let on; but next morning when I see her slip off to the top of one of them grass-waves and stand shading her eyes with her hand and looking away off over the country, I went there and got it all out of her. And it warn't no trouble, either, after she got started. It looked like the mainest trouble was going to be to stop her again.

She had a sweetheart—that was what was the matter of her. He had staid behind, to finish up things, and would be along when he got done. His name was Brace Johnson; big, and fine, and brave, and good, and splendid, and all that, as near as I could make out; twenty-six years old; been amongst the Injuns ever since he was a boy, trapping, hunting, scouting, fighting; knowed all about Injuns, knowed some of the languages, knowed the plains and the mountains, and all the whole country, from Texas to Oregon; and now he was done with all that kind of life, and her and him was going to settle down in Oregon, and get married, and go to farming it. I reckon she thought she only loved him; but I see by her talk it was upwards of that, she worshiped him. She said we was to stay where we was till he come, which might be in a week, and then we would stay as much longer as her pap thought the horses needed to.

There was five of the Injuns, and they had spry little ponies, and was camped tolerable close by. They was big, strong, grand looking fellows, and had on buckskin leggings and moccasins, and red feathers in their hair, and knives and tomahawks, and bows and arrows, and one of them had an old gun and could talk a little English, but it warn't any use to him, he couldn't kill anything with it because it hadn't any flint—I mean the gun. They was naked from the waist up, when they hadn't on their blankets.

They set around our fire till bedtime, the first night, and took supper with us, and passed around the pipe, and was very friendly, and made signs to us, and grunted back, when we signed anything they understood, and pretty much everything they see that they liked, they wanted it. So they got coffee, and sugar, and tobacco, and a lot of little things.

They was there to breakfast, next morning, and then me and Tom went over to their camp with them, and we all shot at a mark with their bows and arrows, and they could outshoot anything I ever see with a bow and arrow, and could stand off a good ways and hit a tree with a tomahawk every time.

They come back with us at noon and eat dinner, and the one with the gun showed it to Peggy, and made signs would she give him a flint, and she got one from her father, and put it in the gunlock and fixed it herself, and the Injun was very thankful, and called her good squaw and pretty squaw, and she was ever so pleased; and another one named Hog Face that had a bad old hurt on his shin, she bandaged it up and put salve on it, and he was very thankful too.

Tom he was just wild over the Injuns, and said there warn't no white men so noble; and he warn't by himself in it, because me and

Jim, and all the rest of us got right down fond of them; and Peggy said she did wish Brace was here, he would change his notions about Injuns, which he was down on, and hated them like snakes, and always said he wouldn't trust one any how or any where, in peace time or war time or any other time. She showed me a little dirk-knife which she got out of her bosom, and asked me what I reckoned it was for, and who give it to her.

"I don't know," says I. "Who did give it to you?"

"Brace." Then she laughed, gay and happy, and says, "You'll never guess what it's for."

"Well, what is it for?" says I.

"To kill myself with!"

"O, good land!" says I, "how you talk."

"Yes," she says, "it's the truth. Brace told me that if I ever fell into the hands of the savages, I mustn't stop to think about him, or the family, or anything, or wait an hour to see if I mightn't be rescued; I mustn't waste *any* time, I mustn't take any chances, I must kill myself right away."

"Goodness," I says, "and for why?"

"I don't know."

"Didn't you ask him why?"

"Of course; and teased him to tell me, but he wouldn't. He kept trying to get me to promise, but I laughed him off, every time, and told him if he was so anxious to get rid of me he must tell me *why* I must kill myself, and then maybe I would promise. At last he said he *couldn't* tell me. So I said, very well, then, I wouldn't promise; and laughed again, but he didn't laugh. By and by he said, very serious and troubled, 'You know I wouldn't ask you to do that or any other thing that wasn't the best for you—you can trust me for that, can't you?' That made me serious, too, because that was true; but I couldn't promise *such* a thing, you know, it made me just shudder to think of it. So then he asked me if I would keep the dirk, as his gift and keepsake; and when I said I would, he said that would do, it was all he wanted."

One of the Injuns, named Blue Fox, come up, just then, and the minute he see the dirk he begun to beg for it; it was their style—

they begged for everything that come in their way. But Peggy wouldn't let him have it. Next day and the next he come teasing around her, wanting to take it to his camp and make a nice new sheath and a belt for her to wear it in, and so she got tired at last and he took it away. But she never let him have it till he promised he would take good care of it and never let it get out of his hands. He was that pleased, that he up and give her a necklace made out of bears' claws; and as she had to give him something back, of course, she give him a Bible, and tried to learn him some religion, but he couldn't understand, and so it didn't do him no particular good—that is, it didn't just then, but it did after a little, because when the Injuns got to gambling, same as they done every day, he put up his Bible against a tomahawk and won it.

They was a sociable lot. They wrastled with Buck and Bill and Sam, and learned them some new holts and throws that they didn't know before; and we all run foot races and horse races with them, and it was prime to see the way their ornery little ponies would split along when their pluck was up.

And they danced dances for us. Two or three times they put on all their fuss and feathers and war paint and danced the war dance, and whooped and jumped and howled and yelled, and it was lovely and horrible. But the one with the gun, named Man-afraid-of-his-Mother-in-law, didn't ever put on any paint and finery, and didn't dance in the war dances, and mostly he didn't come around when they had them, and when he did he looked sour and glum and didn't stay.

Yes, we was all stuck after the Injuns, kind of in love with them, as you may say, and I reckon I never had better times than I had then. Peggy was as good to them as if she was their sister or their child, and they was very fond of her. She was sorry for the one with the gun, and tried to encourage him to put on his war paint and dance the war dance with the others and be happy and not glum; and it pleased him to have her be so friendly, but he never done it. But pretty soon it struck her what maybe the matter was, and she says to me:

"He's in mourning—that's what it is; he has lost a friend. And to think, here I have been hurting him, and making him remember his sorrows, when I wouldn't have done such a thing for the whole world if I had known."

So after that, she couldn't do too much for him, nor be sorry enough for him. And she wished more than ever that Brace was here, so he could see that Injuns was just like other people, after all, and had their sorrows and troubles, and knowed how to love a friend and grieve for him when he was gone.

Tom he was set on having the Injuns take me and him and Jim into their band and let us travel to their country and live in their tribe a week or two; and so, the fourth day, we went over to their camp, me and Tom did, to ask them. But they was fixing for a buffalo hunt next morning, to be gone all day, and maybe longer, and that filled Tom so full of excitement, he couldn't think about anything else, for we hadn't ever seen a buffalo yet. They had a plan for me and Jim and Tom to start before daylight with one Injun and go in one direction, and Buck in another with another Injun, and Bill with another and Sam with another, and leave the other Injun in their camp because he was so lame with his sore leg, and whichever gang found the buffaloes first was to signal the others. So it was all fixed.

Then we see Peggy off there on one of them grass-waves, with Flaxy, looking out over the country with her hand over her eyes, and all the Injuns noticed her at once and asked us what she was looking for. I said she was expecting a lot of friends. The Injun that spoke a little English asked me how many. It's always my disposition to stretch, so I said seven. Tom he kind of smiled, but let it go at that. Man-afraid-of-his-Mother-in-law says:

"Little child (meaning Flaxy, you know,) say only *one*."

I see I was ketched, but in my opinion a body don't ever gain anything by weakening, in them circumstances, so I says:

"*Seven,*" and said it firm, and stuck to it.

The Injuns talked amongst themselves a while, then they told us to go over and ask Bill and Buck and Sam to come and talk about the hunt. We done it, and they went over, and we all set down to wait supper till they come back; they said they reckoned they would be back inside of a half an hour. In a little while four of the Injuns come and said the boys was staying behind to eat supper with Hog Face in their camp. So then we asked the Injuns to eat supper with us, and Peggy she passed around the tin plates and things, and dished out the vittles, and we all begun. They had put their war paint and feathers and fixings on since we left their camp,—all but the one with the gun—so I judged we would have another good time. We eat, and eat, and talked, and laughed, till by and by we was all done, and then still we set there talking.

By and by Tom shoved his elbow into my side, soft and easy, and then got up and took a bucket and said he would fetch some water for Peggy, and went santering off. I said I would help; so I took a bucket and followed along. As soon as we was behind some trees, Tom says:

"Somehow everything don't seem right, Huck. They don't *smoke;* they've always smoked, before. There's only one gun outside the wagon, and a minute or two ago one of them was meddling with it. I never thought anything of it at the time, but I do now, because I happened to notice it just a minute ago, and by George the flint's gone! There's something up, Huck—I'm going to fetch the boys."

Away he went, and what to do I didn't know. I started back, keeping behind the trees, and when I got pretty close, I judged I would watch what was going on, and wait for Tom and the boys. The Injuns was up, and sidling around, the rest was chatting, same as before, and Peggy was gathering up the plates and things. I heard a trampling like a lot of horses, and when it got pretty near, I see that other Injun coming on a pony, and driving the other ponies and all our mules and horses ahead of him, and he let off a long wild whoop, and the minute he done that, the Injun that had a gun, the one that Peggy fixed, shot her father through the head with it and scalped him, another one tomahawked her mother and scalped her, and then these two grabbed Jim and tied his hands together, and the other two grabbed Peggy, who was screaming and crying, and all of them rushed off with her and Jim and Flaxy, and as fast as I run, and as far as I run, I could still hear her, till I was a long, long ways off.

Soon it got dark, and I had to stop, I was so tired. It was an awful long night, and I didn't sleep, but was watching and listening all the time, and scared at every little sound, and miserable. I never see such a night for hanging on, and stringing out, and dismalness.

When daylight come, I didn't dast to stir, at first, being afraid; but I got so hungry I had to. And besides, I wanted to find out about Tom; so I went sneaking for the camp, which was away off across the country, I could tell it by the trees. I struck the line of trees as far up as I could, and slipped along down behind them. There was a smoke, but by and by I see it warn't the camp fire, it was the wagon; the Injuns had robbed it and burnt it. When I got down pretty close, I see Tom there, walking around and looking. I was desperate glad; for I didn't know but the other Injun had got him.

We scratched around for something to eat, but didn't find it, everything being burnt; then we set down and I told Tom everything, and he told me everything. He said when he got to the Injun camp, the first thing he see was Buck and Sam and Bill laying dead —tomahawked and scalped, and stripped; and each of them had as much as twenty-five arrows sticking in him. And he told me how else they had served the bodies, which was horrible, but it would not do to put it in a book. Of course the boys' knives and pistols was gone.

Then Tom and me set there a considerable time, with our jaws in our hands, thinking, and not saying anything. At last I says:

"Well?"

He didn't answer right off, but pretty soon he says:

"I've thought it out, and my mind's made up; but I'll give you the first say, if you want it."

I says:

"No, I don't want it. I've tried, but I can't seem to strike any plan. We're here, and that's all there is to it. We're here, as much as a million miles from any place, I reckon; and we haven't got anything to eat, nor anything to get it with, and no way to get anywhere but just to hoof it, and I reckon we'd play out and die before we got there that way. We're in a fix. That's all I know about it; we're just in a fix, and you can't call it by no lighter name. Whatever your plan is, it'll suit me; I'll do whatever you say. Go on. Talk."

Chapter 4

So he says:

"Well, this is my idea, Huck. I got Jim into this scrape, and so of course I ain't going to turn back towards home till I've got him out of it again, or found out he's dead; but you ain't in fault, like me, and so if we can run across any trappers bound for the States—"

"Never mind about that, Tom," I says, "I'm agoing with you. I want to help save Jim, if I can, and I want to help save Peggy, too. She was good to us, and I couldn't rest easy if I didn't. I'll go with you, Tom."

"All right," he says, "I hoped you would, and I was certain you would; but I didn't want to cramp you or influence you."

"But how are we going?" says I, "walk?"

"No," he says, "have you forgot about Brace Johnson?"

I had. And it made the cold misery go through me to hear his name; for it was going to be sorrowful times for him when he come.

So we was to wait there for him. And maybe two or three days, without anything to eat; because the folks warn't expecting him for about a week from the time we camped. We went off a half a mile to the highest of them grass-waves, where there was a small tree, and took a long look over the country, to see if we could see Brace or anybody coming, but there wasn't a living thing stirring, anywhere. It was the biggest, widest, levelest world—and all dead; dead and still; not a sound. The lonesomest place that ever was; enough to break a body's heart, just to listen to the awful stillness of it. We talked a little sometimes—once an hour, maybe; but mostly we took up the time thinking, and looking, because it was hard to talk against such solemness. Once I said:

"Tom, where did you learn about Injuns—how noble they was, and all that?"

He give me a look that showed me I had hit him hard, very hard, and so I wished I hadn't said the words. He turned away his head, and after about a minute he said "Cooper's novels," and didn't say anything more, and I didn't say anything more, and so that changed the subject. I see he didn't want to talk about it, and was feeling bad, so I let it just rest there, not ever having any disposition to fret or worry any person.

We had started a camp fire in a new place further along down the stream, with fire from the burnt wagon, because the Injuns had burnt the bodies of old Mr. Mills and his wife along with the wagon, and so that place seemed a kind of graveyard, you know, and we didn't like to stay about it. We went to the new fire once in a while and kept it going, and we slept there that night, most starved.

We turned out at dawn, and I jumped up brash and gay, for I had been dreaming I was at home; but I just looked around once over that million miles of gray dead level, and my soul sucked back that brashness and gayness again with just one suck, like a sponge, and then all the miserableness come back and was worse than yesterday.

Just as it got to be light, we see some creatures away off on the prairie, going like the wind; and reckoned they was antelopes or Injuns, or both, but didn't know; but it was good to see some life again, anyway; it didn't seem so lonesome after that, for a while.

We was so hungry we couldn't stay still; so we went loafing off, and run across a prairie-dog village—little low mounds with holes in them, and a sentinel, which was a prairie dog, and looked like a Norway rat, standing guard. We had long cottonwood sticks along, which we had cut off of the trees and was eating the bark for breakfast; and we dug into the village, and rousted out an owl or two and a couple of hatfuls of rattlesnakes, and hoped we was going to get a dog, but didn't, nor an owl, either; but we hived as bully a rattlesnake as ever I see, and took him to camp and cut his head off and skinned him and roasted him in the hot embers, and he was prime; but Tom was afraid, and wouldn't eat any, at first, but I knowed they was all right, because I had seen hogs and niggers eat them, and it warn't no time to be proud when you are starving to death, I reckoned. Well, it made us feel a powerful sight better, and nearly cheerful again; and when we got done we had snake enough left for a Sunday School blowout, for he was a noble big one. He was middling dry, but if we'd a had some gravy or butter or something, it wouldn't a been any slouch of a picnic.

We put in the third day that we was alone talking, and laying around, and wandering about, and snaking, and found it more and more lonesomer and drearier than ever. Often, as we come to a high grass-wave, we went up and looked out over the country, but all we ever saw was buzzards or ravens or something wheeling round and round over where the Injun camp was—and knowed what brought them there. We hadn't been there; and hadn't even been near there.

When we was coming home towards evening, with a pretty likely snake, we stopped and took another long look across country, and didn't see anything at first, but pretty soon we thought we did; but it was away off yonder against the sky, ever so far, and so we warn't certain. You can see an awful distance there, the air is so clear; so we calculated to have to wait a good while. And we did. In about a half an hour, I reckon, we could make out that it was horses or men or something, and coming our way. Then we laid down and kept close, because it might be Injuns, and we didn't want no more Injun then, far from it. At last Tom says:

"There's three horses, sure."

And pretty soon he says:

"There's a man riding one. I don't make out any more men."

And presently he says:

"There's only one man; he's driving three pack mules ahead of him; and coming along mighty brisk. He's got a wide slouch hat on, and I reckon he's white. It's Brace Johnson, I guess; I reckon he's the only person expected this year. Come—let's creep along behind

the grass-waves and get nearer. If it's him, we want to stop him
before he gets to the old camp, and break it to him easy."

But we couldn't. He was too fast for us. There he set, on his
horse, staring. The minute we showed ourselves he had his gun
leveled on us; then he noticed we warn't Injuns, and dropped it, and
told us to come on, and we did.

"Boys," he says, "by the odds and ends that's left, I see that this
was the Mills's camp. Was you with them?"

"Yes."

"What's happened?"

I never said nothing; and Tom he didn't, at first; then he said:
"Injuns."

"Yes," he says, "I see that, myself, by the signs; but the folks got
away, didn't they?—along with you?—didn't they?"

We didn't answer. He jumped off of his horse, and come up to us
quick, looking anxious, and says:

"Where are they?—quick, where are they? Where's Peggy?"

Well, we had to tell him—there warn't no other way. And it was
all he could do to stand it; just all he could do. And when we come
to tell about Peggy, he *couldn't* stand it; his face turned as white as
milk, and the tears run down his cheeks, and he kept saying "Oh,
my God, oh my God." It was so dreadful to see him, that I wanted
to get him away from that part of it, and so I worked around and
got back onto the other details, and says:

"The one with the gun, that didn't have no war paint, he shot
Mr. Mills, and scalped him; and he bloodied his hands, then, and
made blood stripes across his face with his fingers, like war paint,
and then begun to howl war-whoops like the Injuns does in the
circus. And poor old Mrs. Mills, she was down on her knees,
begging so pitiful when the tomahawk—"

"I shall never never see her again—never never any more—my
poor little darling, so young and sweet and beautiful—but thank
God, she's dead!"

He warn't listening to me.

"Dead?" I says; "if you mean Peggy, *she's* not dead."

He whirls on me like a wild-cat, and shouts:

"Not dead! Take it back, take it back, or I'll strangle you! How do *you* know?"

His fingers was working, and so I stepped back a little out of reach, and then says:

"I know she ain't, because I see the Injuns drag her away; and they didn't strike her nor offer to hurt her."

Well, he only just groaned; and waved out his hands, and fetched them together on top of his head. Then he says:

"You staggered me, and for a minute I believed you, and it made me most a lunatic. But it's all right—she had the dirk. Poor child, poor thing—if I had only been here!"

I just had it on my tongue's end to tell him she let Blue Fox have the dirk for a while and I didn't know whether he give it back to her or not—but I didn't say it. Some kind of instinct told me to keep it to myself, I didn't know why. But this fellow was the quickest devil you ever see. He see me hesitate, and he darted a look at me and bored into me like he was trying to see what it was I was keeping back in my mind. But I held my face quiet, and never let on. So then he looked considerable easier, but not entirely easy, and says:

"She had a dirk—didn't you see her have a dirk?"

"Yes," I says.

"Well, then, it's all right. She didn't lose it, nor give it away, nor anything, did she? She had it with her when they carried her away, didn't she?"

Of course I didn't know whether she did or not, but I said yes, because it seemed the thing to say.

"You are sure?" he says.

"Yes, perfectly sure," I says, "I ain't guessing, I *know* she had it with her."

He looked very grateful, then, and drawed a long sigh, and says:

"Ah, the poor child, poor friendless little thing—thank God she's dead."

I couldn't make out why he wanted her to be dead, nor how he could seem to be so thankful for it. As for me, I hoped she wasn't, and I hoped we would find her, yet, and get her and Flaxy away

from the Injuns alive and well, too, and I warn't going to let myself
be discouraged out of that thought, either. We started for the Injun
camp; and when Tom was on ahead a piece, I up and asked Brace if
he actually hoped Peggy *was* dead; and if he did, *why* he did. He
explained it to me, and then it was all clear.

When we got to the camp, we looked at the bodies a minute, and
then Brace said we would bury them presently, but he wanted to
look around and make some inquiries, first. So he turned over the
ashes of the fire, examining them careful, and examining any little
thing he found amongst them, and the tracks, and any little rag or
such like matter that was laying around, and pulled out one of the
arrows, and examined that, and talked to himself all the time,
saying "Sioux—yes, Sioux, that's plain"—and other remarks like
that. I got to wandering around, too, and once when I was a step or
two away from him, lo and behold, I found Peggy's little dirk-knife
on the ground! It just took my breath, and I reckon I made a kind
of a start, for it attracted his attention, and he asked me if I had
found something, and I said yes, and dropped on my knees so that
the knife was under my leg; and when he was coming, I let some
moccasin beads drop on the ground that I had found before, and
pretended to be looking at them; and he come and took them up,
and whilst he was turning them over in his hand examining them, I
slipped the dirk into my pocket; and presently, as soon as it was
dark, I slipped out of our camp and carried it away off about a
quarter of a mile and throwed it amongst the grass. But I warn't
satisfied; it seemed to me that it would be just like that fellow to
stumble on it and find it, he was so sharp. I didn't even dast to bury
it, I was so afraid he'd find it. So at last I took and cut a little hole
and shoved it in betwixt the linings of my jacket, and then I was
satisfied. I was glad I thought of that, for it was like having a
keepsake from Peggy, and something to remember her by, always as
long as I lived.

Chapter 5

THAT NIGHT, in camp, after we had buried the bodies, we set around and talked, and me and Tom told Brace all about how we come to be there, on account of Tom wanting us to go with him and hunt up some Injuns and live with them a while, and Brace said it was just like boys the world over, and just the same way it was with him when he was a boy; and as we talked along, you could see he warmed to us because we thought so much of Peggy and told him so many things she done and said, and how she looked. And now and then, as we spoke of the Injuns, a most wicked look would settle into his face, but at these times he never said nothing.

There was some things which he was a good deal puzzled about; and now and then he would bust into the middle of the talk with a remark that showed us his mind had been wandering to them things. Once he says:

"I wonder what the nation put 'em on the war path. It was perfectly peaceable on the Plains a little while back, or I wouldn't a had the folks start, of course. And I wonder if it's *general* war, or only some little private thing."

Of course we couldn't tell him, and so had to let him puzzle along. Another time, he busted in and says:

"It's the puzzlingest thing!—there's features about it that I can't seem to make head nor tail of, no way. I can understand why they fooled around here three or four days, because there warn't no hurry; they knowed they had from here to Oregon to do the job in, and besides, an Injun is patient; he'd ruther wait a month till he can make sure of his game without any risk to his own skin than attempt it sooner where there's the least risk. I can understand why they planned a buffalo hunt that would separate all the whites from each other and make the mastering of them easy and certain, because five warriors, nor yet fifteen, won't tackle five men and two boys, even by surprise when they're asleep at dawn, when there's a

safer way. Yes, I can understand all that—it's Injun, and easy. But
the thing that gits me, is, what made them throw over the buffalo
plan and act in such a hurry at last—for they did act in a hurry.
You see, an Injun don't kill a whole gang, that way, right out and
out, unless he is mighty mad or in a desperate hurry. After they had
got the young men safe out of the way, they would have saved at
least the old man for the torture. It clear beats me, I can't understand it."

For the minute, I couldn't help him out any; I couldn't think of
anything to make them in a hurry. But Tom he remembered about
me telling the Injuns the Millses was expecting seven friends, and
they looked off and see Peggy and Flaxy on the watch-out for them.
So Brace says:

"That's all right, then; I understand it, now. *That's* Injun—that
would make 'em drop the buffalo business and hurry up things. I
know why they didn't kill the nigger, and why they haven't killed
him yet, and ain't going to, nor hurt him; and now if I only knowed
whether this is general war or only a little private spurt, I would be
satisfied and not bother any more. But—well, hang it, let it go,
there ain't any way to find out."

So we dropped back on the details again, and by and by I was
telling how Man-afraid-of-his-Mother-in-law streaked his face all
over with blood after he killed Mr. Mills, and then—

"Why, he done that for war paint!" says Brace Johnson, excited;
"warn't he in war-outfit before?—warn't they all painted?"

"All but him," I says. "He never wore paint nor danced with the
rest in the war dance."

"Why didn't you tell me that before; it explains everything."

"I did tell you," I says, "but you warn't listening."

"It's all right, now, boys," he says, "and I'm glad it's the way it is,
for I wasn't feeling willing to let you go along with me, because I
didn't know but all the Injuns was after the whites, and it was a
general war, and so it would be bad business to let you get into it,
and we couldn't dare to travel except by night, anyway. But you are
all right, now, and can shove out with me in the morning, for this is
nothing but a little private grudge, and like as not this is the end of

it. You see, some white man has killed a relation of that Injun, and so he has hunted up some whites to retaliate on. It wouldn't be the proper thing for him to ever appear in war fixings again till he had killed a white man and wiped out that score. He was in disgrace till he had done that; so he didn't lose any time about piling on something that would answer for war paint; and I reckon he got off a few war-whoops, too, as soon as he could, to exercise his throat and get the taste of it in his mouth again. They're probably satisfied, now, and there won't be any more trouble."

So poor Peggy guessed right; that Injun was "in mourning;" he had "lost a friend;" but it turns out that he knowed better how to comfort himself than she could do it for him.

We had breakfast just at dawn in the morning, and then rushed our arrangements through. We took provisions and such like things as we couldn't get along without, and packed them on one of the mules, and *cachéd* the rest of Brace's truck—that is, buried it—and then Brace struck the Injun trail and we all rode away, westward. Me and Tom couldn't have kept it; we would have lost it every little while; but it warn't any trouble to Brace, he dashed right along like it was painted on the ground before him, or paved.

He was so sure Peggy had killed herself, that I reckoned he would be looking out for her body, but he never seemed to. It was so strange that by and by I got into a regular sweat to find out why; and so at last I hinted something about it. But he said no, the Injuns would travel the first twenty-four hours without stopping, and then they would think they was far enough ahead of the Millses' seven friends to be safe for a while—so then they would go into camp; and there's where we'd find the body. I asked him how far they would go in that time, and he says:

"The whole outfit was fresh and well fed up, and they had the extra horses and mules besides. They'd go as much as eighty miles —maybe a hundred."

He seemed to be thinking about Peggy *all* the time, and never about anything else or anybody else. So I chanced a question, and says:

"What'll the Injuns do with Flaxy?"

"Poor little chap, she's all right, they won't hurt her. No hurry about her—we'll get her from them by and by. They're fond of children, and so they'll keep her or sell her; but whatever band gets her, she'll be the pet of that whole band, and they'll dress her fine and take good care of her. She'll be the only white child the most of the band ever saw, and the biggest curiosity they ever struck in their lives. But they'll see 'em oftener, by and by, if the whites ever get started to emigrating to Oregon, and I reckon they will."

It didn't ever seem to strike him that Peggy wouldn't kill herself whilst Flaxy was a prisoner, but it did me. I had my doubts; sometimes I believed she would, sometimes I reckoned she wouldn't.

We nooned an hour, and then went on, and about the middle of the afternoon Brace seen some Injuns away off, but we couldn't see them. We could see some little specks, that was all; but he said he could see them well enough, and it was Injuns; but they warn't going our way, and didn't make us any bother, and pretty soon they was out of sight. We made about forty or fifty miles that day, and went into camp.

Well, late the next day, the trail pointed for a creek and some bushes on its bank about a quarter of a mile away or more, and Brace stopped his horse and told us to ride on and see if it was the camp; and said if it was, to look around and find the body; and told us to bury it, and be tender with it, and do it as good as we could, and then come to him a mile further down the creek, where he would make camp—just come there, and only tell him his orders was obeyed, and stop at that, and not tell him how she looked, nor what the camp was like, nor anything; and then he rode off on a walk, with his head down on his bosom, and took the pack mule with him.

It was the Injun camp, and the body warn't there, nor any sign of it, just as I expected. Tom was for running and telling him, and cheering him up. But I knowed better. I says:

"No, the thing has turned out just right. We'll stay here about long enough to dig a grave with bowie knives, and then we'll go and tell him we buried her."

Tom says:

"That's mysterious, and crooked, and good, and I like that much about it; but hang it there ain't any sense in it, nor any advantage to anybody in it, and I ain't willing to it."

So it looked like I'd got to tell him why I reckoned it would be better, all around, for Brace to think we found her and buried her, and at last I come out with it, and then Tom was satisfied; and when we had staid there three or four hours, and all through the long twilight till it was plumb dark, we rode down to Brace's camp, and he was setting by his fire with his head down, again, and we only just said, "It's all over—and done right," and laid down like we wanted to rest; and he only says, in that deep voice of his'n, "God be good to you, boys, for your kindness," and kind of stroked us on the head with his hand, and that was all that anybody said.

Chapter 6

AFTER ABOUT four days, we begun to catch up on the Injuns. The trail got fresher and fresher. They warn't afraid, now, and warn't traveling fast, but we had kept up a pretty good lick all the time. At last one day we struck a camp of theirs where they had been only a few hours before, for the embers was still hot. Brace said we would go very careful, now, and not get in sight of them but keep them just a safe distance ahead. Tom said maybe we might slip up on them in the night, now, and steal Jim and Flaxy away; but he said no, he had other fish to fry, first, and besides it wouldn't win, anyway.

Me and Tom wondered what his other fish was; and pretty soon we dropped behind and got to talking about it. We couldn't make nothing out of it for certain, but we reckoned he was meaning to get even with the Injuns and kill some of them before he took any risks about other things. I remembered he said we would get Flaxy "by and by," and said there warn't no hurry about it. But then for all he talked so bitter about Injuns, it didn't look as if he could actually kill one, for he was the gentlest, kindest-heartedest grown person I ever see.

We killed considerable game, these days; and about this time here comes an antelope scampering towards us. He was a real pretty little creature. He stops, about thirty yards off, and sets up his head, and arches up his neck, and goes to gazing at us out of his bright eyes as innocent as a baby. Brace fetches his gun up to his shoulder, but waited and waited, and so the antelope capered off, zig-zagging first to one side and then t'other, awful graceful, and then stretches straight away across the prairie swift as the wind, and Brace took his gun down. In a little while here comes the antelope back again, and stopped a hundred yards off, and stood still, gazing at us same as before, and wondering who we was and if we was friendly, I reckon. Brace fetches up his gun twice, and then the third time; and this time he fired, and the little fellow tumbled. Me and Tom was starting for him, seeing Brace didn't. But Brace says:

"Better wait a minute, boys, you don't know the antelope. Let him die, first. Because if that little trusting, harmless thing looks up in your face with its grieved eyes when it's dying, you'll never forget it. When I'm out of meat, I kill them, but I don't go around them till they're dead, since the first one."

Tom give me a look, and I give Tom a look, as much as to say, "his fish ain't revenge, that's certain, and so what the mischief is it?"

According to my notions, Brace Johnson was a beautiful man. He was more than six foot tall, I reckon, and had broad shoulders, and he was as straight as a jackstaff, and built as trim as a race-horse. He had the steadiest eye you ever see, and a handsome face, and his hair hung all down his back, and how he ever could keep his outfit so clean and nice, I never could tell, but he did. His buckskin suit looked always like it was new, and it was all hung with fringes, and had a star as big as a plate between the shoulders of his coat, made of beads of all kinds of colors, and had beads on his moccasins, and a hat as broad as a barrel-head, and he never looked so fine and grand as he did a-horseback; and a horse couldn't any more throw him than he could throw the saddle, for when it come to riding, he could lay over anything outside the circus. And as for strength, I never see a man that was any more than half as strong as what he was, and a most lightning marksman with a gun or a bow or a pistol. He had two long-barreled ones in his holsters, and could shoot a pipe out of your mouth, most any distance, every time, if you wanted him to. It didn't seem as if he ever got tired, though he stood most of the watch every night himself, and let me and Tom sleep. We was always glad, for his sake, when a very dark night come, because then we all slept all night and didn't stand any watch; for Brace said Injuns ain't likely to try to steal your horses on such nights, because if you woke up and managed to kill them and they died in the dark, it was their notion and belief that it would always be dark to them in the Happy Hunting Grounds all through eternity, and so you don't often hear of Injuns attacking in the night, they do it just at dawn; and when they do ever chance it in the night, it's only moonlight ones, not dark ones.

He didn't talk very much; and when he talked about Injuns, he talked the same as if he was talking about animals; he didn't seem to have much idea that they was men. But he had some of their ways, himself, on account of being so long amongst them; and moreover he had their religion. And one of the things that puzzled him was how such animals ever struck such a sensible religion. He said the Injuns hadn't only but two Gods, a good one and a bad one, and they never paid no attention to the good one, nor ever prayed to him or worried about him at all, but only tried their level best to flatter up the bad god and keep on the good side of him; because the good one loved them and wouldn't ever think of doing them any harm, and so there warn't any occasion to be bothering him with prayers and things, because he was always doing the very best he could for them, anyway, and prayers couldn't better it; but all the trouble come from the bad god, who was setting up nights to think up ways to bring them bad luck and bust up all their plans, and never fooled away a chance to do them all the harm he could; and so the sensible thing was to keep praying and fussing around him all the time, and get him to let up. Brace thought more of the Great Spirit than he did of his own mother, but he never fretted

about him. He said his mother wouldn't hurt him, would she?—
well then, the Great Spirit wouldn't, that was sure.

Now as to that antelope, it brought us some pretty bad luck.
When we was done supper, that day, and was setting around
talking and smoking, Brace begun to make some calculations about
where we might be by next Saturday, as if he thought this day was
a Saturday, too—which it wasn't. So Tom he interrupted him and
told him it was Friday. They argued over it, but Tom turned out to
be right. Brace set there awhile thinking, and looking kind of
troubled; then he says:

"It's my mistake, boys, and all my fault, for my carelessness.
We're in for some bad luck, and we can't get around it; so the best
way is to keep a sharp look-out for it and beat it if we can—I mean
make it come as light as we can, for of course we can't beat it
altogether."

Tom asked him why he reckoned we would have bad luck, and it
come out that the Bad God was going to fix it for us. He didn't *say*
Bad God, out and out; didn't mention his name, seemed to be afraid
to; said "he" and "him," but we understood. He said a body had got
to perpetuate him in all kinds of ways. Tom allowed he said
propitiate, but I heard him as well as Tom, and he said perpetuate.
He said the commonest way and the best way to perpetuate him
was to deny yourself something and make yourself uncomfortable,
same as you do in any religion. So one of his plans was to try to
perpetuate him by vowing to never allow himself to eat meat on
Fridays and Sundays, even if he was starving; and now he had
gone and eat it on a Friday, and he'd druther have cut his hand off
than done it if he had knowed. He said "he" had got the advantage
of us, now, and you could bet he would make the most of it. We
would have a run of bad luck, now, and no knowing when it would
begin or when it would stop.

We had been pretty cheerful, before that, galloping over them
beautiful Plains, and popping at Jack rabbits and prairie dogs and
all sorts of things, and snuffing the fresh air of the early mornings,
and all that, and having a general good time; but it was all busted
up, now, and we quit talking and got terrible blue and uneasy and

scared; and Brace he was the bluest of all, and kept getting up, all night, and looking around, when it wasn't his watch; and he put out the camp fire, too, and several times he went out and took a wide turn around the camp to see if everything was right. And every now and then he would say:

"Well, it hain't come yet, but it's coming."

It come the next morning. We started out from camp, just at early dawn, in a light mist, Brace and the pack mule ahead, I next, and Tom last. Pretty soon the mist begun to thicken, and Brace told us to keep the procession closed well up. In about a half an hour it was a regular fog. After a while Brace sings out:

"Are you all right?"

"All right," I says.

By and by he sings out again:

"All right, boys?"

"All right," I says, and looked over my shoulder and see Tom's mule's ears through the fog.

By and by Brace sings out again, and I sings out, and he says:

"Answer up, Tom," but Tom didn't answer up. So he said it again, and Tom didn't answer up again; and come to look, there warn't anything there but the mule—Tom was gone.

"It's come," says Brace, "I knowed it would," and we faced around and started back, shouting for Tom. But he didn't answer.

Chapter 7

WHEN we had got back a little ways we struck wood and water, and Brace got down and begun to unsaddle. Says I:

"What you going to do?"

"Going to camp."

"Camp!" says I, "why what a notion. *I* ain't going to camp, I'm going for Tom."

"Going for Tom! Why, you fool, Tom's lost," he says, lifting off his saddle.

"Of course he is," I says, "and you may camp as much as you want to, but I ain't going to desert him, I'm going for him."

"Huck, you don't know what you're talking about. Get off of that mule."

But I didn't. I fetched the mule a whack, and started; but he grabbed him and snaked me off like I was a doll, and set me on the ground. Then he says:

"Keep your shirt on, and maybe we'll find him, but not in the fog. Don't you reckon I know what's best to do?" He fetched a yell, and listened, but didn't get any answer. "We couldn't find him in the fog; we'd get lost ourselves. The thing for us to do is to stick right here till the fog blows off. Then we'll begin the hunt, with some chance."

I reckoned he was right, but I most wanted to kill him for eating that antelope meat and never stopping to think up what day it was and he knowing so perfectly well what consounded luck it would fetch us. A body can't be too careful about such things.

We unpacked, and picketed the mules, and then set down and begun to talk, and every now and then fetched a yell, but never got any answer. I says:

"When the fog blows off, how long will it take us to find him, Brace?"

"If he was an old hand on the Plains, we'd find him pretty easy; because as soon as he found he was lost he would set down and not budge till we come. But he's green, and he won't do that. The minute a greeny finds he's lost, he can't keep still to save his life—tries to find himself, and gets lost worse than ever. Loses his head; wears himself out, fretting and worrying and tramping in all kinds of directions; and what with starving, and going without water, and being so scared, and getting to mooning and imagining more and more, it don't take him but two or three days to go crazy, and then—"

"My land, is Tom going to be lost as long as that?" I says; "it makes the cold shudders run over me to think of it."

"Keep up your pluck," he says, "it ain't going to do any good to lose that. I judge Tom ain't hurt; I reckon he got down to cinch up, or something, and his mule got away from him, and he trotted after it, thinking he could keep the direction where the fog swallowed it up, easy enough; and in about a half a minute he was turned around and trotting the other way, and didn't doubt he was right, and so didn't holler till it was too late—it's the way they always do, consound it. And so, if he ain't hurt—"

He stopped; and as he didn't go on, I says:

"Well? If he ain't hurt, what then?"

He didn't say anything, right away; but at last he says:

"No, I reckon he ain't hurt, and that's just the worst of it; because there ain't no power on earth can keep him still, now. If he'd a broken his leg—but of course he couldn't, with this kind of luck against him."

We whooped, now and then, but I couldn't whoop much, my heart was most broke. The fog hung on, and on, and on, till it seemed a year, and there we set and waited; but it was only a few hours, though it seemed so everlasting. But the sun busted through it at last, and it begun to swing off in big patches, and then Brace saddled up and took a lot of provisions with him, and told me to stick close to camp and not budge, and then he cleared out and begun to ride around camp in a circle, and then in bigger circles, watching the ground for signs all the time; and so he circled wider and wider, till he was far away, and then I couldn't see him any more. Then I freshened up the fire, which he told me to do, and throwed armfuls of green grass on it to make a big smoke; it went up tall and straight to the sky, and if Tom was ten mile off he would see it and come.

I set down, blue enough, to wait. The time dragged heavy. In about an hour I see a speck away off across country, and begun to watch it; and when it got bigger, it was a horseman, and pretty soon I see it was Brace, and he had something across the horse, and I reckoned it was Tom, and he was hurt. But it wasn't; it was a man. Brace laid him down, and says:

"Found him out yonder. He's been lost, nobody knows how long —two or three weeks, I judge. He's pretty far gone. Give him a spoonful of soup every little while, but not much, or it will kill him.

He's as crazy as a loon, and tried to get away from me, but he's all used up, and he couldn't. I found Tom's trail in a sandy place, but I lost it again in the grass."

So away he started again, across country, and left me and this fellow there, and I went to making soup. He laid there with his eyes shut, breathing kind of heavy, and muttering and mumbling. He was just skin and bones and rags, that's all he was. His hands was all scratched up and bloody, and his feet the same and all swelled up and wore out, and a sight to look at. His face—well, I never see anything so horrible. It was baked with the sun, and was splotchy and purple, and the skin was flaked loose and curled, like old wall paper that's rotted on a damp wall. His lips was cracked and dry, and didn't cover his teeth, so he grinned very disagreeable, like a steel-trap. I judged he had walked till his feet give out on him, and then crawled around them deserts on his hands and knees; for his knees hadn't any flesh or skin on them.

When I got the soup done, I touched him, and he started up scared, and stared at me a second, and then tried to scramble away; but I catched him and held him pretty easy, and he struggling and begging very pitiful for me to let him go and not kill him. I told him I warn't going to hurt him, and had made some nice soup for him; but he wouldn't touch it at first, and shoved the spoon away and said it made him sick to see it. But I persuaded him, and told him I would let him go if he would eat a little, first. So then he made me promise three or four times, and then he took a couple of spoonfuls; and straight off he got just wild and ravenous, and wanted it all. I fed him a cup full, and then carried the rest off and hid it; and so there I had to set, by the hour, and him begging for more; and about every half an hour I give him a little, and his eyes would blaze at the sight of it, and he would grab the cup out of my hands and take it all down at a gulp, and then try to crowd his mouth into it to lick the bottom, and get just raging and frantic because he couldn't.

Between times he would quiet down and doze; and then start up wild, and say "Lost, my God, lost!" and then see me, and recollect, and go to begging for something to eat again. I tried to get something out of him about himself, but his head was all wrong, and you couldn't make head nor tail of what he said. Sometimes he seemed to say he had been lost ten years, and sometimes it was ten weeks, and once I judged he said a year; and that is all I could get out of him, and no particulars. He had a little gold locket on a gold chain around his neck, and he would take that out and open it and gaze and gaze at it and forget what he was doing, and doze off again. It had a most starchy young woman in it, dressed up regardless, and two little children in her arms, painted on ivory, like some the widow Douglas had of her old anzesters in Scotland.

This kind of worry and sweat went on the whole day long, and was the longest day I ever see. And then the sun was going down, and no Tom and no Brace. This fellow was sound asleep, for about the first time. I took a look at him, and judged it would last; so I thought I would run out and water the mules and put on their side-lines and get right back again before he stirred. But the pack mule had pulled his lariat loose, and was a little ways off dragging it after him and grazing, and I walked along after him, but every time I got pretty close he throwed up his head and trotted a few steps, and first I knowed he had tolled me a long ways, and I wished I had the other mule to catch him with, but I dasn't go back after him, because the dark would catch me and I would lose this one, sure; so I had to keep tagging along after him afoot, coming as near to cussing the antelope meat as I dast, and getting powerful nervous all the time, and wondering if some more of us was going to get lost. And I would a got lost if I hadn't had a pretty big fire; for you could just barely see it, away back yonder like a red spark when I catched the mule at last, and it was plumb dark too, and getting black before I got home. It was that black when I got to camp that you couldn't see at all, and I judged the mules would get water enough pretty soon without any of my help; so I picketed them closer by than they was before, and put on their side-lines, and groped into the tent, and bent over this fellow to hear if he was there, yet, and all of a sudden it busted on me that I had been gone two or three hours, I didn't know how long, and of course he was out and gone, long ago, and how in the nation would I ever find him in the dark,

and this awful storm coming up, and just at that minute I hear the
wind begin to shiver along amongst the leaves, and the thunder to
mumble and grumble away off, and the cold chills went through
me to think of what I had done and how in the world I was ever
going to find him again in the dark and the rain, dad fetch him for
making all this trouble, poor pitiful rat, so far from home and lost,
and I so sorry for him, too.

So I held my breath and listened over him, and by Jackson he
was there yet, and I hear him breathe—about once a minute. Once
a week would a done me, though, it sounded so good to hear him
and I was so thankful he hadn't sloped. I fastened the flap of the
tent and then stretched out snug on my blankets, wishing Tom and
Brace was there; and thinks I, I'll let myself enjoy this about five
minutes before I sail out and freshen up the camp fire.

The next thing that I knowed anything about, was no telling
how many hours afterwards. I sort of worked along up out of a solid
sleep, then, and when I come to myself the whole earth was rocking
with the smashingest blast of thunder I ever heard in my life and
the rain was pouring down like the bottom had fell out of the sky.
Says I, now I've done it! the camp fire's out, and no way for Tom or
Brace to find the camp. I lit out, and it was so; everything drenched,
not a sign of an ember left. Of course nobody could ever start a new
fire out there in the rain and wind; but I could build one inside and
fetch it out after it got to going good. So I rushed in and went to
bulging around in the dark, and lost myself and fell over this
fellow, and scrambled up off of him, and begged his pardon and
asked if I hurt him; but he never said a word and didn't make a
sound. And just then comes one of them blind-white glares of
lightning that turns midnight to daytime, and there he laid, grin-
ning up at me, stone dead. And he had hunks of bread and meat
around, and I see in a second how it all was. He had got at our grub
whilst I was after the mule, and over-eat himself and died, and I
had been sleeping along perfectly comfortable with his relics I don't
know how long, and him the gashliest sight I ever struck. But I
never waited there to think all that; I was out in the public
wilderness before the flash got done quivering, and I never went

back no more. I let him have it all to his own self; I didn't want no company.

I went off a good ways, and staid the rest of the night out, and got most drownded; and about an hour or more after sun-up Tom and Brace come, and I was glad. I told them how things had went, and we took the gold locket and buried the man and had breakfast, and Brace didn't scold me once. Tom was about used up, and we had to stay there a day or two for him to get straightened up again. I asked him all about it, and he says:

"I got down to cinch up, and I nearly trod on a rattlesnake which I didn't see, but heard him go *bzzz!* right at my heel. I jumped most a rod, I was so scared and taken so sudden, and I run about three steps, and then looked back over my shoulder and my mule was gone—nothing but just white fog there. I forgot the snake in a second, and went for the mule. For ten steps I didn't hurry, expecting to see him all the time; but I picked up my heels, then, and run. When I had run a piece I got a little nervous, and was just going to yell, though I was ashamed to, when I thought I heard voices ahead of me, bearing to the right, and that give me confidence, knowing it must be you boys; so I went heeling it after you on a short-cut; but if I did hear voices I misjudged the direction and went the other way, because you know you can't really tell where a sound comes from, in a fog. I reckon you was trotting in one direction and me in the other, because it warn't long before I got uneasy and begun to holler, and you didn't hear me nor answer. Well, that scared me so that I begun to tremble all over, and I did wish the fog would lift, but it didn't, it shut me in, all around, like a thick white smoke. I wanted to wait, and let you miss me and come back, but I couldn't stay still a second; it would a killed me; I *had* to run, and I did. And so I kept on running, by the hour, and listening, and shouting; but never a sound did ever I hear; and whenever I stopped just a moment and held my breath to listen, it was the awfulest stillness that ever was, and I couldn't stand it and had to run on again.

"When I got so beat out and tired I couldn't run any more, I walked; and when the fog went off at last and I looked over my shoulder and there was a tall smoke going up in the sky miles across

the plain behind me, I says to myself if that was ahead of me it
might be Huck and Brace camping and waiting for me; but it's in
the wrong direction, and maybe it's Injuns and not whites; so I
wouldn't take any chances on it, but kept right on; and by and by I
thought I could see something away off on the prairie, and it was
Brace, but I didn't know it, and so I hid. I saw him, or something,
twice more before night, and I hid both times; and I walked,
between times, further and further away from that smoke and stuck
to ground that wouldn't leave much of a track; and in the night I
walked and crawled, together, because I couldn't bear to keep still,
and was so hungry, and so scratched up with cactuses, and getting
kind of out of my head besides; but the storm drove me up onto a
swell to get out of the water, and there I staid, and took it. Brace he
searched for me till dark, and then struck for home, calculating to
strike for the camp fire and lead his horse and pick his way; but the
storm was too heavy for that, and he had to stop and give up that
notion; and besides you let the fire go out, anyway. I went crawling
off as soon as dawn come, and making a good trail, the ground was
so wet; and Brace found it and then he found me; and the next
time I get down to cinch up a mule in the fog I'll notify the rest of
you; and the next time I'm lost and see a smoke I'll go for it, I don't
care if it comes out of the pit."

Chapter 8

We WAS away along up the North Fork of the Platte, now.
When we started again, the Injuns was two or three days ahead of
us, and their trail was pretty much washed out, but Brace didn't
mind it, he judged he knowed where they was striking for. He had
been reading the signs in their old camps, all these days, and he said
these Sioux was Ogillallahs. We struck a hilly country, now, and
traveled the day through and camped a few miles up a nice valley
late in the afternoon on top of a low flattish hill in a grove of small
trees. It was an uncommon pretty place, and we picked it out on

account of Tom, because he hadn't stood the trip well, and we
calculated to rest him there another day or two. The valley was a
nearly level swale a mile or a mile and a half wide, and had a little
river-bed in it with steep banks, and trees along it—not much of a
river, because you could throw a brick across it, but very deep when
it was full of water, which it wasn't, now. But Brace said we would
find puddles along in its bed, so him and me took the animals and a
bucket, and left Tom in camp and struck down our hill and rode
across the valley to water them. When we got to the river we found
new-made tracks along the bank, and Brace said there was about
twenty horses in that party, and there was white men in it, because
some of the horses had shoes on, and likely they was from out Fort
Laramie way.

There was a puddle or two, but Brace couldn't get down the
banks easy; so he told me to wait with the mules, and if he didn't
find a better place he would come back and rig some way to get up
and down the bank here. Then he rode off down stream and pretty
soon the trees hid him. By and by an antelope darts by me and I
looked up the river and around a corner of the timber comes two
men, riding fast. When they got to me they reined up and begun to
ask me questions. They was half drunk, and a mighty rough looking couple, and their clothes didn't help them much, being old
greasy buckskin, just about black with dirt. I was afraid of them.
They asked me who I was, and where I come from, and how many
was with me, and where we was camped; and I told them my name
was Archibald Thompson, and says:

"Our camp's down at the foot of the valley, and we're traveling
for pap's health, he's very sick, we can't travel no more till he gets
better, and there ain't nobody to take care of him but me and aunt
Mary and Sis, and so we're in a heap of troub—"

"It's all a lie!" one of them breaks in. "You've stole them animals."

"You bet he has," says the other. "Why, I know this one myself;
he belongs to old Vaskiss the trader, up at the Fort, and I'm dead
certain I've seen one of the others somewheres."

"Seen him? I reckon you have. Belongs to Roubidou the blacksmith, and he'll be powerful glad we've found him again. I knowed him in a minute. Come, boy, I'm right down sorry for your sick pap, and poor aunt Mary and Sis, but all the same you'll go along back to our camp, and you want to be mighty civil and go mighty careful, or first you know you'll get hung."

First I didn't know what to do; but I had to work my mind quick, and I struck a sort of an idea, the best I could think of, right off, that way. I says to myself, it's two to one these is horse-thieves, because Brace says there's a plenty of them in these regions; and so I reckon they'd like to get one or two more while they're at it. Then I up and says:

"Gents, as sure as I'm here I never stole the animals; and if I'll prove it to you you'll let me go, won't you?"

"How're you going to prove it?"

"I'll do it easy if you'll come along with me, for we bought two mules that's almost just like these from the Injuns day before yesterday, and maybe they stole 'em, I don't know, but we didn't, that's sure."

They looked at each other, and says:

"Where are they—down at your camp?"

"No; they're only down here three or four hundred yards. Sister Mary she—"

"Has she got them?"

"Yes."

"Anybody with her?"

"No."

"Trot along, then, and don't you try to come any tricks, boy, or you'll get hurt."

I didn't wait for a second invite, but started right along, keeping a sharp lookout for Brace, and getting my yell ready, soon as I should see him. I edged ahead, and edged ahead, all I could, and they notified me a couple of times not to shove along so fast, because there warn't no hurry; and pretty soon they noticed Brace's trail, and sung out to me to halt a minute, and bent down over their saddles, and checked up their speed, and was mightily interested, as I could see when I looked back. I didn't halt, but jogged ahead, and kept widening the distance. They sung out again, and threatened me, and then I brushed by Brace's horse, in the trees, and knowed Brace was down the bank or close by, so I raised a yell and put up my speed to just the highest notch the mules could reach. I looked back, and here they come!—and next comes a bullet whizzing by! I whacked away for life and death, and looked back and they was gaining; looked back again, and see Brace booming after the hind one like a house afire, and swinging the long coils of his lariat over his head; then he sent it sailing through the air, and as it scooped that fellow in, Brace reined back his horse and yanked him out of his saddle, and then come tearing ahead again, dragging him. He yelled to me to get out of range, and so I turned out sudden and looked back, and my man had wheeled and was raising his gun on Brace, but Brace's pistol was too quick for him, and down he went, out of his saddle.

Well, we had two dead men on our hands, and I felt pretty crawly, and didn't like to look at them; but Brace allowed it warn't a very unpleasant sight, considering they tried to kill me. He said we must hurry into camp, now, and get ready for trouble; so we shoved for camp, and took the two new horses and the men's guns and things with us, not waiting to water our animals.

It was nearly dark. We kept a watch-out towards up the river, but didn't see anything stirring. When we got home we still watched from the edge of the grove, but didn't see anything, and no sign of that gang's camp fire; then Brace said we was probably safe from them for the rest of the night, so we would rest the animals three or four hours, and then start out and get as well ahead as we could, and keep ahead as long as this blamed Friday-antelope luck would let us, if Tom could stand the travel.

It come on starlight, a real beautiful starlight, and all the world as still and lovely as Sunday. By and by Brace said it would be a good idea to find out where the thieves was camped, so we could give it a wide berth when we started; and he said I could come along if I wanted to; and he took his gun along, this time, and I took one of the thieves' guns. We took the two fresh horses and rode down across the valley and struck the river, and then went

pretty cautious up it. We went as much as two mile, and not a sign
of a camp fire anywheres. So we kept on, wondering where it could
be, because we could see a long ways up the valley. And then all of
a sudden we heard people laugh, and not very far off, maybe forty
or fifty yards. It come from the river. We went back a hundred
yards, and tied the horses amongst the trees, and then back again
afoot till we was close to the place, where we heard it before, and
slipped in amongst the trees and listened, and heard the voices again,
pretty close by. Then we crept along on our knees, slow and
careful, to the edge of the bank, through the bush, and there was
the camp, a little ways up, and right in the dry bed of the river; two
big buffalo-skins lodges, a band of horses tied, and eight men
carousing and gambling around a fire—all white men, and the
roughest kind, and prime drunk. Brace said they had camped there
so their camp couldn't be seen easy, but they might as well camped
in the open as go and get drunk and make such a noise. He said
they was horse thieves, certain.

We was interested, and stayed looking a considerable time. But
the liquor begun to beat them, and first one and then another went
gaping and stretching to the tents and turned in. And then another
one started, and the others tried to make him stay up, because it was
his watch, but he said he was drunk and sleepy and didn't want to
watch, and said "Let Jack and Bill stand my watch, as long they like
to be up late—they'll be in directly, like as not."

But the others threatened to lick him if he didn't stand his
watch; so he grumbled, but give in, and got his gun and set down;
and when the others was all gone to roost, he just stretched himself
out and went to snoring as comfortable as anybody.

We left, then, and sneaked down to where our horses was, and
rode away, leaving the rapscallions to sleep it out and wait for Jack
and Bill to come, but we reckoned they'd have to wait a most
notorious long time first.

We rode down the river to where Brace was when I yelled to him
when the thieves was after me; and he said he had dug some steps
in the bank there with his bowie, and we could finish the job in a
little while, and when we broke camp and started we would bring

our mules there and water them. So we tied our horses and went down into the river bed to the puddle that was there, and laid down on our breasts to take a drink; but Brace says:

"Hello, what's that?"

It was as still as death before, but you could hear a faint, steady, rising sound, now, up the river. We held our breath and listened. You could see a good stretch up it, and tolerable clear, too, the starlight was so strong. The sound kept growing and growing, very fast. Then all of a sudden Brace says:

"Jump for the bank! I know what that is."

It's always my plan to jump first, and ask afterwards. So I done it. Brace says:

"There's a water-spout broke loose up country somewheres, and you'll see sights mighty soon, now."

"Do they break when there ain't no clouds in the sky?" I says, judging I had him.

"Never you mind," he says, "there was a cloud where this one broke. I've seen this kind of thing before, and I know that sound. Fasten your horse just as tight as you can, or he'll break loose presently."

The sound got bigger and bigger, and away up yonder it was just one big dull thundering roar. We looked up the river a piece, and see something coming down its bed like dim white snakes writhing along. When it went hissing and sizzling by us it was shallow foamy water. About twenty yards behind it comes a solid *wall* of water four foot high, and nearly straight up and down, and before you could wink it went rumbling and howling by like a whirlwind, and carrying logs along, and them thieves, too, and their horses and tents, and tossing them up in sight, and then under again, and grinding them to hash, and the noise was just awful, you couldn't a heard it thunder; and our horses was plunging and pitching, and trying their best to break loose. Well, before we could turn around the water was over the banks and ankle deep.

"Out of this, Huck, and shin for camp, or we're goners!"

We was mounted and off in a second, with the water chasing after us. We rode for life, we went like the wind, but we didn't have to use whip or spur, the horses didn't need no encouragement. Half way across the valley we met the water flooding down from above; and from there on, the horses was up to their knees, sometimes, yes, and even up to their bellies towards the last. All hands was glad when we struck our hill and sailed up it out of danger.

Chapter 9

Our little low hill was an island, now, and we couldn't a got away from it if we had wanted to. We all three set around and watched the water rise. It rose wonderful fast; just walked up the long, gradual slope, as you may say, it come up so fast. It didn't stop rising for two or three hours; and then that whole valley was just a big level river a mile to a mile and a half wide, and deep enough to swim the biggest ship that was ever built, and no end of dim black drift logs spinning around and sailing by in the currents on its surface.

Brace said it hadn't took the water-spout an hour to dump all that ocean of water and finish up its job, but like enough it would be a week before the valley was free of it again; so Tom would have considerable more time than we bargained to give him to get well in.

Me and Tom was down-hearted and miserable on account of Jim and Peggy and Flaxy, because we reckoned it was all up with them and the Injuns, now; and so at last Tom throwed out a feeler to see what Brace thought. He never said anything about the others, but only about the Injuns; said the water-spout must a got the Injuns, hadn't it? But Brace says:

"No, nary an Injun. Water-spouts don't catch any but white folks. There warn't ever a white man that could tell when a water-spout's coming; and how the nation an Injun can tell is something I never could make out, but they can. When it's perfectly clear weather, and other people ain't expecting anything, they'll say, all of a sudden, 'heap water coming,' and pack up in a hurry and shove for high ground. They say they smell it. I don't know whether that's so or not; but one thing I do know, a water-spout often catches a white man, but it don't ever catch an Injun."

Next morning there we was, on an island, same as before; just a level, shining ocean everywheres, and perfectly still and quiet, like it was asleep. And awful lonesome.

Next day the same, only lonesomer than ever.

And next day just the same, and mighty hard work to put in the time. Mostly we slept. And after a long sleep, wake up, and eat dinner, and look out over the tiresome water, and go to sleep again; and wake up again, by and by, and see the sun go down and turn it into blood, and fire, and melted butter, and one thing or another, awful beautiful, and soft, and lovely, but solemn and lonesome till you couldn't rest.

We had eight days of that, and the longer we waited for that ocean to play out and run off, the bigger the notion I got of a water-spout that could puke out such a mortal lot of water as that in an hour.

We left, then, and made a good day's travel, and by sundown begun to come onto fresh buffalo carcases. There was so many of them that Brace reckoned there was a big party of Injuns near, or else whites from the fort.

In the morning we hadn't gone five miles till we struck a big camp where Injuns had been, and hadn't gone more than a day or two. Brace said there was as many as a hundred of them, altogether, men, women and children, and made up from more than one band of Sioux, but Brulé's, mostly, as he judged by the signs. Brace said things looked like these Injuns was camped here a considerable time.

Of course we warn't thinking about our Injuns, or expecting to run across any signs of them or the prisoners, but Tom he found an arrow, broke in two, which was wound with blue silk thread down by the feather, and he said he knowed it was Hog Face's, because he got the silk for him from Peggy and watched him wind it. So Brace begun to look around for other signs, and he believed he found some. Well, I was ciphering around in a general way myself, and outside of the camp I run across a ragged piece of Peggy's dress as big as a big handkerchief, and it had blood on it. It most froze me to see that, because I judged she was killed; and if she warn't, it stood to reason she was hurt. I hid the rag under a buffalo chip, because if Brace was to see it he might suspicion she wasn't dead after all the pains we had took to make him believe she was; and just then he sings out "Run here, boys," and Tom he come running from one way and I the other, and when we got to him, there in the middle of the camp, he points down and says:

"There—that's the shoe-print of a white woman. See—you can see, where she turned it down to one side, how thin the sole is. She's white, and she's a prisoner with this gang of Injuns. I don't understand it. I'm afraid there's *general* trouble broke out between the whites and Injuns; and if that's so, I've got to go mighty cautious from this out." He looks at the track again, and says, "Poor thing, it's hard luck for her," and went mumbling off, and never noticed that me and Tom was most dead with uneasiness, for we could see plain enough it was Peggy's print, and was afraid he would see it himself, or think he did, any minute. His back warn't more than turned before me and Tom had tramped on the print once or twice—just enough to take the clearness out of it, because we didn't know but he might come back for another look.

Pretty soon we see him over yonder looking at something, and we went there, and it was four stakes drove in the ground; and he looks us very straight and steady in the eyes, first me and then Tom, and then me again, till it got pretty sultry; then he says, cold and level, but just as if he'd been asking us a question:

"Well, I believe you. Come along."

Me and Tom followed along, a piece behind; and Tom says:

"Huck, he's so afraid she's alive, that it's just all he can do to believe that yarn of ours about burying her. And pretty soon, now, like enough, he'll find out she ain't dead, after all."

"That's just what's worrying me, Tom. It puts us in a scrape, and I don't see no way out of it; because what can we say when he tackles us about lying to him?"

"I know what to say, well enough."

"You do? Well I wish you'd tell me, for I'm blamed if I see any way out—I wouldn't know a single word to say."

"I'll say this, to him. I'll say, suppose it was likely you was going to get knocked in the head with a club some time or other, but it warn't quite certain; would you want to be knocked in the head straight off, so as to make it certain, or wouldn't you ruther wait and see if you mightn't live your life out and not happen to get clubbed at all? Of course, he would say. Then I would put it at him straight, and say, wasn't you happier, when we made you think she was dead, than you was before? Didn't it keep you happy all this time? Of course. Well, wasn't it worth a little small lie like that to keep you happy instead of awfully miserable many days and nights? Of course. And wasn't it likely she would be dead before you ever run across her again?—which would make our lie plenty good enough. True again. And at last I would up and say, just you put yourself in our place, Brace Johnson: now, honor bright, would you have told the truth, that time, and broke the heart of the man that was Peggy Mills's idol? If you could, you are not a man, you are a devil; if you could and did, you'd be lower and hard-hearteder than the devils, you'd be an Injun. That's what I'll say to him, Huck, if the time ever comes."

Now that was the cleanest and slickest way out that ever was; and who would ever a thought of it but Tom Sawyer? I never seen the like of that boy for just solid gobs of brains and level headedness. It made me comfortable, right away, because I knowed very well Brace Johnson couldn't ever get around *that,* nor under it nor over it nor through it; he would have to answer up and confess he would a told that lie his own self, and would have went on backing it up and standing by it, too, as long as he had a rag of a lie left in him to do it with.

I noticed, but I never said anything, that Tom was putting the Injuns below the devils, now. You see, he had about got it through his noddle, by this time, that book Injuns and real Injuns is different.

Brace was unslinging the pack; so we went to him to see what he was doing it for, and he says:

"Well, I don't understand that white woman being with this band of Injuns. Of course maybe she was took prisoner years ago, away yonder on the edge of the States, and has been sold from band to band ever since, all the way across the Plains. I say of course that may be the explanation of it, but as long as I don't know that that's the way of it, I ain't going to take any chances. I'll just do the other thing: I'll consider that this woman is a new prisoner, and that her being here means that there's trouble broke out betwixt the Injuns and the whites, and so I'll act according. That is, I'll keep shy of Injuns till I've fixed myself up a little, so's to fit the new circumstances."

He had got a needle and some thread out of the pack, and a little paper bag full of dried bugs, and butterflies, and lizards, and frogs, and such like creatures, and he sat down and went to sewing them fast to the lapels of his buckskin coat, and all over his slouch hat, till he was that fantastic he looked like he had just broke out of a museum when he got it all done. Then he says:

"Now if I act strange and foolish, the Injuns will think I'm crazy; so I'll be safe and all right. They are afraid to hurt a crazy man, because they think he's under His special persecution" (he meant the Bad God, you know) "for his sins; and they kind of avoid him, and don't much like to be around him, because they think he's bad medicine, as they call it—'medicine' meaning luck, about as near as you can put it into English. I got this idea from a chap they called a naturalist.

"A war party of Injuns dropped onto him, and if he'd a knowed his danger, he'd a been scared to death; but he didn't know a war party from a peace party, and so he didn't act afraid, and that bothered the Injuns, they didn't know what to make of it; and when they see how anxious and particular he was about his bugs, and how fond of them and stuck after them he seemed to be, they judged he was out of his mind, and so they let him go his own gait, and never touched him. I've gone fixed for the crazy line ever since."

Then he packed the mule again, and says:

"Now we'll get along again, and follow the trail of these Injuns."

But it bore nearly straight north, and that warn't what he was expecting; so he rode off on the desert and struck another trail which bore more to the west, and this one he examined very careful, and mumbled a good deal to himself; but said at last that this was our Injuns, though there was more horses in the party than there was before. He knowed it by signs, he said, but he didn't say what the signs was.

We struck out on this trail, and followed it a couple of days

Jane Lampton Clemens

THIS was my mother. When she died, in October, 1890, she was well along in her eighty-eighth year; a mighty age, a well contested fight for life for one who at forty was so delicate of body as to be accounted a confirmed invalid and destined to pass soon away. I knew her well during the first twenty-five years of my life; but after that I saw her only at wide intervals, for we lived many days' journey apart. I am not proposing to write about her, but merely to talk about her; not give her formal history, but merely make illustrative extracts from it, so to speak; furnish flash-light glimpses of her character, not a processional view of her career. Technically speaking, she had no career; but she had a character, and it was of a fine and striking and lovable sort.

What becomes of the multitudinous photographs which one's mind takes of people? Out of the million which my mental camera must have taken of this first and closest friend, only one clear and strongly defined one of early date remains. It dates back forty-seven years; she was forty years old, then, and I was eight. She held me by the hand, and we were kneeling by the bedside of my brother, two years older than I, who lay dead, and the tears were flowing down her cheeks unchecked. And she was moaning. That dumb sign of anguish was perhaps new to me, since it made upon me a very strong impression—an impression which holds its place still with the picture which it helped to intensify and make memorable.

She had a slender small body, but a large heart; a heart so large that everybody's griefs and everybody's joys found welcome in it and hospitable accommodation. The greatest difference which I find between her and the rest of the people whom I have known, is this, and it is a remarkable one: those others felt a strong interest in a few things, whereas to the very day of her death she felt a strong interest in the whole world and everything and everybody in it. In all her life she never knew such a thing as a half-hearted interest in affairs and people, or an interest which drew a line and left out certain affairs and was indifferent to certain people. The invalid who takes a strenuous and indestructible interest in everything and everybody but himself, and to whom a dull moment is an unknown thing and an impossibility, is a formidable adversary for disease and a hard invalid to vanquish. I am certain it was this feature of my mother's make-up that carried her so far toward ninety.

Her interest in people and the other animals was warm, personal, friendly. She always found something to excuse, and as a rule to love, in the toughest of them—even if she had to put it there herself. She was the natural ally and friend of the friendless. It was believed that, Presbyterian as she was, she could be beguiled into saying a soft word for the devil himself; and so the experiment was tried. The abuse of Satan began; one conspirator after another added his bitter word, his malign reproach, his pitiless censure, till at last, sure enough, the unsuspecting subject of the trick walked into the trap. She admitted that the indictment was sound; that Satan was utterly wicked and abandoned, just as these people had said; *but*, would any claim that he had been treated fairly? A sinner was but a sinner; Satan was just that, like the rest. What saves the rest?—their own efforts alone? No—or none might ever be saved. To their feeble efforts is added the mighty help of pathetic, appealing, imploring prayers that go up daily out of all the churches in Christendom and out of myriads upon myriads of pitying hearts. But who prays for Satan? Who, in eighteen centuries, has had the common humanity to pray for the one sinner that needed it most, our one fellow and brother who most needed a friend yet had not a single one, the one sinner among us all who had the highest and clearest *right* to every Christian's daily and nightly prayers for the plain and unassailable reason that his was the first and greatest need, he being among sinners the supremest?

This Friend of Satan was a most gentle spirit, and an unstudied and unconscious pathos was her native speech. When her pity or her indignation was stirred by hurt or shame inflicted upon some defenceless person or creature, she was the most eloquent person I have heard speak. It was seldom eloquence of a fiery or violent sort, but gentle, pitying, persuasive, appealing; and so genuine and so nobly and simply worded and so touchingly uttered, that many times I have seen it win the reluctant and splendid applause of tears. Whenever anybody or any creature was being oppressed, the fears that belonged to her sex and her small stature retired to the rear, and her soldierly qualities came promptly to the front. One day in our village I saw a vicious devil of a Corsican, a common terror in the town, chasing his grown daughter past cautious male citizens with a heavy rope in his hand, and declaring he would wear it out on her. My mother spread her door wide to the refugee, and then instead of closing and locking it after her, stood in it and stretched her arms across it, barring the way. The man swore, cursed, threatened her with his rope; but she did not flinch or show any sign of fear; she only stood straight and fine, and lashed him, shamed him, derided him, defied him, in tones not audible to the middle of the street, but audible to the man's conscience and dormant manhood; and he asked her pardon, and gave her his rope, and said with a most great and blasphemous oath that she was the bravest woman he ever saw; and so went his way without other word, and troubled her no more. He and she were always good friends after that, for in her he had found a long felt want—somebody who was not afraid of him.

One day in St. Louis she walked out into the street and greatly surprised a burly cartman who was beating his horse over the head with the butt of his heavy whip; for she took the whip away from him and then made such a persuasive appeal in behalf of the ignorantly offending horse that he was tripped into saying he was to blame; and also into volunteering a promise which of course he couldn't keep, for he was not built in that way—a promise that he wouldn't ever abuse a horse again.

That sort of interference in behalf of abused animals was a common thing with her all her life; and her manner must have been without offence and her good intent transparent, for she always carried her point, and also won the courtesy, and often the friendly applause, of the adversary. All the race of dumb animals had a friend in her. By some subtle sign the homeless, hunted, bedraggled and disreputable cat recognized her at a glance as the born refuge and champion of his sort—and followed her home. His instinct was right, he was as welcome as the prodigal son. We had nineteen cats at one time, in 1845. And there wasn't one in the lot that had any character; not one that had a merit, except the cheap and tawdry merit of being unfortunate. They were a vast burden to us all—including my mother—but they were out of luck, and that was enough; they had to stay. However, better these than no pets at all; children must have pets, and we were not allowed to have caged ones. An imprisoned creature was out of the question—my mother would not have allowed a rat to be restrained of its liberty.

In the small town of Hannibal, Missouri, when I was a boy, everybody was poor but didn't know it; and everybody was comfortable, and did know it. And there were grades of society; people of good family, people of unclassified family, people of no family. Everybody knew everybody, and was affable to everybody, and nobody put on any visible airs; yet the class lines were quite clearly drawn, and the familiar social life of each class was restricted to that class. It was a little democracy which was full of Liberty, Equality and Fourth of July; and sincerely so, too, yet you perceive that the aristocratic taint was there. It was there, and nobody found fault with the fact, or ever stopped to reflect that its presence was an inconsistency.

I suppose that this state of things was mainly due to the circumstance that the town's population had come from slave States and still had the institution of slavery with them in their new home. My mother, with her large nature and liberal sympathies, was not intended for an aristocrat, yet through her breeding she was one. Few people knew it, perhaps, for it was an instinct, I think, rather than a principle. So its outward manifestation was likely to be accidental, not intentional; and also not frequent. But I knew of that weak spot. I knew that privately she was proud that the Lambtons, now Earls of Durham, had occupied the family lands for nine hundred years; that they were feudal lords of Lambton Castle and holding the high position of ancestors of hers when the Norman Conqueror came over to divert the Englishry. I argued—cautiously, and with mollifying circumlocutions, for one had to be careful when he was on that holy ground, and mustn't cavort—that there was no particular merit in occupying a piece of land for nine hundred years, with the friendly assistance of an entail; anybody could do it, with intellect or without; therefore, the entail was the thing to be proud of, just the entail and nothing else; consequently, she was merely descended from an entail, and she might as well be proud of being descended from a mortgage. Whereas my own ancestry was quite a different and superior thing, because it had the addition of an ancestor—one Clement—who *did* something; something which was very creditable to him and satisfactory to me, in that he was a member of the court that tried Charles I and delivered him over to the executioner. Ostensibly this was chaff, but at bottom it was not. I had a very real respect for that ancestor, and this respect has increased with the years, not diminished. He did what he could toward reducing the list of crowned shams of his day. However, I can say this for my mother, that I never heard her refer in any way to her gilded ancestry when any person not a member of the family was present, for she had good American sense. But with other Lamptons whom I have known, it was different. "Col. Sellers" was a Lampton, and a tolerably near relative of my mother's; and when he was alive, poor old airy soul, one of the earliest things a stranger was likely to hear from his lips was some reference to the "head of our line," flung off with a painful casualness that was wholly beneath criticism as a work of art. It compelled inquiry, of course; it was intended to compel it. Then followed the whole disastrous history of how the Lambton heir came to this country a hundred and fifty years or so ago, disgusted with that foolish fraud, hereditary aristocracy; and married, and shut himself away from the world in the remotenesses of the wilderness, and went to breeding ancestors of future American Claimants, while at home in England he was given up as dead and his titles and estates turned over to his younger brother, usurper and personally responsible for the perverse and unseatable usurpers of our day. And the Colonel always spoke with studied and courtly deference of the Claimant of his day,—a second cousin of his,—and referred to him with entire seriousness as "the Earl." "The Earl" was a man of parts, and might have accomplished something for himself but for the calamitous accident of his birth. He was a Kentuckian, and a well meaning man; but he had no money, and no time to earn any; for all his time was taken up in trying to get me, and others of the tribe, to furnish him a capital to fight his claim through the House of Lords with. He had all the documents, all the proofs; he knew he could win. And so he dreamed his life away, always in poverty, sometimes in actual want, and died at last, far from home, and was buried from a hospital by strangers who did not know he was an earl, for he did not look it. That poor fellow used to sign his letters "Durham," and in them he would find fault with me for voting the Republican ticket, for the reason that it was unaristocratic, and by consequence un-Lamptonian. And presently along would come a letter from some red-hot Virginian son of my other branch and abuse me bitterly for the same vote—on the ground that the Republican was an aristocratic party and it was not becoming in the descendant of a regicide to train with that kind of animals. And so I used to almost wish I hadn't had any ancestors, they were so much trouble to me.

As I have said, we lived in a slave-holding community; indeed, when slavery perished my mother had been in daily touch with it for sixty years. Yet, kind hearted and compassionate as she was, I think she was not conscious that slavery was a bald, grotesque and unwarrantable usurpation. She had never heard it assailed in any pulpit, but had heard it defended and sanctified in a thousand; her ears were familiar with Bible texts that approved it, but if there were any that disapproved it they had not been quoted by her pastors; as far as her experience went, the wise and the good and the holy were unanimous in the conviction that slavery was right, righteous, sacred, the peculiar pet of the Deity, and a condition which the slave himself ought to be daily and nightly thankful for. Manifestly, training and association can accomplish strange miracles. As a rule our slaves were convinced and content. So, doubtless, are the far more intelligent slaves of a monarchy; they revere and approve their masters the monarch and the noble, and recognize no degradation in the fact that they are slaves; slaves with the name blinked; and less respect-worthy than were our black ones, if to be a slave by meek consent is baser than to be a slave by compulsion—and doubtless it is.

However, there was nothing about the slavery of the Hannibal region to rouse one's dozing humane instincts to activity. It was the mild domestic slavery, not the brutal plantation article. Cruelties were very rare, and exceedingly and wholesomely unpopular. To separate and sell the members of a slave family to different masters was a thing not well liked by the people, and so it was not often done, except in the settling of estates. I have no recollection of ever seeing a slave auction in that town; but I am suspicious that that is because the thing was a common and commonplace spectacle, not an uncommon and impressive one. I vividly remember seeing a dozen black men and women chained to each other, once, and lying in a group on the pavement, awaiting shipment to the southern slave market. Those were the saddest faces I ever saw. Chained slaves could not have been a common sight, or this picture would not have taken so strong and lasting a hold upon me.

The "nigger trader" was loathed by everybody. He was regarded as a sort of human devil who bought and conveyed poor helpless creatures to hell—for to our whites and blacks alike the southern plantation was simply hell; no milder name could describe it. If the threat to sell an incorrigible slave "down the river" would not reform him, nothing would—his case was past cure.

My mother was quite able to pity a slave who was in trouble; but not *because* he was a slave—that would not have emphasized the case any, perhaps. I recal an incident in point. For a time we had as a house servant a little slave boy who belonged to a master back in the country, and I used to want to kill him on account of the noise he made; and I think yet, it would have been a good idea to kill him. The noise was music—singing. He sang the whole day long, at the top of his voice; it was intolerable, it was unendurable. At last I went to my mother in a rage about it. But she said—

"Think; he is sold away from his mother; she is in Maryland, a thousand miles from here, and he will never see her again, poor thing. When he is singing it is a sign that he is not grieving; the noise of it drives me almost distracted, but I am always listening, and always thankful; it would break my heart if Sandy should stop singing."

And she was able to accommodate a slave—even accommodate the whim of a slave, against her own personal interest and desire. A woman who had been "mammy"—that is, nurse—to several of us children, took a notion that she would like to change masters. She wanted to be sold to a Mr. B., of our town. That was a sore trial, for the woman was almost like one of the family; but she pleaded hard —for that man had been beguiling her with all sorts of fine and alluring promises—and my mother yielded, and also persuaded my father.

It is commonly believed that an infallible effect of slavery was to make such as lived in its midst hard-hearted. I think it had no such effect—speaking in general terms. I think it stupefied everybody's humanity, as regarded the slave, but stopped there. There were no hard-hearted people in our town—I mean there were no more than would be found in any other town of the same size in any other country; and in my experience hard-hearted people are very rare everywhere. Yet I remember that once when a white man killed a negro man for a trifling little offence everybody seemed indifferent about it—as regarded the slave—though considerable sympathy was felt for the slave's owner, who had been bereft of valuable property by a worthless person who was not able to pay for it.

My father was a humane man; all will grant this who knew him. Still, proof is better than assertion, and I have it at hand. Before me is a letter, near half a century old, dated January 5, 1842, and written by my father to my mother. He is on a steamboat, ascending the Mississippi, and is approaching Memphis. He has made a hard and tedious journey, in mid winter, to hunt up a man in the far south who has been owing him $470 for twenty years. He has found his man, has also found that his man is solvent and able to pay, but—

—"it seemed so very hard upon him these hard times to pay such a sum, that I could not have the conscience to hold him to it. On the whole I consented to take his note, payable 1st March next, for $250 and let him off at that. I believe I was quite too lenient, and ought to have had at least that amount down."

Is not this a humane, a soft-hearted man? If even the gentlest of us had been plowing through ice and snow, horseback and per steamboat, for six weeks to collect that little antiquity, wouldn't we have collected it, and the man's scalp along with it? I trust so. Now, lower down on the same page, my father—proven to be a humane man—writes this:

"I still have Charley; the highest price I was offered for him in New Orleans was $50, and in Vicksburg $40. After performing the journey to Tennessee I expect to sell him for whatever he will bring when I take water again, viz., at Louisville or Nashville."

And goes right on, then, about some indifferent matter, poor Charley's approaching eternal exile from his home, and his mother, and his friends, and all things and creatures that make life dear and the heart to sing for joy, affecting him no more than if this humble comrade of his long pilgrimage had been an ox—and somebody else's ox. It makes a body homesick for Charley, even after fifty years. Thank God I have no recollection of him as house servant of ours; that is to say, playmate of mine; for I was playmate to all the niggers, preferring their society to that of the elect, I being a person of low-down tastes from the start, notwithstanding my high birth, and ever ready to forsake the communion of high souls if I could strike anything nearer my grade.

She was of a sunshiny disposition, and her long life was mainly a holiday to her. She was a dancer, from childhood to the end, and as capable a one as the Presbyterian church could show among its communicants. At eighty-seven she would trip through the lively and graceful figures that had been familiar to her more than seventy years before. She was very bright, and was fond of banter and playful duels of wit; and she had a sort of ability which is rare in men and hardly existent in women—the ability to say a humorous thing with the perfect air of not knowing it to be humorous. Whenever I was in her presence, after I was grown, a battle of chaff was going on all the time, but under the guise of serious conversation. Once, under pretence of fishing for tender and sentimental reminiscences of my childhood—a sufficiently annoying childhood for other folk to recal, since I was sick the first seven years of it and lived altogether on expensive allopathic medicines— I asked her how she used to feel about me in those days. With an almost pathetic earnestness she said, "All along at first I was afraid you would die"—a slight, reflective pause, then this addition, spoken as if talking to herself—"and after that I was afraid you wouldn't." After eighty her memory failed, and she lived almost entirely in a world peopled by carefree mates of her young girlhood whose voices had fallen silent and whose forms had mouldered to dust many and many a year gone by; and in this gracious companionship she walked pleasantly down to the grave unconscious of her gray head and her vanished youth. Only her memory was stricken; otherwise her intellect remained unimpaired. When I arrived, late at night, in the earliest part of her last illness, she had been without sleep long enough to have worn a strong young person out, but she was as ready to talk, as ready to give and take, as ever. She knew me perfectly, but to her disordered fancy I was not a gray-headed man, but a school-boy, and had just arrived from the east on vacation. There was a deal of chaff, a deal of firing back and forth, and then she began to inquire about the school and what sort of reputation I had in it—and with a rather frankly doubtful tone about the questions, too. I said that my reputation was really a wonder; that there was not another boy there whose morals were anywhere near up to mine; that whenever I passed by, the citizens stood in reverent admiration, and said: "There goes the model boy." She was silent a while, then she said, musingly: "Well, I wonder what the rest are like."

She was married at twenty; she always had the heart of a young girl; and in the sweetness and serenity of death she seemed somehow young again. She was always beautiful.

Villagers of 1840–3

Judge *Draper,* dead without issue.

Judge *Carpenter.* *Wife,* Joanna. Sons: Oscar, Burton, Hartley, Simon. Daughter, Priscella.

Dr. Meredith. Sons, Charley and John. Two old-maid sisters. He had been a sailor, and had a deep voice. Charley went to California and thence to hell; John, a meek and bashful boy, became the cruelest of bushwhacker-leaders in the war-time.

Dr. Fife. Dr. Peake.

Lawyer Lakenan.

Captain Robards. Flour mill. Called rich. George (flame, Mary Moss,) an elder pupil at Dawson's, long hair, Latin, grammar, etc. Disappointed, wandered out into the world, and not heard of again for certain. Floating rumors at long intervals that he had been seen in South America (Lima) and other far places. Family apparently not disturbed by his absence. But it was known that Mary Moss was.

John Robards. When 12, went to California across the plains with his father. Gone a year. Returned around Cape Horn. Rode in the Plains manner, his long yellow hair flapping. He said he was appointed to West Point and couldn't pass because of a defect in his eye. Probably a lie. There was always a noticeable defect in his veracity. Was a punctual boy at the Meth. Sunday school, and at Dawson's; a good natured fellow, but not much *to* him. Became a lawyer. Married a Hurst—new family. Prominent and valued citizen, and well-to-do. Procreated a cloud of children. Superintendent of the Old Ship of Zion Sunday school.

Clay Robards. A good and daring rebel soldier. Disappeared from view.

Sally Robards. Pupil at Dawson's. Married Bart Bowen, pilot and captain. Young widow.

Russell Moss. Pork-house. Rich. Mary, very sweet and pretty at 16 and 17. Wanted to marry George Robards. Lawyer Lakenan the rising stranger, held to be the better match by the parents, who were looking higher than commerce. They made her engage herself to L. L. made her study hard a year to fit herself to be his intellectual company; then married her, shut her up, the docile and heart-hurt young beauty, and continued her education rigorously. When he was ready to trot her out in society 2 years later and exhibit her, she had become wedded to her seclusion and her melancholy broodings, and begged to be left alone. He compelled her—that is, commanded. She obeyed. Her first exit was her last. The sleigh was overturned, her thigh was broken; it was badly set. She got well with a terrible limp, and forever after stayed in the house and produced children. Saw no company, not even the mates of her girlhood.

Neil Moss. The envied rich boy of the Meth. S. S. Spoiled and of small account. Dawson's. Was sent to Yale—a mighty journey and an incomparable distinction. Came back in swell eastern clothes, and the young men dressed up the warped negro bell ringer in a travesty of him—which made him descend to village fashions. At 30 he was a graceless tramp in Nevada, living by mendicancy and borrowed money. Disappeared. The parents died after the war. Mary Lakenan's husband got the property.

Dana Breed. From Maine. Clerk for old T. R. Selmes, an Englishman. Married Letititia Richmond. Collins and Breed—merchants. This lot all dead now.

Lot Southard. Clerk. Married Lucy Lockwood. Dead.

Jesse Armstrong. Clerk for Selmes. Married -------. After many years she fell in love with her physician. One night somebody entered the back door—A. jumped out of bed to see about it and was chopped to pieces with an axe brought from his own woodpile. The widow and the physician tried for the murder. Evidence insufficient. Acquitted, but Judge, jury and all the town believed them guilty. Before the year was out they married, and were at once and rigorously ostracised. The physician's practice shrunk to nothing, but Armstrong left wealth, so it was no matter.

Bill Briggs. Drifted to California in '50, and in '65 was a handsome bachelor and had a woman. Kept a faro-table.

John Briggs. (Miss Torrey and Miss Newcomb and Mrs. Horr.) Worked as stemmer in Garth's factory. Became a 6-footer and a capable rebel private.

Artemissa Briggs. (Miss Torrey, N. and Mrs. H.) Married Richmond the mason, Miss Torrey's widower.

Miss Newcomb—old maid and thin. Married Davis, a day laborer.

Miss Lucy Davis. Schoolmarm.

Mrs. Hawkins. Widow about 1840. 'Lige—became rich merchant in St Louis and New York.

Ben. City marshal. Shot his thumb off, hunting. Fire marshal of Big 6 Company.

Jeff. Little boy. Died. Buried in the old graveyard on the hill.

Sophia. Married ----- the prosperous tinner.

Laura. Pretty little creature of 5 at Miss Torrey's. At the Hill street school she and Jenny Brady wrote on the slate that day at the noon recess. Another time Laura fell out of her chair and Jenny made that vicious remark. Laura lived to be the mother of six 6-foot sons. Died.

Little Margaret Striker.

----- Striker the blacksmith.

McDonald the desperado (plasterer.)

Mrs. Holiday. Was a MacDonald, born Scotch. Wore her father's ivory miniature—a British General in the Revolution. Lived on Holiday's Hill. Well off. Hospitable. Fond of having parties of young people. Widow. Old, but anxious to marry. Always consulting fortune-tellers; always managed to make them understand that she had been promised 3 by the first fraud. They always confirmed the prophecy. She finally died before the prophecies had a full chance.

Old Stevens, jeweler. Dick, Upper Miss. pilot. Ed, neat as a new pin. Miss Newcomb's. Tore down Dick Hardy's stable. Insurrection-leader. Brought before Miss N., brickbats fell out of his pockets and J. Meredith's. Ed was out with the rebel company sworn in by Col. Ralls of the Mexican war.

Ed. Hyde, Dick Hyde. Tough and dissipated. Ed. held his uncle down while Dick tried to kill him with a pistol which refused fire.

Eliza Hyde. "Last Link is Broken." Married a stranger. Thought drifted to Texas. Died.

Old Selmes and his Wildcat store. Widower. His daughter married well—St Louis.

'Gyle Buchanan. Robert, proprietor of Journal. Shouting methodists. Young Bob and Little Joe, printers. Big Joe a fighter and steamboat engineer after apprenticeship as a moulder. Somebody hit young Bob over the head with a fire-shovel.

Sam Raymond—fire company, and editor of (Journal?) St Louis swell. Always affected fine city language, and said "Toosday." Married Mary Nash?

Tom Nash. Went deaf and dumb from breaking through ice. Became a house-painter; and at Jacksonville was taught to talk, after a fashion. His 2 young sisters went deaf and dumb from scarlet fever.

Old Nash. Postmaster. His aged mother was Irish, had family jewels, and claimed to be aristocracy.

Blankenships. The parents paupers and drunkards; the girls charged with prostitution—not proven. Tom, a kindly young heathen. Bence, a fisherman. These children were never sent to school or church. Played out and disappeared.

Captain S. A. Bowen. Died about 1850. His wife later.

John, steamboat agent in St Louis; army contractor, later—rich.

Bart. Pilot and Captain. Good fellow. Consumptive. Gave $20, time of Pennsylvania disaster. Young McManus got it. Left young widow.

Mary. Married lawyer Green, who was Union man.

Eliza—stammered badly, and was a kind of a fool.

Will. Pilot. Diseased. Mrs. Horr and all the rest (including Cross?) Had the measles that time. Baptist family. Put cards in minister's baptising robe. Trouble in consequence. Helped roll rock down that jumped over Simon's dray and smashed into coopershop. He died in Texas. Family.

Sam. Pilot. Slept with the rich baker's daughter, telling the adoptive parents they were married. The baker died and left all his wealth to "Mr. and Mrs. S. Bowen." They rushed off to a Carondolet magistrate, got married, and bribed him to antedate the marriage. Heirs from Germany proved the fraud and took the wealth. Sam no account and a pauper. Neglected his wife; she took up with another man. Sam a drinker. Dropped pretty low. Died of yellow fever and whisky on a little boat with Bill Kribben the defaulting secretary. Both buried at the head of 82. In 5 years 82 got washed away.

Rev. Mr. Rice. Presbyterian. Died.

Rev. Tucker. Went east.

Roberta Jones. Scared old Miss ------ into the insane asylum with a skull and a doughface. Married Jackson. "Oh, on Long Island's Sea-girt Shore."

Jim Quarles. Tinner. Set up in business by his father—$3,000 —a fortune, then. Popular young beau—dancer—flutist—serenader—envied—a great catch. Married a child of 14. Two babies the result. Father highly disapproved the marriage. Dissipation—often drunk. Neglected the business—and the child-wife and babies. Left them and went to California. The little family went to Jim's father. Jim became a drunken loafer in California, and so died.

Jim Lampton. A popular beau, like the other. Good fellow, very handsome, full of life. Young doctor without practice, poor, but good family and considered a good catch. Captured by the arts of Ella Hunter, a loud vulgar beauty from a neighboring town—one of the earliest chipper and self-satisfied and idiotic correspondents of the back-country newspapers—an early Kate Field. Moved to St Louis. Steamboat agent. Young Dr. John McDowell boarded with them; followed them from house to house; an arrant scandal to everybody with eyes—but Jim hadn't any, and believed in the loyalty of both of them. God took him at last, the only good luck he ever had after he met Ella. Left a red-headed daughter, Kate. Doctor John and Ella continued together.

In sixty years that town has not turned out a solitary preacher; not a U.S. Senator, only 2 congressmen, and in no instance a name known across the river. But one college-man.

Wales McCormick. J—s H. C.

Dick Rutter.

Pet McMurry. His medicine bottle—greasy auburn hair—Cuba sixes. Quincy. Family. Stove store.

Bill League. Married the gravestone-cutter's daughter. "Courier." Became its proprietor. Made it a daily and prosperous. Children. Died.

The two young sailors—Irish.

Urban E. Hicks. Saw Jenny Lind. Went to Oregon; served in Indian war.

Jim Wolf. The practical jokes. Died.

Letitia Honeyman. School. Married a showy stranger. Turned out to be a thief and swindler. She and her baby waited while he served a long term. At the end of it her youth was gone, and her cheery ways.

Sam. Lost an arm in the war. Became a policeman.

Pavey. "Pigtail done." A lazy, vile-tempered old hellion. His wife and daughters did all the work and were atrociously treated. Pole —went to St Louis. Gone six months—came back a striker, with wages, the envy of everybody. Drove his girl Sunday in buggy from Shoot's stable, $1.50 a day. Introduced poker—cent ante. Became second engineer. Married a pretty little fat child in St. Louis. Got drowned.

Becky. Came up from St Louis a sweet and pretty young thing —caused many heart-breaks. Silver pencil—$1.50—she didn't care for it. Davis a widower, married her sister Josephine, and Becky married Davis's son. They went to Texas. Disappeared. The "long dog."

The other sisters married—Mrs. Strong went to Peoria. One of them was Mrs. Shoot—married at 13, daughter (Mrs. Hayward) born at 14. Mrs. Hayward's daughter tried the stage at home, then at Daly's, didn't succeed. Finally a pushing and troublesome London newspaper correspondent.

Jim Foreman. Clerk. Pomeroy Benton & Co. Handkerchief.

Mrs. Sexton (*she* pronounced it *Saxton* to make it finer, the nice, kind-hearted, smirky, smily dear Christian creature—Methodist.)

Margaret. Pretty child of 14. Boarders in 1844 house. Simon and Hartley, rivals. Mrs. S. talked much of N-Yorliuns; and hints and sighs of better days there, departed never to return. Sunday-school.

[*Cloak of the time,* flung back, lined with bright plaid. Worn with a swagger. Most rational garment that ever was.

Slouch hat, worn gallusly.

Hoop-skirts coming in.

Literature. Byron, Scott, Cooper, Marryatt, Boz. Pirates and knights preferred to other society. Songs tended to regrets for bygone days and vanished joys: Oft in the Stilly Night; Last Rose of Summer; The Last Link; Bonny Doon; Old Dog Tray; for the lady I love will soon be a bride; Gaily the Troubadour; Bright Alfarata.

Negro melodies the same trend: Old Kentucky Home; (de day goes by like a shadow on de wall, wid sorrow where all was delight;) Massa's in de Cold Ground; Swanee River.

The gushing Crusaders admired; the serenade was a survival or a result of this literature.

Any young person would have been proud of a "strain" of Indian blood. Bright Alfarata of the blue Juniata got her strain from "a far distant fount."

All that sentimentality and romance among young folk seem puerile, now, but when one examines it and compares it with the ideals of to-day, it was the preferable thing. It was soft, sappy, melancholy; but money had no place in it. To get rich was no one's ambition—it was not in any young person's thoughts. The heroes of these young people—even the pirates—were moved by lofty impulses: they waded in blood, in the distant fields of war and adventure and upon the pirate deck, to rescue the helpless, not to make money; they spent their blood and made their self-sacrifices for "honor's" sake, not to capture a giant fortune; they married for love, not for money and position. It was an intensely sentimental age, but it took no sordid form. The Californian rush for wealth in '49 introduced the change and begot the lust for money which is the rule of life to-day, and the hardness and cynicism which is the spirit of to-day.

The three "rich" men were not worshiped, and not envied. They were not arrogant, nor assertive, nor tyrannical, nor exigeant. It was California that changed the spirit of the people and lowered their ideals to the plane of to-day.

Unbeliever. There was but one—Blennerhasset, the young Kentucky lawyer, a fascinating cuss—and they shuddered to hear him talk. They expected a judgment to fall upon him at any moment. They believed the devil would come for him in person some stormy night.

He was very profane, and blasphemous. He was vain of being prayed for in the revivals; vain of being singled out for this honor always by every new revivalist; vain of the competition between these people for his capture; vain that it was the ambition of each in his turn to hang this notable scalp at his belt. The young ladies were ambitious to convert him.

Chastity. There was the utmost liberty among young people— but no young girl was ever insulted, or seduced, or even scandalously gossiped about. Such things were not even dreamed of in that society, much less spoken of and referred to as possibilities.

Two or three times, in the lapse of years, married women were whispered about, but never an unmarried one.

Ouseley. Prosperous merchant. Smoked fragrant cigars—regalias —5 apiece. Killed old Smar. Acquitted. His party brought him huzzaing in from Palmyra at midnight. But there was a cloud upon him—a social chill—and he presently moved away.

The Hanged Nigger. He raped and murdered a girl of 13 in the woods. He confessed to forcing 3 young women in Va, and was brought away in a feather bed to save his life—which was a valuable property.

The Stabbed Cal. Emigrant. Saw him.

Judge Carpenter knocked MacDonald down with a mallet and saved Charley Schneider. Mac in return came near shooting Col. Elgin in the back of the head.

Clint Levering drowned. His less fortunate brother lived to have a family and be rich and respected.

Garth. Presbyterians. Tobacco. Eventually rich. David, teacher in S. school. Later, Supt.

John. Mrs. Horr and the others. He removed to New York and became a broker, and prosperous. Returned, and brought Helen Kercheval to Brooklyn in '68. Presently went back to St P. and remained. Banker, rich. Raised 2 beautiful daughters and a son.

Old Kercheval the tailor. Helen did not like his trade to be referred to.

His apprentice saved Simon Carpenter's life—aged 9—from drowning, and was cursed for it by Simon for 50 years.

Daily Packet Service to Keokuk. The merchants—envied by all the untraveled town—made trips to the great city (of 30,000 souls). St. L papers had pictures of Planters House, and sometimes an engraved letter-head had a picture of the city front, with the boats sardined at the wharf and the modest spire of the little Cath Cathedral showing prominently; and at last when a minor citizen realized the dream of his life and traveled to St. Louis, he was thrilled to the marrow when he recognized the rank of boats and the spire and the Planters, and was amazed at the accuracy of the pictures and at the fact that the things were realities and not inventions of the imagination. He talked St Louis, and nothing but S L and its wonders for months and months afterward. "Call *that* a fire-uniform! you ought to see a turn-out in St L.—blocks and blocks and blocks of red shirts and helmets, and more engines and hosecarts and hook and ladder Co's—my!"

4th July. Banners. Declaration and Spreadeagle speech in public square. Procession—Sunday schools, Masons, Odd Fellows, Temperance Society, Cadets of Temperance, the Co of St P Greys, the Fantastics (oh, so funny!) and of course the Fire Co and Sam R. Maybe in the woods. Collation in the cool shade of a tent. Gingerbread in slabs; lemonade; ice cream. Opened with prayer—closed with a blessing.

Circus.

Mesmerizer.

Nigger Show. (the swell pet tenor) Prendergast

Bell-Ringers (Swiss)

Debating Society.

National Intelligencer. Dr. Peake.

St. L. Republican.

Old Pitts, the saddler. Always rushed wildly down street putting on coat as he went—rushed aboard—nothing for him, of course.

John Hannicks, with the laugh. See black smoke rising beyond point—"Steeammmmboat a coming!" Laugh. Rattle his dray.

Bill Pitts, saddler, succeeded his father.

Ben Coontz—sent a son to W. Point.

Glover (protégé of old T. K. Collins) really did become a famous lawyer in St L., but St P always said he was a fool and nothing *to* him.

The Mock Duel.

Lavinia Honeyman captured "celebrated" circus-rider—envied for the unexampled brilliancy of the match—but he got into the penitentiary at Jefferson City and the romance was spoiled.

Ratcliffes. One son lived in a bark hut up at the stillhouse branch and at intervals came home at night and emptied the larder.

Back door left open purposely; if notice was taken of him he would not come.

Another son had to be locked into a small house in corner of the yard—and chained. Fed through a hole. Would not wear clothes, winter or summer. Could not have fire. Religious mania. Believed his left hand had committed a mortal sin and must be sacrificed. Got hold of a hatchet, nobody knows how, and chopped it off. Escaped and chased his stepmother all over the house with carving knife. The father arrived and rescued her. He seemed to be afraid of his father, and could be cowed by him, but by no one else. He died in that small house.

One son became a fine physician and in California ventured to marry; but went mad and finished his days in the asylum. The old Dr., dying, said, "Don't cry; rejoice—shout. This is the only valuable day I have known in my 65 years." His grandfather's generation had been madmen—then the disease skipped to his. He said Nature laid a trap for him: slyly allowed all his children to be born before exposing the taint.

Blennerhasset enlarged upon it and said Nature was *always* treacherous—did not single *him* out, but spared nobody.

B. went to K. to get married. All present at the wedding but himself. Shame and grief of the bride; indignation of the rest. A year later he would be found—bridally clad—shut into the family vault in the graveyard—spring lock and the key on the outside. His mother had but one pet and he was the one—because he was an infidel and the target of bitter public opinion. He always visited her tomb when at home, but the others didn't. So the judgment hit him at last. He was found when they came to bury a sister. There had been a theft of money in the town, and people managed to suspect him; but it was not found on him.

Judge Carpenter. Married in Lexington in '23; he 24, his wife 20. She married him to spite young Dr. Ray, to whom she was engaged, and who wouldn't go to a neighboring town, 9 miles, in the short hours of the night, to bring her home from a ball.

He was a small storekeeper. Removed to Jamestown and kept a

store. Entered 75,000 acres of land (oil land, later). Three children born there. The stray calf.

Removed to village of Florida. M. born there—died at 10. Small storekeeper. Then to St P middle of 1838. Rest of the family born there—Han and B. died there. The mother made the children feel the cheek of the dead boy, and tried to make them understand the calamity that had befallen. The case of memorable treachery.

Still a small storekeeper—but progressing. Then Ira Stout, who got him to go security for a large sum, "took the benefit of the bankrupt law" and ruined him—in fact made a pauper of him.

Became justice of the peace and lived on its meagre pickings.

Stern, unsmiling, never demonstrated affection for wife or child. Had found out he had been married to spite another man. Silent, austere, of perfect probity and high principle; ungentle of manner toward his children, but always a gentleman in his phrasing—and never punished them—a look was enough, and more than enough.

Had but one slave—she wanted to be sold to Beebe, and was. He sold her down the river. Was seen, years later, ch. on steamboat. Cried and lamented. Judge whipped her once, for impudence to his wife—whipped her with a bridle.

It was remembered that he went to church—once; never again. His family were abandoned Presbyterians. What his notions about religion were, no one ever knew. He never mentioned the matter; offered no remarks when others discussed it. Whoever tried to drag a remark out of him failed; got a courteous answer or a look which discouraged further effort, and that person understood, and never approached the matter again.

If he had intimates at all, it was Peake and Draper. Peake was very old in the 40s, and wore high stock, pigtail and up *to* '40, still wore kneebreeches and buckle-shoes. A courtly gentleman of the old school—a Virginian, like Judge C.

Judge C. was elected County Judge by a great majority in '49, and at last saw great prosperity before him. But of course caught his death the first day he opened court. He went home with pneumonia, 12 miles, horseback, winter—and in a fortnight was dead.

First instance of affection: discovering that he was dying, chose his daughter from among the weepers, who were kneeling about the room and crying—and motioned her to come to him. Drew her down to him, with his arms about her neck, kissed her (for the first time, no doubt,) and said "Let me die"—and sunk back and the death rattle came. Ten minutes before, the Pres. preacher had said, "Do you believe on the Lord Jesus Christ, and that through his blood only you can be saved?" "I do." Then the preacher prayed over him and recommended him. He did not say good-bye to his wife, or to any but his daughter.

The autopsy.

Jimmy Reagan, from St Louis.

Carey Briggs, from Galena and also from Bayou Lafourche.

Priscella. Old maid at 25, married W. Moffett, mouldy old bachelor of 35—a St L commission merchant and well off. He died 1865, rich ($20,000) leaving little boy and girl.

Oscar. Born Jamestown, 1825. About 1842, aged 17, went to St. L to learn to be a printer, in Ustick's job office.

At 18, wrote home to his mother, that he was studying the life of Franklin and closely imitating him; that in his boarding house he was confining himself to bread and water, and was trying to persuade the other young boarders and Ustick's other cubs, to eschew beer. They called him Parson Snivel and gave him frank and admirable cursings, and urged him to mind his own business. All of which pleased him, and made him a hero to himself: for he was turning his other cheek, as commanded, he was being reviled and persecuted for righteousness' sake, and all that. Privately his little Presbyterian mother was not pleased with this too-literal loyalty to the theoretical Bible-teachings which he had acquired through her agency, for, slender and delicately moulded as she was, she had a dauntless courage and a high spirit, and was not of the cheek-turning sort. She believed fervently in her religion and strenuously believed it was a person's duty to turn the cheek, but she was quite open and aboveboard in saying that she wouldn't turn her own cheek nor respect anybody that did. "Why, how do you reconcile that with—" "I don't reconcile it with anything. I am the way I am made. Religion is a jugfull; I hold a dipperfull; you can't crowd a jugful of ANYthing into a dipper—there's no way. I'm holding what I can, and I'm not going to cry because I can't crowd the rest in. I know that a person that can turn his cheek is higher and holier than I am, and better every way. And of course I reverence him; but I despise him, too, and I wouldn't have him for a doormat."

We know what she meant. Her attitude is easily understandable, but we get our comprehension of it not through her explanation of it but in spite of it. Her language won't scan, but its meaning is clear, all the same.

She did not show Oscar's letter to his father; the Judge would have taken no great interest in it. There were few points of contact between him and his son; there were few or no openings for sympathy between the two. The father was as steady as a church-tower, the son as capricious as the weather-vane on its top. Steady people do not admire the weather-vane sort.

But the mother answered the letter; and she poured out her affection upon her boy, and her praises, too; praises of his resolution to be a Franklin and become great and good and renowned; for she always said that he was distrustful of himself and a prey to despondences, and that no opportunity to praise him and encourage him must be lost, or he would lose heart and be defeated in his struggles to gain the front in the race of life. She had to do all the encouraging herself; the rest of the family were indifferent, and this wounded her, and brought gentle reproaches out of her that were strangely eloquent and moving, considering how simple and unaffected her language was, and how effortless and unconscious. But there was a subtle something in her voice and her manner that was irresistibly pathetic, and perhaps that was where a great part of the power lay; in that and in her moist eyes and trembling lip. I know now that she was the most eloquent person whom I have met in all my days, but I did not know it then, and I suppose that no one in all the village suspected that she was a marvel, or indeed that she was in any degree above the common. I had been abroad in the world for twenty years and known and listened to many of its best talkers before it at last dawned upon me that in the matter of moving and pathetic eloquence none of them was the equal of that untrained and artless talker out there in the western village, that obscure little woman with the beautiful spirit and the great heart and the enchanted tongue.

Oscar's mother praised in her letter what she was able to praise; and she praised forcefully and generously and heartily, too. There was no uncertain ring about her words. But her gorge rose at the cheek-turning heroisms, and since she could not commend them and be honest, she skipped them wholly, and made no reference to them.

Oscar's next week's letter showed further progress. He was now getting up at four in the morning, because that was Franklin's way; he had divided his day on the Franklin plan—eight hours for labor, eight for sleep, eight for study, meditation and exercise; he had pinned Franklin's rules up in a handy place, and divided the hours into minutes, and distributed the minutes among the rules, each minute sacred to its appointed duty: so many minutes for the morning prayer; so many for the Bible chapter; so many for the dumb-bells; so many for the bath; so many for What did I do yesterday that was morally and mentally profitable? What did I do which should have been left undone? What opportunity did I neglect of doing good? Whom did I injure, whom did I help, whose burden did I lighten? How shall I order this day to the approval of God, my own spiritual elevation, and the betterment of my fellow beings? And so on, and so on, all the way through: sixteen waking hours cut up into minutes, and each minute labeled with its own particular duty-tag.

He wrote it all home to his mother; and added that he found that life was a noble and beautiful thing when reduced to order and system; that he was astonished to see what briskness, mentally and physically, early rising gave him, and what a difference he could already notice between himself and the late-rising boarders—the greatest difference in the world, and all in four days.

But he said he had taken to his lamp again, for he had found that he could not read his fine-print books by the Franklin tallow candle. Also, he had been to a lecture, and was now a vegetarian, and an enthusiastic one. He had discarded bread, and also water; vegetables, pure and simple, made the most effective and inspiring diet in the world, and the most thoroughly satisfying; he wondered how his intellect had ever survived the gross food with which he had formerly burdened it; but he sometimes almost feared that it had suffered impairment. He had mentioned this fear to the foreman of the office, but the foreman had said, almost with enthusiasm, considering what a lifeless and indifferent man he usually was, "Don't worry—nothing can impair your intellect."

The mother's face flushed when she read that, and the foreman was better off where he was than he would have been, here, in reach of her tongue.

Hellfire Hotchkiss

Chapter 1

"But James, he is our son, and we must bear with him. If we cannot bear with him, how can we expect others to do it?"

"I have not said I expected it, Sarah. I am very far from expecting it. He is the most trying ass that was ever born."

"James! You forget that he is our son."

"That does not save him from being an ass. It does not even take the sting out of it."

"I do not see how you can be so hard toward your own flesh and blood. Mr. Rucker does not think of him as you do."

"And why should he? Mr. Rucker is an ass himself."

"James—do think what you are saying. Do you think it becoming to speak so of a minister—a person called of God?"

"Who said he was?"

"Who *said* he was? Now you are becoming blasphemous. His office is proof that he was called."

"Very well, then, perhaps he was. But it was an error of judgment."

"James, I might have known you would say some awful thing like that. Some day a judgment will overtake you when you least expect it. And after saying what you have said about Mr. Rucker, perhaps you will feel some natural shame when you learn what he has been saying to me about our Oscar."

"What was it? What did he say?"

"He said there was not another youth of seventeen in the Sunday School that was so bright."

"Bright. What of that? He is bright enough, but what is brightness worth when it is allied to constitutional and indestructible instability of character? Oscar's a fool."

"For pity's sake! And he your own son."

"It's what he is. He is a fool. And *I* can't help his being my son. It is one of those judgments that overtake a person when he is least expecting it."

"James, I wonder how you can say such things. The idea of calling your own son a judgment."

"Oh, call him a benefaction if you like."

"I do call him one, James; and I bless the day that God in his loving thoughtfulness gave him to us."

"That is pure flattery."

"James Carpenter!"

"That is what it is, and you know it. What is there about it to suggest loving thoughtfulness—or any kind of thoughtfulness? It was an inadvertence."

"James, such language is perfectly shocking. It is profanity."

"Profanity is better than flattery. The trouble with you Presbyterians and other church-people is that you exercise no discrimination. Whatever comes, you praise; you call it praise, and you think it praise; yet in the majority of cases it is flattery. Flattery, and undignified; undignified and unworthy. Your singular idea that Oscar was a result of thoughtfulness—"

"James, I won't listen to such talk! If you would go to church yourself, instead of finding fault with people who do, it would be better."

"But I don't find fault with people who do."

"Didn't you just say that they exercise no discrimination, and all that?"

"Certainly, but I did not say that that was an *effect* of going to church. It probably is; and now that you press me, I think it *is;* but I didn't quite say it."

"Well, James, you as good as said it; and now it comes out that at bottom you thought it. It shows how staying away from church makes a person uncharitable in his judgments and opinions."

"Oh, come!"

"But it does."

"I dissent—distinctly."

"Now James, how can you know? In the nineteen years that we have been married, you have been to church only once, and that was nearly nineteen years ago. You have been uncharitable in your judgments ever since—more or less so."

"I do not quite catch your argument. Do you mean that going to church only once made me uncharitable for life?"

"James, you know very well that I meant nothing of the kind. You just said that to provoke me. You know perfectly well that I meant—I meant—now you have got me all confused, and I don't know what I did mean."

"Don't trouble about it, Sarah. It's not like having a new experience, you know. For—"

"That will do, James. I do not wish to hear anything more about it. And as for Oscar—"

"Good—let us have some more Oscar for a change. Is it true that he has resigned from the Cadets of Temperance?"

"Ye-s."

"I thought he would."

"Indeed? And what made you think it?"

"Because he has been a member three months."

"What has that to do with it?"

"It's his limit."

"What do you mean by that, James?"

"Three months is his limit—in most things. When it isn't three weeks or three days or three hours. You must have noticed that. He revolves in threes—it is his make. He is a creature of enthusiasms. Burning enthusiasms. They flare up, and light all the region round. For three months, or weeks, or days. Then they go out and he

catches fire in another place. You remember he was the joy of the
Methodist Sunday school at 7—for three months. Then he was the
joy of the Campbellite Sunday school—for three months. Then of
the Baptist—for three months. Then of the Presbyterian—for three
months. Then he started over again with the Methodist contingent,
and went through the list again; and yet again; and still again; and
so on. He has been the hope and joy of each of those sources of
spiritual supply nine times in nine years; and from Mr. Rucker's
remark I gather that he is now booming the Presbyterian interest
once more. As concerns the Cadets of Temperance, I was just
thinking that his quarterly period—"

"James, it makes me sick to hear you talk like that. You have
never loved your boy. And you never encourage him. You know
how sensitive he is to slights and neglect, yet you have always
neglected him. You know how quickly he responds to praise, and
how necessary praise and commendation and encouragement are to
him—indeed they are his very life—yet he gets none of these helps
from you. How can you expect him to be steadfast; how can you
expect him to keep up his heart in his little affairs and plans when
you never show any interest in them and never applaud anything
he does?"

"Applaud? What is there to applaud? It is just as you say: praise
is his meat and bread—it is his life. And there never was such an
unappeasable appetite. So long as you feed him praise, he gorges,
gorges, gorges, and is obscenely happy; the moment you stop he is
famished—famished and wretched; utterly miserable, despondent,
despairing. You ought to know all about it. You have tried to keep
him fed-up, all his life, and you know what a job it is. I detest that
word—encouragement—where the male sex is concerned. The boy
that needs much of it is a girl in disguise. He ought to put on
petticoats. Praise has a value—when it is earned. When it isn't
earned, the male creature receiving it ought to despise it; and will,
when there is a proper degree of manliness in him. Sarah, if it is
possible to make anything creditable out of the boy, only a strong
hand can do it. Not yours, and not mine. You are all indulgence, I
all indifference. The earlier the strong hand takes him in charge, the

better. And not here in Dawson's Landing, where he can be always running home for sympathy and pettings, but in some other place—as far off as St Louis, say. You gasp!"

"Oh, James, James, you can't mean what you say! Oh, I never could bear it; oh, I know I never could."

"Now come, don't cry, Sarah. Be reasonable. *You* don't want the boy ruined. Now do you?"

"But oh, to have him away off there, and I not by if anything should happen."

"Nothing's going to happen. He—"

"James—he might get sick. And if I were not there—"

"But you can go there, if he gets sick. Let us not borrow trouble—there is time enough. Other boys go from home—it is nothing new—and if Oscar doesn't, he will be ruined. Now you know Underwood—a good man, and an old and trusty friend of mine."

"The printer?"

"Yes. I have been corresponding with him. He is willing to take Oscar as an apprentice. Now doesn't that strike you pleasantly?"

"Why—yes. If he *must* go away from home—oh, dear, dear, dear!—why of course I would rather have him with Mr. Underwood than with anyone else. I want to see Oscar succeed in the world; I desire it as much as you can. But surely there are other ways than the one proposed; and ways more soothing to one's pride, too. Why should our son be a common mechanic—a printer? As far back as we can go there have been no mechanics in your family, and none in mine. In Virginia, for more than two centuries they have been as good as anybody about them; they have been slave-holding planters, professional men, politicians—now and then a merchant, but never a mechanic. They have always been gentlemen. And they were that in England before they came over. Isn't it so?"

"I am not denying it. Go on."

"Don't speak in that tired way, James. You always act annoyed when I speak of our ancestors, and once you said 'Damn the ancestors.' I remember it very well. I wonder you could say such a horrid thing about them, knowing, as you do, how brief this life is, and how soon you must be an ancestor yourself."

"God forgive me, I never thought of that."

"I *heard* that, James—heard every word of it; and you said it ironically, too, which is not good taste—no better taste than muttering it was—muttering to yourself like that when your wife is talking to you."

"Well, I'm sorry; go on, I won't do it again. But if the irony was the thing that pinched, that was a quite unnecessary unkindness; I could have said it seriously, and so saved you the hurt."

"Seriously? How do you mean?"

"Oh, sometimes I feel as if I could give anything to give it all up and lie down in the peace and the quiet and be an ancestor, I do get so tired of being posterity. It is when things go wrong and I am low spirited that I feel like that. At such times—peculiarly dark times, times of deep depression, when the heart is bruised and sore and the light of life is veiled in shadows—it has seemed to me that I would rather be a dog's ancestor than a lieutenant governor's posterity."

"For shame! James, it is the same as saying I am a disappointment to you, and that you would be happier without me than with me. Oh, James, how could you say such a thing?"

"I didn't say it."

"What *did* you say?"

"I said that sometimes I would rather be an ancestor than posterity."

"Well, isn't that separating us?"

"No—for I included you."

"That is different. But James you didn't *say* so. It sounded as if you only wanted to be an ancestor by yourself, and of course that hurt me. Did you *always* think of me, James? Did you always include me? Did you wish I was an ancestor as often as you wished you were one?"

"Yes. Oftener. Twice as often."

"How good you are, James—when you *want* to be. But you are not always good; I wish you were. Still, I am satisfied with you, just as you are; I don't want you changed. You don't want me changed, do you, James?"

"No, I don't think of any change that I would want to risk."

"How lovely of you!"

"Don't mention it. Now, as I remember it, your argument had reached the point where—well, I think you had about finished with the ancestry, and—"

"Yes—and was coming to you. You are county judge—the position of highest dignity in the gift of the ballot—and yet you would see your son become a mechanic."

"I would see him become a *man*. He needn't *remain* a mechanic, if you think it would damage his chances for the peerage."

"The peerage! I never said anything about the peerage. He would never get rid of the stain. It would always be remembered that he had been a mechanic."

"To his discredit? Nonsense. Who would remember it as a smirch?"

"Well, I would, for one. And so would the widow Buckner—"

"Grand-daughter of a Hessian corporal, whom she has painted up in a breastpin as an English general. *She* despise mechanics! Why, her ancestors were bought and sold in shoals in Cassel, at the price of a pound of candles apiece. And it was an overcharge."

"Well, there's Miss Rector—"

"Bosh!"

"It isn't bosh! She—"

"Oh, I know all about that old Tabby. She claims to be descended in an illegal and indelicate way from Charles II. That is no distinction; we are all that. Come, she is no aristocracy. Her opinion is of no consequence. That poor scraggy old thing—why, she is the descendant of an interminable line of Presbyterian Scotch fishermen, and is built, from the ground up, out of hereditary holiness and herring-bones."

"James, it is scandalous to talk so. She—"

"Get back on your course, Sarah. We can discuss the Hessian and the osteological remains another time. You were coming to some more reasons why Oscar should not be a printer."

"Yes. It is not a necessity—either moneywise or otherwise. You are comfortably off and need no help from earnings of his. By grace of his grandfather he has a permanent income of four hundred dollars a year, which makes him rich—at least for this town and region."

"Yes; and fortunately for him it is but a life-interest and he can never touch the principal; otherwise I would rather have a hatful of smoke than that property."

"Well, that is neither here nor there. He has that income; and has six hundred dollars saved from it and laid up."

"Don't let him find it out, Sarah."

"I—I—he already knows it, James. I did not mean to tell him; it escaped me when I wasn't thinking. I'm sorry."

"I am, too. But it is no matter—yet awhile. It is out of his reach until he is of age."

Sarah said nothing, but she was a little troubled. She had lent trifles of money to Oscar from time to time, against the day of his financial independence.

Judge Carpenter mused a while, then said—

"Sarah, I think your objections to my project are not very strong. I believe we must let it stand, unless you can suggest something better. What is your idea about the boy?"

"I think he ought to be trained to one of the professions, James."

"Um-m. Medicine and surgery?"

"Oh, dear no! not surgery. He is too kind-hearted to give pain, and the sight of blood distresses him. A physician has to turn out of his bed at all hours and expose himself to all weathers. I should be afraid of that—for his health, I mean. I should prefer the law. There is opportunity for advancement in that; such a long and grand line of promotions open to one who is diligent and has talent. James, only think of it—he could become Chief Justice of the Supreme Court of the United States!"

"*Could? Would*, you mean."

"Oh, James, do you think he would?"

"Undoubtedly."

"Oh, James, what makes you think so?"

"I don't know."

"You don't *know?*"

"No."

"Then what made you say so?"

"I don't know."

"James, I think you are the most provoking man that ever— James, are you trifling with me? But I know you are—I can see it. I don't see how you can act so. *I* think he would be a great lawyer. If you have doubts—"

"Well, Sarah, I have. He has a fair education; good enough for the business—here in a region where lawyers are hardly ever college-bred men; he has a brighter mind than the average, hereabouts—very much brighter than the average, indeed; he is honest, upright, honorable, his impulses are always high, never otherwise—but he would make a poor lawyer. He has no firmness, no steadfastness, he is as changeable as the wind. He will stick at a thing no longer than the novelty of it lasts, and the praises—then he is off again. When his whole heart is in something and all his fires blazing, anybody can squirt a discouraging word on them and put them out; and any wordy, half-clever person can talk him out of his dearest opinion and make him abandon it. This is not the stuff that good lawyers are made of."

"James, you *cannot* be right. It cannot be as bad as you think; you are prejudiced. You never would consent to see any but the most unfavorable side of Oscar. Do you believe he is unfitted for *all* the professions?"

"All but one."

"Which one?"

"The pulpit."

"James, I could hug you for that! It was the secret wish of my heart—my day-dream all these years; but I never dared to speak of it to *you*, of all creatures. Oh, James, do you think, do you really and seriously think that he would make a name for himself in the pulpit —be spoken of, written about?"

"I *know* it."

"Oh, it is *too* good, too lovely! Think of it—our Oscar famous! You really believe he would be famous!"

"No. Notorious."

"Well—what is the difference?"

"There is a good deal."

"Well, what *is* it?"

"Why, fame is a great and noble thing—and permanent. Notoriety is a noise—just a noise, and doesn't last."

"So *that* is what you think our Oscar would reach. Then pray, why do you think him suited for the pulpit?"

"The law is a narrow field, Sarah; in fact it is merely a groove. Or, you may call it a house with only one room in it. But in religion there are a hundred sects. It is a hotel. Oscar could move from room to room, you know."

"James!"

"Yes, he could. He could move every quarter, and take a fresh start. And every time he moved, there would be a grand to-do about it. The newspapers would be full of it. That would make him happy. It is my opinion that he ought to be dedicated to this career of sparkling holiness, usefulness and health-giving theological travel."

Sarah's face flushed and all her frame quivered with anger. Her breath came in gasps; for the moment she could not get her voice. Then she got it, but before she could use it the thin pipe of a boy calling to a mate pierced to her ear through the still and murky air—

"Thug Carpenter's got drownded!"

"Oh, James, our Oscar—drowned!" She sank into a chair, pallid and faint, and muttered, "The judgment—I warned you."

Chapter 2

"Drownded, you say?" This from another boy.

"Well, not just entirely, but he's goin' to be. The ice is breaking up, and he's got caught all by himself on t'other side of the split, about a half a mile from shore. He's a goner!"

Sarah Carpenter was on her feet in a moment, and fumbling with bonnet and shawl with quaking hands. "Quick, James, there's hope yet!" The Judge was getting into his overcoat with all haste.

Outside, the patter of hurrying footsteps was heard, and a confusion of excited voices; through the window one could see the village population pouring out upon the white surface of the vast Mississippi in a ragged long stream, the further end of it, away toward the middle of the river, reduced by distance to a creeping swarm of black ants.

Now arose the ringing sound of flying hoofs, and a trim and fair young girl, bareheaded and riding bareback and astride, went thundering by on a great black horse.

"There goes Hellfire Hotchkiss! Oh, James, he's saved, if anybody can save him!"

"You've said the truth, Sarah. She has saved him before, and she will do it again. Keep up your heart, it will all come right."

By this time the couple had crossed the river road and were starting down the ice-paved slope of the bank. Ahead, on the level white plain, the black horse was speeding past detachment after detachment of plodding citizens; and all along the route hats and handkerchiefs went up in welcome as the young girl swept by, and burst after burst of cheers rose and floated back, fainter and fainter, as the distance grew.

Far out toward the middle of the river the early arrivals were massed together on the border of a wide rift of indeterminable length. They could get no further. In front of them was the water; beyond it, clear to the Illinois shore, a moaning and grinding drift and turmoil of monster ice-cakes, which wandered apart at times, by compulsion of the swirling currents, then crashed thunderously together again, piling one upon another and rising for a moment into rugged hillocks, then falling to ruin and sagging apart once more. It was an impressive spectacle, and the people were awed by the sight and by the brooding spirit of danger and death that was in the air, and they spoke but little, and then in low voices. Most of them said nothing at all, but gazed fixedly out over the drifting plain, searching it for the missing boy. Now and then, through the vague steam that rose from the thawing ice they caught sight of a black speck away out among the recurrent up-bursting hillocks under the lowering sky, and then there would be a stir among the crowd, and eager questions of "Where? which is it? where do you

see it?" and answers of "There—more to the right—still more—
look where I am pointing—further out—away out—just a black
speck—don't you see it now?" But the speck would turn out to be a
log or some such thing, and the crowd would fall silent again.

By and by distant cheering was heard, and all turned to listen.
The sound grew and grew, approached nearer and nearer, the black
horse was sighted, the people fell apart, and down the lane the
young girl came flying, with her welcome roaring about her.
Evidently she was a favorite. All along, from the beginning of her
flight, as soon as she was recognised the cry went up—

"It's Hellfire Hotchkiss—stand back and give her the road!" and
then the cheers broke out.

She reined up, now, and spoke—

"Where is he?"

"Nobody knows. Him and the other boys were skating, along
about yonder, somewheres, and they heard a rip, and the first they
knew their side of the river begun to break up. They made a rush,
and got through all right; but he was behind, and by the time he got
here the split was too wide for him—for *him,* you understand—so
they flew home to tell, and get help, and he broke for up the river to
hunt a better place, and—"

The girl did not wait for the rest, but rode off up stream, peering
across the chasm as she went, the people following her with their
eyes, and commenting.

"She's the only person that had enough presence of mind to come
fixed to *do* something in case there was a chance. She's got a life-
preserver along." It was Miss Hepworth, the milliner, that said that.
Peter Jones, the blacksmith, said—

"It ought to do some good, seeing she took the trouble and had
the thoughtfulness to fetch it, but there's never any telling which
way Thug Carpenter is going to act. Take him as a rule, he is afraid
of his shadow; and then again, after a mighty long spell, he'll up
and do a thing which is brave enough for most anybody to be proud
of. If he is just his ordinary natural self to-day, the life-preserver
ain't going to be any good; he won't dare use it when Hellfire
throws it to him."

"That's about the size of it," said Jake Thompson, the baker. "There's considerable difference betwixt them two—Thug and her. Pudd'nhead Wilson says Hellfire Hotchkiss is the only genuwyne male man in this town and Thug Carpenter's the only genuwyne female girl, if you leave out sex and just consider the business facts; and says her pap used to—hey, she's stopped."

"So she has. Maybe she's found him."

"No, only thought she had. She's moving on, again. Pudd'nhead Wilson says Thug's got the rightest heart and the best disposition of any person in this town, and pretty near the quickest brains, too, but is a most noble derned fool just the same. And *he* says Hellfire's a long sight the prettiest human creature that ever lived, and the trimmest built, too, and as graceful as a fish; and says he'd druther see her eyes snap when she's mad, or water up when she's touched than—'y George, she's stopped again. Say—she's faced around; she's coming this way."

"It's so. Stopped again. She's found him, sure. Seems to be talking across the rift—don't you see? Got her hand up to her mouth for a trumpet. Ain't it so?"

"Oh, yes, there ain't any doubt. She's got off of her horse. Hi!—come along, everybody. Hellfire's found him!"

The crowd set out at a pace which soon brought them to the girl; then they faced about and walked along with her. Oscar was abreast, prisoner on a detached and independent great square of ice, with a couple of hundred yards of water and scattered ice-cakes between him and the people. His case had a bad look. Oscar's parents arrived, now, and when his mother realized the situation she put out her hands toward him and began to wail and sob, and call him by endearing names, and implore him not to leave her, not to take away the light of her life and make it desolate; and then she looked beseechingly into the faces about her, and said, "Oh, will nobody save him? he is all the world to me; oh, I cannot give him up." She caught sight of the young girl, now, and ran to her and said, "Oh, Rachel, dear, dear Rachel, you saved him before, you'll not let him die now, *will* you?"

"No."

"Oh, you precious child! if ever—"

" 'Sh! What is he saying? Listen."

Oscar was shouting something, but the words could not be made out with certainty.

"Wasn't it something about snags?" asked the girl. "Are there snags down yonder?"

"Snags? Yes," said the baker, "there's a whole rack-heap of them. That is what he's talking about, sure. He knows they are there, and he knows they'll wreck him."

"Then it won't do to wait any longer for the rift to get narrower," said Rachel. "He must be helped now or it will be too late."

She threw off her winter wrap, and began to take off her shoes.

"What are you going to do?" said old Uncle Benny Stimson, Indian doctor and tavern keeper.

"Take him the preserver. He isn't much of a swimmer, and couldn't ever make the trip without it."

"You little fool, you'll freeze to death."

"Freeze to death—the idea!"

"Well, you will. You let some of these young fellows do it."

"When I want anybody's help, I'll ask for it, Uncle Benny. I am one of the young fellows myself, I'll let you know."

"Right you are. The pig-headedest little devil, for a parson's daughter, I ever saw. But a brick just the same; I'll say that for you, H. H.,—every time."

"Thank you, dear. Please lead my horse and carry my things, and go along down yonder and stand by. Thug is pretty well chilled by this time; somebody please lend me a whisky-flask."

Thirty-five were offered. She took one, and put it in her bosom. Uncle Benny said—

"No use in that, he's teetotal—he won't touch it, girly."

"That was last week. He has reformed by this time."

She plunged in and struck out. Somebody said "Let us pray," but no one heard; all were absorbed in watching. The girl made good progress both ways—forward, by her own strength, and downstream by the force of the current. She made her goal, and got a cheer when she climbed out of the water. Oscar had been in a state of exhausting fright for an hour and more, and he said he was weak and chilled and helpless and unmanned, and would rather die where he was than chance the desperate swim—he knew he couldn't make it.

"Yes you can. I'll help you, Thug, and the preserver will keep you up. Here, take some of this—it will hearten you."

"What is it?"

"Milk."

He took a drain.

"Good milk, too," he said. "It is so comforting, and I was so cold. I will take some more. How thoughtful it was of you to bring the flask; but you always think of everything."

"Hurry. Get off your overcoat, Thug."

But he glanced at the water and the wide distance, and said, "Oh, I don't dare to venture it. I never could make it."

"Yes you can. Trust to me. I'll help you with the coat. There, it's off. Now the boots. Sit down—I'll help. Now the preserver; hold still, I'll strap it around you. We are ready, now. Come—you are not afraid to trust to me, Thug?"

"I am going to do it, if I die—but I wouldn't risk it with any other person. You'll go through safe, I know that; and you'll fetch me through if anybody can." He added, tearfully, "But it may be that I'll never get across; I don't feel that I shall. And if these are my last words, I want to say this. If I go down, you must tell my mother that I loved her and thought of her to the last; and I want you to remember always that I was grateful to you. I think you are the best, best girl that ever lived; and if I pass from this troubled life this day, I shall enter heaven with a prayer on my lips for you, Hellfire. I am ready."

"You are a dear good boy, Thug, but it is not wise to be thinking about death at such a time as this. Come along, and don't be afraid; your mother is yonder, and you will be with her in a very little while. Quick, here are the snags."

They were away in time; in a few moments more their late refuge went to wreck and ruin with a crash.

"Rest your right hand on my shoulder, Thug, and keep the same stroke with me. And no matter what happens, don't get rattled. Slack up a little—we mustn't hurry." After a little she said, "We are half way, now—are you getting tired?"

"Yes, and oh, so cold! I can't hold out, Rachel."

"Yes you can. You *must*. We are doing well; we are going to make it. Turn on your back and float a little—two minutes. There, that will do; you mustn't get cramps."

"Rachel, they are cheering us. How that warms a person up! If they'll keep that up, I believe I can make it."

"They'll do it—hear that!"

"Rachel—"

"What?"

"I'm afraid there's a cramp coming."

"Hush—put it out of your mind!"

"I can't, Rachel—it's coming."

"Thug, you *must* put it out of your mind. Brace up—we are almost there. It is no distance at all, now. Two minutes more. Brace up. Don't give in—I know we are safe."

Both were well spent when they were hauled out on the ice, and also fairly well frozen; but a warm welcome and good whisky refreshed them and made them comfortable; and the attentions and congratulations and interest and sympathy and admiration lavished upon them deeply gratified Oscar's love of distinction and made him glad the catastrophe had happened to him.

Chapter 3

VESUVIUS, isolated, conspicuous, graceful of contour, is lovely when it is at peace, with the sunshine pouring upon its rich vineyards and its embowered homes and hamlets drowsing in the drift of the cloud-shadows; but it is subject to irruptions. Rachel was a Vesuvius, seen through the butt-end of the telescope. She was largely made up of feeling. She had a tropically warm heart, a right spirit and a good disposition; but under resentment her weather could change with remarkable promptness, and break into tempests of a surprising sort. Still, while the bulk of her was heart and impulse, the rest of her was mental, and good in quality. She had a business head, and practical sense, and it had been believed from the first, by Judge Carpenter and other thoughtful people, that she would be a valuable person when she got tame.

Part of what she was was born to her, the rest was due to environment and to her up-bringing. She had had neither brothers nor sisters; there was no young society for her in the house. Her mother was an invalid and kept her room the most of the time. She could not endure noise, nor tempers, nor restless activities; and from the cradle her child was a master hand in these matters. So, in her first years she was deprived of the society of her mother. The young slave woman, Martha, was superstitious about her, thinking at first that she was possessed of a devil, and later that he had found the accommodations to his mind and had brought his family. She petted and spoiled the child, partly out of her race's natural fondness for children of any sort or kind, and partly to placate and pacify the devils; but she had a world of work to do and could give but little time to play, so the child would soon find the kitchen a dull place and seek elsewhere for amusement.

The father was sweetness and amiability itself, and greatly loved the child, but he was no company for the volatile creature, nor she for him. He was always musing, dreaming, absorbing himself in his books, or grinding out sermons, and while the child was present these industries suffered considerable interruption. There was conversation—abundance of it—but it was of a wearing and nerve-racking kind.

"Can I have this, fa'r?" (father.)

"No, dear, that is not for lit—"

"Could I have that?"

"No, dear, please don't handle it. It is very frail and you might—"

"What is *this* for, fa'r? Can Wildcat have it?" This was Martha's love-name for Rachel.

"Oh, *dear* no! My child, you must *not* put your hands on things without asking *beforehand* whether you may or—"

"Ain't there anything for me to play with?—and it's so lonesome; and there isn't any place to go."

"Ah, poor child, I wish—there! Oh, I knew you would; the whole inkstand emptied onto your nice clean clothes. Run along, dear, and tell Martha to attend to you—quick, before you smear it over everything."

There was no one to govern Rachel, no one to train her, so she drifted along without these aids; and such rearing as she got was her own handiwork and was not according to any familiar pattern. She was never still when awake, she was stored to the eyelids with energies and enthusiasms, her mind, her hands, her feet, her body, were in a state of constant and tireless activity, and her weather was about equally divided between brilliant and happy sunshine and devastating tempests of wrath. Martha said she was a "sudden" child—the suddenest she had ever seen; that when anything went wrong with her there was no time to provide against consequences: she had smashed every breakable thing she could get her hands on before a body could say a word; and then as suddenly her fury was over and she was gathering up the wreckage and mourning over it remorsefully.

By the law of her nature she had to have society; and as she could not get it in the house she forsook that desert early and found it outside. And so while she was as yet a toddling little thing it became a peaceful house—a home of deep and slumberous tranquillity, and for a good while perhaps forgot that it had ever been harassed and harried and terrorised by her family of uneasy devils.

She was a stranger outside, but that was nothing; she soon had a reputation there. She laid its foundations in her first week at Miss Roper's school, when she was six years old and a little past. At first she took up with the little girls, but they were a disappointment; she found their society a weariness. They played with dolls; she found that dull. They cried for a pin-scratch: she did not like that. When they quarreled, they took it out in calling each other names; according to her ideas, this was inadequate. They would not jump from high places; they would not climb high trees; they were afraid of the thunder; and of the water; and of cows; and would take no perilous risks; and had no love of danger for its own sake. She tried to reform them, but it failed. So she went over to the boys.

They would have none of her, and told her so. They said they were not going to play with girls—they despised them. Shad Stover threatened her with a stout hickory, and told her to move along or she would catch it. She perceived, now, that she could be happy, here, and was sorry she had ·wasted so much time with the little girls. She did not say anything to the boy, but snatched his switch away and wore it out on him. She made him beg. He was nearly twice her own age and size, and as he was the bully of the small-fry side of the school, she had established her ability to whip the whole of his following by whipping him—and if she had been a boy this would have been conceded and she would have succeeded to the bully's captainship without further balloting; but she was a girl, and boys have no manly sense of fairness and justice where girls are concerned; so she had to whip two or three of the others before opposition was quenched and her wish to play with the gang granted. Shad Stover withdrew and took a minor place in a group of somewhat larger boys.

Thenceforth Rachel trained with the boys altogether, and found in their rough play and tough combats and dangerous enterprises the contentment and joy for which she long had hungered. She took her full share in all their sports, and was a happy child. All through the summer she was encountering perils, but she had luck, and disappointed all the prophets. They all said she would get herself killed, but in no instance did her damages reach quite to that, though several times there were good hopes. She was a hardy and determined fighter, and attacked anything that came along, if it offended. By and by when the cool October came and the news went about that the circus was coming, on its way to the South, she was on hand outside the village, with many others, at sunrise, to get a look at the elephant free of charge. With a cake in her hand for the animal, she sat with the crowd on the grass by the country road. When the elephant was passing by, he scooped up a snoutful of dust and flung it over his back, then scooped up another and discharged it into the faces of the audience. They were astonished and frightened, and all except Rachel flitted promptly over the rail fence with a rush, gasping and coughing; but the child was not moved to run away. The little creature was in a towering rage; for she had come to offer hospitality, and this was the thanks she got. She sprang into the road with the first stick that came handy and began to fiercely bang and hammer the elephant's hind legs and scream at him all the injurious epithets she could think of. But the elephant swayed along, and was not aware of what was happening. This offensive indifference set fire to all the child's reserves of temper, and she ran forward to see if she could get any attention at that end. She gave the trunk a cordial bang, saying, "Now let *that* learn you!" and raised her stick for another stroke; but before she could deliver it the elephant, without changing his gait, gathered her gently up and tossed her over the fence among the crowd. She was beside herself at this new affront, and was for clearing out after him again; and struggled to get free, but the people held her. They reasoned with her, and said it was no use to fight the elephant, for he didn't mind a stick. "I know it," she said, "but I've got a pin, now, and if I can get to him I will stick it in him."

A few months later her mother died. Rachel was then seven years old. During the next three years she went on playing with the boys, and gradually building up a perfect conflagration of a reputation, as far as unusual enterprises and unsafe exploits went. Then at last arguments and reasonings began to have an effect upon her, and she presently stopped training with the boys.

She played with the girls six months, and tried to get used to it and fond of it, but finally had to give it up. The amusements were not rugged enough; they were much too tame, not to say drowsy. Kissing parties and candy pullings in the winter, and picnics in the summer: these were good romps and lively, but they did not happen often enough, and the intermediate dissipations seemed wholly colorless to Rachel.

She withdrew. She did not go back to the boys at once, but tried to get along by herself. But nature was too strong for her; she had to have company; within two months she was a tomboy again, and her life was once more a satisfaction to her, a worry to her friends, and a marvel to the rest of the community.

Before the next four and a half years were out she had learned many masculine arts, and was more competent in them than any boy of her age in the town. All alone she learned how to swim, and with the boys she learned to skate. She was the only person of her sex in the county who had these accomplishments—they were taboo. She fished, boated, hunted, trapped, played "shinny" on the ice and ball on the land, and ran foot races. She broke horses for pastime, and for the risk there was in it. At fifteen she ranked as the strongest "boy" in the town, the smartest boxer, a willing and fearless fighter, and good to win any fight that her heart was in. The firemen conferred an honorary membership upon her, and allowed her to scale the roofs of burning houses and help handle the hose; for she liked that sort of employment, she had good judgment and coolness in danger, she was spry and active, and she attended strictly to business when on the roof. Whenever there was a fire she and her official belt and helmet were a part of the spectacle— sometimes lit up with the red flush of the flames, sometimes dimly glimpsed through the tumbling volumes of smoke, sometimes helping to get out the inmates, sometimes being helped out herself in a suffocated condition. Several times she saved lives, several times her own life was saved by her mates; and once when she was overcome by the smoke they penetrated to her and rescued her when the chance of success was so slender that they would not have taken the risk for another.

She kept the community in an unrestful state; it could settle to no permanent conclusion about her. She was always rousing its resentment by her wild unfeminine ways, and always winning back its forgiveness again by some act or other of an undeniably creditable sort.

By the time she was ten she had begun to help about the house, and before she was thirteen she was become in effect its mistress— mistress and assistant housekeeper. She kept the accounts, checked wastage, and was useful in other ways. But she had earned her picturesque nickname, and it stayed by her. It was a country where nicknames were common; and once acquired, they were a life-property, and inalienable. Rachel might develop into a saint, but that would not matter: the village would acknowledge the saintship and revere the saint, but it would still call her Hellfire Hotchkiss. Old use and habit would take care of that.

Along in her sixteenth year she accidentally crossed the orbit of her early antagonist, Shad Stover, and this had good results for her; or rather it led up to something which did her that service. Shad Stover was now twenty, and had gone to the dogs, along with his brother Hal, who was twenty-one. They were dissipated young loafers, and had gotten the reputation of being desperadoes, also. They were as vain of this dark name as if they had legitimately earned it—which they hadn't. They went armed—which was not the custom of the town—and every now and then they pulled their pepper-box revolvers and made some one beg for his life. They traveled in a pair—two on one—and they always selected their man with good discretion, and no bloodshed followed. It was a cheap way to build up a reputation, but it was effective. About once a month they added something to it in an inexpensive way: they got drunk and rode the streets firing their revolvers in the air and scaring the people out of their wits. They had become the terror of the town. There was a sheriff, and there was also a constable, but they could never be found when these things were going on. Warrants were not sued out by witnesses, for no one wanted to get into trouble with the Stovers.

One day there was a commotion in the streets, and the cry went about that the Stovers had picked a quarrel with a stranger and were killing him. Rachel was on her way home from a ball-game, and had her bat in her hand. She turned a corner, and came upon the three men struggling together; at a little distance was gathered a crowd of citizens, gazing spell-bound and paralyzed. The Stovers had the stranger down, and he had a grip upon each of them and was shouting wildly for help. Just as Rachel arrived Shad snatched himself free and drew his revolver and bent over and thrust it in the man's face and pulled the trigger. It missed fire, and Rachel's bat fell before he could pull again. Then she struck the other brother senseless, and the stranger jumped up and ran away, grateful but not stopping to say so.

A few days later old Aunt Betsy Davis paid Rachel a visit. She was no one's aunt in particular, but just the town's. The title indicated that she was kind and good and wise, well beloved, and in age. She said—

"I want to have a little talk with you, dear. I was your mother's friend, and I am yours, although you are so headstrong and have never done as I've tried to get you to do. But I've got to try again, and you must let me; for at last the thing has happened that I was afraid might happen: you are being talked about."

Rachel's expression had been hardening for battle; but she broke into a little laugh, now, and said—

"Talked about? Why, aunt Betsy, I was always talked about."

"Yes, dear, but not in this new way."

"New way?"

"Yes. There is one kind of gossip that this town has never dealt in before, in the fifty-two years that I've lived in it—and has never had any occasion to. Not in one single case, if you leave out the town drunkard's girls; and even that turned out to be a lie, and was stopped."

"Aunt Betsy!" Rachel's face was crimson, and an angry light rose in her eyes.

"There—now don't lose your temper, child. Keep calm, and let us have a good sensible talk, and talk it out. Take it all around, this is a fair town, and a just town, and has been good to you—very good to you, everything considered, for you *have* led it a dance, and you know it. Now ain't that so?"

"Ye-s, but—"

"Never mind the buts. Leave it just so. The town has been quite reasonably good to you, everything considered. Partly it was on account of your poor mother, partly on your father's account and your own, and partly because it's its natural and honorable disposition to stand by all its old families the best it can. Now then, haven't you got your share to do by *it?* Of course you have. Have you done it? In some ways you haven't, and I'm going to tell you about it. You've always preferred to play with the boys. Well, that's all right, up to a certain limit; but you've gone away beyond the limit. You ought to have stopped long ago—oh, long ago. And stopped being fireman, too. Then there's another thing. It's all right for you to break all the wild horses in the county, as long as you like it and are the best hand at it; and it's all right for you to keep a wild horse of your own and tear around the country everywhere on it all alone; but you are fifteen years old, now, and in many ways you are seventeen and could pass for a woman, and so the time has gone by for you to be riding astraddle."

"Why, I've not done it once since I was twelve, aunt Betsy."

"Is that so? Well, I'm glad of it; I hadn't noticed. I'll set that down to your credit. Now there's another thing. If you *must* go boating, and shooting, and skating, and all that—however, let that go. I reckon you couldn't break yourself. But anyway, you don't need the boys' company—you can go alone. You see, if you had let the boys alone, why then these reports wouldn't ever—"

"Aunt Betsy, does anybody *believe* those reports?"

"Believe them? Why, how you talk! Of course they don't. Our people don't believe such things about our old families so easy as all that. They don't believe it *now*, but if a thing goes on, and on, and on, being talked about, why that's another matter. The thing to do is to stop it in time, and that is what I've come to plead with you to do, child, for your own sake and your father's, and for the sake of your mother who is in her grave—a good friend to me she was, and I'm trying to be hers, now."

She closed with a trembling lip and an unsteady voice. Rachel was not hearing; she was lost in a reverie. Presently a flush crept into her face, and she muttered—

"And they are talking about me—like that!" After a little she glanced up suddenly and said, "You spoke of it as new talk; how new is it?"

"Two or three days old."

"Two or three days. Who started it?"

"Can't you guess?"

"I think I can. The Stovers."

"Yes."

"I'll horsewhip them both."

The old lady said with simplicity—

"I was afraid you would. You are a dear good child, and your heart is always in the right place. And so like your grandfather. Dear me but he was a topper! And just as splendid as he could be."

After aunt Betsy took her leave, Rachel sat a long time silent and thinking. In the end, she arrived at a conclusion, apparently.

"And they are talking about me—like that. Who would ever have dreamed it? Aunt Betsy is right. It *is* time to call a halt. It is a pity, too. The boys are such good company, and it is going to be so dull without them. Oh, everything seems to be made wrong, nothing seems to be the way it ought to be. Thug Carpenter is out of his sphere, I am out of mine. Neither of us can arrive at any success in life, we shall always be hampered and fretted and kept back by our misplaced sexes, and in the end defeated by them, whereas if we could change we should stand as good a chance as any of the young people in the town. I wonder which case is the hardest. I am sorry for him, and yet I do not see that he is any more entitled to pity than I am."

She went on thinking at random for a while longer, then her thoughts began to settle and take form and shape, and she ended by making a definite plan.

"I will change my way of life. I will begin now, and stick to it. I will not train with the boys any more, nor do ungirlish things except when it is a duty and I ought to do them. I mean, I will not do them for mere pleasure. Before this I would have horsewhipped the Stovers just as a pleasure; but now it will be for a higher motive —a higher motive, and in every way a worthier one.

"That is for Monday. Tomorrow I will go to church. I will go every Sunday. I do not want to, but it must be done. It is a duty.

"Withdraw from the boys. The Stovers. Church. That makes three. Three in three days. It is enough to begin with; I suppose I have never done three in three weeks before—just *as* duties."

And being refreshed and contented by this wholesale purification, she went to bed.

Tom Sawyer's Conspiracy

Chapter 1

Well, we was back home and I was at the Widow Douglas's up on Cardiff Hill again getting sivilised some more along of her and old Miss Watson all the winter and spring, and the Widow was hiring Jim for wages so he could buy his wife and children's freedom some time or other, and the summer days was coming, now, and the new leaves and the wind-flowers was out, and marbles and hoops and kites was coming in, and it was already barefoot time and ever so bammy and soft and pleasant, and the damp a-stewing out of the ground and the birds a-carrying on in the woods, and everybody taking down the parlor stoves and stowing them up garret, and speckled straw hats and fish-hooks beginning to show up for sale, and the early girls out in white frocks and blue ribbons, and schoolboys getting restless and fidgetty, and anybody could see that the derned winter was over. Winter is plenty lovely enough when it *is* winter and the river is froze over and there's hail and sleet and bitter cold and booming storms and all that, but spring is no good—just rainy and slushy and sloppy and dismal and ornery and uncomfortable, and ought to be stopped. Tom Sawyer he says the same.

Me and Jim and Tom was feeling good and thankful, and took

the dug-out and paddled over to the head of Jackson's island early Saturday morning where we could be by ourselves and plan out something to do. I mean it was Tom's idea to plan out something to do—me and Jim never planned out things to do, which wears out a person's brains and ain't any use anyway, and is much easier and more comfortable to set still and let them happen their own way. But Tom Sawyer said it was a lazy way and put double as much on Providence as there was any use in. Jim allowed it was sinful to talk like that, and says—

"Mars Tom, you ought not to talk so. *You* can't relieve Prov'dence none, en he doan need yo' help, nohow. En what's mo', Mars Tom, if you's gwyne to try to plan out sump'n dat Prov'dence ain' gwyne to 'prove of, den ole Jim got to pull out, too."

Tom seen that he was making a mistake, and resking getting Jim down on his projects before there was any to get down on. So he changed around a little, and says—

"Jim, Providence appoints everything beforehand, don't he?"

"Yessah—'deed he do—fum de beginnin' er de worl'."

"Very well. If I plan out a thing—*thinking* it's me that's planning it out, I mean—and it don't *go;* what does that mean? Don't it mean that it wasn't Providence's plan and he ain't willing?"

"Yessah, you can 'pen' 'pon it—dat's jes' what it mean, every time."

"And if it *does* go, it means that it *was* Providence's plan, and I just happened to hit it right, don't it?"

"Yessah, it's jes' what it mean, dead sho'."

"Well, then, it's right for me to go ahead and keep on planning out things till I find out which is the one he wants done, ain't it?"

"W'y, sutt'nly, Mars Tom, dat's all right, o' course, en ain' no sin en no harm—"

"That is, I can *suggest* plans?"

"Yassah, sutt'nly, you can *sejest* as many as you want to, Prov'dence ain' gwyne to mine dat, if he can look 'em over fust, but doan you *do* none of 'em, Mars Tom, excep' only jes' de right one—becase de sin is shovin' ahead en *doin'* a plan dat Prov'dence ain't satisfied wid."

Everything was satisfactry again. You see he just fooled Jim along and made him come out at the same hole he went in at, but Jim didn't know it. So Tom says—

"It's all right, now, and we'll set down here on the sand and plan out something that 'll just make the summer buzz, and worth being alive. I've been examining the authorities and sort of posting up, and there's two or three things that look good, and would just suit, I reckon—either of them."

"Well," I says, "what's the first one?"

"The first one, and the biggest, is a civil war—if we can get it up."

"Shucks," I says, "dern the civil war. Tom Sawyer, I might a knowed you'd get up something that's full of danger and fuss and worry and expense and all that—it wouldn't suit you, if it warn't."

"And glory," he says, excited, "you're forgetting the glory—forgetting the main thing."

"Oh, cert'nly," I says, "it's got to have that in, you needn't tell a person that. The first time I ketch old Jimmy Grimes fetching home a jug that hain't got any rot-gut in it, I'll say the *next* mericle that's going to happen is Tom Sawyer fetching home a *plan* that hain't got any glory in."

I said it very sarcastic. I just *meant* it to make him squirm, and it done it. He stiffened up, and was very distant, and said I was a jackass.

Jim was a studying and studying, and pretty soon he says—

"Mars Tom, what do dat word mean—*civil?*"

"Well, it means—it means—well, anything that's good, and kind, and polite, and all that—Christian, as you may say."

"Mars Tom, doan dey fight in de wars, en kill each other?"

"Of course."

"Now den, does you call dat civil, en kind en polite, en does you call it Christian?"

"Well—you see—well, you know—don't you understand, it's only just a *name.*"

"Hi-yah! I was a layin' for you, Mars Tom, en I got you dis time, sho'. Jist a name! *Dat's* so. *Civil* war! Dey ain' no sich war. De idear!—people dat's good en kind en polite en b'long to de church a-marchin' out en slashin' en choppin' en cussin' en shootin' one another—lan', I knowed dey warn't no sich thing. You done 'vent it yo' own self, Mars Tom. En you want to take en drap *dat* plan, same as if she was hot. Don't you git up no civil war, Mars Tom—Prov'dence ain' gwyne to 'low it."

"How do *you* know, till it's been tried?"

"How does I know? I knows becase Prov'dence ain' gwyne to let *dat* kind o' people fight—he ain' never hearn o' no sich war."

"He has heard of it, too; it's an old thing; there's been a million of them."

Jim couldn't speak, he was so astonished. And so hurt, too. He judged it was a sin for Tom to say such a thing. But Tom told him it was so, and everybody knowed it that had read the histories. So Jim had to believe it, but he didn't want to, and said he didn't believe Providence would allow it any more; and then he got doubtful and troubled and ontrustful, and asked Tom to lay low and not sejest it. And he was so anxious that he couldn't be comforted till Tom promised him he wouldn't.

So Tom done it; but he was disappointed. And for a while he couldn't keep from talking about it and hankering after it. It shows what a good heart he had; he had been just dead set on getting up a civil war, and had even planned out the preparations for it on the biggest scale, and yet he throwed it all aside and give it up to accommodate a nigger. Not many boys would a done such a thing as that. But that was just his style; when he liked a person there wasn't anything he wouldn't do for them. I've seen Tom Sawyer do a many a noble thing, but the noblest of all, I think, was the time he countermanded the civil war. That was his word—and not a half a mouthful for him, either, but I don't fat up with such, they give me the dry gripes. He had the preparations all made, and was going to have a billion men in the field, first and last, besides munitions of war. I don't know what that is—brass bands, I reckon; sounds like it, anyway, and I knowed Tom Sawyer well enough to know that if he got up a war and was in a hurry and overlooked some of the things, it wouldn't be the brass bands, not by a blame sight. But he give up the civil war, and it is one of the brightest things to his credit. And he could a had it easy enough if he had sejested it, anybody can see it now. And it don't seem right and fair that Harriet Beacher Stow and all them other second-handers gets all the credit of starting that war and you never hear Tom Sawyer mentioned in the histories ransack them how you will, and yet he was the first one that thought of it. Yes, and years and years before ever they had the idea. And it was all his own, too, and come out of his own head, and was a bigger one than theirs, and would a cost forty times as much, and if it hadn't been for Jim he would a been in ahead and got the glory. I know, becuz I was there, and I could go this day and point out the very place on Jackson's island, there on the sand-bar up at the head where it begins to shoal off. And where is Tom Sawyer's monument, I would like to know? There ain't any. And there ain't ever going to be any. It's just the way, in this world. One person *does* the thing, and the other one gets the monument.

So then I says, "What's the next plan, Tom?"

And he said his next idea was to get up a revolution. Jim licked his chops over that, and says—

"Hit's a pow'ful big word, Mars Tom, en soun' mighty good. What 's a revolution?"

"Well, it's where there ain't only nine-tenths of the people satisfied with the gov'ment, and the others is down on it and rises up full of patriotic devotion and knocks the props from under it and sets up a more different one. There's nearly about as much glory in a revolution as there is in a civil war, and ain't half the trouble and expense if you are on the right side, because you don't have to have so many men. It's the economicalest thing there is. Anybody can get up a revolution."

"Why lookyhere, Tom," I says, "how can one-tenth of the people pull down a gov'ment if the others don't want them to? There ain't any sense in that. It can't be done."

"It can't, can't it? Much you know about history, Huck Finn. Look at the French revolution; and look at ourn. I reckon that 'll show you. Just a handful started it, both times. You see, *they* don't know they're going to revolute when they start *in,* and they don't know they *are* revoluting till it's all over. Our boys started in to get taxation by representation—it's all they wanted—and when they got through and come to look around, they see they had knocked out the king. And besides, had more taxation and liberty and things than they knowed what to do with. Washington found out towards the last that there had been a revolution, but *he* didn't know when it happened, and yet he was there all the time. The same with Cromwell, the same with the French. That's the peculiarity of a revolution—there ain't anybody intending to do anything when they start in. That's one of the peculiarities; and the other one is, that the king gets left, every time."

"Every time?"

"Of course; it's all there is *to* a revolution—you knock out the gov'ment and start a fresh kind."

"Tom Sawyer," I says, "where are you going to get a king to knock out? There ain't any."

"Huck Finn, you don't have to have any to knock out, this time —you put one *in.*"

He said it would take all summer, and break up school and everything, and so I was willing for us to start the revolution; but Jim says—

"Mars Tom, I's gwyne to object. I hadn't nothing agin kings ontel I had dat one on my han's all las' summer. Dat one's enough for me. He *was* de beatenes' ole cuss—now warn't he, Huck? Warn't he de wust lot you ever see?—awluz drunk en carryin' on, him en de duke, en tryin' to rob Miss Mary en de Hair-lip—*no* sah, I got enough; I ain' gwyne to have nothing more to do wid kings."

Tom said that that warn't no regular king, and couldn't be took as a sample; and tried his level best to argufy Jim into some kind of reasonableness, but it warn't any use; he was set, and when he was set once, he was set for good. He said we would have all the trouble and worry and expense, and when we got the revolution done our old king would show up and hog the whole thing. Well, it begun to sound likely, the way Jim put it, and it got me to feeling oneasy, and I reckoned we was taking too much of a resk; so I pulled out

and sided with Jim, and that let the stuffing out of the revolution. I
was sorry to have Tom so disappointed again, and him so happy and
hopeful; but ever since, when I look back on it I know I done for
the best. Kings ain't in our line; we ain't used to them, and
wouldn't know how to keep them satisfied and quiet; and they don't
seem to do anything much for the wages, anyway, and don't pay no
rent. They have a good heart, and feel tender for the poor and for
the best charities, and they leg for them, too, and pass the hat pretty
frequent, I can say that for them; but now and then they don't put
anything in it themselves. They let *on* to economise, but that is
about all. If one of them has got something on hand the other side
of the river, he will go over in about nine ships; and the ferry-boat a
laying there all the time. But the worst is the trouble it is to keep
them still; it can't be done. They are always in a sweat about the
succession, and the minute you get that fixed to suit them they bust
out in another place. And always, rain or shine, they are hogging
somebody else's land. Congress is a cuss, but we better get along
with it. We always know what it will do, and that is a satisfaction.
We can change it when we want to. And get a worse one, most of
the time; but it is a change, anyway, and you can't do that with a
king.

So Tom he give up the revolution, and said the next best thing
would be to start an insurrection. Well, me and Jim was willing to
that, but when we come to look it over we couldn't seem to think
up anything to insurrect about. Tom explained what it was, but
there didn't seem to be any way to work it. He had to give in,
himself, that there wasn't anything definite about an insurrection.
It wasn't either one thing nor t'other, but only just the middle stage
of a tadpole. With its tail on, it was only just a riot; tail gone, it was
an insurrection; tail gone and legs out, it was a revolution. We
worried over it a little, but we see we couldn't do anything with it,
so we let it go; and was sorry about it, too, and low spirited, for it
was a beautiful name.

"Now then," I says, "what's the next?"

Tom said the next was the last we had in stock, but was the best
one of all, in some ways, because the hide and heart of it was

mystery. The hide and heart of the others was glory, he said, and glory was grand and valuable; but for solid satisfaction, mystery laid over it. It warn't worth while his telling us he was fond of mysteries, we knowed it before. There warn't anything he wouldn't do to be connected with a mystery. He was always that way. So I says—

"All right, what is your idea?"

"It's a noble good one, Huck. It's for us to get up a conspiracy."

"Is it easy, Mars Tom? Does you reckon we can do it?"

"Yes, anybody can."

"How does you go at it, Mars Tom? What do de word mean?"

"It means laying for somebody—private. You get together at night, in a secret place, and plan out some trouble against somebody; and you have masks on, and passwords, and all that. Georges Cadoudal got up a conspiracy. I don't remember what it was about, now, but anyway he done it, and we can do it, too."

"Is it cheap, Mars Tom?"

"Cheap? Well, I should reckon! Why, it don't cost a cent. That is, unless you do it on a big scale, like Bartholomew's Day."

"What is dat, Mars Tom? What did dey do?"

"I don't know. But it was on a big scale, anyway. It was in France. I think it was the Presbyterians cleaning out the missionaries."

Jim was disappointed, and says, kind of irritated—

"So, den, blame de conspiracy, down *she* goes. We got plenty Presbyterians, but we ain't got no missionaries."

"Missionaries, your granny—we don't need them."

"We don't, don't we? Mars Tom, how you gwyne to run yo' conspiracy if you ain' got but one end to it?"

"Why, hang it, can't we have somebody in the *place* of missionaries?"

"But would dat be right, Mars Tom?"

"Right? Right hasn't got anything to do with it. The wronger a conspiracy is, the better it is. All we've got to do is to have somebody in the place of the missionaries, and then—"

"But Mars Tom, will dey *take* de place, onless you explains to them how it is, en how you couldn't help yoself becase you couldn't git no mish—"

"Oh, shut up! You make me tired. I never see such a nigger to argue, and argue, and argue, when you don't know anything what you are talking about. If you'll just hold still a minute I'll get up a conspiracy that 'll make Bartholomew sick—and not a missionary in it, either."

Jim knowed it wouldn't do for him to chip in any more for a spell, but he went on a mumbling to himself, the way a nigger does, and saying *he* wouldn't give shucks for a conspiracy that was made up out of just any kinds of odds and ends that come handy and hadn't anything lawful about it. But Tom didn't let on to hear; and it's the best way, to let a nigger or a child go on and grumble itself out, then it's satisfied.

Tom bent his head down, and propped his chin in his hands, and begun to forget us and the world; and pretty soon when he got up and begun to walk the sand and bob his head and wag it, I knowed the conspiracy was beginning to bile; so I stretched out in the sun and went to sleep, for I warn't going to be needed in that part of the business. I got an hour's nap, and then Tom was ready, and had it all planned out.

Chapter 2

I SEE in a minute that he had struck a splendid idea. It was to get the people in a sweat about the ablitionists. It was the very time for it. We knowed that for more than two weeks past there was whispers going around about strangers being seen in the woods over on the Illinois side, and then disappearing, and then seen again; and everybody reckoned it was ablitionists laying for a chance to run off some of our niggers to freedom. They hadn't run off any yet, and most likely they warn't even thinking about it and warn't ablitionists anyway; but in them days a stranger couldn't show himself and not start an uneasiness unless he told all about his business straight off and proved it hadn't any harm in it. So the town was considerable worried, and all you had to do was to slip up behind a man and say Ablitionist if you wanted to see him jump, and see the cold sweat come.

And they had tightened up the rules, and a nigger couldn't be out after dark at night, pass or no pass. And all the young men was parceled out into paterollers, and they watched the streets all night, ready to stop any stranger that come along.

Tom said it was a noble good time for a conspiracy—it was just as if it was made for it on a contract. He said all we had to do was to start it, and it would run itself. He believed if we went at it right and conscientious, and done our duty the best we could, we could have the town in a terrible state in three days. And I believed he was right, because he had a good judgment about conspiracies and those kind of things, mysteries being in his line and born to it, as you may say.

For a beginning, he said we must have a lot of randyvoozes—secret places to meet at and conspire; and he reckoned we better kind of surround the town with them, partly for style and partly so as there would always be one of them handy, no matter what part of town we might be in. So, for one he appointed our old hanted house, in the lonesome place three miles above town where Crawfish creek comes in out of Catfish hollow. And for another, mine and Jim's little cave up in the rocks in the deep woods on Jackson's island. And for another, the big cave on the main land three miles below town—Injun Joe's cave, where we found the money that the robbers had hid. And for another, the old deserted slaughterhouse on Slaughterhouse Point at the foot of town, where the creek comes in. The polecats couldn't stand that place, it smelt like the very nation; and so me and Jim tried to get him to change, but he wouldn't. He said it was a good strattyjick point, and besides was a good place to retreat to and hide, because dogs couldn't follow us there, on account of our scent not being able to beat the competition, and even if the dogs could follow us the enemy couldn't follow the dogs because they would suffocate. We seen that it was a good idea and sound, so then we give in.

Me and Jim thought there ought to be more conspirators if there was going to be much work, but Tom scoffed, and said—

"Lookyhere—what busted up Guy Fawkes? And what busted up Titus Oates?"

He looked at me very hard. But I warn't going to give myself away. Then he looked at Jim very hard—but Jim warn't going to, either. So then there wasn't anything more said about it.

Tom appointed our cave on Jackson's island for the high chief headquarters, and said common business could be done in the other randyvoozes, but the Council of State wouldn't ever meet anywhere but there—and said it was sacred. And he said there would have to be two Councils of State to run a conspiracy as important as this one—a Council of Ten and a Council of Three; black gowns for the Ten and red for the Three, and masks for all. And he said all of us would be the Council of Ten, and he would be the Council of Three. Because the Council of Three was supreme and could abrogate anything the other Council done. That was his word—one of his pile-drivers. I sejested it would save wages to leave out the Council of Ten, and there warn't hardly enough stuff for it anyway; but he only said—

"If I didn't know any more about conspiracies than you do, Huck Finn, I wouldn't expose myself."

So then he said we would go to the Council Chamber now, and hold the first meeting without any gowns or masks, and pass a resolution of oblivion next meeting and justify it; then it would go on the minutes all regular, and nobody could be put under attainder on account of it. It was his way, and he was born so, I reckon. Everything had to be regular, or he couldn't stand it. Why, I could steal six watermelons while he was chawing over authorities and arranging so it would be regular.

We found our old cave just as me and Jim had left it the time we got scared out and started down the river on the raft. Tom called up the Council of Ten, and made it a speech about the seriousness of the occasion, and hoped every member would reconnize it and put his hand sternly to the wheel and do his duty without fear or favor. Then he made it take an oath to run the conspiracy the best it knowed how in the interests of Christianity and sivilization and to get up a sweat in the town; and God defend the right, amen.

So then he elected himself President of the Council and Secretary, and opened the business. He says—

"There's a lot of details—no end of them—but they don't all come first, they belong in their places; they'll fall in all right, as we go along. But there's a first detail, and that is the one for us to take hold of now. What does the Council reckon it is?"

I was stumped, and said so. Jim he said the same.

"Well, then, I'll tell you. What is it the people are a-worrying about? What is it they are afraid of? You can answer that, I reckon."

"Why, they're afraid there's going to be some niggers run off."

"That is right. Now, then, what is our duty as a conspiracy?"

Jim didn't know, and I didn't.

"Huck Finn, if you would think a minute you would know. There's a lack—we've got to supply it. Ain't that plain enough? We've got to run off a nigger."

"My lan', Mars Tom! W'y, dey'll hang us."

"Well, what do you *want*? What is a conspiracy *for*? Do you reckon it's to propagate immortality? We've *got* to run risks, or it ain't any conspiracy at all, and no honor in it. The honor of a conspiracy is to do the thing you are after, but do it right and smart and *not* get hung. Well, we will fix that. Now then, come back to business. The first thing is, to pick out the nigger, and the next is, to arrange about running him off."

"Why, Tom, we can't ever do it. There ain't a nigger in the town that 'll listen to it a minute. It would scare him out of his life, and he would run straight to his master and tell on us."

He looked as if he was ashamed of me; and says—

"Now, Huck Finn, do you reckon I didn't know that?"

I couldn't understand what he was getting at. I says—

"Well, then, Tom Sawyer, if there ain't a nigger in the town that will let us run him off, how can we manage?"

"Very easy. We'll *put* one there."

"Oh, cert'nly—that's very easy. Where are we going to get him?"

"He's here; I'm the one."

Me and Jim laughed; but Tom said he had thought it all out, and it would work. So then he told us the plan, and it was a very good one, sure enough. He would black up for a runaway nigger and hide in the hanted house, and I would betray him and sell him to old Bradish, up in Catfish hollow, which was a nigger trader in a little small way, and the orneriest hound in town, and then we would run him off and the music would begin, Tom said. And I reckoned it would.

But of course, just as everything was fixed all ship-shape and satisfactry, Jim's morals begun to work again. It was always happening to him. He said he belonged to the church, and couldn't do things that warn't according to religion. He reckoned the conspiracy was all right, he wasn't worried about that, but oughtn't we to take out a licence?

It was natural for him to think that, you know, becuz he knowed that if you wanted to start a saloon, or peddle things, or trade in niggers, or drive a dray, or give a show, or own a dog, or do most any blame thing you could think of, you had to take out a licence, and so he reckoned it would be the same with a conspiracy, and would be sinful to run it without one, becuz it would be cheating the gover'ment. He was troubled about it, and said he had been praying for light. And then he says, in that kind of pitiful way a nigger has that is feeling ignorant and distressed—

"De prar hain't ben answered straight en squah, but as fur as I can make out fum de symptoms, hit's agin de conspiracy onless we git de licence."

Well, I could see Jim's side, and knowed I oughtn't to fret at a poor nigger that didn't mean no harm, but was only going according to his lights the best he could, and yet I couldn't help being aggeravated to see our new scheme going to pot like the civil war and the revolution and no way to stop it as far as I could see—for Jim was set; you could see it; and of course when he was set, that was the end; arguments couldn't budge him. I warn't going to try; breath ain't given to us for to be wasted. I reckoned Tom would try, becuz the conspiracy was the last thing we had in stock and he

would want to save it if he could; and I judged he would flare up
and lose his temper right at the start, becuz it had had so much
strain on it already—and then the fat would be in the fire of course,
and the last chance of a conspiracy along with it.

But Tom never done anything of the kind. No, he come out of it
beautiful. I hardly ever seen him rise to such grandure of wisdom as
he done that time. I've seen him in delicate places often and often,
when there warn't no time to swap horses, and seen him pull
through all right when anybody would a said he couldn't, but I
reckon they warn't any delicater than this one. He was catched
sudden—but no matter, he was all there. When I seen him open
his mouth I says to myself wherever one of them words hits it's
agoing to raise a blister. But it warn't so. He says, perfectly cam and
gentle—

"Jim, I'll never forget you for thinking of that, and reminding us.
I clean forgot the licence, and if it hadn't been for you we might
never thought of it till it was too late and we'd gone into a conspiracy that warn't rightly and lawfully sanctified." Then he speaks out
in his official voice, very imposing, and says, "Summons the Council
of Three." So then he mounted his throne in state, which was a
nail-kag, and give orders to grant a licence to us to conspire in the
State of Missouri and adjacent realms and apinages for a year,
about anything we wanted to; and commanded the Grand Secretary to set it down in the minutes and put the great seal to it.

Jim was satisfied, then, and full of thankfulness, and couldn't
find words enough to say it; though I thought then and think yet
that the licence warn't worth a dern. But I didn't say anything.

There was only one more worry on Jim's mind, and it didn't take
long to fix that. He was afeared it wouldn't be honest for me to sell
Tom when Tom didn't belong to me; he was afeared it looked like
swindling. So Tom didn't argue about it. He said wherever there
was a doubt, even if it was ever so little a one, but yet had a look of
being unmoral, he wanted it removed out of the plan, for he would
not be connected with a conspiracy that was not pure. It looked to
me like this conspiracy was a-degenerating into a Sunday school.
But I never said anything.

So then Tom changed it and said he would get out handbills and offer a reward for himself, and I could find him, and not sell him but betray him over to Bat Bradish for part of the reward. Bat warn't his name; people called him that becuz he couldn't more than half see. Jim was satisfied with that, though I couldn't see where was the difference between selling a *boy* that don't belong to you and selling shares in a *reward* that was a fraud and warn't ever going to be paid. I said so to Tom, private, but he said I didn't know as much as a catfish; and said did I reckon we warn't going to pay the money *back* to Bat Bradish? Of course we would, he said.

I never said anything; but I reckoned to myself that if I got the money and Tom forgot and didn't interfere, me and Bat Bradish would settle that somehow amongst ourselves.

Chapter 3

WE PADDLED over to town, and Jim went home and me and Tom went to the carpenter shop and got a lot of smooth pine blocks that Tom wanted, and then to a shop and got an awl and a gouge and a little chisel, and took them to Tom's aunt Polly's and hid them up garret, and I stayed for supper and for all night; and in the middle of the night we slipped out and trapsed all over town to see the paterollers; and it was dim and quiet and still, except a dog or two and a cat that warn't satisfied, and nobody going about, but everybody asleep and the lights out except where there was sickness, then there would be a pale glow on the blinds; and a pateroller stood on every corner, and said "Who goes there?" and we said "Friends," and they said "Halt, and give the countersign," and we said we didn't have any, and they come and looked, and said, "Oh, it's you; well, you better get along home, no time for young trash like you to be out of bed."

And then we watched for a chance and slipped up stairs into the printing office, and put down the blinds and lit a candle, and there was old Mr. Day, the traveling jour. printer, asleep on the floor under a stand, with his old gray head on his carpet-sack for a pillow; but he didn't stir, and we shaded the light and tip-toed around and got some sheets of printing paper, blue and green and red and white, and some red printing ink and some black, and snipped off a little chunk from the end of a new roller to dab it with, and left a quarter on the table for pay, and was thirsty, and found a bottle of something and drunk it up for lemonade, but it turned out it was consumption medicine, becuz there was a label on it, but it was very good and answered. It was Mr. Day's; and we left another quarter for it, and blowed out the light, and got the things home all right and was very well satisfied, and hooked a hairbrush from Tom's aunt Polly to do the printing with and went to sleep.

Tom warn't willing to do business on Sunday, but Monday morning we went up garret and got out all our old nigger-show things, and Tom tried on his wig and the tow-linen shirt and ragged britches and one suspender, and straw hat with the roof caved in and part of the brim gone, and they was better than ever, becuz the shirt hadn't been washed since the cows come home and the rats had been sampling the other things.

Then Tom wrote out the handbill, "$100 Reward, Elegant Deef and Dumb Nigger Lad run away from the subscriber," and so on, and described himself to a dot the way he would look when he was blacked and dressed up for business, and said the nigger could be returned to "Simon Harkness, Lone Pine, Arkansaw;" and there warn't no such place, and Tom knowed it very well.

Then we hunted out the old chain and padlock and two keys that we used to play the Prisoner of the Basteel with, and some lampblack and some grease, and put them with the other things— "properties," Tom called them, which was a large name for truck which was not rightly property at all, for you could buy the whole outfit for forty cents and get cheated.

We had to have a basket, and there wasn't any that was big enough except aunt Polly's willow one, which she was so proud of and particular about, and it wasn't any use asking her to lend us that, becuz she wouldn't; so we went down stairs and got it while she was pricing a catfish that a nigger had to sell, and fetched it up and put the outfit in it, and then had to wait nearly an hour before we could get away, becuz Sid and Mary was gone somewheres and there wasn't anybody but us to help her hunt for the basket. But at last she had suspicions of the nigger that sold her the catfish, and went out to hunt for him, so then we got away. Tom allowed the hand of Providence was plain in it, and I reckoned it was, too, for it did look like it, as far as we was concerned, but I couldn't see where the nigger's share come in, but Tom said wait and I would see that the nigger would be took care of in some mysterious inscrutable way and not overlooked; and it turned out just so, for when aunt Polly give the nigger a raking over and then he proved he hadn't took the basket she was sorry and asked him to forgive her, and bought another catfish. And we found it in the cubberd that night and traded it off for a box of sardines to take over to the island, and the cat got into trouble about it; and when I said, now then the nigger is rectified but the cat is overlooked, Tom said again wait and I would see that the cat would be took care of in some mysterious inscrutable way; and it was so, for while aunt Polly was gone to get her switch to whip her with she got the other fish and et it up. So Tom was right, all the way through, and it shows that every one *is* watched over, and all you have to do is to be trustful and everything will come out right, and everybody helped.

We hid the outfit up stairs in the hanted house that morning, and come back to town with the basket, and it was very useful to carry provisions to Jim's big boat in, and cooking utensils. I stayed in the boat to take care of the things, and Tom done the shopping —not buying two basketfuls in one shop, but going to another shop every time, or people would have asked questions. Last of all, Tom fetched the pine blocks and printing ink and stuff from up garret, and then we pulled over to the island and stowed the whole boatload in the cave, and knowed we was well fixed for the conspiracy now.

We got back home before night and hid the basket in the woodshed, and got up in the night and hung it on the front door knob, and aunt Polly found it there in the morning and asked Tom how it come there, and he said he reckoned it was angels, and she said she reckoned so too, and suspicioned she knowed a couple of them and would settle with them after breakfast. She would a done it, too, if we had stayed.

But Tom was in a hurry about the handbills, and we took the first chance and got away and paddled down the river seven miles in the dugout to Hookerville, where there was a little printing office that had a job once in four years, and got a hundred and fifty Reward bills printed, and paddled back in the dead water under the banks, and got home before sundown and hid the bills up garret and had a licking, not much of a one, and then supper and family worship, and off to bed dog tired; but satisfied, becuz we had done every duty.

We went straight to sleep, for it ain't any trouble to go to sleep when you are tired and have done everything there was time to do, and done it the best you could, and so nothing on your conscience and nothing to trouble about. And we didn't take any pains about waking up, becuz the weather was good, and if it stayed so we couldn't do anything more till there was a change; and if a change come it would wake us. And it did.

It come on to storm about one in the morning, and the thunder and lightning woke us up. The rain come down in floods and floods; and ripped and raced along the shingles enough to deefen you, and would come slashing and thrashing against the windows, and make you feel so snug and cosy in the bed, and the wind was a howling around the eaves in a hoarse voice, and then it would die down a little and pretty soon come in a booming gust, and sing, and then wheeze, and then scream, and then shriek, and rock the house and make it shiver, and you would hear the shutters slamming all down the street, and then there'd be a glare like the world afire, and the thunder would crash down, right at your head and seem to tear everything to rags, and it was just good to be alive and tucked up comfortable to enjoy it; but Tom shouts "Turn out, Huck, we can't ever have it righter than this," and although he shouted it I could hardly hear him through the rattle and bang and roar and racket.

I wished I could lay a little bit longer, but I knowed I couldn't, for Tom wouldn't let me; so I turned out and we put on our clothes by the lightning and took one of the handbills and some tacks and got out of the back window onto the L, and crope along the comb of the roof and down onto the shed, and then onto the high board fence, and then to the ground in the garden the usual way, then down the back lane and out into the street.

It was a-drenching away just the same, and blowing and storming and thundering, a wild night and just the weather for ockult business like ourn, Tom said. I said yes; and said we ought to brought all the bills, becuz we wouldn't have another such a night soon. But he said—

"What do we want of any more? Where do they stick up bills, Huck?"

"Why, on the board that leans up against the postoffice door, where they stick up strayeds and stolens, and temperance meetings, and taxes, and niggers for sale, and stores to rent, and all them things, and a good place, too, and don't cost nothing, but an advertisement does, and don't anybody read it, either."

"Of course. They don't put up two bills, do they?"

"No. Only one. You can't read two at a time, except people that is cross-eyed, and there ain't enough of them for to make it worth the trouble."

"Well, then, that's why I fetched only one."

"What did you get 150 for, then? Are we going to stick up a new one every night for six months?"

"No, we ain't ever going to stick up any but the one. One's a plenty."

"Why, Tom, what *did* you spend all that money for, then? Why didn't you get only one printed?"

"On account of its being the regular number. If I had got only one, the printer would a gone soliloquising around to himself, saying 'This is curious; he could get 150 for the same money, and he takes only one; there's something crooked about this, and I better get him arrested.'"

Well, that was Tom Sawyer all over; always thought of everything. A long head; the longest I ever see on a boy.

Then come a glare that didn't leave a thimbleful of darkness betwixt us and heaven, and you could see everything, plumb to the river, the same as day. By gracious, not a pateroller anywheres; the streets was empty. And every gutter was a creek, and nearly washed us off of our feet the water run so deep and strong. We stuck up the bill, and then stood there under the awning a while listening to the storm and watching bunches of packing-straw and old orange boxes and things sailing down the gutter when it lightened, and wanted to stay and see it out, but dasent; becuz we was afraid of Sid. The thunder might wake him up; and he was scared of thunder and might go to the nearest room for comfort, which was ourn, and find out we was gone, and watch and see how long we was out, so he could tell on us in the morning, and give all the facts, and get us into trouble. He was one of them kind that don't commit no sin themselves, but ain't satisfied with that, but won't let anybody else have a good time if they can help it. So we had to get along home. Tom said he was too good for this world, and ought to be translated. I never said anything, but let him enjoy his word, for I think it is mean to take the tuck out of a person just to show how much you know. But many does it, just the same. I knowed all about that word, becuz the Widow told me; I knowed you can translate a book, but you can't translate a boy, becuz translating means turning a thing out of one language into another, and you can't do that with a boy. And besides it has to be a foreign one, and Sid warn't a foreign boy. I am not blaming Tom for using a word he didn't know the meaning of; becuz he warn't dishonest about it, he used a many a one that was over his size, but he didn't do it to deceive, he only done it becuz it tasted good in his mouth.

So we got home hoping Sid hadn't stirred; and kind of calculating on it, too, seeing how we was being looked out for in inscrutable ways and how many signs there was that Providence was satisfied with the conspiracy as far as we had got. But there come a little hitch, now. We was on the roof of the L, and clawing along the comb in the dark, and I was in the lead and was half way to our window, and had set down frog-fashion, very gentle and soft, to feel for a nail that was along there, becuz I had set down on it hard, sometimes, when I warn't wanting to, and it was that kind of a nail

which the more you don't set down on it at all the more comfortable
you can set down somewheres else next day, when there come a
sudden sharp glare of lightning that showed up everything keen
and clear, and there was Sid at his window watching.

We clumb into our window and set down and whispered it over.
We had to do something, and we didn't know what. Tom said, as a
general thing he wouldn't care for this, but it wasn't a good time,
now, to be attracting attention. He said if Sid could have a holiday
out on his uncle Fletcher's farm, thirty miles in the country, for
about four weeks, it would clear the decks and be the very thing,
and the conspiracy would glide along and be in smooth water and
safe, by that time. He didn't reckon Sid was suspicioning anything
yet, but would start in to watch us, and pretty soon he would. I
says—

"When are you going to ask your aunt Polly to let him have the
holiday, Tom—in the morning?"

"Why, I ain't going to ask her at all. That's not the way. She
would ask me what was interesting *me* in Sid's comfort all of a
sudden, and she would suspicion something. No, we must cunjer
up some way to make her invent the idea herself and send him
away."

"Well," I says, "I'll let you have the job—it ain't in my line."

"I'll study it over," he says, "I reckon it can be fixed."

I was going to pull off my clothes, but he says, "Don't do that,
we'll sleep with them on."

"What for?"

"It's nothing but shirt and nankeen pants, and they'll dry in
three hours."

"What do we want them dry for, Tom?"

But he was listening at Sid's door, to hear if he was snoring.
Then he slipped in there and got Sid's clothes and fetched them
and hung them out of the window till they was soaked, then he
carried them back and come to bed. So then I understood. We
snuggled up together, and pulled up the blankets, and wasn't overly
comfortable, but of course we had to stand it. After a long thinking
spell, Tom says—

"Huck, I believe I've got it. I know where I can get the measles. We've all got to have them some time or other anyway, and I better have them now, when they can do some good."

"How?"

"Aunt Polly wouldn't let Sid and Mary stay in the house if we had measles here; she would send them to uncle Fletcher's—it's the only place."

I didn't like the idea, it made me half sick; and I says—

"Tom, don't you do it; it's a fool idea. Why, you might die."

"Die, you pelican? I never heard such foolishness. Measles never kills anybody except grown people and babies. You never heard of a case."

I was worried, and tried to talk him out of it, and done my best, but it didn't do any good. He was full of it, and bound to try it, and wanted me to help him; so I give it up and said I would. So he planned it out how we was to manage it, and then we went to sleep.

We got up dry, but Sid's things was wet; and when he said he was going to tell on us, Tom told him he could go and tell, as fast as he wanted to, and see if him and his wet clothes could beat our dry ones testifying. Sid said he hadn't been out, but knowed we had, becuz he seen us. Tom says—

"You ought to be ashamed of yourself. You are always walking in your sleep and dreaming all kinds of strange things that didn't happen, and now you are at it again. Can't you see, perfectly plain, it's nothing but a dream? If you didn't walk, how comes your clothes wet? and if we did, how comes ourn dry?—you answer me that."

Sid was all puzzled and mixed up, and couldn't make it out. He felt of our clothes, and thought and thought; but he had to give it up. He said he judged he could see, now, it was only a dream, but it was the amazingest vividest one he ever had. So the conspiracy was saved, and out of a close place, too, and Tom said anybody could see it was approved of. And he was awed about it, and said it was enough to awe anybody and make them better, to see the inscrutable ways that that conspiracy was watched over and took care of, and I felt the same. Tom resolved to be humbler and gratefuller from this out, and do everything as right as he could, and said so; and after breakfast we went down to Captain Harper's to get the measles, and had a troublesome time, but we got it. We didn't go at it the best way at first, that was the reason. Tom went up the back stairs and got into the room all right, where Joe was laying sick, but before he could get into bed with him his mother come in to give him the medicine, and was scared to see him there, and says—

"Goodness gracious, what *are* you doing here! Clear out, you little idiot, don't you know we've got the measles?"

Tom wanted to explain that he come to ask how Joe was, but she shoo'd and shoo'd him to the door and out, and wouldn't listen, and says—

"Oh, do go away and save yourself. You've frightened the life out of me, and your aunt Polly will never forgive me, and yet it's nobody's fault but yourn, for not going to the front door, where anybody would that had any sense of discretion," and then she slammed the door and shut Tom out.

But that give him an idea. So in about an hour he sent me to the front door to knock and fetch her there; and she would have to go, becuz the children was with the neighbors on account of the measles, and the captain out at his business; and so, whilst I kept her there asking her all about Joe for the Widow Douglas, Tom got in the back way again and got into bed with Joe, and covered up, and when she come back and found him there, she had to drop down in a chair or she would a fainted; and she shut him up in another room until she sent word to aunt Polly.

So aunt Polly was frightened stiff, and shook so she could hardly pack Sid and Mary's things. But she had them out of the house in a half an hour and into the tavern to stay there over night and take the stage for her brother Fletcher's at four in the morning, and then went and fetched Tom home, and wouldn't let me come in the house; and she hugged him and hugged him, and cried, and said she would lick him within an inch of his life when he got well.

So then I went up on the hill to the Widow's, and told Jim, but he said it was a right down smart plan, and he hadn't ever seen a plan work quicker and better; and Jim warn't worried, he said measles didn't amount to anything, everybody has them and everybody's got to; so I stopped worrying, too.

After a day or two Tom had to go to bed and have the doctor. Me and Jim couldn't work the conspiracy without Tom, so we had to let it lay still and wait, and I reckoned it was going to be dull times for me for a spell. But no, Tom warn't hardly to bed before Joe Harper's medicine fetched his measles out onto the surface, and then the doctor found it warn't measles at all, but scarlet fever. When aunt Polly heard it she turned that white she couldn't get her breath, and was that weak she couldn't see her hand before her face, and if they hadn't grabbed her she would have fell. And it just made a panic in the town, too, and there wasn't a woman that had children but was scared out of her life.

But it crossed off the dull times for me, and done that much good; for I had had scarlet fever, and come in an ace of going deef and dumb and blind and baldheaded and idiotic, so they said; and so aunt Polly was very glad to let me come and help her.

We had a good doctor, one of them old fashioned industrious kind that don't go fooling around waiting for a sickness to show up and call game and start fair, but gets in ahead, and bleeds you at one end and blisters you at the other, and gives you a dipperful of castor oil and another one of hot salt water with mustard in it, and so gets all your machinery agoing at once, and then sets down with nothing on his mind and plans out the way to handle the case.

Along as Tom got sicker and sicker they shut off his feed, and closed up the doors and windows and made the room snug and hot and healthy, and as soon as the fever was warmed up good and satisfactry, they shut off his water and let him have a spoonful of panada every two hours to squench his thirst with. Of course that is dreadful when you are burning up, and nice cool water there for other people to drink and you can't touch it but need it more than anybody else; so Tom arranged to wink when he couldn't stand it any longer, and I watched my chance and give him a good solid drink when aunt Polly's back was turned; and after that it was more comfortable, for I kept an eye out sharp and filled him up every time he wunk. The doctor said water would kill him, but I knowed that when you are blazing with scarlet fever you don't mind that.

Tom was sick two weeks, and got very bad, and then one night he begun to sink, and sunk pretty fast. All night long he got worse and worse, and was out of his head, and babbled and babbled, and give the conspiracy plumb away, but aunt Polly was that beside herself with misery and grief that she couldn't take notice, but only just hung over him, and cried, and kissed him and kissed him, and bathed his face with a wet rag, and said oh, she could not *bear* to lose him, he was the darling of her heart and she couldn't ever live without him, the world wouldn't ever be the same again and life would be so empty and lonesome and not worth while; and she called him by all the pet names she could think of, and begged him to notice her and say he knowed her, but he couldn't, and once when his hand went groping about and found her face and stroked it and he took it for me, and said "good old Huck," she was broken-hearted, and cried so hard and mourned so pitiful I had to look away, I couldn't bear it. And in the morning when the doctor come and looked at him and says, kind of tender and low, "He doeth all things for the best, we must not repine," she—but I can't tell it, it would a made anybody cry to see her. Then the doctor motioned, and the preacher was there and had been praying, and we all went and stood around the bed, waiting and still, and aunt Polly crying, and nobody saying anything. Tom was laying with his eyes shut, and very quiet. Then he opened them, but didn't seem to notice, much, or see anything; but they kind of wandered about, and fell on me; and steadied there. And one of them begun to sag down, went shut, and t'other one begun to work and twist, and twist and work, and kind of squirm; and at last he got it, though pretty lame and out of true—it was a wink. I jumped for the fresh cold water, tin pail and all, and says "Hold up his head!" and put it to his lips, and he drunk and drunk and drunk—the very first I had had a chance to give him in a whole day and night. The doctor said, "Poor boy, give him all he wants, he is past hurting, now."

It warn't so. It saved him. He begun to pull back to life again from that very minute, and in five days he was setting up in bed, and in five more was walking about the floor; and aunt Polly was that full of joy and gratefulness that she told me, private, she wished he *would* do something he had no business to, so she could forgive him; and said she never would a knowed how dear he was to her if she hadn't come so near losing him; and said she was glad it happened and she'd got her lesson, she wouldn't ever be rough on him again, she didn't care what he done. And she said it was the way we feel when we've laid a person in the grave that is dear to us and we wish we could have them back again, we wouldn't ever say anything to grieve them any more.

Chapter 4

ALL THE first week that Tom was sick he wasn't very sick, and then for a while he was, and after that he wasn't, again, but was getting well; so he lost only the between-time. Both of the other times he worked on the conspiracy—first to get it all shaped out so me and Jim could finish it if he died, and leave it behind him for his monument; and the other time to boss it himself. So the minute I come down to help take care of him he said he wanted some type, and to learn how to set them up; and told me to go to Mr. Baxter about it. He was the foreman of the printing office, and had Mr. Day and a boy under him and was one of the most principal men in the town, and looked up to by everybody. There warn't nothing agoing for the highsting up of the human race but he was under it and a-shoving up the best he could—being a pillow of the church and taking up the collection, Sundays, and doing it wide open and square, with a plate, and setting it on the table when he got done where everybody could see, and never putting his hand anear it, never pawing around in it the way old Paxton always done, letting on to see how much they had pulled in; and he was Inside Sentinel of the Masons, and Outside Sentinel of the Odd Fellows, and a kind a head bung-starter or something of the Foes of the Flowing

Bowl, and something or other to the Daughters of Rebecca, and something like it to the King's Daughters, and Royal Grand Warden to the Knights of Morality, and Sublime Grand Marshal of the Good Templars, and there warn't no fancy apron agoing but he had a sample, and no turnout but he was in the procession, with his banner, or his sword, or toting a bible on a tray, and looking awful serious and responsible, and yet not getting a cent. A good man, he was, they don't make no better.

And when I come he was setting at his table with his pen, and leaning low down over a narrow long strip of print with wide margins, and he was crossing out most everything that was in it and freckling-up the margins with his pen and cussing. And I told him Tom was sick and maybe going to die, and—

There he shut me off sudden, and says, prompt and warm—

"*Him* die? We can't have it. There's only one Tom Sawyer, and the mould's busted. Can I do anything? Speak up."

I says—

"Tom says, can he have—"

"*Yes;* he can have anything he wants. Speak out," he says, all alive and hearty and full of intrust.

"He'd like to have about a handful of old type that you hain't got any use for, and—"

Then he broke in again and sung out to Mr. Day, and says—

"Tell the devil to go to hell and fetch a hatful; and quick about it."

It give me the cold shivers to hear him. In about a minute Mr. Day says—

"The devil says hell's empty, sir."

"All right, fetch a hatful of pie."

That made my mouth water, and I was glad I come. Then the boy fetched a couple of oyster cans full of old type; it had to be old, there warn't any new in the place; and Mr. Baxter told him to fetch a stick and a rule.[1] And last, he told him to fetch an old half-case,

---

1. *Hell,* printer's term for broken and otherwise disabled type. 2. *Printer's Devil,* apprentice. 3. *Pi,* printer's term for a mass of mixed-up type. 4. The (composing) stick and rule are used in setting the type.—EDITOR.

which he done; it was the size of a wash-board, and was all separated up into little square boxes. Then they pasted A's and B's and C's and so on on the boxes, to show which boxes they belonged in —two sets, capital letters and little ones; and Mr. Baxter told the boy to go with me and help carry the things and learn Tom how to set the type. And he done it.

He learnt Tom, and Tom set up all the type in the oyster cans and then put all the letters where they belonged in the case, setting up in bed and using up about two days at it. Bright? Tom Sawyer? I should reckon so. Inside of five days he had learnt himself the whole trade, and could set up type as well as anybody; and I can prove what I am saying. Becuz, that day he set up this, and I took it over and Mr. Baxter printed it, and when he took up the print he was astonished, and said so; and give me a copy for myself, and one for Tom, and I've got mine yet.

COMPOSITION

The noble art of ¶rinting cailed by some typograPhy the art preservative of Arts was fistr discover3d up a lane in a tower by cutting lettars on birch pegs not knowing they woud print and n0t expecting it but they did by aacident hence theGerman name for type to this day Buchstaben although made of metal ever since let all tha nations bless the name fo Guttingburg andFowst which done it aMen

TOM SAWYER
Printer

When Mr. Baxter printed it and took it up and looked at it the tears come in his eyes, and he says—

"Derned if any comp. in christiandum can lay over it but old Day, and *he* can't when he's sober."

It made Tom mighty proud when I told him, and well it might. But the strain of composing of it out of his head thataway, and setting it up without anybody's help, and the general excitement of it and anxiousness it cost him to get it ackurate, was too many for him and knocked him silly and laid him out, and the sickness went for him savage; and so that was the last thing he ever done till the day the doctor says—

"Huck, he's convalescent."

I warn't prepared, and fell flat in my tracks where I was. But when they throwed water on me and I come to and they told me what the doctor was trying to mean when the word fell out of him, I see it warn't so bad as I reckoned.

Now some boys quits repenting as soon as they are getting well, and goes to getting worldly again, and judging they hadn't ought to have got flustered so soon, it wasn't necessary, but it warn't so with Tom, he said he had a close shave and ought to be grateful to Providence, and was; and man's help warn't worth much, and man's wisdom warn't anything at all—look at ourn, he says.

"Look at ourn, Huck. We went for measles. It shows how little we knowed and how blind we was. What good was measles, when you come to look at it? None. As soon as it's over you wash up the things and air out the house and send for the children home again, and a person has been sick all for nothing. But you take the scarlet fever and what do you find? You scour out the place, and burn up every rag when it's over and you're well again, and from that very day no Sid and no Mary can come anear it for six solid useful weeks. Now who thought of scarlet fever for us, Huck, and arranged it, when we was ignorant and didn't know any better than to go for measles? Was it us? You know it warn't. Now let that learn you. This conspiracy is being took care of by a wiser wisdom than ourn, Huck. Whenever you find yourself getting untrustful and worried, don't you be afraid, but recollect about the scarlet fever, and remember that where that help come from there's more to be had. All you want is faith; then everything will come out right, and better than you can do it yourself."

Well, it did look so; there wasn't any way to get around it. It was the scarlet fever that saved the game and kept Sid up country, and it wasn't us that thought of it.

It was real summer by now, and Tom was well and hearty, and the weather and everything suitable and ready for us to go ahead. So we took our little printing office over to the island to have it handy any time we might want it; and I fished all the afternoon, and smoked and swum and napped, whilst Tom took his chisels and things and one of his blocks, and carved this on it.

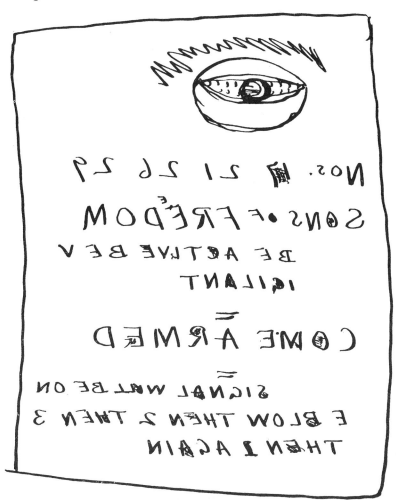

Then he dabbed it over with black ink, and dampened some white printer's paper and laid it on, and a piece of blanket on that and a heavy smooth block on top of that and give it a good hammering with his mallet, and then took off the paper and it was

printed very beautiful, but by gracious it was all wrong-end first
and you had to stand on your head to read it. Well, it beat me, and
it beat Tom. There warn't any way to understand how it come like
that. We took and looked at the block, but the block was all right, it
was only the printing that was crazy. We printed it again, but it
come wrong again, just the same. So then we studied it out and
judged we had got at the trouble this time; we put the paper
underneath and turned the block upside down on it and printed it.
But it never done any good; it was as crazy as it was before.

Tom said that when he set up type in the stick it read from left to
right and upside down, but he hadn't reckoned Mr. Baxter would
leave it so, but would fix it right before he printed it, and of course
he done it, becuz it was right when it come back printed, but *we*
couldn't learn that juglery out of our own heads, we would have to
wait and get him to tell us the secret; and we reckoned he would, if
we swore we wouldn't tell anybody; and Tom was willing to do
that, and so was I.

Tom was ever so disappointed, after all his hard work, and I was
very sorry for him, to see him setting there all tired and idle and low
spirited; but all of a sudden he got excited and glad, and said it was
the luckiest thing that ever happened, and the very thing for a
conspiracy, becuz it was so strange and grisly and mysterious, and
looked so devilish; and said it would scare the people twice as much
as it would if it was in its right mind, and all ship-shape and
regular, the common old way; and says—

"Huck, it's a new thing, and we've discovered it, and will go
down to prosperity along with Guttingburg and Fowst, and be
celebrated everywheres, and can take out a patent on it and not let
anybody use it except for conspiracies, and not even then unless
they have a pure character and are the best people in the business."

So it come out right, after all. And it's mostly so, when things is
looking the darkest, Tom said, you only have to wait, and be
trustful, and keep your shirt on.

And I asked him who was the Sons of Freedom, and he said the
people would think it was the ablitionists, and it would scare the

cold sweat out of them. And I asked him what that nut was for, at
the top, and he said it wasn't a nut, it was an eye and an eyebrow,
and stood for vigilance and was emblumatic. That was him—all
over; if a thing hadn't a chance in it somewheres for the emblum-
atics it warn't in his line, and he would shake it and hunt up
something else.

He said we must have a horn of a solemn deep sound, for the
Sons of Freedom to make the signal with; so we chopped down a
hickory sapling and skinned it and got a wide strip of bark that was
plenty long enough, and went home to supper, and carried it to Jim
that night, and he twisted it into a tapering long horn, and we took
it into the Widow Douglas's woods on the front slope of the hill
towards the town and Jim clumb the highest tree and hid it there.
Then home and to bed; and slid out, away in the night, and down
to the river street, and slipped into Slater's alley when the paterollers was asleep, and so up back behind the blocks and come out
through that crack that was betwixt the julery shop and the postoffice, and tacked our bill onto the board, and back the way we come,
and home again.

At breakfast in the morning a person could see that aunt Polly
was kind of excited about something, becuz she was nervous and
absent minded, and kept getting up and going to the window and
looking out, and muttering to herself; and once she sweetened her
coffee with salt and it made her choke and strangle; and she would
take up her toast and start to butter it and forget what she was
doing and lay it down; and when Tom put the little Webster
spelling book in the place of it when she was staring haggard
towards the window she buttered that and took a bite, and lost her
temper and throwed the book across the house, and says—

"There, hang the thing, I'm that upset I don't know what I'm a
doing. And reason enough. Oh, dear, you little know what danger
you're in, poor things, and what danger we're all in."

"Why, what is it, aunt Polly," Tom says, like he was surprised.

"Don't you see the people flocking down street and flocking back,
and talking so excited, and most of them gone half crazy? Why

there's an awful bill sticking up, down at the postoffice, and the ablitionists are going to burn the town and run off the niggers."

"Goodness, aunt Polly, it ain't as bad as that, I reckon."

"What do you know about it, you numscull! Hain't Oliver Benton been here, and Plunket the editor, and Jake Flacker, and told me all about it, and do you reckon you are going to lay abed asleep and then come down here a-reckoning and a-reckoning and a-reckoning, and suppose that *that* is going to count for anything when a person has been listening to grown people that don't go reckoning around, but digs up the cold facts and examines them and *knows?*"

She wouldn't let him say a word, but said if we was done breakfast, clear out and get hold of everything that was going on, and come and tell her, so she could prepare for the worst. We was glad of the chance; and when we got out in the street we see that everything was working prime, and couldn't be no better; and Tom said if he had died he would always regretted it.

Down at the postoffice you couldn't get anear it. Everybody was there, and scrowging in to get a look at the bill, going in red and coming out pale and telling all about it to them that was on the outside edge pawing and shouldering to get in.

Jake Flacker the detective was the biggest man in town, now, and everybody was cringing to him and trying to get something out of him, but he was mum, and only wagged his head as much as to say, "Never you mind, just leave this thing to me, don't you worry;" and people whispered around and said, "I bet you he knows them rascals, and every move they make in the game, and can put his hand on them whenever he wants to—look at that eye of his'n; you can't hide nothing from an eye like that." And Colonel Elder said the bill was a most remarkable one and proved that these warn't no common ornery canail, but blackhearted biggots of the highest intelligents. It pleased Tom to hear him say that, for he was the most looked up to of any man in town, and come from old Virginia and belonged to the quality. Colonel Elder said the bill was done in a new and ockult and impossible way, and showed what we was coming to in these abandund days; and that seemed to make every-body shudder.

And that warn't all the shuddering they done. They shivered every time the signals was mentioned. They said they would wake up some night with their throats cut and them awful sounds dinging in their ears. And then somebody noticed that the *kind* of sound it was going to be warn't named distinct in the bill. Mostly they reckoned it was a horn, but said there warn't no proof of it; it might be blows on a anvil, Pete Kruger the German blacksmith said; and Abe Wallace the sexton said yes, and it might be blows on a bell, too. And then they *all* up and cussed the uncertainty of it, and said they could stand it better, and maybe get some sleep, too, if they knowed what it was.

Colonel Elder spoke up again, and said yes, that was bad, but the uncertainty about the date was worse.

"That's so," they said; "we don't know when they're coming—the bill don't say. Maybe it's weeks, maybe it's days,—"

"And maybe it's to-night," says the Colonel, and that made them shiver again. "We must take time by the firelock, friends; we must get ready; not next week, not to-morrow, but to-day." They give a little shout, and said the Colonel was right. He went on and made them a speech and braced them up, then Claghorn the justice of the peace made one, and by this time everything was booming and the most of the town was there and they turned it into a public meeting; and whilst the iron was hot, Plunket the editor got up and spoke, and praised up Colonel Elder, which was in the last war and at the battle of New Orleans, and knowed all about soldiering, and was the man they needed now. And he moved to elect him Provo Marshal and set up martial law in the town, and they done it. And then the Colonel he thanked them for the honor they done him, and ordered Captain Haskins and Captain Sam Rumford to call out their companies and go into camp in the public square, and put details all about town to guard it, and issue ball cartridge, and have them in uniform, and all that. So then the meeting broke up, and we started along.

Tom said everything was working splendid, but it didn't seem so to me. I says—

"How are we going to get around, nights? Won't the soldiers watch us and meddle with us? We are tied, Tom, we can't do a thing."

"No," he says, "it's going to be better for us than ever, now."

"How?'"

"They'll want spies, and they can't get them. They know it. And Jake Flacker's no good. He don't know enough to follow the fence and find the corner. I've got a ruputation, on account of beating the Dunlaps and getting the di'monds, and I'll manage for us—you'll see."

He done it, too. The Colonel was glad to have him, and wanted him to get some more, if he could, and he would put them under him. So Tom said all he wanted was me and Jim. He said he wanted Jim to spy amongst the niggers. The Colonel said it was a good idea, and everybody knowed Jim and could trust him; so he give Tom passes, for us and him, and that fixed us all right.

Then we went home and told about everything except spying and the passes; and soon we heard drums and a fife away off, and it come nearer, and pretty soon Sam Rumford's company went a marching by—tramp, tramp, tramp, all the feet a-rumbling down just as regular, and Sam a-howling the orders, "Shoul---*der*—ARMS! by the left file, for----*word!*" and so on, and the fifes a-screaming and the drums a-banging and a-crashing so you couldn't hear yourself think, by George it was splendid and stirred a person up, and there was more children along than soldiers; and the uniforms was beautiful, and so was the flag, and every time Sam Rumford whirled his sword in the air and yelled, it catched the sun and made the prettiest flash you ever see. But aunt Polly she stood there white and quivery, and looked perfectly gashly. And she says—

"Goodness only knows what is coming to us. I am *so* thankful Sid and Mary—oh, Tom, if you was only with them."

It was Tom's turn to shiver—and mine, too; and we done it. The next thing, she would be arranging for him to go out somewheres in the country where some family had had scarlet fever and would take him. Tom knowed it, and knowed there wasn't any time to waste; so we went out back to fetch some wood for the kitchen, and paddled over to the island to think up what we better do to get around this trouble; and Tom set down, off by himself, and thought it out, and took a pine block and carved this on it and printed a lot of them with red ink.

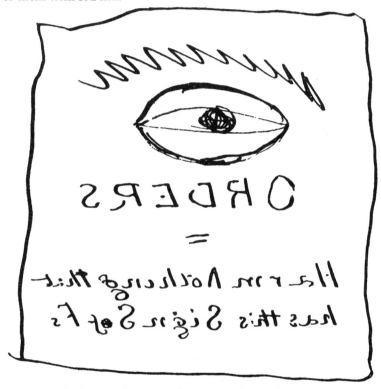

We fetched them home, and away in the night we went spying around and showing the passes when the soldiers stopped us, and stuck one on Judge Thatcher's door and fifteen others, and on aunt Polly's; becuz Tom said if we didn't stick them on anybody's door but aunt Polly's the people might suspicion something. We had lots of them left, but Tom said he reckoned we would need them.

In the morning—it was Wednesday—it made another big stir, and them that had them on their doors was thankful and glad, and them that hadn't was scared and mad, and said pretty rough things about the others, and said if they warn't ablitionists they was pets of them, anyway, and they reckoned it was about the same thing. And everybody was astonished to see how the S. of F. gang had managed to come right into the town and stick up the things under the soldiers's noses; and of course they was troubled and worried about it, and got suspicious of one another, not knowing who was a friend and who wasn't; and some begun to say they believed the town was full of traitors; and then they shut up, all of a sudden, and got afraid to say *anything;* and got a notion that they had already said too much, and maybe to the wrong people.

I never see a person do such a noble job of cussing as the Colonel; and Tom he said the same. And he had up the captains to headquarters and said it was scandlous, and said he couldn't have things going on like this, and they'd got to keep better watch, and they promised they would.

Tom told me to set down the name of everybody I heard talking against people that had our protection-paper on their doors, and he done the same.

Aunt Polly was comforted to have the paper on her door, and not scared any more, like she was; but Mrs. Lawson the lawyer's wife come in, in the morning, and made her feel bad about it. She let on she didn't know aunt Polly had one, and said thank goodness *she* hadn't any, and didn't want it, but at the same time whoever wished to be protected by ablition secret gangs and warn't ashamed of it was welcome for all *her.* And when aunt Polly colored up a little and couldn't say anything, she got up and says "but maybe I'm indiscreet, please forgive me," and went out very grand, and aunt Polly's comfort was most all gone.

That night we stuck the papers on all the doors we took the names of, and stuck one on Mrs. Lawson's, too. It shut up a lot of people's mouths, and made Mrs. Lawson quiet; and comfortabler, too, than she was before, I reckon. And we found Jake Flacker standing watch asleep down by the lumber yard, and stuck one on his back. Me and Tom went about town in the morning, and lo and behold some of the papers was missing from some of the doors— five—and there was five papers on doors that we hadn't put them on.

And he said wait till next morning and we would see something more that was fresh. And it was so. Everybody that had a paper had wrote his name on it to keep people from stealing it, for it was all over town how they was being smouched. Aunt Polly had her name on her paper, wrote large and plain, and the same with Mrs. Lawson.

When Saturday come all the town that hadn't the papers was tuckered out and looked seedy, becuz they had set up the most of three nights listening for the signals, and then laid down to sleep in their clothes when they couldn't keep awake any more. Then, just as the excitement was wavering a little and getting ready to go down, on account of no signals yet, the paper come out and started it all up again; for it was full of it, and just wild about it; and it had extracts from papers in Illinois and St Louis about it, and showed how it was traveling and making the town celebrated; and so everybody was proud as well as worried, and read the paper all through, and Tom said they hadn't ever done that before. So he was proud, too, and said it was a good conspiracy, and we would go ahead, now, and give it another boom.

Chapter 5

So EVERYTHING was all right, now, and we went around in the night and stuck up the reward-bill for the runaway nigger-boy; and Jim was along, on spy-business. Then we laid the plans for next afternoon—like this. Towards evening me and Tom would go up to the hanted house on Crawfish Branch, and whilst Tom was in there dressing to play nigger, I would go on up to Bat Bradish's and tell him I knowed where the nigger was that was advertised, and would show him the place if he would give me some of the money when he got the reward. Then I would fetch him and turn Tom over to him, chain and all, and Tom was to have the extra key along, and unlock the chain in the night and escape and go back to the hanted house and change clothes again and wash up, in the Branch, and carry his nigger clothes home; and Jim would blow the horn-signals in the high tree at midnight and set the town wild; and in the morning of course Bat would come to town and tell about his nigger that was escaped, and that would make everybody sure that the ablishonists *was* on hand to a certainty; and that would fire things up worse than ever and make the conspiracy the best success we ever had; and Tom could be a detective and help hunt for himself, and have a grand time.

So next afternoon towards dusk we come in sight of the hanted house, and was about to step out of the woods into the open, but Tom pulled me back, and said somebody was coming down the Branch. And it was so. It was Bat Bradish. So Tom told me to go and meet up with him and tell him, and then get him out of the way until Tom could go and dress in the hanted house. I left Tom waiting in the bushes and went out and when I got to where Bat was I told him about the nigger. But stead of jumping at the chance he looked kind of bothered; and scratched his head and cussed a little, and said he had just *got* one runaway nigger a half an hour ago, and couldn't manage two in these skittish times; did I reckon I could keep watch of mine a few days and then come?

I didn't know anything else to do, and of course it could take some of the tuck out of the conspiracy and Tom wouldn't like that, so I done the best I could the way things stood and told him I reckoned I could manage it. That cheered him up and he said I wouldn't lose anything by it, he would look out for that; and said the nigger he had got was a splendid one and had a five hundred dollar reward on him, and he had bought the chance off of the man that found him for two hundred cash and would clear about three hundred, and a profitable good job, too. He was going down to town now to see the sheriff and make his arrangements. As soon as he was out of sight down the Cold Spring road I whistled to Tom and he come and I told him the bad news.

It just broke his heart. I knowed it would. He had been imagining all kinds of adventures and good times he was going to have when he was washed up and hunting for himself, and he couldn't seem to get over it. It looked to me, in a private way, like Providence was drawing out of the conspiracy; and so, by and by I made a mistake and said so. It made him pretty fierce, and he turned on me and said I ought to be ashamed of myself—a person without any trust, and not deserving any blessings; and then he went on and give me down the banks; and said how could *I* know but this was one of the most mysterious and inscrutablest moves connected with the whole conspiracy? He had got a good start, now, so I knowed everything was going to be comfortable again; for if I let him alone and didn't interrupt, he would hammer right along with his arguments till he proved to himself that this *was* a planned-out move and belonged in the game. And sure enough, he done it. Then he was gay and cheerful right away, and said he was glad it happened and said he was foolish and wicked for losing pluck merely because *he* couldn't see the design straight off. I let him alone and he rattled along, and finally he got the notion that maybe he had guessed out what the new design was—it was for him to go yonder and trade places with that nigger. And so he was going straight to dress and get ready; but I says—

"Tom Sawyer, that's a five-hundred-dollar nigger; you ain't a five-hundred-dollar nigger, I don't care *how* you dress up."

He couldn't get around that, you know; there warn't any way. But he didn't like to let on that I had laid him out; so he talked random a minute, trying to work out, then he said we couldn't tell anything about it till we had *seen* the nigger. And said, come along.

I didn't think there was any sense in it, but I was willing to let him down as easy as I could, so we struck out up the hollow. It was dark, now, but we knowed the way well enough. It was a log house, and no light in it; but there was a light in the lean-to, and we could see through the chinks. Sure enough it was a man, and a hearty good strong one—a thousand-dollar nigger, and worth it anywhere. He was stretched out on the ground, chained, and snoring hard.

So then Tom wanted us to go in and look at him good. But I wouldn't do it. I warn't going to fool with a strange nigger in the night in a lonesome place like that, I will get you to excuse me, I says. Tom said, all right, I needn't if I didn't want to, nobody was forcing me. Then he pulled the latch-string easy and got down on his hands and knees and crope in, and I kept my eye to the chink to see what would happen. When Tom got to the other end where the nigger was, he took up the candle and shaded it with his hand and examined the nigger, which had his mouth wide open to let the snore out. I see Tom look surprised at something; and I reckoned it was something the nigger said in his sleep, becuz I heard him growl out something. Then Tom took up the nigger's old battered shoes and turned them this way and that, examining them like a detective, and something fell out of one of them, and he picked it up, and looked around the place a little, here and there, same as a detective would, then set the candle back and crope out, and says come along.

So we went to the hanted house and struck up over Cardiff Hill, and Tom says—

"I reckon this 'll learn you to have trust next time, Huck Finn."

"What will?"

"Well, there was a plan and a program, wasn't there?"

"There *was*, yes—and it got busted."

"Did, did it? According to the plan and the program a runaway nigger was going to escape from there to-night—ain't that so?"

"Yes."

"Well, it's going to happen."

"Shucks—what are you talking?"

"It was going to be a white nigger wasn't it?"

"Yes."

"All right, *that's* going to happen."

"Tom, you don't mean it."

"Yes I do."

"Honest Injun, Tom, is that man white?"

"Honest Injun, Huck, he is."

"Why, it's the most astonishing thing I ever see."

"Huck, it's the very same game we laid out to play ourselves. Providence hasn't changed anything in the program except just the *person*—that's all. *Now* I reckon you'll have trust hereafter."

"Why Tom, it's the strangest thing that ever—"

"Happened? I *told* you it was the most mysterious and inscrutablest design in the whole conspiracy. I reckon you believe me now. *We* don't know what the change is made for Huck, but we know one thing—it was for the best."

He said it very solemn, and it made me feel thataway. Well, it was all very wonderful and strange. It made us kind of quiet a while, then I says—

"Tom, how'd you know he is white?"

"Oh, a lot of things. They couldn't fooled old Bat if he had good eyesight. Huck, for one thing, the inside of that nigger's hands are black."

"Well, what's the matter of that?"

"Why, you idiot, the inside of a nigger's hands *ain't* black."

"That's so, Tom, I didn't think of it."

"And he talked some words in his sleep; he talked white, not nigger; hasn't learnt to talk nigger in his sleep, yet."

"Tom, what makes you think he's going to get out to-night."

"Evidence of it in his shoe."

"Something fell out of it; was that it?"

"Two things fell out; I put one back. It was a key. But I tried it in his padlock first, and it fitted."

"By gracious!"

"He's playing our scheme to a dot, don't you see?"

"Why, Tom, it just beats anything that ever was. Say—what was the other thing that fell out?"

"I didn't put that back—I've got it yet."

"Lemme see it, Tom; what is it?"

But he put me off, and said it was too dark to see it; so I knowed he was working one of his mysteries and I'd got to wait till it suited him to come out with it. I asked him how he come to look in the nigger's shoe. He sniffed, and says—

"Huck Finn, hain't you got any reasoning powers at all? Where

would a detective look? He looks everywheres—he don't make any
exceptions. First, he looks where he ain't likely to find anything—
becuz that is where he'd druther find it, of course, on account of the
showiness of it; and if he is disappointed he turns to and hunts in
the likely places. But he's *got* to examine everything—it's his business; and he must remember all about it at the trial, too. I didn't
want to find the things in the shoe, of course—"

"Why, Tom?"

"Didn't I just *tell* you why? Becuz it was the likely place. A
white nigger that's playing a swindle knows his new marster might
take a notion to search him; so *he* don't hide his suspiciousest things
in his pockets, does he?"

"Well, now, I wouldn't a thought of that, but I reckon it's so,
Tom. You think of everything and you notice everything."

"A detective's got to. I noticed everything in that lean-to, and can
tell all about it, from the musket on the hooks with no flint in the
lock to Bat's old silver-plated watch hanging under the shelf
with the minute-hand broke off the same length as the hour-hand
and you can't come within two weeks of telling what time of day it
is, to save you; and I noticed—"

All of a sudden I thought of something—

"Tom!"

"Well?"

"We are just foolish."

"How?"

"To be fooling along here like this. The thing for us to do is to
rush to the sheriff's and tell him, so he can slip up here and catch
this humbug and jail him for swindling Bat."

He stopped where he was, and says, very sarcastic—

"You think so, do you?"

It made me feel sheepish, but I said "Yes," anyway, though I
didn't say it very confident.

"Huck Finn," he says, kind of sorrowful, "you can't ever seem to
see the noblest opportunities. Here is this conspiracy weaving along
just perfect, and you want to turn him in in this ignorant way and
spoil it all."

"How is that going to spoil it, Tom Sawyer?"

"Well, just look at it a minute," he says, "and I reckon you'll see. How would a detective act? I'll ask you that. Would he go in that simple girly way and catch this humbug and make him tell where the other one is, and then catch the other one and make him hand out the two hundred dollars, and have the whole thing over and done with before morning and not a rag of glory in it anywhere? I never see such a mud turtle as you, Huck Finn."

"Well, then," I says, "what *would* he do? It looks like the common sense way, to me, Tom Sawyer."

"Common sense!" he says, as scornful as he could. "What's common sense got to do with detecting, you leatherhead? It ain't got *anything* to do with it. What is wanted is genius and penetration and marvelousness. A detective that had common sense couldn't ever make a ruputation—couldn't even make his living."

"Well, then," I says, "what *is* the right way?"

"There's only one. Let these frauds go ahead and play their game and get away, then follow them up by *clews*—that's the way. It may take weeks and weeks, but is full of glory. Clews is the thing."

"All right," I says, ruther aggravated, "have it your own way, but I think it's an assful way."

"What is there assful about it, Huck Finn?"

"It's assful because you mayn't ever catch them at all, and when you do they've spent all of Bat's two hundred and he can't get it back. Where's the sense in that?"

"Don't I tell you there ain't any sense *in* detecting,—I never see such a clam. It's nobler—and higher—and grander; and who cares for the money, anyway?—the glory's the thing."

"All right," I says, "go it—I ain't interfering. What's your plan?"

"Now you're getting into your right mind. Come along, and I'll tell you as we climb. These two frauds think they are safe—they don't know there's any detectives around, in a little back settlement like ourn. They'd never think of such a thing. It makes them our meat. Why? Becuz the nigger will wash up, and both of them will

get up some new disguises so as Bat and anybody else won't know
them, and like as not they'll stay here a while and try to play some
more swindles. Now then, the plan is this. Whenever you and Jim
sees a stranger, you let me know. If he's the nigger, I'll reconnize
him; and I'll let him alone till I catch him with another stranger—
then we'll take them into camp."

"You might get the wrong ones."

"You leave it to me—I'll show you."

"Is that the whole plan, Tom?"

"You'll find it's a plenty. You lay for strangers and tell me—that's
all I want."

So then we went ahead and clumb the tree and found Jim there
and told him the whole thing, and he said it was splendid, and
believed it was the best conspiracy that ever was, and was coming
along judicious and satisfactory. And about half past one in the
morning he blowed the signals and it was a perfectly horrible noise,
enough to make a person turn in his grave; and then we pulled out
for town to sample the effects.

Chapter 6

IT COULDN'T a been better, it couldn't a been finer. Tom said so
his own self, and Jim said the same. The whole town was out in the
streets, taking on like it was the Last Day. There was lights in all
the houses, and people ranting up and down and carrying on and
prophecying, and that scared they didn't know what they was
about. And the drums was rumbling and the fifes tooting and the
soldiers tramp-tramping, and Colonel Elder and Sam Rumford
shouting the orders, and the dogs howling—it was all beautiful and
glorious.

When it got to be about an hour before dawn Tom said he must
get back to Bat's place, now, so as to get footprints and other clews
while they was fresh, so he could begin to track out the escaped
nigger. He knowed his aunt Polly would be uneasy about him, but

it wouldn't do for him to go there, he might get locked up for safety, and that could make no end of trouble with the conspiracy, so he told Jim to go and explain to her how he was out on detective work, and ask her permission and comfort her up; then he could rush and overtake us. Me and Tom struck out up the river road, then, and got to Bat's just in the gray of the dawn.

And by gracious! Right before the lean-to was Bat Bradish stretched out on the ground, and seemed to be dead, and was all bloody; and his old musket was laying there with blood and hair on the barrel; and the lean-to was open and the nigger gone, and things upset and smashed around in a great way, and plenty of footprints and clews and things, all a person could want. Tom told me to rush for the undertaker—not the new one, give the job to the old one, Jake Trumbull, which was a friend of ourn—and said he would come along and catch up with me as soon as he had got the clews tallied up.

He was always quick, Tom was. I warn't out of sight at the turn of the river road when I looked back and see him waving his hat for me. So I run back, and he says—

"We needn't go for help, Huck, it's been 'tended to."

"What makes you reckon so, Tom?"

"I don't reckon anything about it, I know it. Jim's been here."

And sure enough he had. Tom had found his tracks. Of course he had come the short way over the hill and beat us, becuz we come the long way, up the river road. I was dog-tired, and glad we didn't have to go for anybody. I went behind the house, out of sight of the dead man, and set down and rested whilst Tom examined around amongst the clews. It warn't but a few minutes till he come and said he was through, and said there'd been four men there besides Bat and Jim, and he had their prints, but nobody's prints was inside the lean-to except Bat's and the white nigger's and another man's —the nigger's pal, he reckoned. He said Jim and two of the men was gone for help by the short way over the hill, and the nigger and his pal had made for the creek, and we would take out after them—come along.

It was an easy trail, through mangy poor little grass-patches with bare dust between; and where the tracks struck the dust they bored in heavy and showed that the men was running as hard as they could go. Tom says—

"They don't know the country very well, you see; or they're too excited; or they've got pointed a little wrong on account of it's being dark. Anyway, if they don't slew to the left pretty soon they'll get into trouble."

"Looks like it," I says; "they're aiming for the jumping-off place."

The jumping-off place was twelve foot high, and had low bushes on it, and even in the daytime an ignorant person wouldn't know it was there till he was over it. We chased the tracks plumb to the edge. Then we pulled off to the left and clumb down and got the trail again at the jumping-off place and followed it fifty yards to the Branch. The Branch was uncommon high but had begun to fall; so there was a flat wide belt of half-dry mud at the edge, shriveling and stinking, and Tom says—

"Good luck, Huck, the pal hurt his left leg when he fell over the jumping-off place, it only makes a dragging-print here, and the nigger had to help him along. It's a clew, don't you know!"

He would trade pie for a clew, any time. Next, he says—

"They've got old Cap. Haines's canoe; hooked it, I reckon."

Said he knowed it by the print the bow made in the mud. It might be—I didn't know. I had stole the canoe lots of times, but never noticed. I says—

"Now we can go home. They're safe in Illinois by this time and we ain't going to hear of them no more."

But he said no, it might be and it mightn't be; he wouldn't jump to no conclusions about it—best way was to go ahead and find out; and says—

"The only way to ascertain a thing is to *ascertain;* guessing ain't any good. And besides—look at it all around. Suppose this pal's leg is broke? Is he going to strike for Illinois and the everlasting woods? No; he'll want a doctor. They haven't been in town—they'd have been in jail in two minutes, becuz they're strangers; it ain't any healthy place for strangers in these conspiracy times. They've come from up river or over river; they know Bat; they've traded with him before, some time or other. *If* the leg's broke they've got to have a doctor—"

"Well then, they've gone to town, Tom."

"In Cap. Haines's canoe?—from close to the murder?—a canoe that they stole, you can bet on it—it's the kind of folks they are. *I* don't think they've gone to town."

"Well, I don't, nuther, come to think. What will they do, Tom?"

We was tramping along down the Branch, all this time. Tom thought a while, then says—

"Huck, if they had plenty of time, they could manage, but I reckon they haven't. Nearest town up-stream, twenty-five miles— an all-day trip with one paddle; nearest town down-stream, twenty-one miles—five hours; but it wouldn't do any good; the news of the murder will be there to-day, and even if they sunk Haines's canoe and stole another, people would still want to know where they got that leg." After studying a little, he says "I hope they've done that. I hope they've had the time. We'd have them before night, dead sure!"

"Good!" says I.

We went tramping along, Tom a-watching for clews. Pretty soon he shook his head and pulled a long breath, and says—

"No, it won't work, Huck; they're around here somewheres— they hadn't the time."

"How do you know?"

"Well, the nigger overslept or something, the pal didn't turn up till hours after he oughter, and so the thing didn't come off till towards dawn."

"What makes you think that, Tom?"

"Becuz Bat was warm yet, when we got there; I felt of him, under his waistcoat."

It give me the cold shivers; I wouldn't a done it.

"Go on," I says.

"The nigger has got to wash up and change to white folks' clothes before he can go and smuggle a doctor to his pal, and like enough the pal's got a disguise, too. The nigger's got another suit, anyway—that's sure. He would want to make his change pretty soon after he escaped, before he met up with anybody. So I reckon the clothes must be hid around here somewheres, not very far. Well, by the time the washing and dressing and paddling three miles was done it would be daylight and they would be chased and caught as they passed the town, I don't care which side of the river they went down. If they've tried it they've made a mistake."

Well, when we had gone along down about a half a mile and was abreast the stretch of bushes back of the hanted house, right there we struck the trail again. Tom says—

"Ain't it curious? They got in ahead of us on our scheme all around: play counterfeit-nigger like we was going to do, and jump our dressing-room, too. They've been around here before, Huck."

The canoe warn't anywhere in sight; they had hid her or turned her loose, we didn't know which, and didn't care anyway, it warn't any matter. We crope through the bushes and there was the trail plowing straight for the house through the high weeds where the garden used to was. The windows was still boarded up the way me and Tom done it the summer before, the time we let on to be a gang of counterfeiters and used to go there and cut out tin money in the night and contribbit it to the mishonary business Sundays, and she was looking awful lonesome and mournful, the way she always done. Tom said we'd got to get down on our hands and knees and crawl through the weeds, and go very, very slow, and not make the least noise or they might hear us. I says—

"Who? Me? I reckon I see myself a doing it. If you want to go and get into trouble with them hellions," I says, "it's your instincts and it's all right, and I'll wait for you; but nary a peg do I budge."

So he took his course with his little compass and started, and I watched, out of the shadder of the bushes. He done it first rate. You would see the tops of the weeds wiggle a little, and after a quiet spell they would wiggle again, a little further along—the slowest business; but always I could keep track of him, and always he was getting ahead. So he got there by and by, and I waited the dullest longest time, and got afraid they had grabbed him and choked him to death; but at last I see by the weeds that he was coming again, and I was awful glad. As soon as he got to me he says—

"Come along, it's all right—they're there. I crep' through the hole where the hogs get under the house, and it was dark as pitch in there and in the house, and I stuck my head up through the busted place in the floor—"

"What a fool!"

"Fool yourself!—they couldn't see me; and couldn't if it had been light—our old counterfeiter-chest was in the way. And I didn't see them, either, but I've heard them talk. I was 'most as close to them as I am to you, now. If I had had a walking stick I could a punched them with it. But I wouldn't."

"Well, then, you've got *some* sense left, but not enough to hurt, Tom Sawyer. What did they say?"

"Talked about the scrimmage."

"Like enough—but what did they *say?*"

"Lots."

Then he said he was too tired to walk down to town, and no hurry anyway—we must jump in the river and float down on our backs—which was satisfactry to me; but I knowed I had got all I was going to get about that talk for just now. Them old roosters had laid another mystery, and he warn't ready to have it hatched out yet.

Just where the Branch goes into the river we struck a mortal piece of good luck. Some person had come ashore and left his skiff pulled up, with the oars in the rollocks, and warn't anywhere in sight; so we borrowed it, Tom saying something grateful about Providence, and we got in and pulled out a good piece and laid down in her and lit the pipes and let her float. It was very comfortable after all the hard work we'd been through. By and by Tom says—

"It warn't in the plan, but of course it's there for the best."

"What ain't in the plan?"

"The murder. It's a kind of a pity, becuz there warn't any real harm in Bat Bradish, but as long as it had to be somebody I reckon it's as well it's him, and it *does* give this conspiracy a noble lift, now *don't* it, Huck? We'd be mean not to be grateful. And more trustful than ever, too. Why, Huck, a body wouldn't think it, but a person can see, now, that a conspiracy that is conducted right is just as good as a revolution. Just as good and ain't half the trouble."

"Looks so to me, Tom."

"Huck, it's just like a revolution in some ways—a person that hadn't had any experience couldn't tell it from a revolution. You see, it starts in for one thing, and comes out another; starts in in a little small way to worry a village, and murders a nigger-trader. Yes, sir, it's got all the marks of a revolution; and the way it's prospering along now, I believe it could be nursed up and turned *into* a revolution. All it wants now is capital, and something to revolute about."

Well, he was started, and so I let him alone. It was the best way. He would think it out, and gild it up, and put the ruffles on it, and I could lay still and rest, and that suited me.

Just as we struck into town and went ashore by the Cold Spring where the flour mill is, here comes Higgins's Bill, the one-legged nigger, hopping along on his crutch, very much excited and all out of breath and says—

"Marse Tom, ole Jim want you en Huck to come to de jail quick as you kin—dey's got him, en jammed him in, seh."

"What for?"

"Killin' ole Bat Bradish."

I says—

"Great jeeminy!"

But Tom's face lit up pious and happy—it made me shiver to see it; and he give Bill a dime, and says, quite ca'm—

"All right; run along; we are a coming." Bill cleared out and we hurried up, and Tom says, kind of grateful, "Ain't it beautiful, the way it's developing out?—*we* couldn't ever thought of that, and it's the splendidest design yet. *Now* you'll be trustful, I reckon, and quit fretting and losing confidence."

"Tom Sawyer," I says, "what in the nation is there splendid about it?" I was mad, and grieved, and most crying. "There's our old Jim, the best friend we ever had, and the best hearted, and the whitest man inside that ever walked, and now he's going to get hung for a murder he never done, I just *know* he never done it, and whose fault is it but this blame conspiracy, I wish it was in—"

"Shut up!" he says, "you can't tell a blessing from a bat in the eye, I never see such an idiot—always flying at everything Providence does, you ought to be ashamed of yourself. Who's running this conspiracy?—you? Blame it, you are hendering it every way you can think of. Old Jim get hung? Who's going to let him get hung, you tadpole?"

"Well, but—"

"Hush up! there ain't any well about it. It's going to come out all right, and the grandest thing that ever was, and just oceans of glory for us all—and here you are finding fault with your blessings, you catfish. Old Jim get hung! He's going to be a hero, that's what he's going to be. Yes, and a brass band and a torchlight procession on top of it, or *I* ain't no detective."

It made me feel good and satisfied again, I couldn't help it. It was always just so. He had so much confidence it was catching, and a person always had to knock under and come to his notions.

We had our passes, and was officials, so we shouldered through the crowd at the jail door and the sheriff let us in, though he wouldn't let anybody else. Tom told me private not to know anything, and he wasn't going to know anything himself—he would do the talking for us both, to the sheriff. He done it. The sheriff didn't get anything out of him. Old Jim was scared most to death, and was sure he was going to be hung; but Tom was ca'm, and told him he needn't worry, it warn't going to happen; and so it warn't ten minutes till Jim was ca'm, too, and all cheered up and comfortable. Tom told Jim the officers wouldn't ask him any questions, and if visitors got in and asked him questions he must say he couldn't answer anybody but his lawyer. Then Jim went ahead and told us his tale.

He didn't find aunt Polly at home, of course she was out getting her share of the scare; so he was after us pretty soon, and hurried up, reckoning he could catch up with us, but we went the long way by the river road and he went the short one over Cardiff Hill; so it wasn't light, yet, when he got to Bat's place, and he stumbled over Bat and fell on him; and just as he was getting up a couple of men come running, and grabbed him, and it was Buck Fisher and old Cap. Haines, and they said they had heard the murdersome row and was glad they catched him in the act. He was going to explain, but they shut him up and wouldn't let him say a word—said a nigger's word warn't any account anyway. They felt of Bat's heart and said he was dead, then they took Jim back over the hill and down to the jail, and spread the news, and then the town was that beside itself it didn't know *what* to do. Tom studied a while, and says, kind of thoughtful—

"It could be better. Still, it ain't bad, the way it is."

"Good lan', Mars Tom, how you's a talkin'! Here I is, wid de man's blood all over me, en you—"

"That's all right, as far as it goes—a good point, a very good point; but it don't go far enough."

"How does you mean, Marse Tom?"

"By itself it ain't any evidence of a motive. What we want's, a motive."

"What's a motive, Marse Tom?"

"A *reason* for killing the man."

"My goodness, Marse Tom, I never *killed* him."

"I know. That's the weak place. It's easy to show that you *probably* killed him, and of course that is pretty good, but it can't hang a man—a white one, anyway. It would be ever so much stronger if you had a *motive* to kill him, you see."

"Marse Tom, is I in my right mine, or is it you? Blame my cats if I kin understan'."

"Why, plague take it, it's plain enough. Look at it. I'm going to save you—that's all right, and perfectly easy. But where's the glory of saving a person merely just from jail. To save him from the gallows is the thing. It's got to be murder in the first degree—you get the idea? You've got to have a *motive* for killing the man—*then* we're all right! Jim, if you can think up a rattling good motive, I can get you put up for murder in the first degree just as easy as turning your hand over."

He was all excitement and hope, but Jim—why, Jim could hardly get out his words he was that astonished and scared.

"Why, Marse Tom—why, bless yo' heart, honey, I ain't in no sweat to hunt up dish-yer—"

"Hold still, I tell you, and think of a motive! I could have thought up a dozen while you are fooling away all this time. Look here, did Bat Bradish like you?—did you like Bat?"

That seemed to jostle Jim. Tom saw it, and followed it right up. Jim dodged this and that and t'other way, but it didn't do any good, Tom chased him up and found out it was Bradish that was at the bottom of it the time old Miss Watson come so near selling Jim down the river and Jim heard about it and run away and me and him floated down to Arkansaw on the raft. It was Bradish that persuaded her to sell Jim and give him the job of doing it for her. So at last Tom says—

"That's enough. That's a motive. We are all right, now, it's murder in the first degree, and we'll have a grand time out of it and when we get through you'll be a hero, Jim. I wouldn't take a thousand dollars for your chances."

But Jim didn't like it a bit, and said he would sell out for ten cents, and glad to. Tom was very well satisfied, now, and said we would tell the district attorney—which is the lawyer for the prostitution—all about the motive, and then things would go right along. Then he arranged with the sheriff for Jim to have pipes and good vittles and everything he wanted, and said good-bye to Jim, promising we would come every day and amuse him some more. Then we left.

Chapter 7

THE TOWN was booming. Everybody was raging about the murder, and didn't doubt but Jim was in with the Sons of Freedom and been paid by the gang to murder the nigger-trader, and there'd be more—every man that owned niggers was in danger of his life; it was only just the beginning, the place was going to swim in blood, you'll see. That is what they said. It was foolish talk, that talk about Jim, becuz he had always been a good nigger, and everybody knowed it; but you see he was a free nigger this last year and more, and that made everybody down on him, of course, and made them forget all about his good character. It's just the way with people. And the way they was taking on about Bat Bradish you would a thought they had lost a angel; they couldn't seem to get over grieving about him and telling one another no end of sweet little beautiful things he had done, one time or another, which they had forgot till now; and it warn't no trouble, nuther, becuz they hadn't ever happened. Yesterday there wouldn't anybody say a good word for the nigger-trader nor care a dern about him, becuz everybody despised nigger-traders, of course; but to-day, why, they couldn't seem to get over the loss of him, nohow. Well, it's people's way; they're mostly puddnheads—looks so to me.

Of course they was going to lynch Jim, everybody said it; and they just packed all the streets around the jail, and talked excited, and couldn't hardly wait to commence. But Cap'n Ben Haskins, sheriff, was inside, and the mob that started in there without an invite would have a sickly time, and knowed it; and Colonel Elder was outside, and that warn't healthy for a mob, and they knowed it. So me and Tom went along; we warn't worried about Jim. Tom let the *motive* leak out where it would get to the attorney for the prostitution; then we got in the back way at his aunt Polly's and got something to eat and didn't have any trouble becuz she was out enjoying the excitements and hunting for Tom; and from there we went up in the woods on the hill to get some sleep where we wouldn't be in the way, and Tom made his plans.

He said we would 'tend the inquest to-day, and be on hand at the Grand Jury to-morrow, but our evidence wouldn't go for anything against Cap. Haines's and Buck Fisher's, and Jim would be brought in for first degree all right. His trial would come off in about a month. It would take that long for the pal's leg to get so he could walk on it. Then we must have it fixed so that when the trial was just going against Jim we could snatch the two frauds into court and clear Jim and make a noble sensation, and Jim would be a hero and we would all be heroes.

I didn't like it; I was scared of it; it was too risky; something might happen; any little hitch, and Jim's a goner! A nigger don't stand any show. I said we ought to tell the sheriff and let him go and get the men *now*—and jail them, and then we'd have them when we wanted them.

But Tom wouldn't listen to it for a minute. There warn't anything stunning about it. He wanted to get the men into the court without them suspicioning anything—and then make the grand pow-wow, the way he done in Arkansaw. That Arkansaw business had just pisoned him, I could see it plain; he wouldn't ever be satisfied to do things in a plain common way again.

Well, we couldn't keep awake any longer, so we reckoned we would sleep an hour, and then step down to the inquest. And of course when we woke it was too late. When we got down there it was over, and everybody gone—corpse and all. But it warn't much matter, we could go to the Grand Jury to-morrow.

Why, we had slept away past the middle of the afternoon and it was coming on sundown. Time to go home for supper; but Tom said no, he wanted to make sure of his men; so we would wait till night and he would step to the hanted house and listen again. I was very willing for him to do it, it would make me feel easier; so we struck down the Branch and slid past, and down to the river and up it a quarter of a mile under the bluff and went in swimming and stayed in till an hour after dark, then come back and Tom crope through the weeds to the house, and I waited.

I waited and waited, and it was awful lonesome and still and creepy there in the dark, and the hanted house so close. It wasn't actually very long, but it seemed so, you know. At last Tom come a tearing through the weeds and says—

"Oh, poor Jim, poor Jim, he'll be hung— they're gone!"

I just fell flat, where I was. Everything was swimming, it seemed to me I was going to faint. Then I let go and cried, I couldn't help it and didn't want to. And Tom was crying, too, and said—

"What did I ever do it for?—Huck what *did* I do it for! I had them safe, and I could a saved Jim spite of anything anybody could do, if I only hadn't been a fool. Oh, Huck you wanted me to tell the sheriff, and I was an idiot and wouldn't listen, and now they've got away and we'll never see them again, and nothing can save Jim, and it's all my fault, I wish I was dead."

He took it so hard, and said so many hard things about himself that I hadn't the heart to say any myself, though I was going to, and had them on my tongue's end, but you know how it is, that way. I begun to try to comfort him, but he couldn't bear it, and said call him names, call him the roughest ones I knowed, it was the only thing could do him any good; and then he broke out and abused himself for taking for *granted* the man's leg was broke, and maybe it was only sprained—of *course* it was only sprained, it was perfectly plain, now. Then he had a sudden idea, and said—

"Come!"

So we went tearing down the road for town; said maybe the men would make for the next town below, and we would catch the steamboat and beat them. As we passed the Cold Spring the boat went by; when we got to the wharf she was pulling in the stage, but we jumped for it and made it. People yelled at us to know where we was bound for, but we never took any notice, and went up on the harricane roof and away aft, and set down in the sparks to watch for the canoe, and forgot all about the Grand Jury, but Tom said it wasn't any matter, nothing could save Jim but to find the *men*.

Tom couldn't talk straight and connected, he was gone clean off of his head by the disastersomeness of what was come to Jim on accounts of him letting the men get away; and pretty soon he seen, himself, that his mind was upside down, becuz he says—

"Huck, I'm so miserable it has knocked all the judgment out of me. Don't you know there ain't any sense in us being on this boat?"

"Why, Tom?"

"Becuz it's in the plan I made on the broken-leg theory, and the leg *ain't* broke. The man don't have to hunt a doctor, and he can go wherever he wants to. And they *have* gone to Illinois and the everlasting woods—it's the rightest place and the safest for them. Huck, they went the minute it was dark, and if we had went in swimming at the mouth of the Branch 'stead of a quarter of a mile above, we'd a *seen* them. I wish we was back to town, I'd give a million dollars. We would get on their trail and tree them in their camp quick and easy, because the pal's leg is hurt and he can't go a yard without help. Huck, we've got to get back there the minute we can—what a fool I've been to forget that broken-leg theory and come on this boat."

Well, I could see it now, myself; I didn't think of it before. But I didn't say anything mean; his mind warn't to blame for getting out of true, when you come to think. Anybody's would. I was starting in to encourage him up, but he busted out bitter and aggravated, and says—

"The luck has turned against us, there ain't any getting around it —look at this!"

It was rain. I was sorry enough for him to cry.

"It's going to wipe out the trail." He begun to get perfectly desprate, and said if any harm come to Jim he would square up the best he could—he would blow his brains out, he wouldn't miss them.

I couldn't bear to see him in so much trouble, so I tried to soothe him up, and told him *we* couldn't know where the men went to, becuz we didn't know the men, and so how could we know how they would act? Mightn't they belong to Burrell's Gang?

"Yes—prob'ly *do*. What of it?"

"Wouldn't they be safe if they was with the Gang?"

"Perfectly. Go on."

"Fox island is their den, ain't it?"

"Yes."

"How far from here?"

"Hundred and seventy mile."

"They can make it in four nights in a canoe and lay up and hide daytimes, and so how do *we* know they ain't making for home?"

"Lemme hug you, Huck! There's one level head left, anyway. If we can head them off before they get there, and have a sheriff with us—Huck, if they are ahead of us we'll catch up on them inside of an hour and make this boat chase them down. I bet you we're all right, Huck. Rush! Go down on the foc'sle and watch; I'll go in the pilot house and watch. If you see them, give three whoops as loud as you can, and I'll have the pilot all ready and anxious for business. Rush!"

So we both rushed. He was all right again and hopeful, and I was glad I thought of that idea, though I didn't take no stock in it, much. I knowed Tom's notion that the men had broke for Illinois was worth six of it. He would know it, too, when his mind got settled, then we would go home, and if that pal's leg was much hurt there would be new trails in a day or two, and not so very deep in the woods, either.

It was as dark as pitch on the foc'sle, and I fell over a man, and he storms out—

"What in hell are you doin'!" and grabbed me by the leg.

I sunk right down where I was, pulpy and sick, and begun to whimper, for it was the King's voice! Another voice says—

"Seems to be only a boy, you old hog—*he* didn't do it a-purpose. You've got no bowels—and never had any."

By George, it was the Duke!

And there I was!

The King spoke up again—

"A boy, are ye? Why didn't you *say* so? I took you for a cow. What do you want here—hey? Who are ye? What's your name?"

Of course I didn't want to answer, but I knowed I had to. But I tried to make my voice different—

"Bill Parsons, please sir."

"Ger-reat Scott!" says the Duke, setting up, and poking his face in mine, "what's brought *you* here, Huck Finn?"

He talked ruther thick, and I judged he was drunk; but that was all right, becuz if the Duke was more good-natureder one time than another it was when he was drunk. I had to tell them about myself, I knowed there warn't any way to get around it; so I done it as judicious as I could, caught sudden thataway, and unloaded considerable many lies onto them. When I got done they grunted, and the Duke says—

"Now tell some truth for a change."

I started painting again, but the Duke stopped me, and says—

"Wait, Huckleberry, you better let me help, I reckon."

My time was come, and I knowed it. He was sharp, and he would begin to chase me up with questions and follow me right to my hole. Of course I knowed his game, and was scared. The time I let Jim get away, down there in Arkansaw, it took a pile of money out of him and the King's pocket, and they had me, now. They wouldn't let up till they found out where Jim was—that was certain. The Duke begun; then the King begun to shove in questions, but the Duke shut him up and told him he was only botching the business, and didn't know enough to come in when it rained. It made the King pretty grouty.

It warn't long till they had it out of me—Jim was in jail, in our town.

"What for?"

Now the minute the Duke asked that, I see my way perfectly clear. If Jim was to get clear they could come with their sham papers and run him South and sell him, but if I showed them he was going to get hung, and hung for sure, they wouldn't bother about him no more, and we would be shut of them. I was glad I had that idea, and I made up my mind to put the murder on Jim and do it strong.

"What for?" the Duke says.

"Murder," I says, perfectly ca'm.

"Great guns!"

"Yes," I says, "he done it, and he done right—but he *done* it, ain't any doubt about that."

"It's an awful pity, becuz he warn't a bad nigger at bottom; but how do you know he done it?"

"Becuz old Cap. Haines and Buck Fisher come on him in the very act. He had hit a nigger-trader over the head with his own musket, and stumbled and fell on him, and was getting up when the men come running. It was dark, but they heard the row and warn't far off. I wisht they had been somewheres else. If Jim hadn't fell he might a got away."

"Too bad. Is the man really dead?"

"I reckon so. They buried him this afternoon."

"It's awful. Does Jim give in that he done it?"

"No. Only just says it ain't any use for a nigger to talk when there's two white men against him."

"Well, that's so—hey, Majesty?"

"Head's level for a nigger—yes."

"Why, maybe he *didn't* kill the man. Any suspicious characters around?"

"Nary."

"Hasn't anybody seen any?"

"No. And besides, if there'd been any, where's their *motive?* They wouldn't kill a man just for fun, would they?"

"Well, no. And maybe Jim hadn't any motive, either."

"Why, your grace, the motive's the very worst thing against him. Everybody knows what he done to Jim once, and two men heard Jim tell him he was going to lay him out for it one of these days. It was only talk, and I know it, but that ain't any difference, it's white man's talk and Jim's only a nigger."

"It does look bad for Jim."

"Poor old Jim, he knows it. Everybody says he'll be hung, and of course he hain't got any friends, becuz he's free."

Nobody said anything, now, and I judged I had put it home good and strong, and they would quit bothering about Jim, and me and Tom would be let alone to go ahead and find the men and get Jim out of his scrape. So I was feeling good and satisfied. After a little bit the Duke says—

"I've been a thinking. I'll have a word with you, Majesty."

Him and the King stepped to the side and mumbled together, and come back, and the Duke says—

"You like Jim, and you're sorry for him. Now which would you druther—let him get sold down South, or get hung?"

Chapter 8

I<small>T WAS</small> sudden. It knocked me silly. I couldn't seem to understand what his idea was. Before I could come to myself, he says—

"It's for you to say. Now and then and off and on me and the King have struck Jim's trail and lost it again; for we've got a requisition for Jim from the Governor of Kentucky onto the Governor of Missouri and his acceptans of the same—all bogus, you know, but the seals and the paper, which is genuwyne—and on them papers we can go and grab Jim wherever we find him and there ain't anybody can prevent us. First and last we've followed that trail but first and last we've followed it to Elexandry, sixty mile above here. Lost it again, and give it up for good and all, and took this boat there towards the middle of the afternoon to-day—"

"Not knowin' that a righteous overrulin' Providence—"

"Shut up, you old rum-barrel, and don't interrupt. It's with you, Huck, to save him or hang him. Which is it?"

"Oh, goodness knows, your grace, I'm anxious enough—tell me how."

"It's easy. Spose Jim murdered a man down yonder in Tennessee or Mississippi or Arkansaw fourteen months ago when you and Jim was helping me and the King run the raft, and me and the King was going to sell Jim for *our* nigger, becuz he *was* ourn, by rights of discovery, we having found him floating down the river without any owner—"

"Yes, and he's ourn *yit,*" says the King, in that snarly way of his'n.

"Stick your feet in your mouth and stop some of your gas from escapin', Majesty. Spose Jim done that, Huck—murdered a planter or somebody down there. Take it in? Get the idea?"

"Not by a blame' sight I don't. Jim never done it. Jim warn't scasely ever out of my sight a day on a stretch; and if he—"

"There—don't be a fool. Of course he never done it; *that* ain't the idea. The idea is—*spose* he done it. See? Spose he *had* a done it. *Now* you see?"

"No, I don't."

"Shucks! Why, blame it, you couldn't try him up here till *after* you had tried him down there, could you? Got to take his murders in the order of preseedence, hain't you? 'Course. Any idiot knows that much. Very good. Now then, here's the scheme that'll give us back our nigger and save your black chum's life. To-morrow in Sent Louis we'll go to a friend of ourn that's in a private business up a back alley and got up our papers for us, and he'll change them so as to fit the case the way it stands now; change them from nigger 'escaped from service' to murder—murder done by Jim down South, you know. Then we'll come straight up here to-morrow or next day and show the papers and take Jim down South and sell him—not in Kentucky, of course, but 'way down towards the mouth of the river, where Missouri couldn't ever get on his track when she found she'd been played. See it *now*, don't you?"

By gracious I felt that good, I reckon the angels don't feel no better when they looks down Sabberday morning and sees the Catholic kids getting roped into the Presbyterium Sunday school. Well, the world, it's curious, thataway. One minute your heart is away down and miserable, and don't seem to be no way out of your troubles, and next minute some little thing or another happens you warn't looking for and just lifts her to your teeth with a bounce, and all your worries is gone and you feel as happy and splendid as Sodom and Gomorrah or any other of them patriarchs. I says to myself, it's nuts for Tom Sawyer, this is. And it's nuts for Jim, too. Jim's life's safe by this game, if they play it good, and if he ain't in England and free again three months after they sell him it'll be becuz we've forgot how to run niggers out of slavery and better quit the business.

So I told them to count me in, the 'rangement was satisfactry to me. They was very much pleased, and shuck me by the hand; the first time they ever come down onto my level like that, I reckon.

And I said I wanted to help if they'd tell me how; and the Duke says—

"You can be a prime help, Huck, and you won't lose nothing by it, nuther. All you got to do is, keep mum—don't talk."

"All right, I won't."

"Tell Jim, if you want to; tell him to look awful scared and guilty when he sees us and finds we are sheriff's officers and hears what we've come for—it'll have a good effect; but he mustn't show that he has seen us before. And *you* mustn't. You want to be particular about that."

"I won't let on to know you, your grace—I'll be particular."

"That's the idea. Say—what are you doing on this boat?"

It took me ruther sudden, and I didn't know what to say, so I said I was traveling for my health. But they was feeling good, now, and unparticular; so they laughed and asked me where was the resort, and I said the town down yonder where the lights is showing; so they let me go, then, and told me good-bye and said there was going to be trouble in the chicken coops of that resort before morning, but they reckoned I would pull through all right.

I cleared for the pilot house, feeling first rate; then I remembered I had forgot to watch for the canoe, but I didn't care; I knowed there hadn't been any or the pilot and Tom would a seen it and chased it down. The mud-clerk was up there collecting our passages, and me and Tom come down on the texas roof, and I whispers and says—

"What do you think—the King and the Duke's down on the foc'sle!"

"Go 'long—you don't mean it!"

"Wish I may never die. You want to have a sight of them?"

"Well, I should reckon! Come along."

So we flew down. They was celebrated in our town on accounts of me and Jim's adventures with them, and there wasn't a person but would give his shirt for a look at them—including Tom. The time Tom saw them down in Arkansaw it was night, and they was tarred and feathered and the public was riding them on a rail in a torchlight procession and they was looking like the pillar of cloud that led Moses out of the bulrushers; but of course he would like to see them without the feathers on, becuz with the feathers on you couldn't tell them from busted bolsters.

But we didn't make it. The boat was sidling in to the wharfboat, and of course the mates had cleared the foc'sle and there warn't anybody there but a crowd of deckhands, now, bustling with the freight. They was red and vivid in the shine of the fire-doors and the torch-basket, but it was pitch dark everywheres else and you couldn't see anything. So we hopped ashore and took out to the upper end of the town and found a long lumber raft there and went out and set down on the outside edge of it with our legs in the water and listened to the quietness and the little waves slapping soft against it, and begun to talk, and watch out for the canoe, and it was ever so summery and bammy and comfortable, and the mosquitoes a singing and the frogs a going it, the way they do, such nights.

So then I told Tom the scheme and said we must keep mum, and not tell anybody but Jim. It cheered him up and nearly made him gay; and he said Jim was safe now; if we didn't find the men the Duke's plan would save him, sure, and we would have good times running him out of slavery again, and then we would take him over to England and hand him over to the Queen ourselves to help in the kitchen and wait on table and be a body-guard and celebrated; and we would have the trip, and see the Tower and Shackspur's grave and find out what kind of a country we all come from before we struck for taxation and misrepresentation and raised Cain becuz we couldn't get it.

But he said he'd got his lesson, and warn't going to throw any more chances away for glory's sake; no, let glory go, he was for business, from this out. He was going to save Jim the *quickest* way, never mind about the showiest.

It sounded good, and I loved to hear it. He hadn't ever been in his right mind before; I could see it plain. Sound? He was as sound as a nut, now. Why, he even said he wished the King and the Duke would come and take Jim out of jail and out of town in the *night*, so there wouldn't be nary a sign of gaudiness and showiness about it, he was done with pow-wow, and didn't want no more. By gracious that made me uncomfortable again, it looked like he'd gone off his balance the *other* way, now. But I didn't say nothing.

He said the new scheme was a hundred times the most likeliest, but he warn't going to set down and take it easy on that account, becuz who knows but the Duke and the King will get into jail down there, which is always to be expected, and mightn't get out till it was too late for Jim's business—

"*Don't*, Tom!" says I, breaking in, "don't let's talk about it, don't let's even *think* about it."

"We've got to, Huck; it's in the chances, and we got to give all the doubts a full show from this out—there ain't going to be any more taking things for granted. We'll hunt for the *men* a couple of days while we're waiting—we won't throw any chance away." After a spell he drawed a sorrowful deep breath and says, "it was a prime good chance before the rain—I wish we hadn't come down here."

We watched faithful, all night till most daylight, and warn't going to go to sleep at all, but we did; and when we woke up it was noon and we was disgusted; and peeled and had a swim, and went down to town and et about 64 battercakes and things and felt crowded and better; and inquired around and didn't hear of the canoe, and a steamboat come along late and we got home at dark and Jim was slated for first degree and Bat was in the ground, and everybody was talking about the watchful inscrutableness of Providence, and thankful for it and astonished at it, but didn't das't to say so right out.

And after 64 more we went to jail and comforted Jim up and told him about the new plan, and it joggled him considerable, and he couldn't tell straight off whether to be glad or not, and says—

"By jimminies, I don't mo'n git outer one scrape tell I gits in a wuss one." But when he see how down-hearted it made Tom to hear him say that, he was sorry, and put his old black hand on Tom's head and says, "but I don't mine, I don't mine, honey, don't you worry; I knows you's gwyne to do de bes' you kin, en it don't make no diffunce what it is, ole Jim ain't gwyne to complain."

Of course it was awful to him, the idea of the King and the Duke getting a grip on him again, and he could scasely bear to talk about it; still, he knowed me and Tom wouldn't let him be a slave long if industriousness and enterprise and c'ruption was worth anything; so he quieted down, and reckoned if the Queen was satisfied with him after she tried him and found he was honest and willing, she would raise his wages next year; and Tom said she was young and inexperienced and would, he knowed it. So it was all satisfactry, and Tom went along home, and told me to come too, and I done it.

His aunt Polly give him a hiding, but it didn't hurt—nor me, neither; we didn't care for it. She was in a towering way, but when we explained we had been over on t'other side of the river fishing, about a couple of days and nights, and didn't know the horn-signal had blowed and scared the town to death and there'd been a murder and a funeral and Jim done it, she forgot she was mad at us, and wouldn't a sold out her chance for a basket of money, she being just busting to tell the news.

So she started in, and never got a dern thing right, but enjoyed herself, and it took her two solid hours; and when she got done painting up the show it was worth four times the facts, and I reckon Tom was sorry he didn't get her to run the conspiracy herself. But she was right down sorry for Jim, and said Bat must a tried to kill Jim or he never would a blowed his brains out with the musket.

"*Did* blow them out, did he, aunt Polly?"

"Such as he had—yes."

Then company come in to spend the evening, and amongst them was Flacker the detective, and he had been working up his clews and knowed all about the murder, same as if he'd seen it; and they all set with their mouths open a listening and holding their breath and wondering at his talents and marvelousness whilst he went on.

Why, it was just rot and rubbage—clean, straight foolishness, but them people couldn't see it. According to him, the Sons of Freedom was a sham—it was Burrell's Gang, and he had the clews

that would prove it. Burrell's Gang—it made them fairly shudder
and hitch their chairs clos'ter together when he said it. He said
there was six members of it right here in town, friends of you all,
you meet up and chat with them every day—it made them shudder
again. Said he wouldn't mention no names, he warn't ready yet, but
he could lay his hands on them whenever he wanted to. Said they
had a plan to burn the town and rob it and run off the niggers, he
had the proofs; and so they went on a shuddering, enough to shake
the house and sour the milk. Said Jim was in leagues with them, he
had the facts and could prove it any day; and said he had shaddered
the Sons to their den—wouldn't say where it was, just now; and he
come onto provisions there cal'lated to feed sixteen men six weeks
—(ourn, by jings!) And found their printing 'rangements, too, and
lugged them off and hid them, and could show them whenever he
got ready. Said he knowed the secret of the figures that was printed
on the bills with red ink, and it was too awful to tell where there
was senstive scary women. That made everybody scrunch together
and look sick. And he said the man that got up them bills warn't
any common ornery person, he was a gigantic intelleck, and was
prob'ly the worst man alive; and he knowed by some little marks on
the bills that another person wouldn't notice and wouldn't understand them if he did, that it was Burrell his own self that done it;
and said there warn't another man in America could get up them
bills but Burrell. And that very Burrell was in this town this
minute, in disguise and running a shop, and it was him that blowed
the signal-horn. Old Miss Watson fainted and fell onto the cat
when she heard that, and she yowled, becuz it was her tail that got
hurt, and they had a lot of trouble to fetch her to. And last of all, he
said Jim had two 'complices to the murder and he seen their
footprints—dwarfs, they was, one cross-eyed and t'other left-
handed; didn't say how he knowed it, but he was shaddering them,
and although they had escaped out of town for now, he warn't
worrying, he allowed he would take them into camp when they was
least expecting of it.

Why that was me and Tom—I never see such an idiot. But the
company was charmed to death with that stuff, and said it was the

most astonishing thing the way a detective could read every little sign he come across same as if it was a book, and you couldn't hide nothing from him. And they said this town would a lived and died and never knowed what started the row and who done it if it hadn't been for Flacker, and they was all under obligations to him; but he said it warn't nothing, it was his perfeshon, and anybody could do it that had practice and the gifts.

"*And* the gifts! you may well say *that*," says Tom's aunt Polly; and then they all said it.

She was soft on detectives, becuz Tom had an ambitiousness thataway, and she was proud about what he done that time down at his uncle Silas's.

Chapter 9

W E W A S over the river before daylight next morning, and as soon as the dawn come we begun to search for them foot-tracks. Tom had the measures of the two men's tracks—length and width; and he had the heels exact, just as they was printed in the ground in the lean-to, becuz he had run tallow into them from the candle and made thin moulds, and then traced them around on a leaf which he tore out of Bat's grocery-store book and done it with Bat's pen. The prints was like anybody else's to me, except the pal's left heel, which had a little of the north-east corner gone, and it oughter been the other one, to do us any good, I reckoned, becuz it was the left one he dragged after he hurt it falling down the jumping-off place, and the corner wouldn't show, now, if he was still a-dragging it; but Tom said I was a sap-head, and said if it dragged couldn't we see the drag-mark. Well, that was so; so then I didn't say no more.

We started work about a mile above the ferry on the Illinois shore. There was a low place where you could land a lame man there, and it was the only one above the ferry—the rest was all bluff bank ten foot high, like a wall, at this stage of the river. There was considerable many tracks, some fresh and some old, but if the ones we wanted was there they was too old to show up, now. We went out in the woods a piece and struck down-stream and went as far as the ferry, and found tracks in places, but they warn't the right ones. There wasn't a place for miles below the ferry where they could land; so we struck out on the ferry road and hunted the ground on both sides of it away out double as far as a lame man could get to in the time they had, since they started, but we hadn't any luck.

We stuck to it all day, and went back next day and ransacked again—rummaged the whole country betwixt the landings, plum till dark. It warn't any good. Next day we went down and rummaged Jackson's island—no tracks there but Flacker's; and he had lugged off our print-works, and some of our feed, too. So then we crossed to our shore and went to the cave, but that warn't any use, becuz the soldiers was there that Colonel Elder sent on accounts of the pow-wow the conspiracy made, and if any strangers had tried to get in there it would a been hark from the tomb for them.

We had to give it up, then, and paddled along home. Tom was down in the mouth again, becuz Jim would have to go down South with the King and the Duke, now, and could have a terrible rough time before we could run him out of slavery and break for England. But pretty soon he jumps up, all excited and glad, and says—

"We're fools, Huck, just fools!"

"Tain't no news," I says, "but what's the matter now?"

"Why, we're in luck—that's what's the matter."

"Skin it to me," I says, "I'm a listening."

"Well, you see, we didn't find the men, and ain't ever going to; so Jim hangs, for dead sure, now, if he stays here—ain't it so? And so it's splendid that he's going to be sold South, and I'm glad you run across the Duke and the King. It's the best thing that ever happened, becuz—"

"Shucks," I says, "is it any more splendider now than it was two minutes ago? You was 'most sick about it, then. How is it such good luck?"

"Becuz he ain't agoing to *be* sold South."

It sounded so good I come near jumping up and cracking my heels; but I held in, becuz I don't like disapp'intments, and says—

"How you going to prevent it?"

"Easy. We're just fools for not thinking of it sooner. We'll go down the river with them on the same boat, and when we get to Cairo we're in a free State, and we'll say, now then, the most you can get for Jim down South is a thousand dollars—you can get that right *here* for him!"

So then I *did* jump up and crack my heels, and says—

"It's splendid, Tom. I'm in for half of the money."

"No you ain't."

"Yes I am."

"No you ain't. If it hadn't been for the conspiracy Jim wouldn't been at that place, and wouldn't be in no trouble now. It's my fault, and I foot the bill."

"It ain't fair," I says. "How did I come to hog half of the robber's money and get so rotten flush? Was it my smartness? No, it was yourn. By rights you ought to took it all, and you wouldn't."

And I stuck to him till he give in.

"Now then," I says, "we ain't such fools as you think, for not thinking about this sooner. We couldn't buy Jim *here,* becuz he's free and there ain't anybody to buy him of. We couldn't buy him of anybody *but* the King and the Duke, and can't buy him of *them* till he's on free ground where we can run him up the Ohio and into Canada and over to England—so we've thought of it plenty soon enough, and ain't fools, nuther."

"All right, then, we ain't fools, but ain't it lucky that we went down the river when there warn't the least sense in it, and yet it was the very thing that met us up with the King and the Duke, and we can see, now, Jim would be hung, sure, if it hadn't happened. Huck—something else in it, ain't there?"

He said it pretty solemn. So I knowed he had treed the hand of Providence again, and said so.

"I reckon you'll learn to trust, before long," he says.

I started to say "I wisht *I* could get the credit for everything another person does," but pulled it in and crowded it down and didn't say nothing. It's the best way. After he had studied a while he says—

"We got to neglect the conspiracy, Huck, our hands is too full to run it right."

I was graveled, and was agoing to say "Long's we ain't running it anyway—'least don't get none of the credit of it—it ain't worth the trouble it is to us," but pulled it in and crowded it down like I done before. Best way, I reckon.

After supper we went to the jail and took Jim a pie and one thing and another and told him how we was going to buy him at Cairo and run him to England, and by Jackson he busted out and cried; and the pie went down the wrong way and we had to beat him and bang him or he would a choked to death and might as well a been hung.

Jim was all right, now, and joyful, and his mournfulness all went away, and took his banjo, and 'stead of singing "Ain't got long to stay here," the way he done since he got into jail, he sung "Jinny git de hoecake done," and the gayest songs he knowed; and laughed and laughed about the King and the Duke and the Burning Shame till he 'most died; it was good to see him; and then danced a nigger breakdown, and said he hadn't been so young in his heart since he was a boy.

And he was willing for his wife and children to come and see him now, if their marsters would let them—and the sheriff; he couldn't bear the idea of it before. So we said we would try for it, and hoped we'd have them there in the morning so he could see them and say good-bye before the King and the Duke come up on the boat.

That night we packed our things, and in the morning I went to Judge Thatcher and drawed eight hundred dollars, and he *was* surprised, but he didn't get no information out of me; and Tom drawed the same, and then we went to 'range about Jim's wife and children, and their marsters was very good and kind, but couldn't spare them now, but would let them come before long—maybe next week—was there any hurry? Of course we had to say no, that would answer very well.

Then we went to the jail and Jim was dreadful sorry, but knowed it couldn't be helped and he had to get along the way things was; but he didn't take on, becuz niggers is used to that.

We chattered along pretty comfortable till we heard the boat coming, but after that we was too excited to talk, but only fidgeted up and down; and every time the bolts and chains on the jail door rattled I catched my breath and says to myself, that's them a-coming! But it wasn't.

They didn't come at all. We was disappointed, and so was Jim, but it warn't any matter, they was prob'ly in the calaboose for getting drunk and raising a row, and would turn up to-morrow. So then we hid the money and went a-fishing.

Next day Jim's trial was set for three weeks ahead.

No Duke and no King, yet.

So we allowed we would wait one more day, and then if they didn't come we would go down to Sent Louis and go to the calaboose and find out how long they was in for.

Well, they didn't come; so we went down. And by George they warn't in the calaboose, and *hadn't* been!

It was perfectly awful. Tom was that sick he had to set down on something—he couldn't stand.

What to do we didn't know; becuz the calaboose was the only address them bilks ever had.

Then we went and tried the jail. No use—they hadn't been there, either.

It was getting to look right down scary; I knowed it, and Tom knowed it. But we'd got to keep moving, we couldn't rest. It was a powerful big town—some said it had sixty thousand people in it, prob'ly a lie; but we searched it high and low for four days just the same, particularly the worst parts, like what they call Hell's Half-Acre. But we couldn't run across them; they was gone—clean gone, just the same as if they had been blowed out, like a candle.

We got downer and downer in the mouth, we couldn't make it out nohow. Something had gone and happened to them, of course, but there warn't no guessing what, only we knowed it was serious. And could be mighty serious for Jim, too, if it went on so. I reckoned they was dead, but I didn't say so, it wouldn't help Tom feel any better.

We had to give it up, and we went back home. And not talking much; there warn't anything to talk about, but plenty to think. And mainly what to say to Jim, and how to let on to be hopeful.

Well, we went to the jail every day, and pretended we warn't uneasy, and let on to be pretty gay, and done it the best we could, but it was pretty poor and wouldn't fooled anybody but old Jim, which believed in us. We kept it up more than two weeks, and it was the hardest work we ever had and the sorrowfulest. And always we said it was going to come out all right, but towards the last we couldn't say it hearty and strong, and that made Jim suspicion something, and he turned in and went to bracing *us* up and trying to make us cheerful, and it 'most broke us down, and was the hardest of all for us to bear, becuz it showed he had as good as found out we hadn't any real hope, and so he was forgetting to be troubled about himself he was so sorry for us.

But there was one part of the day that we warn't ever in the jail. It was when the boat come. We was always there, and seen everybody that come ashore. And every now and then, along at first, as the boat sidled in I would think I saw them bilks in the jam on the foc'sle and nudge Tom and say "There they are!" but it was a mistake; and so towards the last we only went becuz we couldn't help it, and looked at the passengers without any intrust, and turned around and went away without saying anything when they had all come ashore. It seemed kind of strange: last month I would a broke my neck getting away from the King and the Duke, but now I would druther see them than the angels.

Tom was pale, and hadn't any appetite for his vittles, and didn't sleep good, and hadn't any spirits and wouldn't talk, and his aunt Polly was worried out of her life about him, and believed the Sons of Freedom and their bills and their horn had scared Tom into a sickness; and every day she loaded him up with any kind of medicine she could get aholt of; and she watched him through the keyhole, and 'stead of giving it to the cat he took it himself, and that just scared her crazy; and she said if she could get her hands on the Son of Freedom that scattered them bills around she believed to gracious she would break his leg if it was the last act.

Me and Tom had to be witnesses, and Jim's lawyer was a young man and new to the village, and hadn't any business, becuz of course the others didn't want the job for a free nigger, though we offered to pay them high. They hated to go back on Tom, but they was plenty right enough, they had to get their living and the prejudices was pretty strong, which was natural. Tom reconnized that; he wouldn't be lawyer for a free nigger himself, unless it was Jim.

Chapter 10

THE MORNING of the trial Tom's aunt Polly stopped him and warn't going to let him go; she said it warn't any place for boys, and besides, they wouldn't be allowed—everybody was going and there wouldn't be room; but Tom says—

"There'll be room for me and Huck. We're going to be witnesses."

She was that astonished you could a knocked her down with a brickbat; and shoved her spectacles up on her forehead and says—

"*You* two! What do *you* know about it, I'd like to know!"

But we didn't stop to talk, but cleared out and left her finishing fixing up; becuz she was coming, of course—everybody was.

The court-house was jammed. Plenty of ladies, too—seven or eight benches of them; and aunt Polly and the Widow Douglas and Miss Watson and Mrs. Lawson, they all set together, and the Thatchers and a lot more back of them—all of the quality. And Jim was there, and the sheriff.

Then the judge come in and set down very solemn, and opened court; and Mr. Lawson made a speech and said he was going to prove Jim done it by two witnesses, and he had a *motive*, and would prove that, too. I knowed it didn't make Tom feel good to hear him say that.

Jim's young lawyer made a speech and said he was going to prove an *allyby*—prove it by two witnesses; and that it warn't done by Jim but by a stranger unknown. It made everybody smile; and I was sorry for that young man, becuz he was nervous and scared, and knowed he hadn't any case, and so couldn't talk out bold and strong like Mr. Lawson done. And he knowed everybody was making fun of him, too, and didn't think much of him for being a free nigger's lawyer and a nobody to boot.

Flacker he went on the stand and give his idea of how it all happened; and mapped it out and worked his clews, and everybody held their breath and was full of wonderment to hear him make it so plain and clear, and nothing in the world to do it with but just his intellects.

Then Cap. Haines and Buck Fisher told how they catched Jim as good as in the very act; and how poor old Bat was laying there dead, and Jim just getting up, having caved his head in with the musket and slipped and fell on him.

And then the musket was showed, with rust and hair on the barrel, and the people shuddered; and when they held up the bloody clothes they shuddered some more.

Then I told all I knowed and got back out of the way; and hadn't done no good, becuz there wasn't anybody there believed any of it, and the most of them *looked* it.

Then they called Tom Sawyer, and people around me mumbled and said, " 'Course—couldn't happen 'thout *him* being in it; couldn't do an eclipse successful if Tom Sawyer was took sick and couldn't superintend." And his aunt Polly and the women perked up and got ready to wonder what kind of 'sistance he was going to contribbit and who was going to get the benefit of it.

"Thomas Sawyer, where was you on the Saturday night before the Sunday that this deed was done?"

"Running a conspiracy."

"Doing what?" says the judge, looking down at him over his pulpit.

"Running a conspiracy, your honor."

"This sounds like a dangerous candor. Tell your story; and be careful and not reveal things that can hurt you."

So Tom went on and told the whole thing, how we got up the conspiracy and run it for all it was worth; and Colonel Elder and Captain Sam set there looking ashamed and pretty mad, for 'most everybody was laughing; and when he showed that it was us that was the Sons of Freedom and got up the scare-bills and stuck them on the doors, and not Burrell, which Flacker said it was, they laughed again, and it was Flacker's turn to look sick, and he done it.

So he went on telling it, straight out and square, and no lies, all the way down to where Jim come down out of the tree after he blowed the signal-horn and we all went into the town and sampled the excitement—and you could see the people was believing it all, becuz it sounded honest and didn't have a made-up look; and so the *alliby* was getting to look right down favorable, and people was nodding their heads at one another as much as to say so, and looking more friendlier at Jim, too, and Mr. Lawson warn't looking so comfortable as he was before; but at last come the question—

"You say the prisoner was to go and report to your aunt, and then follow you. What time was that?"

And by Jackson Tom couldn't tell him. We hadn't noticed. Tom had to guess; it was all he could do, and guessing warn't worth much. It was mighty bad—and it showed in people's faces. Mr. Lawson was looking comfortable again.

"Why were you three going to Bradish's house?"

Then Tom told them *that* part of the conspiracy; how he was going to play runaway nigger and I was going to play him onto Bradish, but Bradish had already got one—and so on; and how Tom examined the nigger in the night and see that he warn't a nigger at all, and had a key in his shoe, and he judged he was going to escape, and he wanted to be there and get the clews and hunt him down after he got away. And the people and the judge listened right along, and it was just as good as a tale out of a book.

And he told how me and him got there at daylight and see Bat laying dead, and he told me to go for the undertaker, and then found Jim's track and called me back and said it was all right, Jim had been there and of course *he* was gone to tell about the murder.

A lot of them smiled at that, and Mr. Lawson laughed right out.

But Tom went right along, and told how we followed the tracks to the hanted house and he crope in under there and listened and heard the murderers talk, but didn't see them.

"Didn't see them?"

"No, sir;" and he told why.

"Imaginary ones, maybe," says Mr. Lawson, and laughed; and a lot of the others laughed, too, and a fellow close to me says to a friend, "he better stopped when he was well off—he's got to embroiderin', now." "Yes," says the other one, "he's spiling it."

"Go on," says the judge; "tell what you heard."

"It was like this. One was a thrashing around a little now and then and growling, and the other one was groaning; and by and by the one that thrashed around says in a low voice, 'Shut up, you old cry-baby, and let a person get some sleep.' Then the groaner says, 'If your leg was hurt as bad as mine, you'd be a cry-baby too, I reckon, and it's all your fault, anyway; when Bradish come and catched us escaping, if you had a helped me 'stead of trying to prevent me, I would a busted his head right there in the lean-to, 'stead of outside, and he wouldn't a had a chance to yell and fetch them men a-running, and we wouldn't a had to take a short cut and hurt my leg and have to lay up here and p'raps get catched before the day's over—and yet here you are a-growling about cry-babies, and it shows you hain't got no real heart, and no Christian sentiments and bringing up.' Then the other one says, 'The whole blame's your own, for coming three or four hours late—drunk, as usual.' 'I warn't drunk, neither; I got lost—ain't no crime in that, I don't reckon.' 'All right,' says the other one, 'have it your own way, but shut up and keep still now; you want to be thinking up your last dying speech, becuz you're going to need it on the gallows for this piece of work, which was just unnecessary blame foolishness, and I'll be hung too, and serve me right, for being in such dam company.' The other one wanted to growl some more about his leg, but this one said if he didn't shut up he would pull it out and belt him over the head with it. So then they quieted down and I come away."

When Tom got done it was dead still, just the way it always is when people has been listening to a yarn they don't take no stock in and are sorry for the person that has told it. It was kind of miserable, that stillness. At last the judge he cleared his throat and says, very grave—

"If this is true, how is it you didn't come straight and tell the sheriff? How do you explain that?"

Tom was working at a button with his fingers and looking down at the floor. It was too many for him, that question, and I knowed it. How was he going to tell them he didn't do it becuz he was going to work the thing out on detective principles and git glory out of it? And how was he going to tell them he wanted to make the glory bigger by making it seem Jim killed the man, and even crowded him into a *motive,* and then went and told about the motive where Mr. Lawson could get on it—and so just by reason of him and his foolishness the murderers got away and now Jim was going to be hung for what they done. No, sir, he couldn't say a word. And so when the judge waited a while, everybody's eyes on Tom a fooling with his button, and then asked him again why he didn't go and tell the sheriff, he swallowed two or three times, and the tears come in his eyes, and he says, very low—

"I don't know, sir."

It was still again, for a minute, then the lawyers made their speeches, and Mr. Lawson was terrible sarcastic on Tom and his fairy tale, as he called it, and so then the jury fetched Jim in guilty in the first degree in two minutes, and old Jim stood up and the judge begun to make his speech telling him why he'd got to die; and Tom he set there with his head down, crying.

And just then, by George, the Duke and the King come a-working along through the crowd, and worked along up front, and the King says—

"Pardon a moment, your honor," and Tom glanced up; and the Duke says—

"We've got a little matter of business which—"

Tom jumps up and shouts—

"I reconnize the voices—it's the murderers!"

Well, you never see such a stir. Everybody rose up and begun to stretch their necks to get a view, and the sheriff he stormed at them and made them set down; and the King and the Duke looked perfectly astonished, and turned pretty white, I tell you; and the judge says—

"Why do you make such a charge as this?"

"Becuz I know it, your honor," Tom says.

"How do you know it—you said, yourself, you didn't see the men?"

"It ain't any difference, I've got the proofs."

"Where?"

He fetched out the leaf from Bat's book and showed the drawing, and says—

"If this one hasn't changed his shoes, this is the print of the left one."

And it *was*, sure enough, and the King looked very sick.

"Very good indeed," says the judge. "Proceed."

Tom fetched a set of false teeth out of his pocket, and says—

"If they don't fit the other one's mouth he ain't the white nigger that was in the lean-to."

Schoolhouse Hill

Chapter 1

I T W A S not much short of fifty years ago—and a frosty morning. Up the naked long slant of Schoolhouse Hill the boys and girls of Petersburg village were struggling from various directions against the fierce wind, and making slow and difficult progress. The wind was not the only hindrance, nor the worst; the slope was steel-clad in frozen snow, and the foothold offered was far from trustworthy. Every now and then a boy who had almost gained the schoolhouse stepped out with too much confidence, thinking himself safe, lost his footing, struck upon his back and went skimming down the hill behind his freed sled, the straggling schoolmates scrambling out of his way and applauding as he sailed by; and in a few seconds he was at the bottom with all his work to do over again. But this was fun; fun for the boy, fun for the witnesses, fun all around; for boys and girls are ignorant and do not know trouble when they see it.

Sid Sawyer, the good boy, the model boy, the cautious boy, did not lose his footing. He brought no sled, he chose his steps with care, and he arrived in safety. Tom Sawyer brought his sled and he, also, arrived without adventure, for Huck Finn was along to help, although he was not a member of the school in these days; he merely came in order to be with Tom until school "took in." Henry

Bascom arrived safely, too—Henry Bascom the new boy of last year, whose papa was a "nigger" trader and rich; a mean boy, he was, and proud of his clothes, and he had a play-slaughterhouse at home, with all the equipment, in little, of a regular slaughterhouse, and in it he slaughtered puppies and kittens exactly as beeves were done to death down at the "Point;" and he was this year's school-bully, and was dreaded and flattered by the timid and the weak and disliked by everybody. He arrived safely because his slave-boy Jake helped him up the hill and drew his sled for him; and it wasn't a home-made sled but a "store" sled, and was painted, and had iron-tyred runners, and came from St. Louis, and was the only store-sled in the village.

All the twenty-five or thirty boys and girls arrived at last, red and panting, and still cold, notwithstanding their yarn comforters and mufflers and mittens; and the girls flocked into the little school-house and the boys packed themselves together in the shelter of its lee.

It was noticed now that a new boy was present, and this was a matter of extraordinary interest, for a new boy in the village was a rarer sight than a new comet in the sky. He was apparently about fifteen; his clothes were neat and tasty above the common, he had a good and winning face, and he was surpassingly handsome—handsome beyond imagination! His eyes were deep and rich and beautiful, and there was a modesty and dignity and grace and graciousness and charm about him which some of the boys, with a pleased surprise, recognised at once as familiar—they had encountered it in books about fairy-tale princes and that sort. They stared at him with a trying backwoods frankness, but he was tranquil and did not seem troubled by it. After looking him over, Henry Bascom pushed forward in front of the others and began in an insolent tone to question him:

"Who are you? What's your name?"

The boy slowly shook his head, as if meaning by that that he did not understand.

"Do you hear? Answer up!"

Another slow shake.

"Answer up, I tell you, or I'll make you!"

Tom Sawyer said—

"That's no way, Henry Bascom—it's against the rules. If you want your fuss, and can't wait till recess, which is regular, go at it right and fair; put a chip on your shoulder and dare him to knock it off."

"All right; he's got to fight, and fight now, whether he answers or not; and I'm not particular about how it's got at." He put a flake of ice on his shoulder and said, "There—knock it off if you dare!"

The boy looked inquiringly from face to face, and Tom stepped up and answered by signs. He touched the boy's right hand, then flipped off the ice with his own, put it back in its place, and indicated that that was what the boy must do. The lad smiled, put out his hand, and touched the ice with his finger. Bascom launched a blow at his face which seemed to miss; the energy of it made Bascom slip on the ice, and he departed on his back for the bottom of the hill, with cordial laughter and mock applause from the boys to cheer his way.

The bell began to ring, and the little crowd swarmed into the schoolhouse and hurried to their places. The stranger found a seat apart, and was at once a target for the wondering eyes and eager whisperings of the girls. School now "began." Archibald Ferguson, the old Scotch schoolmaster, rapped upon his desk with his ruler, rose upon his dais and stood, with his hands together, and said "Let us pray." After the prayer there was a hymn, then the buzz of study began, and the multiplication class was called up. It recited, up to "twelve times twelve;" then the arithmetic class followed and exposed its slates to much censure and little commendation; next came the grammar class of parsing parrots, who knew everything about grammar except how to utilize its rules in common speech.

"Spelling class!" The schoolmaster's wandering eye now fell upon the new boy, and he countermanded that order. "Hm—a stranger? Who is it? What is your name, my boy?"

The lad rose and bowed, and said—

"Pardon, monsieur—je ne comprends pas."

Ferguson looked astonished and pleased, and said, in French—

"Ah, French—how pleasant! It is the first time I have heard that tongue in many years. I am the only person in this village who speaks it. You are very welcome; I shall be glad to renew my practice. You speak no English?"

"Not a word, sir."

"You must try to learn it."

"Gladly, sir."

"It is your purpose to attend my school regularly?"

"If I may have the privilege, sir."

"That is well. Take English only, for the present. The grammar has about thirty rules. It will be necessary to learn them by heart."

"I already know them, sir, but I do not know what the words mean."

"What is it you say? You know the rules of the grammar, and yet don't know English? How can that be? When did you learn them?"

"I heard your grammar class recite the rules before entering upon the rest of their lesson."

The teacher looked over his glasses at the boy a while, in a puzzled way, then said—

"If you know no English words, how did you know it was a grammar lesson?"

"From similarities to the French—like the word grammar itself."

"True! You have a headpiece! You will soon get the rules by heart."

"I know them by heart, sir."

"Impossible! You are speaking extravagantly; you do not know what you are saying."

The boy bowed respectfully, resumed his upright position, and said nothing. The teacher felt rebuked, and said gently—

"I should not have spoken so, and am sorry. Overlook it, my boy; recite me a rule of grammar—as well as you can—never mind the mistakes."

The boy began with the first rule and went along with his task quite simply and comfortably, dropping rule after rule unmutilated from his lips, while the teacher and the school sat with parted lips and suspended breath, listening in mute wonder. At the finish the boy bowed again, and stood, waiting. Ferguson sat silent a moment or two in his great chair, then said—

"On your honor—those rules were wholly unknown to you when you came into this house?"

"Yes, sir."

"Upon my word I believe you, on the veracity that is written in your face. No—I don't—I can't. It is beyond the reach of belief. A memory like that—an ear for pronunciation like that, is of course im— why, *no* one in the earth has such a memory as that!"

The boy bowed, and said nothing. Again the old Scot felt rebuked, and said—

"Of course I don't mean—I don't really mean—er—tell me: if you could *prove* in some way that you have never until now—for instance, if you could repeat other things which you have heard here. Will you try?"

With engaging simplicity and serenity, and with apparently no intention of being funny, the boy began on the arithmetic lesson, and faithfully put into his report everything the teacher had said and everything the pupils had said, and imitated the voices and style of all concerned—as follows:

"Well, I give you my word it's enough to drive a man back to the land of his fathers, and make him hide his head in the charitable heather and never more give out that *he* can teach the race! Five slates—five of the chiefest intelligences in the school—and look at them! Scots wha hae wi' Wallace bled—Harry Slater! *Yes, sir.* Since when, is it, that 17, and 45, and 68 and 21 make 155, ye unspeakable creature? *I—I—if you please, sir, Sally Fitch hunched me and I reckon it made me make a figure 9 when I was intending to make a—* There's not a 9 in the sum, you blockhead!—and ye'll get a black mark for the lie you've told; a foolish lie, ill wrought and clumsy in the invention; you have no talent—stick to the truth. Becky Thatcher! *Yes, sir, please.* Make the curtsy over again, and do it better. *Yes, sir.* Lower, still! *Yes, sir.* Very good. Now I'll just ask you how you make out that 58 from 156 leaves 43? *If you please, sir, I subtracted the 8 from the 6, which leaves—which leaves—I* THINK *it leaves 3—and then—* Peace! ye banks and braes o' bonny Doon but it's a rare answer and a credit to my patient teaching! Jack Stillson! *Yes, sir.* Straighten up, and don't d-r-a-w-l like that—it's a fatigue to hear ye! And what *have* you been setting down here: If a horse travel 96 feet in 4 seconds and two-tenths of a second, how much will a barrel of mackerel cost when potatoes are 22 cents a bushel? Answer—eleven dollars and forty-six cents. You incurable ass, don't you see that ye've mixed three questions into one? The gauds and vanities o' learning! Oh, here's a hand, my trusty fere, and gie's a hand o' thine, and we'll—out of my sight, ye maundering idiot!—"

The show was become unendurable. The boy had forgotten not a word, nor a tone, nor a look, nor a gesture, nor any shade or trifle of detail—he was letter-perfect, and the house could shut its eyes anywhere in the performance and know which individual was being imitated. The boy's deep gravity and sincerity made the exhibition more and more trying the longer he went on. For a time, in decorous, disciplined and heroic silence, house and teacher sat bursting to laugh, with the tears running down, the regulations requiring noiseless propriety and solemnity; but when the stranger recited the answer to the triple sum and then put his hands together and raised his despairing eyes toward heaven in exact imitation of Mr. Ferguson's manner, the teacher's face broke up; and with that concession the house let go with a crash and laughed its fill thenceforth. But the boy went tranquilly on and on, unheeding the screams and throes and explosions, clear to the finish; then made his bow and straightened up and stood, bland and waiting.

It took some time to quiet the school; then Mr. Ferguson said—

"It is the most extraordinary thing I have seen in my life. In this world there is not another talent like yours, lad; be grateful for it, and for the noble modesty with which you bear about such a treasure. How long would you be able to keep in your memory the things which you have been uttering?"

"I cannot forget anything that I see or hear, sir."

"At all?"

"No, sir."

"It seems incredible—just impossible. Let me experiment a little

—for the pure joy of it. Take my English-French dictionary and sit down and study it while I go on with the school's exercises. Shall you be disturbed by us?"

"No, sir."

He took the dictionary and began to skim the pages swiftly, one after another. Evidently he dwelt upon no page, but merely gave it a lick from top to bottom with his eye and turned it over. The school-work rambled on after a fashion, but it consisted of blunders, mainly, for the fascinated eyes and minds of school and teacher were oftener on the young stranger than elsewhere. At the end of twenty minutes the boy laid the book down. Mr. Ferguson noticed this, and said, with a touch of disappointment in his tone—

"I am sorry. I saw that it did not interest you."

The boy rose and said—

"Oh, sir, on the contrary!" This in French; then in English, "I have now the words of your language, but the forms not—perhaps, how you call?—the pronunciation also."

"You have the words? How many of the words do you know?"

"All, sir."

"No—no—there are 645 octavo pages—you couldn't have examined a tenth of them in this short time. A page in two seconds?—it is impossible."

The boy bowed respectfully, and said nothing.

"There—I am in fault again. I shall learn of you—courtesy. Give me the book. Begin. Recite—recite!"

It was another miracle. The boy poured out, in a rushing stream, the words, the definitions, the accompanying illustrative phrases and sentences, the signs indicating the parts of speech—everything; he skipped nothing, he put in all the details, and he even got the pronunciations substantially right, since it was a pronouncing-dictionary. Teacher and school sat in a soundless and motionless spell of awe and admiration, unconscious of the flight of time, unconscious of everything but the beautiful stranger and his stupendous performance. After a long while the juggler interrupted his recitation to say—in rather cumbrous and booky English—

"It is of necessity—what you call 'of course,' n'est-ce pas?—that I now am enabled to apply the machinery of the rules of the grammar, since the meanings of the words which constitute them were become my possession—" Here he stopped, quoted the violated rule, corrected his sentence, then went on: "And it is of course that I now understand the languages—language—appropriated to the lesson of arithmetic—yet not all, the dictionary being in the offensive. As for example, to-wit, 'Scots wha hae wi' Wallace bled, Sally Fitch *hunched* me, ye banks and braes o' bonny Doon, oh here's a hand my trusty fere and gie's a hand o' thine.' Some of these words are by mischance omitted from the dictionary, and thereby results confusion. Without knowledge of the signification of *hunched* one is ignorant of the nature of the explanation preferred by the mademoiselle Thatcher; and if one shall not know what a Doon is, and whether it is a financial bank or other that is involved, one is still yet again at a loss."

Silence. The master roused himself as if from a dream, and lifted his hands and said—

"It is not a parrot—it *thinks!* Boy, ye are a marvel! With listening an hour and studying half as long, you have learned the English language. You are the only person in America that knows all its words. Let it rest, where it is—the construction will come of itself. Take up the Latin, now, and the Greek, and short-hand writing, and the mathematics. Here are the books. You shall have thirty minutes to each. Then your education will be complete. But tell me! How do you manage these things? What is your method? You do not read the page, you only skim it down with your eye, as one wipes a column of sums from a slate. You understand my English?"

"Yes, master—perfectly. I have no method—meaning I have no mystery. I see what is on the page—that is all."

"But you see it at a glance."

"But is not the particulars of the page—" He stopped to apply the rule and correct the sentence: "are not the particulars of the page the same as the particulars of the school? I see all the pupils at once; do I not know, then, how each is dressed, and his attitude and expression, and the color of his eyes and hair, and the length of his nose, and if his shoes are tied or not? Why shall I glance twice?"

Margaret Stover, over in the corner, drew her untied shoe back out of sight.

"Ah, well, I have seen no one else who could individualize a thousand details with one sweep of the two eyes. Maybe the eyes of the admirable creature the dragon-fly can do it, but that is another matter—he has twelve thousand, and so the haul he makes with his multitudinous glance is a thing within reason and comprehension. Get at your Latin, lad." Then with a sigh, "We will proceed with our poor dull ploddings."

The boy took up the book and began to turn the pages, much as if he were carefully counting them. The school glanced with an evil joy at Henry Bascom, and was pleased to note that he was not happy. He was the only Latin pupil in the school, and his pride in this distinction was a thing through which his mates were made to endure much suffering.

The school droned and buzzed along, with the bulk of its mind and its interest not on its work but fixed in envy and discouragement upon the new scholar. At the end of half an hour it saw him lay down his Latin book and take up the Greek; it glanced contentedly at Henry Bascom, and a satisfied murmur dribbled down the benches. In turn the Greek and the mathematics were mastered, then "The New Short-Hand Method, called Phonography" was taken up. But the phonographic study was short-lived—it lasted but a minute and twenty seconds; then the boy played with several other books. The master noticed this, and by and by said—

"So soon done with the Phonography?"

"It is only a set of compact and simple *principles*, sir. They are applicable with ease and certainty—like the principles of the mathematics. Also, the examples assist; innumerable combinations of English words are given, and the vowels eliminated. It is admirable, this system, for precision and clarity; one could write Greek and Latin with it, making word-combinations with the vowels excised, and still be understood."

"Your English is improving by leaps and bounds, my boy."

"Yes, sir. I have been reading these English books. They have furnished me the forms of the language—the moulds in which it is cast—the idioms."

"I am past wondering! I think there is no miracle that a mind like this cannot do. Pray go to the blackboard and let me see what Greek may look like in phonographic word-combinations with the vowel-signs left out. I will read some passages."

The boy took the chalk, and the trial began. The master read very slowly; then a little faster; then faster still; then as fast as he could. The boy kept up, without apparent difficulty. Then the master threw in Latin sentences, English sentences, French ones, and now and then a hardy problem from Euclid to be ciphered out. The boy was competent, all the while.

"It is amazing, my child, amazing—stupefying! Do me one more miracle, and I strike my flag. Here is a page of columns of figures. Add them up. I have seen the famous lightning-calculator do it in three minutes and a quarter, and I know the answer. I will hold the watch. Beat him!"

The boy glanced at the page, made his bow and said,—

"The total is 4,865,493 if the blurred twenty-third figure in the fifth column is a 9; if it is a 7, the total is less by 2."

"Right, and he is beaten by incredible odds; but you hadn't time to even see the blurred figure, let alone note its place. Wait till I find it—the twenty-third, did you say? Here it is, but I can't tell which it is—it may be a 9, it may be a 7. But no matter, one of your answers is right, according to which name we give the figure. Dear me, can my watch be right? It is long past the noon recess, and everybody has forgotten his dinner. In my thirty years of school-teaching experience this has not happened before. Truly it is a day of miracles. Children, we dull moles are in no condition to further plod and grub after the excitements and bewilderments of this intellectual conflagration—school is dismissed. My wonderful scholar, tell me your name."

The school crowded forward in a body to devour the stranger at close quarters with their envying eyes; all except Bascom, who remained apart and sulked.

"Quarante-quatre, sir. Forty-four."

"Why—why—that is only a number, you know, not a name."

The boy bowed. The master dropped the subject.

"When did you arrive in our town?"

"Last night, sir."

"Have you friends or relatives among us?"

"No, sir—none. Mr. Hotchkiss allows me to lodge in his house."

"You will find the Hotchkisses good people, excellent people. Had you introductions to them?"

"No, sir."

"You see I am curious; but we are all that, in this monotonous little place, and we mean no harm. How did you make them understand what you wanted?"

"Through my signs and their compassion. It was cold, and I was a stranger."

"Good—good—and well stated, without waste of words. It describes the Hotchkisses; it's a whole biography. Whence did you come—and how?"

Forty-four bowed. The master said, affably—

"It was another indiscretion—you will not remember it against —no, I mean you will forget it, in consid— what I am trying to say is, that you will overlook it—that is it, overlook it. I am glad you are come, grateful that you are come."

"I thank you—thank you deeply, sir."

"My official character requires that I precede you in leaving this house, therefore I do it. This is an apology. Adieu."

"Adieu, my master."

The school made way, and the old gentleman marched out between the ranks with a grave dignity proper to his official state.

Chapter 2

THE GIRLS went vivaciously chattering away, eager to get home and tell of the wonders they had seen; but outside of the schoolhouse the boys grouped themselves together and waited; silent, expectant, and nervous. They paid but little attention to the bitter weather, they were apparently under the spell of a more absorbing interest. Henry Bascom stood apart from the others, in the neigh-

borhood of the door. The new boy had not come out, yet. Tom
Sawyer had halted him to give him a warning.

"Look out for him—he'll be waiting. The bully, I mean—Hen
Bascom. He's treacherous and low down."

"Waiting?"

"Yes—for you."

"What for?"

"To lick you—whip you."

"On what account?"

"Why, he's the bully this year, and you're a fresh."

"Is that a reason?"

"Plenty—yes. He's got to take your measure, and do it to-day—
he knows that."

"It's a custom, then?"

"Yes. He's got to fight you, whether he wants to or not. But he
wants to. You've knocked his Latin layout galley-west."

"Galley west? Je ne—"

"It's just a word, you know. Means you've knocked his props
from under him."

"Knocked his props from under him?"

"Yes—trumped his ace."

"Trumped his—"

"Ace. That's it—pulled his leg."

"I assure you this is an error. I have not pulled his leg."

"But you don't understand. Don't you see? You've graveled him,
and he's disgruntled."

The new boy's face expressed his despair. Tom reflected a moment, then his eye lighted with hope, and he said, with confidence—

"Now you'll get the idea. You see, he held the age on Latin—just
a lone hand, don't you know, and it made him Grand Turk and
Whoopjamboreehoo of the whole school, and he went in procession
all by himself, like Parker's hog. Well, you've walked up to the
captain's office with *your* Latin, now, and pulled in high, low, jack
and the game, and it's taken the curl out of his tail. There—that's
the idea."

The new boy hesitated, passed his hand over his forehead, and began, haltingly—

"It is still a little vague. It was but a poor dictionary—that French-English—and over-rich in omissions. Do you perhaps mean that he is jealous?"

"Score *one!* That's it. Jealous—the very word. Now then, there'll be a ring, and you'll fight. Can you box? do you know the trick of it?"

"No."

"I'll show you. You'll learn in two minutes and less; it don't *begin* with grammar for difficulties. Put up your fists—so. Now then, hit me . . . . . You notice how I turned that off with my left? Again . . . . . . See?—turned it with my right. Dance around; caper—like this. Now I'm coming for you—look sharp . . . . . . That's the ticket—I didn't arrive. Once more . . . . . . Good! You're all right. Come on. It's a cold day for Henry."

They stepped outside, now. As they walked past Bascom he suddenly thrust out his foot, to trip Forty-four. But the foot was no obstruction, it did not interrupt Forty-four's stride. Necessarily, then, Bascom was himself tripped. He fell heavily, and everybody laughed privately. He got up, all a-quiver with passion, and cried out—

"Off with your coat, Know-it-all—you're going to fight or eat dirt, one or t'other. Form a ring, fellows!"

He threw off his coat. The ring was formed.

"May I keep my coat on? Do the rules allow it?"

"Don't!" said Tom; "it's a disadvantage. Pull it off."

"Keep it on, you wax doll, if you want to," said Henry, "it won't do you any good either way. Time!"

Forty-four took position, with his fists up, and stood without moving, while the lithe and active Bascom danced about him, danced up toward him, feinted with his right, feinted with his left, danced away again, danced forward again—and so-on and so-on, Tom and others putting in frequent warnings for Forty-four: "Look out for him—look *o-u-t!*" At last Forty-four opened his guard for an instant, and in that instant Henry plunged, and let drive with all his force; but Forty-four stepped lightly aside, and Henry's impulse and a slip on the ice carried him to the ground. He got up lame but eager, and began his dance again; he presently lunged again, hit vacancy and got another fall. After that he respected the slippery ground, and lunged no more, and danced cautiously; he fought with energy, interest and smart judgment, and delivered a sparkling rain of blows, but none of them got home—some were dodged by a sideward tilt of the head, the others were neatly warded. He was getting winded with his violent exercise, but the other boy was still fresh, for he had done no dancing, he had struck no blows, and had had no exercise of consequence. Henry stopped to rest and pant, and Forty-four said—

"Let us not go on with it. What good can come of it?"

The boys murmured dissent; this was an election for Bully; they were personally interested, they had hopes, and their hopes were getting the color of certainties. Henry said—

"You'll stay where you are, Miss Nancy. You don't leave this ground till I know who wears the belt."

"Ah, but you already know—or ought to; therefore, where is the use of going on? You have not struck me, and I have no wish to strike you."

"Oh, you haven't, haven't you? How kind! Keep your benevolences to yourself till somebody asks you for them. Time!"

The new boy began to strike out, now; and every time he struck, Henry went down. Five times. There was great excitement among the boys. They recognised that they were going to lose a tyrant and perhaps get a protector in his place. In their happiness they lost their fears and began to shout—

"Give it him, Forty-four! Let him have it! Land him again! Another one! Give it him good!"

Henry was pluck. He went down time after time, but got patiently up and went at his work again, and did not give up until his strength was all gone. Then he said—

"The belt's yours—but I'll get even with you, yet, girly, you see if I don't." Then he looked around upon the crowd, and called eight of them by name, ending with Huck Finn, and said: "You're spotted, you see. *I* heard you. To-morrow I'll begin on you, and I'll lam the daylights out of you."

For the first time, a flash of temper showed in the new boy's eye. It was only a flash; it was gone in a moment; then he said, without passion—

"I will not allow that."

"*You* won't allow it! Who's asking you? Who cares what you allow and what you don't allow? To show you how much I care, I'll begin on them *now*."

"I cannot have it. You must not be foolish. I have spared you, till now; I have struck you only lightly. If you touch one of the boys, I will hit you *hard*."

But Henry's temper was beyond his control. He jumped at the nearest boy on his black-list, but he did not reach him; he went down under a sounding slap from the flat of the new boy's hand, and lay motionless where he fell.

"I saw it! I saw that!" This shout was from Henry's father, the nigger-trader—an unloved man, but respected for his muscle and his temper. He came running from his sleigh, with his whip in his hand and raised to strike. The boys fell back out of his way, and as he reached Forty-four he brought down the whip with an angry "*I'll* learn you!" Forty-four dodged deftly out of its course and seized the trader's wrist with his right hand. There was a sound of crackling bones and a groan, and the trader staggered away, saying—

"Name of God, my wrist is crushed!"

Henry's mamma arrived from the sleigh, now and broke into frenzies of lamentation over her collapsed son and her crippled husband, while the schoolboys looked on, dazed, and rather frightened at the woman's spectacular distress, but fascinated with the show and glad to be there and see it. It absorbed their attention so entirely that when Mrs. Bascom presently turned and demanded the extradition of Forty-four so that she might square accounts with him they found that he had disappeared without their having noticed it.

Chapter 3

Within an hour afterward people began to drop in at the Hotchkiss house; ostensibly to make a friendly call, really to get sight of the miraculous boy. The news they brought soon made the Hotchkisses proud of their prize and glad that they had caught him. Mr. Hotchkiss's pride and joy were frank and simple; every new marvel that any comer added to the list of his lodger's great deeds made him a prouder and happier man than he was before, he being a person substantially without jealousies and by nature addicted to admirations. Indeed he was a broad man in many ways; hospitable to new facts and always seeking them; to new ideas, and always examining them; to new opinions and always adopting them; a man ready to meet any novelty half way and give it a friendly trial. He changed his principles with the moon, his politics with the weather, and his religion with his shirt. He was recognized as being limitlessly good-hearted, quite fairly above the village average intellectually, a diligent and enthusiastic seeker after truth, and a sincere believer in his newest belief, but a man who had missed his vocation—he should have been a weather-vane. He was tall and handsome and courteous, with winning ways, and expressive eyes, and had a white head which looked twenty years older than the rest of him.

His good Presbyterian wife was as steady as an anvil. She was not a creature of change. When she gave shelter to an opinion she did not make a transient guest of it, but a permanency. She was fond and proud of her husband, and believed he would have been great if he had had a proper chance—if he had lived in a metropolis, instead of a village; if his merits had been exposed to the world instead of being hidden under a bushel. She was patient with his excursions after the truth. She expected him to be saved—thought she knew that that would happen, in fact. It could only be as a

Presbyterian, of course, but that would come—come of a certainty. All the signs indicated it. He had often been a Presbyterian; he was periodically a Presbyterian, and she had noticed with comfort that his period was almost astronomically regular. She could take the almanac and calculate its return with nearly as much confidence as other astronomers calculated an eclipse. His Mohammedan period, his Methodist period, his Buddhist period, his Baptist period, his Parsi period, his Roman Catholic period, his Atheistic period— these were all similarly regular, but she cared nothing for that. She knew there was a patient and compassionate Providence watching over him that would see to it that he died in his Presbyterian period. The latest thing in religions was the Fox-girl Rochester rappings; so he was a Spiritualist for the present.

Hannah Hotchkiss exulted in the wonders brought by the visitors, and the more they brought the happier she was in the possession of that boy; but she was very human in her make-up, and she felt a little aggravated over the fact that the news had to come from the outside; that these people should know these things about her lodger before she knew them herself; that she must sit and do the wondering and exclaiming when in all fairness she ought to be doing the telling and they the applauding; that they should be able to contribute all the marvels and she none. Finally the widow Dawson remarked upon the circumstance that all the information was being furnished from the one side; and added—

"Didn't he do anything out of the common here, sister * Hotchkiss—last night or this morning?"

Hannah was ashamed of her poverty. The only thing she was able to offer was colorless compared with the matters which she had been listening to.

"Well, no—I can't say that he did; unless you consider that we couldn't understand his language but *did* understand his signs about as easy as if they had been talk. We were astonished at it, and spoke of it afterwards."

Her young niece, Annie Fleming, spoke up and said—

---

* "Sister" in the Methodist, or Presbyterian, or Baptist, or Campbellite church— nothing more. A common form, in those days.

"Why, auntie, that wasn't all. The dog doesn't allow a stranger to come to the door at night, but he didn't bark at the boy; he acted as if he was ever so glad to see him. You said, yourself, that that never happened with a stranger before."

"It's true, as sure as I live; it had passed out of my mind, child."

She was happier, now. Then her husband made a contribution—

"I call to mind, now, that just as we stepped into his room to show him its arrangements I knocked my elbow against the wardrobe and the candle fell and went out, and—"

"Certainly!" exclaimed Hannah, "and the next moment he had struck a match and was lighting—"

"Not the stub I had dropped," cried Hotchkiss, "but a whole candle! Now the marvel is that there was only one whole candle in the room—"

"And it was clear on the *other side* of the room," interrupted Hannah, "and moreover only just the end of it was showing, where it lay on the top of the bookcase, and he had noticed it with that lightning eye of his—"

"Of course, of course!" exclaimed the company, with admiration.

"—and gone right to it in the dark without disturbing a chair. Why, sister Dawson, a *cat* couldn't have done it any quicker or better or surer! Just think of it!"

A chorus of rewarding astonishment broke out which made Hannah's whole constitution throb with pleasure; and when sister Dawson laid her hand impressively upon Hannah's hand, and then walled her eyes toward the ceiling, as much as to say, "it's beyond words, beyond words!" the pleasure rose to ecstasy.

"Wait!" said Mr. Hotchkiss, breaking out with the kind of laugh which in the back settlements gives notice that something humorous is coming, "I can tell you a wonder that beats that to pieces— beats anything and everything that has been told about him up to date. He paid four weeks' board in advance—cash down! Petersburg can believe the rest, but you'll never catch it taking *that* statement at par."

The joke had immense success; the laugh was hearty all around. Then Hotchkiss issued another notifying laugh, and added—

"And there's another wonder on top of that; I tell you a little at a time, so as not to overstrain you. He didn't pay in wildcat at twenty-five discount, but in a currency you've forgotten the look of —minted gold! Four yellow eagle-birds—and here they are, if you don't believe me."

This was too grand and fine to be humorous; it was impressive, almost awe-inspiring. The gold pieces were passed from hand to hand and contemplated in mute reverence. Aunt Rachel, elderly slave woman, was passing cracked nuts and cider. She offered a contribution, now.

"Now, den, dat 'splain it! I uz a wonderin' 'bout dat cannel. You is right, Miss Hannah, dey uz only one in de room, en she uz on top er de bookcase. Well, she dah *yit*—she hain't been tetched."

"Not been touched?"

"No, m'am; she hain't been tetched. A ornery po' yaller taller cannel, ain't she?"

"Of course."

"Yes'm. I mould' dat cannel myself. Kin we 'ford *wax* cannels— half a dollar a pound?"

"Wax! The idea!"

"Dat new cannel's *wax!*"

"Oh, come!"

"Fo' Gawd she is. White as Miss Guthrie's store-teeth."

A delicate flattery-shot, neatly put. The widow Guthrie, 56 and dressed for 25, was pleased, and exhibited a girlish embarrassment that was very pretty. She was excusably vain of her false teeth, the only ones in the town; a costly luxury, and a fine and showy contrast with the prevailing mouth-equipment of both old and young—the kind of sharp contrast which white-washed palings make with a charred stump-fence.

Everybody wanted to see the wax candle; Annie Fleming was hurried away to fetch it, and aunt Rachel resumed—

"Miss Hannah, dey's sump'n pow'ful odd 'bout our young gent-man. In de fust place, he ain't got no baggage. Ain't dat so?"

"It hasn't come yet, but I reckon it's coming. I've been expecting it all day, of course."

"Well, don't you give yourself no mo' trouble 'bout it, honey. In my opinion he ain't got no baggage, en none ain't a-coming."

"What makes you think that, Rachel?"

"Caze he ain't got no use for it, Miss Hannah."

"Why?"

"I's gwyne tell you. Warn't he dress' beautiful when he come?"

"Yes." Then she added—to the company: "Plain, but of finer materials than anybody here is used to. Nicely made, too, and spick and span new."

"You's got it down 'cording to de facts. Now den, I went to his room dis mawnin to fetch his clo'es so Jeff could bresh 'em en black his boots, en dey warn't no clo'es dah. Nary a rag. En no boots en no socks, nuther. He uz soun' asleep, en I search de place all over. Tuck his breakfus after you-all uz done—didn't he?"

"Yes."

"Prim en slick en combed up nice as a cat, warn't he?"

"Yes. I think so. I had only a glimpse of him."

"Well, he was; en dey ain't no comb ner bresh ner nothing in dat room. How you reckon he done it?"

"I don't know."

"En *I* don't. But dem is de facts. Did you notice his clo'es, honey?"

"No. Only that they were neat and handsome."

"Now den, I did. *Dey warn't de same dat he come in.*"

"Why, Rachel—"

"Nemmine, I knows what I's a talkin' 'bout. Dey warn't de same. Every rag of 'em jist a little diffunt; not much, but diffunt. His overcoat uz on a cheer by him, en *it* uz *entirely* diffunt. Las' night it uz long en brown, dis mawnin' it uz short en blue; en dah he sot, wid *shoes* on, not boots—I swah to it!"

The explosions of astonishment that followed this charmed Mrs. Hotchkiss's ear; the family's shares in the wonder-market were accumulating satisfactorily.

"Now, den, Miss Hannah, dat ain't all. I fotch him some mo' batter-cakes, en whilst I uz a butterin' 'em for him I happens to look around, en dah uz ole Sanctified Sal, as Marse Oliver calls her, a loafin' along in, perfeckly comfortable. When I see dat, I says to myself, By jimminy dey's bewitchment here som'ers, en it's time for me to light out, en I done it. En I tole Jeff, en he didn't b'lieve me, so me en him slip back en peep, for to see what uz gwyne to happen. En Jeff uz a sayin' 'She'll tah de livers en lights outer him, dat's what she'll do; she ain't friendly to no stranger any time, en now she's got kittens, she won't stan' 'em nohow.' "

"Rachel, it was shame of you to leave her there; you knew perfeckly well what could happen."

"I knowed it warn't right, Miss Hannah, but I couldn't he'p it, I uz scairt to see de cat so ca'm. But don't you worry, honey. You 'member 'bout de dog? De dog didn't fly at him, de dog uz glad to see him. Jist de same wid de cat. Me en Jeff seen it. She jump' up in his lap, en he stroke her, en she uz happy, en raise her back up en down comfortable, en wave her tail, en scrape her head along under his chin, en den jump on de table en set down, en den dey talk together."

"*Talk* together!"

"Yes'm. I wisht I may die if it ain't so."

"The foreign talk that he began with, last night?"

"No'm. Cat-talk."

"Nonsense!"

"Shore's you born. Cat-talk. Bofe of 'em talked cat-talk—sof' en petting—jist like a ole cat en a young cat—cats dat's relations. Well, she tuck a chance at de vittles, en didn't like 'em, so den he tuck truck outer his pocket en fed it to her—en you bet you she didn't go back on *dat*! No'm—'deed she didn't. She laid into it like she hain't had nothin' to eat for four years. He tuck it all outer de same pocket. Now, den, Miss Hannah, I reckon you knows how much Sanctified Sal kin hold? Well, he loaded her chock up to de chin—yes'm, till her eyes fairly bug out. She couldn't wag her tail she's so full. Look like she'd swallered a watermillion she uz dat crammed. Tuck it all outer dat one pocket. Now, den, Miss Hannah, dey ain't no pocket, en dey ain't no saddle-bags dat kin hold enough to load up Sanctified Sal, en you knows it. Well, he tuck it all outer de one pocket—I swah to it."

Everybody was impressed; there was a crackling fire of ejacula-tions; sister Dawson walled her eyes again, and Dr. Wheelright, that imposing oracle, nodded his head slowly up and down, as one who could deliver a weighty thought an' he would.

"Well, a mouse come a-running, en run up his leg en into his bosom, en Sanctified Sal was nodding, but she seen it en forgot she uz loaded, en made a jump for it en fell off the table, en laid there on her back a-waving her hands in the air, en waved a couple of times or so en went to sleep jist so—couldn't keep her eyes open. Den he loaded up de mouse—outer dat same pocket; en put his head down en dey talked mouse-talk together."

"Oh, stop—your imagination's running away with you."

"Fo' Gawd it's true. Me en Jeff heard 'em. Den he put de mouse down en started off, en de mouse was bound she'd foller him; so he put her in de cubberd en shet de do'; den he cler'd out de back way."

"How does it come you didn't tell us these things sooner, Rachel?"

"*Me* tell you! Hm! You reckon you'd a b'lieved me? You reckon you'd a b'lieved Jeff? *We* b'lieves in bewitchments, caze we knows dey's so; but you-all only jist laughs at 'em. Does you reckon you'd a b'lieved me, Miss Hannah?—does you?"

"Well—no."

"Den you'd a laughed at me. Does a po' nigger want to git laughed at any mo' d'n white folks? No, Miss Hannah, dey don't. We's got our feelins, same as *you*-all, alldough we's ign'ant en black."

Her tongue was hung in the middle and was easier to start than to stop. It would have gone on wagging, now, but that the wax candle had long ago been waiting for exhibition. Annie Fleming sat with it in her hand, with one ear drinking in aunt Rachel's fairy-tales, and the other one listening for the click of the gate-latch; for she had lost her tender little inexperienced heart to the new boy without suspecting it; awake and asleep she had been dreaming of his beautiful face ever since she had had her first glimpse of it and she was longing to see it again and feel that enchanting and mysterious ecstasy which it had inspired in her before. She was a dear and sweet and pretty and guileless creature, she was just turned eighteen, she did not know she was in love, she only knew that she worshiped—worshiped as the fire-worshipers worship the sun, content to see his face and feel his warmth, unworthy of a nearer intimacy, unequal to it, unfitted for it, and not requiring it or aspiring to it. Why didn't he come? Why had he not come to dinner? The hours were so slow, the day so tedious; the longest she had known in her eighteen years. All were growing more and more impatient for his coming, but their impatience was pale beside hers; and besides, they could express it, and did, but she could not have that relief, she must hide her secret, she must put on the lie of indifference and act it the best she could.

The candle was passed from hand to hand, now, and its material admired and verified; then Annie carried it away.

It was well past mid-afternoon, and the days were short. Annie and her aunt were to sup and spend the night with sister Guthrie on the hill, a good mile distant. What should be done? Was it worth while to wait longer for the boy? The company were reluctant to go without seeing him; sister Guthrie hoped she might have the distinction of his presence in her house with the niece and the aunt, and would like to wait a little longer and invite him; so it was agreed to hold on a while.

Annie returned, now, and there was disappointment in her face and a pain at her heart, though no one detected the one nor suspected the other. She said—

"Aunty, he has been here, and is gone again."

"Then he must have come the back way. It's *too* bad. But are you sure? How do you know?"

"Because he has changed his clothes."

"Are there clothes there?"

"Yes; and not the ones he had this morning, nor the ones he wore last night."

"Dah, now, what I tell you? En dat baggage not come *yit!*"

"Can we see them?"

"Can't we see them?"

"Do let us go and look at them!"

Everybody wanted to see the clothes, everybody begged. So, sentries were posted to look out for the boy's approach and give notice—Annie to watch the front door and Rachel the back one—and the rest went up to Forty-four's chamber. The clothes were there, new and handsome. The coat lay spread upon the bed. Mrs. Hotchkiss took it by the skirts and held it up to display it—a flood of gold and silver coin began to pour out of the inverted pockets; the woman stood aghast and helpless; the coin piled higher and higher on the floor—

"Put it down!" shouted her husband; "drop it, can't you!" But she was paralysed; he snatched the coat and threw it on the bed, and the flood ceased. "Now we are in a fine fix; he can come at any moment and catch us; and we'll have to explain, if we can, how we happen to be here. Quick, all you accessories after the fact and before it—turn to; we must gather it up and put it back."

So all those chief citizens got down on their hands and knees and scrambled all around and everywhere for the coins, raking under the bed and the sofa and the wardrobe for estrays, a most undignified spectacle. The work was presently finished, but that did not restore happiness, for there was a new trouble, now: after the coat's pockets had been stuffed there was still half a peck of coin left. It was a shameful predicament. Nobody could get command of his wits for a moment or two; then sister Dawson made a suggestion—

"No real harm is done, when you come to look at it. It is natural that we should have some curiosity about the belongings of such a wonderful stranger, and if we try to satisfy it, not meaning any harm or disrespect—"

"Right," interrupted Miss Pomeroy, the schoolm'am; "he's only a boy, and he wouldn't mind, and he wouldn't think it anything odd if people as old as we are should take a little liberty which he mightn't like in younger folks."

"And besides," said Judge Taylor the magistrate, "he hasn't suffered any loss, and isn't going to suffer any. Let us put the whole of the money in his table drawer and close it, and lock the room door; and when he comes we will all tell him just how it was, and apologise. It will come out all right; I think we don't need to worry."

It was agreed that this was probably as good a plan as could be contrived in the difficult circumstances of the case; so the company took all the comfort from it they could, and were glad to get out of the place and clear for their homes without waiting longer for the boy, in case he shouldn't arrive before they got their wraps on. They said Hotchkiss could do the explaining and apologising, and depend upon them to indorse and stand by all his statements.

"And besides," said Mrs. Wheelright, "how do we know it is real money? He may be a juggler out of India; in that case the drawer is empty, or full of sawdust by this time."

"I am afraid it's not going to happen," said Hotchkiss; "the money was rather heavy for sawdust. The thing that mainly interests me is, that I shan't sleep very well with that pile of money in the house—I shan't sleep at all if you people are going to tell about it, and so I'll ask you to keep the secret until morning; then I will make the boy send it to the bank, and you may talk as freely as you please, then."

Annie put on her things and she and her aunt departed with the rest. Darkness was approaching; the lodger was not come. What could the matter be? Mrs. Hotchkiss said he was probably coasting with his schoolmates and paying no attention to more important things—boy-like. Rachel was told to keep his supper warm and let him take his own time about coming for it; "boys will be boys, and late by nature, nights and mornings; let them be boys while they can, it's the best of life and the shortest."

It had turned warm, and clouds were gathering fast, with a promise of snow—a promise which would be kept. As Doctor Wheelright, the stately old First-Family Virginian and imposing Thinker of the village was going out at the front door, he unloaded a Thought. It seemed to weigh a good part of a ton, and it impressed everybody—

"It is my opinion—after much and careful reflection, sir—that the indications warrant the conjecture that in several ways this youth is an extraordinary person."

That verdict would go around. After such an endorsement, from such a source, the village would think twice before it ventured to think small potatoes of that boy.

Chapter 4

As the darkness closed down an hour later, what is to this day called the Great Storm began. It was in reality a Blizzard, but that expressive word had not then been invented. It was this storm's mission to bury the farms and villages of a long narrow strip of country for ten days, and do it as compactly and as thoroughly as the mud and ashes had buried Pompeii nearly eighteen centuries before. The Great Storm began its work modestly, deceptively. It made no display, there was no wind and no noise; whoever was abroad and crossed the lamp-glares flung from uncurtained windows noticed that the snow came straight down, and that it laid its delicate white carpet softly, smoothly, artistically, thickening the substance swiftly and equably; the passenger noticed also that this snow was of an unusual sort, it not coming in an airy cloud of great feathery flakes, but in a fog of white dust-forms—mere powder; just powder; the strangest snow imaginable. By 8 in the evening this snow-fog had become so dense that lamp-glares four steps away were not visible, and without the help of artificial light a passenger could see no object till he was near enough to touch it with his hand. Whosoever was abroad now was practically doomed, unless he could soon stumble upon somebody's house. Orientation was impossible; to be abroad was to be lost. A man could not leave his own door, walk ten steps and find his way back again.

The wind rose, now, and began to sing through this ghastly fog; momently it rose higher and higher, soon its singing had developed into roaring, howling, shrieking. It gathered up the snow from the ground and drove it in massy walls ahead of it and distributed it here and there across streets and open lots and against houses, in drifts fifteen feet deep.

There were disasters now, of course. Very few people were still out, but those few were necessarily in bad case. If they faced the wind, it caked their faces instantly with a thick mask of powder which closed their eyes in blindness and stopped their nostrils and their breath, and they fell where they were; if they tried to move with the wind they soon plunged into a drift and the on-coming wall of snow buried them. Even in that little village twenty-eight persons perished that night, some because they had heard cries of distress and went out to help, but got lost within sixty seconds, and then, seeking their own doors, went in the wrong direction and found their graves in five minutes.

At 8, just as the wind began to softly moan and whimper and wheeze, Mr. Hotchkiss laid his spiritualistic book down, snuffed the candle, threw an extra log on the fire, then parted his coat tails and stood with his back to the blaze and began to turn over in his mind some of the information which he had been gathering about the manners and customs and industries of the spirit land, and to repeat and try to admire some of the poetry which Byron had sent thence through the rapping-mediums. He did not know that there was a storm outside. He had been absorbed in his book for an hour and a half. Aunt Rachel appeared, now, with an armful of wood, which she flung in the box and said—

"Well, seh, it's de wust I ever see; and Jeff say de same."

"Worst what?"

"Storm, seh."

"Is there a storm?"

"My! didn't you know it, seh?"

"No."

"Why, it's de beatenes' storm—tain't like nothin' you ever see, Marse Oliver—so fine—like ashes a-blowin'; why, you can't see no distance scasely. Me en Jeff was at de prar meetin', en come back a little bit ago, en come mighty near miss'n de house; en when we look out, jist dis minute it's a heap wuss'n ever. Jeff he uz a sayin'—" She glanced around; an expression of fright came into her face and she exclaimed, "Why, I reckoned of cose he uz here—en he ain't!"

"Who?"

"Young Marse Fawty-fo'."

"Oh, he's playing somewhere; he'll be along presently."

"You hain't seen him, seh?"

"No."

"O, my Gawd!"

She fled away, and in five minutes was back again, sobbing and panting.

"He ain't in his room, his supper ain't tetched, he ain't anywhers; I been all over de house. O, Marse Oliver de chile's lost, we ain't never gwyne to see him no mo'."

"Oh, nonsense, you needn't be afraid—boys don't mind a storm."

Uncle Jeff arrived at this moment, and said—

"But Marse Oliver *dis* ain't no common storm—has you been to look at it?"

"No."

Hotchkiss was alarmed, at last, and ran with the others to the front door and snatched it open. The wind piped a high note, and they disappeared in a world of snow which was discharged at them as if from steam-shovels.

"Shut it, shut it!" gasped the master. It was done. A blast of wind came, that rocked the house. There was a faint and choking cry outside. Hotchkiss blenched, and said, "What can we do? It's death to go out there. But we *must* do something—it may be the boy."

"Wait, Marse Oliver, I'll fetch a clo'es line, en Jeff he—" She was gone, and in a moment brought it and began to tie an end around uncle Jeff's waist. "Now, den, out wid you! me en Marse Oliver 'll hole on to de yuther end."

Jeff was ready; the door was opened for the plunge, and the plunge was made; but in the same instant a suffocating assault of snow closed the eyes and took away the breath of the master and Rachel and they sank gasping to the floor and the line escaped from their hands. They threw themselves on their faces, with their feet toward the door; their breath returned, and Rachel moaned, *"He's gone, now!"* By the light from the hall lamp over the door she caught a dim vision of the new boy, coming from toward the dining room, and said "Thank de good Gawd for *dat* much—how ever did he find de back gate?"

The boy came through against the wind and shut the front door. The master and Rachel rose out of their smother of snow, and the former said—

"I'm so grateful! I never expected to see you again."

By this time Rachel's sobs and groans and lamentations were rising above the clamors of the storm, and the boy asked what the trouble was. Hotchkiss told him about Jeff.

"I will go and fetch him, sir. Get into the parlor, and close the door."

"You will venture out? Not a step—stay where you are! I wouldn't allow—"

The boy interrupted—not with words, but only a look—and the man and the servant passed into the parlor and closed the door. Then they heard the front door close, and stood looking at each other. The storm raged on; every now and then a gust of wind burst against the house with a force which made it quake, and in the intervals it wailed like a lost soul; the listeners tallied the gusts and the intervals, losing heart all the time, and when they had counted five of each, their hopes died.

Then they opened the parlor door—to do they didn't know what —the street door sprang open at the same moment, and two snow-figures entered: the boy carrying the unconscious old negro man in his arms. He delivered his burden to Rachel, shut the door, and said—

"A man has found refuge in the open shed over yonder; a slender, tall, wild-looking man with thin sandy beard. He is groaning. It is not much of a shelter, that shed."

He said it indifferently, and Hotchkiss shuddered.

"Oh, it is awful, awful!" he said, "he will die."

"Why is it awful?" asked the boy.

"*Why?* It—it—why of *course* it's awful!"

"Perhaps it is as you say; I do not know. Shall I fetch him?"

"Great guns, no! Don't dream of such a thing—one miracle of the sort is enough."

"But if you want him— Do you want him?"

"Want him? I—why, I don't *want* him—*that* isn't it—I mean, why, don't you understand?—it's a pity he should *die*, poor fellow; but we are not in a position to—"

"I will fetch him."

"Stop, stop, are you mad!—come back!"

But the boy was gone.

"Rachel, why the devil did you let him get out? Can't you see that the lad's a rank lunatic?"

"O, Marse Oliver, gim it *to* me, I deserve it! I's so thankful to git my ole Jeff back I ain't got no sense en can't take notice of nothin'. I's so shamed, en O, my Gawd, I—"

"We had him, and now we've lost him again; and this time for good; and it's all your fault, for being a—"

The door fell open, a snow image plunged in upon the floor, the boy's voice called, "There he is—there's others, yet," and the door closed again.

"Oh, well," cried Hotchkiss with a note of despair, "we've got to give him up, there's no saving him. Rachel!" He was flapping the snow from the new take, with a "tidy." "Bless my soul, it's Crazy Meadows! Rouse up, Jeff! lend a hand, both of you—drag him to my fire." It was done. "Now, then, blankets, food, hot water, whisky—fly around! we'll save him, he isn't more than half dead, yet."

The three worked over Crazy Meadows half an hour, and brought him around. Meantime they had kept alert ears open, listening; but their listening was unblessed, no sounds came but the rumbling and blustering of the storm. Crazy Meadows gazed around confusedly, gradually got his bearings, recognized the faces, and said—

"I am saved! Hotchkiss, it seems impossible. How did it happen?"

"A boy did it—the most marvelous boy on the planet. It was lucky you had a lantern."

"Lantern? I hadn't any lantern."

"Yes, you had. *You* don't know. The boy described your build and beard."

"I *hadn't* any lantern, I tell you. There wasn't any light around."

"Marse Oliver," said Rachel, "didn't Miss Hannah say de young marster kin see in de dark?"

"Why, certainly—now that you mention it. But how could he see through that blanket of snow? My gracious, I wish he would come! Oh, but he'll never come, poor young chap, he'll never come— never any more."

"Marse Oliver, don't you worry, de good Lawd kin take care of him."

"In this storm, you old idiot? You don't know what you're talking about. Wait—I've got an idea! Quick—get around the table; now then, take hold of hands. Banish all obstructive influences—you want to be particular about that; the spirits can't do anything against doubt and incredulity. Silence, now, and concentrate your minds. Poor boy, if he is dead he will come and say so."

He glanced up, and perceived that there was a hiatus in the circle; Crazy Meadows said, without breach of slave-State politeness, and without offence to the slaves present, since they had been accustomed to the franknesses of slave-State etiquette all their lives—

"I'll go any reasonable length to prove my solicitude for the fate of my benefactor, for I am not an ungrateful man, and not a soured one, either, if the children *do* chase me and stone me for the fun they get out of it; but I've got to draw the line. I'm willing to sit at a table with niggers for just this once, for your sake, Oliver Hotchkiss, but that is as far as I can go—I'll get you to excuse me from taking them by the hand."

The gratitude of the two negroes was deep and honest; this speech promised relief for them; their situation had been a cruelly embarrassing one; they had sat down with these white men because they had been ordered to do it, and it was habit and heredity to obey, but their seats had not been more comfortable than a hot stove would have been. They hoped and expected that their master would be reasonable and rational, now, and send them away, but it didn't happen. He could manage his *seance* without Meadows, and would do it. He didn't mind holding hands with negroes, for he was a sincere and enthusiastic abolitionist; in fact had been an abolitionist for five weeks, now, and if nothing happened would be one for a fortnight longer. He had confirmed the sincerity of his new convictions in the very beginning by setting the two slaves free—a generosity which had failed only because they didn't belong to him but to his wife. As she had never been an abolitionist it was impossible that she could ever become one.

By command the slaves joined hands with their master and sat trembling and silent, for they were miserably afraid of spectres and spirits. Hotchkiss bowed his head solemnly to the table, and said in a reverent tone:

"Are there any spirits present? If so, please rap three times."

After a pause the response came—three faint raps. The negroes shrunk together till their clothes were loose upon their bodies, and begged pathetically to be released.

"Sit still! and don't let your hands shake like that."

It was Lord Byron's spirit. Byron was the most active poet on the other side of the grave in those days, and the hardest one for a medium to get rid of. He reeled off several rods of poetry now, of his usual spiritual pattern—rhymy and jingly and all that, but not good, for his mind had decayed since he died. At the end of three-quarters of an hour he went away to hunt for a word that would rhyme with silver—good luck and a long riddance, Crazy Meadows said, for there wasn't any such word. Then Napoleon came and explained Waterloo all over again and how it wasn't his fault—a thing which he was always doing in the St. Helena days, and latterly around the festive rapping-table. Crazy Meadows scoffed at him, and said he didn't even get the dates right, let alone the facts; and he laughed his wild mad laugh—a reedy and raspy and horrid explosion which had long been a fright to the village and its dogs, and had brought him many a volley of stones from the children.

Shakspeare arrived and did some rather poor things, and was followed by a throng of Roman statesmen and generals whose English was the only remarkable thing about their contributions; then at last, about eleven o'clock, came some thundering raps which made the table and the company jump.

"Who is it, please?"

"Forty-four!"

"Ah, how sad!—we are deeply grieved, but of course we feared it and expected it. Are you happy?"

"Happy? Certainly."

"We are so glad! It is the greatest comfort to us. Where are you?"

"In hell!"

"O, de good Lawd!—please, Marse Oliver, lemme go, oh, please lemme go—oh, Marse Oliver, me en Rachel *can't* stan' it!"

"Hold still, you fool!"

"Oh, please, *please*, Marse Oliver!"

"*Will* you keep still, you puddnhead! Ah, now, if we can only persuade him to materialize! I've never seen one yet. Forty-four, dear lost lad, *would* you mind appearing to us?"

"Oh, *don't*, Marse Oliver!—please, don't!"

"Shut up! *Do* materialize! Do appear to us, if only for a moment!"

Presto! There sat the boy, in their midst! The negroes shrieked, and went over on their backs on the floor and continued to shriek. Crazy Meadows fell over backwards, too, but gathered himself up in silence and stood apart with heaving breast and flaming eyes, staring at the boy. Hotchkiss rubbed his hands together in gratitude and delight, and his face was transfigured with the glory-light of triumph.

"*Now* let the doubter doubt and the scoffer scoff if they want to —but they've had their day! Ah, Forty-four, dear Forty-four, you've done our cause a noble service."

"What cause?"

"Spiritualism. *Stop* that screeching and screaming, will you!"

The boy stooped and touched the negroes, and said—

"There—go to sleep. Now go to bed. In the morning you will think it was a dream." They got up and wandered somnambulistically away. He turned and looked at Crazy Meadows, whose lids at once sank down and hid his wild eyes. "Go and sleep in my bed; in the morning it will be a dream to you, too." Meadows drifted away like one in a trance, and followed after the vanished negroes. "What is spiritualism, sir?"

Hotchkiss eagerly explained. The boy smiled, made no comment, and changed the subject.

"Twenty-eight have perished in your village by the storm."

"Heavens! Can that be true?"

"I saw them; they are under the snow—scattered over the town."

"*Saw* them?"

The boy took no notice of the inquiry in the emphasised word.

"Yes—twenty-eight."

"What a misfortune!"

"Is it?"

"Why—how can you ask?"

"I don't know. I could have saved them if I had known it was desirable. After you wanted that man saved I gathered the idea that it was desirable, so I searched the town and saved the rest that were straggling—thirteen."

"How noble! And how beautiful it was to die in such a work. Oh, sainted spirit, I worship your memory!"

"Whose memory?"

"Yours; and I—"

"Do you take me for dead?"

"Dead? Of course. Aren't you?"

"Certainly not."

Hotchkiss's joy was without limit or measure. He poured it eloquently out until he was breathless; then paused, and added pathetically—

"It is bad for spiritualism—yes, bad, bad—but let it go—go and welcome, God knows I'm glad to have you back, even on those costly terms! And by George, we'll celebrate! I'm a teetotaler—been a teetotaler for years—months, anyway—*a* month—but at a time like this—"

The kettle was still on the fire, the bottle which had revived Meadows was still at hand, and in a couple of minutes he had brewed a pair of good punches—"anyway, good enough for a person out of practice," he said.

The boy began to sip, and said it was pleasant, and asked what it was.

"Why, bless your heart, whisky of course—can't you tell by the smell of it? And we'll have a smoke, too. I don't smoke—haven't for years—I *think* it's years—because I'm president of the Anti-Smoking League—but at a time like this—" He jumped up and threw a log on the fire, punched the pile into a roaring blaze, then filled a couple of cob pipes and brought them. "There, now, ain't it cosy, ain't it comfortable?—and just *hear* the storm! My, but she's booming! But snug here?—it's no name for it!"

The boy was inspecting his pipe with interest.

"What shall I do with it, sir?"

"*Do* with it? Do you mean to say you don't smoke? I never saw such a boy. Next you'll say you don't break the Sabbath."

"But what is the material?"

"That? Tobacco—of course."

"Oh, I see. Sir Walter Raleigh discovered it among the Indians; I read about it in the school. Yes, I understand now."

He applied the candle and began to smoke, Hotchkiss gazing at him puzzled.

"You've *read* about it! Upon my word! Now that I come to think about it, you don't seem to know anything except what you've read about in that school. Why how in the world could you be born and raised in the State of Missouri and never—"

"But I wasn't. I am a foreigner."

"You don't say!—and speak just like an educated native—not even an accent. Where *were* you raised?"

The boy answered naïvely—

"Partly in heaven, partly in hell."

Hotchkiss's glass fell from one hand, his pipe from the other, and he sat staring stupidly at the boy, and breathing short. Presently he murmured dubiously—

"I reckon the punch—out of practice, you know—maybe both of us—and—" He paused, and continued to gaze and blink; then shook his thoughts together and said, "Can't tell anything about it —it is too undeveloped for me; but it's all right, we'll make a night of it. It's my opinion, speaking as a prohibitionist—" He stooped and picked up his glass and his pipe, and went rambling on in a broken and incoherent way while he filled them, glancing furtively at the boy now and then out of the corner of his eye and trying to settle his disturbed and startled mind and get his bearings again. But the boy was not disturbed; he smoked and sipped in peace, and quiet, and manifest contentment. He took a book out of his pocket, and began to turn the pages swiftly; Hotchkiss sat down, stirring his new punch, and keeping a wistful and uneasy eye upon him. After a minute or two the book was laid upon the table.

"Now I know all about it," said the boy. "It is all here—tobacco, and liquors, and such things. Champagne is placed at the head of everything; and Cuban tobacco at the head of the tobaccos."

"Oh, yes, they are the gems of the planet in those lines. Why—I don't recognise this book; did you bring it in to-night?"

"Yes."

"Where from?"

"The British Museum."

Hotchkiss began to blink again, and look uneasy.

"It is a new work," added the boy. "Published yesterday."

The blinking continued. Hotchkiss started to take a sip of punch, but reconsidered the motion; shook his head and put the glass down. Upon pretext of examining the print and the binding, he opened the book; then closed it at once and pushed it away. He had seen the Museum stamp—bearing date of the preceding day. He fussed nervously at his pipe a moment; then held it to the candle with a hand that trembled and made some of the tobacco spill out, then asked timidly—

"How did you get the book?"

"I went after it myself."

"Your—self. Mercy! When?"

"While you were stooping for your pipe and glass."

Hotchkiss moaned.

"Why do you make that noise?"

"Be—because I—I am afraid."

The boy reached out and touched the trembling hand and said gently—

"There—it is gone."

The troubled look passed from the old prohibitionist's face, and he said, in a sort of soft ecstasy of relief and contentment—

"It tingles all through me—all through me. De—licious! Every fibre—the root of every hair—it is enchantment! Oh magician of the magicians, talk to me—talk! tell me everything."

"Certainly, if you like."

"Now, that is lovely! First I will rout out old Rachel and we'll have a bite and be comfortable and freshen up; I am pretty sharp-set after all these hours, and I reckon you are, too."

"Wait. It is not necessary. I will order something."

Smoking dishes began to descend upon the table; it was covered in a moment.

"It's the Arabian Nights come again! And I am not scared, now. I don't know why—it was that magic touch, I think. But you didn't fetch them yourself, this time; I was noticing, and you didn't go away."

"No, I sent my servants."

"I didn't see them."

"You can if you wish."

"I'd give anything!"

The servants became visible; all the room was crowded with them. Trim and shapely little fellows they were; velvety little red fellows, with short horns on their heads and spiked tails at the other end; and those that stood, stood in metal plates, and those that sat—on chairs, in a row upon settees, and on top of the bookcase with their legs dangling—had metal plates under them—"to keep from scorching the furniture," the boy quietly explained, "these have come but this moment, and of course are hot, yet."

Hotchkiss asked, a little timidly—

"Are they little devils?"

"Yes."

"Real ones?"

"Oh, yes—quite."

"They—are they safe?"

"Perfectly."

"I don't need to be afraid?"

"Oh, not at all."

"Then I won't be. I think they are charming. Do they understand English?"

"No, only French. But they could be taught it in a few minutes."

"It is wonderful. Are they—you won't mind my asking—relatives?"

"Of mine? No; sons of my father's subordinates. You are dismissed, young gentlemen, for the present."

The little fiends vanished.

"Your father is—er—"

"Satan!"

"Good land!"

Chapter 5

Hotchkiss sank into his chair weak and limp, and began to pour out broken words and disjointed sentences whose meanings were not always clear but whose general idea was comprehensible. To this effect: from custom bred of his upbringing and his associations he had often talked about Satan with a freedom which was regrettable, but it was really only talk, mere idle talk, he didn't mean anything by it; in fact there were many points about Satan's character which he greatly admired, and although he hadn't said so, publicly, it was an oversight and not intentional—but from this out he meant to open his mouth boldly, let people say what they might and think what they chose—

The boy interrupted him, gently and quietly—

"I don't admire him."

Hotchkiss was hard aground, now; his mouth was open, and remained so, but no words came; he couldn't think of anything judicious to say. Presently he ventured to throw out a feeler—cautiously, tentatively, feelingly, persuasively:

"You see—well, you know—it would be only natural, if I was a devil—a good, kind, honorable devil, I mean—and my father was a good, kind, honorable devil against whom narrow and perhaps wrongful or at least exaggerated prejudices—"

"But I am not a devil," said the boy, tranquilly.

Hotchkiss was badly confused, but profoundly relieved.

"I—er—I—well, you know, I suspected as much, I—I—indeed I hadn't a doubt of it; and—although it—on the whole—oh, good land, I can't understand it, of course, but I give you my word of honor I like you all the better for it, I do indeed! I feel good, now—good, and comfortable, and in fact happy. Join me—take something! I wish to drink your health; and—and your family's."

"With pleasure. Now eat—refresh yourself. I will smoke, if you don't mind. I like it."

"Certainly; but eat, too; aren't you hungry?"

"No, I do not get hungry."

"Is that actually so?"

"Yes."

"Ever? Never?"

"No."

"Ah, it is a pity. You miss a great deal. Now tell me about yourself, won't you?"

"I shall be glad to do it, for I have a purpose in coming to the earth, and if you should find the matter interesting, you can be useful to me."

Then the talking and eating began, simultaneously.

———————

"I was born before Adam's fall—"

"Wh-at!"

"It seems to surprise you. Why?"

"Because it caught me unprepared. And because it is six thousand years ago, and you look to be only about fifteen years old."

"True—that is my age, within a fraction."

"Only fifteen, and yet—"

"Counting by *our* system of measurement, I mean—not yours."

"How is that?"

"A day, with us, is as a thousand years with you."

Hotchkiss was awed. A seriousness which was near to solemnity settled upon his face. After a meditative pause he said—

"Surely it cannot be that you really and not figuratively mean—"

"Yes—really, not figuratively. A minute of our time is 41⅔ years

of yours. By our system of measurement I am fifteen years old; but
by yours I am five million, lacking twenty thousand years."

Hotchkiss was stunned. He shook his head in a hopeless way,
and said, resignedly—

"Go on—I can't realize it—it is astronomy to me."

"Of course you cannot realize these things, but do not be troubled; measurements of time and eternity are merely conveniences,
they are not of much importance. It is about a week ago that Adam
fell—"

"A week?— Ah, yes, *your* week. It is awful—that compression
of time! Go on."

"I was in heaven; I had always lived in heaven, of course; until a
week ago, my father had always lived there. But I saw this little
world created. I was interested; we were all interested. There is
much more interest attaching to the creation of a planet than
attaches to the creation of a sun, on account of the life that is going
to inhabit it. I have seen many suns created—many indeed, that
you are not yet acquainted with, they being so remotely situated in
the deeps of space that their light will not reach here for a long
time yet; but the planets—I cared the most for them; we all did; I
have seen millions of them made, and the Tree planted in the
Garden, and the man and the woman placed in its shade, with the
animals about them. I saw your Adam and Eve only once; they
were happy, then, and innocent. This could have continued forever,
but for my father's conduct. I read it all in the Bible in Mr. Ferguson's school. As it turned out, Adam's happiness lasted less than
a day—"

"Less than one day?"

"By our reckoning, I mean; by yours he lived nine hundred and
twenty years—the bulk of it unhappily."

"I see; yes, it is true."

"It was my father's fault. Then hell was created, in order that
Adam's race might have a place to go to, after death—"

"They could go to heaven, too."

"That was later. Two days ago. Through the sacrifice made for
them by the son of God, the Savior."

"Is hell so new?"

"It was not needed before. No Adam in any of the millions of other planets had ever disobeyed and eaten of the forbidden fruit."

"It is strange."

"No—for the others were not tempted."

"How was that?"

"There was no tempter until my father ate of the fruit himself and became one. Then he tempted other angels and they ate of it also; then Adam and the woman."

"How did your father come to eat of it this time?"

"I did not know at the time."

"Why didn't you?"

"Because I was away when it happened; I was away some days, and did not hear of it at all and of the disaster to my father until I got back; then I went to my father's place to speak with him of it; but his trouble was so new, and so severe, and so amazing to him that he could do nothing but grieve and lament—he could not bear to talk about the details; I merely gathered that when he made the venture it was because his idea of the nature of the fruit was a most erroneous one."

"Erroneous?"

"Quite erroneous."

"You do not know in what way it was erroneous?"

"Yes, I think I know now. He probably—in fact unquestionably —supposed that the nature of the fruit was to reveal to human beings the knowledge of good and evil—that, and nothing more; but not to Satan the great angel; he had that knowledge before. We always had it—always. Now why he was moved to taste it himself is not clear; I shall never know until he tells me. But his error was—"

"Yes, what was his error?"

"His error was in supposing that a knowledge of the difference between good and evil was *all* that the fruit could confer."

"Did it confer more than that?"

"Consider the passage which says *man is prone to evil as the sparks to fly upward*. Is that true? Is that really the nature of man? —I mean your man—the man of this planet?"

"Indeed it is—nothing could be truer."

"It is not true of the men of any other planet. It explains the mystery. My father's error stands revealed in all its nakedness. The fruit's office was not confined to conferring the mere knowledge of good and evil, it conferred also the passionate and eager and hungry *disposition to* DO *evil.* Prone as sparks to fly upward; in other words, prone as water to run down hill—a powerful figure, and means that man's disposition is wholly evil, uncompromisingly evil, inveterately evil, and that he is as undisposed to do good as water is undisposed to run *up* hill. Ah, my father's error brought a colossal disaster upon the men of this planet. It *poisoned* the men of this planet—poisoned them in mind and body. I see it, plainly."

"It brought death, too."

"Yes—whatever that may be. I do not quite understand it. It seems to be a sleep. You do not seem to mind sleep. By my reading I gather that you are not conscious of either death *or* sleep; that nevertheless you fear the one and do not fear the other. It is very stupid. Illogical."

Hotchkiss put down his knife and fork and explained the difference between sleep and death; and how a person was not sorry when asleep, but sorry when dead, because—because—

He found it was not so easy to explain why as he had supposed it was going to be; he floundered a while, then broke down. But presently he tried again, and said that death *was* only a sleep, but that the objection to it was that it was so *long;* then he remembered that time stands still when one sleeps, and so the difference between a night and a thousand years is really no difference at all so far as the sleeper is personally affected.

However, the boy was thinking, profoundly, and heard none of it; so nothing was lost. By and by the boy said, earnestly—

"The fundamental change wrought in man's nature by my father's conduct must remain—it is permanent; but a part of its burden of evil consequences can be lifted from your race, and I will undertake it. Will you help?"

He was applying in the right quarter. Lifting burdens from a whole race was a fine and large enterprize, and suited Oliver

Hotchkiss's size and gifts better than any contract he had ever taken hold of yet. He gave in his adhesion with promptness and enthusiasm, and wanted the scheme charted out at once. Privately he was immeasurably proud to be connected in business with an actual angel and son of a devil, but did what he could to keep his exultation from showing. The boy said—

"I cannot map out a definite plan yet; I must first study this race. Its poisoned condition and prominent disposition to do evil differentiate it radically from any men whom I have known before, therefore it is a new race to me and must be exhaustively studied before I shall know where and how to begin. Indefinitely speaking, our plan will be confined to ameliorating the condition of the race in some ways in *this* life; we are not called upon to concern ourselves with its future fate; that is in abler hands than ours."

"I hope you will begin your studies right away."

"I shall. Go to bed, and take your rest. During the rest of the night and to-morrow I will travel about the globe and personally examine some of the nationalities, and learn languages and read the world's books in the several tongues, and to-morrow night we will talk together here. Meantime the storm has made you a prisoner. Will you have one of my servants to wait on you?"

A genuine little devil all for his own! It was a lovely idea, and swelled Hotchkiss's vanity to the bursting point. He was lavish with his thanks.

"But he won't understand what I say to him."

"He will learn in five minutes. Would you like any particular one?"

"If I could have the cunning little rascal that sat down in the fire after he got cooled off—"

There was a flash of scarlet and the little fiend was present and smiling; and he had with him some books from the school; among them the French-English dictionary and the phonographic shorthand system.

"There. Use him night and day. He knows what he is here for. If he needs help he will provide it. He requires no lights; take them, and go to bed; leave him to study his books. In five minutes he will be able to talk broken English in case you want him. He will read twelve or fifteen of your books in an hour and learn shorthand besides; then he will be a capable secretary. He will be visible or invisible according to your orders. Give him a name—he has one already, and so have I, but you would not be able to pronounce either of them. Good-bye."

He vanished.

Hotchkiss stood smiling all sorts of pleasant smiles of intricate and variegated pattern at his little devil, with the idea of making him understand how welcome he was; and he said to himself, "It's a bitter climate for him, poor little rascal, the fire will go down and he will freeze; I wish I knew how to tell him to run home and warm himself whenever he wants to."

He brought blankets and made signs to him that these were for him to wrap up in; then he began to pile wood on the fire, but the red stranger took that work promptly off his hands, and did the work like an expert—which he was. Then he sat down on the fire and began to study his book, and his new master took the candle and went away to bed, meditating a name for him. "He is a dear little devil," he said, "and must have a nice one." So he named him Edward Nicholson Hotchkiss—after a brother that was dead.

Chapter 6

In the morning the world was still invisible, for the powdery snow was still sifting thickly down—noiselessly, now, for the wind had ceased to blow. The new devil appeared in the kitchen and scared aunt Rachel and uncle Jeff out of it, and they fled to the master's room with the tale. Hotchkiss explained the situation and told them there was no harm in this devil, but a great deal of good; and that he was the property of the wonderful boy, who had strongly recommended him.

"Is he a slave, Marse Oliver?" asked Rachel.

"Yes."

"Well, den, dey oughtn't to be much harm in him, I reckon; but is he a *real* devil?"

"Yes, genuine."

"Den how kin he be good?"

"Well, he is, anyway. We have been misinformed about devils. There's a great deal of ignorant prejudice around, concerning them. I want you to be friends with this one."

"But how kin we, Marse Oliver?" asked uncle Jeff; "we's afraid of him. We'd *like* to be friends wid him, *becase* we's afraid of him, en if he stays on de place, 'course we gwyne to do de bes' we kin; but when he come a skippin' into de kitchen all red hot like a stack of fire-coals, bless you *I* didn't want nothin' to do wid him. Still, if *he's* willin' to be friends it ain't gwyne to answer for *us* to hold back, for Gawd on'y knows what he might do."

"S'pose things don't go to suit him, Marse Oliver," said Rachel, "what he gwyne do *den?*"

"Really, you needn't worry, Rachel, he has a kind disposition, and moreover he wants to be useful—I know it."

"Why, Marse Oliver, he'll take en tear up all de hymn-books en—"

"No he won't; he's perfectly civil and obliging, and he'll do anything he is asked to do."

"Is dat so?"

"I know it."

"But what *kin* he do, Marse Oliver? he's so little, en den he don't know our ways."

"Oh, he can do anything—shovel snow, for instance."

"My! kin he do dat?" asked Jeff. "If he'll do dat, *I's* his friend, for one—right on de spot!"

"Yes, and he can run errands—any errand you want, Rachel."

"Dat 'ud come mighty handy, Marse Oliver," said Rachel, relenting; "he can't run none now, 'course, but if de snow 'uz gone—"

"He'll run them for you, I know he will; I wish he were here, I—"

Edward Nicholson Hotchkiss appeared in their midst, and the

negroes scrambled for the door, but he was there first and barred the way. He smiled an eager and fiery smile, and said—

"I've been listening. I want to be friends—don't be afraid. Give me an errand—I'll show you."

Rachel's teeth chattered a little, and her breath came short and she was as pale as bronze; but she found her tongue, and said—

"I's yo' friend—I is, I swah it. Be good to me en ole Jeff, honey—don't hurt us; don't do us no harm, for yo' ma's sake."

"Hurt you?—no. Give me an errand—I'll show you."

"But chile, dey ain't no errand; de snow's so deep, en you'd catch cold, anyway, de way you's been raised. But sakes, if you'd been here yistiddy evenin'—Marse Oliver I clean forgot de cream, en dey ain't a drop for yo' breakfast."

"I'll fetch it," said Edward, "go down—you'll find it on the table."

He disappeared. The negroes were troubled, and did not know what to make of this. They were afraid of him again; he must be off his balance, for he could not run errands in this weather. Hotchkiss smoothed away their fears with persuasive speeches, and they presently went below, where they found the new servant trying to tame the cat and not succeeding; but the cream was there, and their respect for Edward and his abilities received a great impulse.

Huck Finn

Well, I had a noble big bullfrog that I had traded a hymn-book for, and was all profit, becuz it never cost me anything, deacon Kyle give it to me for saving his daughter's life time she fell in the river off of the ferry boat going down to the picnic in Cave Holler, and warn't any use to me on account of my being able to get along without hymns, and I traded the bullfrog for a cat, and sold the cat for a false-face, a horrible thing that was awful to look at and cost fifteen cents when it was new, and so I was prospering right along and was very well satisfied.

But I lent it to Tom Sawyer and he lent it to Miss Rowena Fuller, which was a beautiful young lady and a favorite and full of spirits and never quiet but always breaking out in a new place with her inventions and making the whole town laugh, for she just lived for fun and was born for it. She was lovely in her disposition and the happiest person you ever see, and people said it took the sorrow out of life to see that girl breeze around and carry on, and hear her laugh, and certainly she done a lot of it, she was that lively and gay and pranksome.

She never meant any harm with her jokes, poor thing, but she never laughed any more after that time. She wouldn't ever done what she done if she had thought what was going to come of it. But she didn't think, she got right to work on her project, and she was so full of it she *couldn't* think; and she was so full of laugh that she couldn't hold still, but kept breaking out in a fresh place all the time, just with antissipations. She was going to scare old Miss Wormly, which was a superstitious old maid and lived all alone and was that timid she was afraid of everything, specially of ghosts, and was always dreading them, she couldn't help it. Miss Rowena put on the false-face and got herself up in a shroud and started for Miss Wormly's about eleven at night, with a lot of young people trailing after her to see the fun; and she tiptoed in, and Miss Wormly was sitting by her lamp sort of half dozing, and she crept up behind her and bent around and looked her in the face, still and solemn and awful. Miss Wormly turned white like a dead person, and stared and gasped for a second, then she begun to scream and shriek, and jumped up and started to run, but fainted and fell on the floor. She was gone mad, poor old harmless lady, and never got over it. Spent all her days in the sylum, and was always moaning and crying, and many a time jumping out of her bed in the night, thinking the ghost was after her again. Poor Miss Rowena's life was spoilt, too, she never got up any more jokes and couldn't ever laugh at anything any more.

REFERENCE
MATERIAL

Explanatory Notes

These notes give dates and general circumstances of composition for each work reprinted here, and they discuss topical allusions, furnish historical background, and define words or phrases not readily found in *Webster's Third New International Dictionary of the English Language*. Whenever Mark Twain modeled a fictional character after someone he knew, a note names the person. Names printed in SMALL CAPITALS indicate the person is more fully identified in the Biographical Directory.

Notes are keyed to page and line of the text: 4.10 means page 4, line 10 (chapter titles are not included when counting lines). Works are cited either by an abbreviation or by the author's last name, followed by a page (or page and volume) number: (*MTBus*, 24) or (Conard, 4:192). If more than one work by an author is cited by last name, the year of publication is used to distinguish them: (Dodge 1877, 12) means page 12 of the volume Dodge published in 1877, rather than the one he published in 1883, cited elsewhere as (Dodge 1883). Complete bibliographical information for all works cited is provided in References.

Previously unpublished words by Mark Twain are identified by a dagger (†) in the citation and are © 1989 by Edward J. Willi and Manufacturers Hanover Trust Company as Trustees of the Mark Twain Foundation, which reserves all reproduction or dramatization rights in every medium.

Boy's Manuscript
(1868)

"Boy's Manuscript" is the earliest of Mark Twain's fictional works to draw extensively upon his boyhood memories of Hannibal. It is, in Bernard DeVoto's phrase, "the embryo of *Tom Sawyer*," which Mark Twain began to write some four or five years later. In it the author demonstrates his evocative powers and his special gift for colloquial speech, as well as his intuitive preference for stories told "autobiographically," like *Huckleberry Finn*.

Mark Twain completed "Boy's Manuscript," but did not publish it. The first two pages of the manuscript (and thus the author's own title) are lost and have been missing at least since Albert Bigelow Paine, Mark Twain's first posthumous literary editor, found the surviving fifty-eight pages among the Mark Twain Papers. Typed on the envelope in which Paine stored the manuscript is the following: "Boy's Manuscript, beginning page 3   Probably written about 1870." When DeVoto first published the story in 1942, he adopted Paine's phrase as the title, and later editors accepted that decision. Paine's guess about the date of composition—"about 1870"— was also accepted by DeVoto and others (DeVoto 1942, 5–6, 7; *TS*, 419), but the physical evidence of the manuscript—paper, ink, and handwriting style—suggests a much earlier date, probably sometime between October and late November 1868. The paper is a type that Mark Twain used with some frequency in letters written between September 1868 and early January 1869, and then only infrequently until June 1869, when he stopped using it entirely. The compact handwriting and black ink make the manuscript, in overall appearance, nearly identical to letters he wrote in October 1868.

   This physical evidence is reinforced by biographical fact. In the fall of 1868, Clemens was assiduously courting Olivia Langdon, of Elmira, New York. Early in September, she turned down his initial proposal of marriage, but by the end of November, after two more refusals, she had changed her mind. (The pair became formally engaged in February 1869 and were married a year later.) Clearly some of the vicissitudes of Clemens's own courtship are reflected, obliquely and with gentle satire, in Billy Rogers's wooing of "Darling Amy."

1.5   Amy]   Anna Laura Hawkins.

2.7–9   Jimmy Riley . . . lick him again]   The now missing pages of the manuscript presumably informed the reader that the keeper of this journal was Billy Rogers, and that he had just had a fight with Jimmy Riley. Riley may have been modeled on Jim Reagan.

2.24–27   they would have carried me into her house . . . I would have had to stay there till I got well]   Billy's fantasy is clearly based on an experience that Clemens had shortly before writing this sketch. On 28 September 1868, after a brief stay at Olivia Langdon's Elmira home, Clemens, accompanied by her brother, Charles, was preparing to depart for the railroad depot: "Charley & I got into the wagon at 8 PM, to leave for New York, & just as we sat down on the aftermost seat the horse suddenly started, the seat broke loose, & we went over backwards, Charley falling in all sorts of ways & I lighting exactly on my head in the gutter & breaking my neck in eleven different places. I lay there about four or five minutes, completely insensible. . . . They took us in the library & laid us out" (SLC to Mary Mason Fairbanks, 5 Oct 68, CSmH, in *MTMF*, 39–40). Almost forty years later, in his autobiography, Clemens confessed that he had only feigned injury and unconsciousness in order to prolong his visit and further his courtship (AD, 14 Feb 1906, CU-MARK, in *MTA*, 2:106–9). Gladys Bellamy in 1950 was the first to notice this and other similarities between events in Clemens's own courtship and events represented in the story (Bellamy, 333).

3.16   twenty-two commas and a white alley]   Small marbles made from common clay were called "commas," or "commies." Superior and often larger marbles used for shooting were called "alleys," originally made from alabaster, but frequently of glass in imitation of alabaster (Cassidy, 1:39–40, 741).

4.29   a sure-enough china]   A marble made from genuine porcelain (Cassidy, 1:627).

4.29   spool cannon]   A toy cannon made by attaching elastic material to one end of a spool so that a pencil or similar projectile can be shot through the spool hole (*TS*, 473).

4.34   potato-gun]   A blowgun which uses pieces of potato as missiles. It is prepared by sharpening a large, hollow goose quill and pushing the sharpened end into a potato, a piece of which is then expelled by blowing on the other end of the quill (Howard and Howard, 24).

5.21   blue mass pills]   A preparation of mercury, used as a laxative (Wood and Bache, 929–31).

6.2–3   the water treatment—douche, sitz, wet-sheet and shower-bath]   In the 1840s and 1850s, the United States was swept by the "water cure" craze, a medical regimen using various ostensibly therapeutic applications of cold water. Here, Billy Rogers names several of the more popular treatments: the douche, in which patients stood or sat under a strong stream of water falling from a height of five to twenty feet; the sitz bath, which required sitting in a washtub roughly one-third full of water, with the feet outside the tub; the wet-sheet pack, in which patients were tightly wrapped in a sheet that had been dipped in cold water and wrung out, then bundled in blankets until warm, and finally immersed in a cold or tepid bath; and the shower bath, in which water was sprayed on the patient from overhead (Cayleff, 37–38; Weiss and Kemble, 18, 22; *OED* 1933, 9:769). In 1901, addressing a New York state legislative committee on public health, Clemens recalled that he was about nine years old when "the cold water cure was first talked about. . . . I remember how my mother used to stand me up naked in the back yard every morning and throw buckets of cold water on me, just to see what effect it would have. . . . And then, when the dousing was over, she would wrap me up in a sheet wet with ice water and then wrap blankets around that and put me to bed. . . . I would get up a perspiration that was something worth seeing" (Fatout, 386–87).

8.18   turned down foot]   Sent to the end of the line. In a spelling bee such as the one described in chapter 6 of *Tom Sawyer*, students lined up in accord with their standing at the end of the previous contest, the winner first. Each misspelling caused a player to move one place lower in the line, so that by missing enough words even the winner of the previous contest could end up at the opposite end, or foot, of the line (*TS*, 80, 480). The rules of the spelling bee described by Billy

Rogers were evidently more draconian, since Billy is "turned down foot" for missing a single word.

12.2–4   Capt. Kydd . . . Morgan . . . Gibbs . . . Lafitte . . . Black Avenger of the Spanish Main!]   Billy invokes one fictional pirate and four real, if legendary, ones. William Kidd (1645?–1701) was commissioned in 1696 by King William III to suppress piracy, particularly off the coast of America, but later was charged with piracy himself. He admitted that acts of piracy had been committed, but claimed that he had been overpowered by a mutinous crew. Despite inconclusive evidence, he was found guilty and hanged. Sir Henry Morgan (1635?–88) was a British buccaneer who raided Spanish possessions in the West Indies and Central America. Charles Gibbs (1794–1831), from Rhode Island, plundered merchant vessels along the coast of Cuba and was known for slaughtering the crews of ships he took. Jean Laffite or Lafitte (1780?–?1826), a Frenchman, led a band of privateers and smugglers headquartered off the coast of Louisiana. During the War of 1812 Laffite and his men helped General Andrew Jackson defend New Orleans and, as a reward, were pardoned for past crimes (Gosse, 222–28, 133–34). *The Black Avenger of the Spanish Main; or, The Fiend of Blood* (1847) was a sensational adventure novel by Ned Buntline (Edward Z. C. Judson).

12.35–13.3   Bill Bowen, he bought a louse from Archy Thompson . . . and begun to stir him up with a pin]   A true incident that involved Clemens's Hannibal schoolmates WILLIAM BOWEN and ARCHIBALD FUQUA. "I still remember the louse you bought of poor Arch Fuqua," Clemens wrote Bowen on 25 January 1868. "I told about that at a Congressional dinner in Washington the other day, & Lord, how those thieves laughed! It *was* a gorgeous old reminiscence. I just expect I shall publish it yet, some day" (TxU, in *MTLBowen*, 17). He included the incident in chapter 7 of *Tom Sawyer*, where Tom and his "bosom friend" Joe Harper (who is based on Bowen) torment a tick.

15.12   nigger-show business . . . he wanted to be bones]   In minstrel shows "Bones" was the character who played bones or castanets. He and the tambourine (or banjo) player were known in minstrel parlance as "end men"; they sat at opposite ends of the stage, sang comic songs, and engaged in banter with the "middleman," who sat between them and who was generally made the butt of their jokes. Clemens recalled that the "first negro-minstrel show" he ever saw came to Hannibal in the early 1840s, when he was ten years old or less. "It was a new institution . . . and it burst upon us as a glad and stunning surprise. . . . 'Bones' and 'Banjo' were the prime jokers and whatever funniness was to be gotten out of paint and exaggerated clothing they utilized to the limit" (AD, 30 Nov 1906, CU-MARK, in *MTE*, 110–11, 112).

17.24   fox or baste or three-cornered cat or hide'n'whoop]   "Fox" and "baste the bear" are essentially games of tag; "three-cornered cat" is a ball game in which there are three batters; and "hide'n'whoop" is a form of hide-and-seek (Routledge, 7–8, 24, 69; Mathews, 1:279, 2:1726).

Letter to William Bowen
(1870)

Four days after his marriage to Olivia Langdon on 2 February 1870, Clemens wrote this letter to William Bowen. The Clemenses had just settled into their house in Buffalo, a wedding gift from Olivia's father, Jervis. Clemens, occupied as co-owner and co-editor of the Buffalo *Express*, was enjoying the success of his second book, *The Innocents Abroad*, a copy of which he had sent to Bowen. Published in late July 1869, *Innocents* had been very widely and favorably reviewed, and by the time of this letter had sold almost 40,000 copies, earning Clemens royalties of approximately $7,300 (Hirst, 285, 491 n. 17; American Publishing Company, 46–52). Bowen and the other Hannibal villagers named in the letter are identified in the Biographical Directory.

20.6   The fountains of my great deep are broken up] Genesis 7:11: "the same day were all the fountains of the great deep broken up, and the windows of heaven were opened."

21.4   Holliday's Hill] Just north of Hannibal, this rise overlooking the Mississippi River was presumably named for its owners, the family of MELICENT S. HOLLIDAY. It is called Cardiff Hill in *Tom Sawyer* and in "Tom Sawyer's Conspiracy."

21.5   still-house branch] A stream emptying into the Mississippi River from the valley just north of Holliday's Hill, it provided water for one of Hannibal's early distilleries (Hagood and Hagood 1986, 205, 206).

21.7   "the Bay"] The Bay de Charles was a large inlet on the Mississippi about two miles north of Hannibal and extending some five miles to the northwest.

21.32–33   that poor fellow in the calaboose] DENNIS MCDERMID.

22.21–22   as well as we used to know "boils" from "breaks."] A boil is a turbulent swirl or eddy in a river. A break, which looks like a streak on the water's surface, is an ominous sign of a snag or other submerged obstacle (Cassidy, 1:323; *Lex*, 27; *Life on the Mississippi*, chapter 9).

23.1   Mollie] WILLIAM BOWEN's wife.

Tupperville-Dobbsville
(1876–80)

This depiction of a sleepy Arkansas town on the banks of the Mississippi was probably written between the fall of 1876 and the spring of 1880. Although Mark Twain abandoned the story after writing only nine and a half pages, he revived its imagery for *Huckleberry Finn* (1885). The dilapidated houses and the muddy streets lined with the town loafers reappear in chapter 21 of the novel, and the widow Bennett's home shares several characteristics with the Phelps farm (modeled after JOHN ADAMS

QUARLES's farm) in chapter 32. Mark Twain left the fragment untitled. The editorial title used here joins the two names Mark Twain gave to the village; he initially called it Tupperville, but in the final paragraph, which he added at a later time, he called it Dobbsville.

Clairvoyant
(1883 or 1884)

This unfinished tale is a curious blend of fact and fantasy. Set in Hannibal, most of its characters bear names of actual residents: a jeweler named Stevens, storekeepers named Selmes and Brittingham, and a lunatic boy named Ratcliff who tries to murder his mother are all mentioned in "Villagers of 1840–3" (and identified in the Biographical Directory). The story is a product of Mark Twain's continuing interest in psychic phenomena. In 1878 he wrote an article he called "Mental Telegraphy" (his term for thought transference), in which he claimed to believe in telepathic communication, despite never having seen a convincing clairvoyant performance. Fearing he would not be taken seriously, however, he did not publish the article for thirteen years (SLC 1891). Meanwhile, in 1884 he joined the Society for Psychical Research in London, writing its founder, William Fletcher Barrett, that he was convinced "people can have crystal-clear mental communication with each other over vast distances" (SLC to Barrett, 4 Oct 84, in Barrett, 167). And in 1895 he confirmed his belief in telepathy in a second article on the subject, "Mental Telegraphy Again" (SLC 1895b).

Albert Bigelow Paine supplied the title "Clairvoyant" on the manuscript of this story, dating it only "80^s." The physical evidence—paper, pencil, and handwriting—suggests late 1883 or 1884 as the most likely date of composition.

27.2   John H. Day]   No John H. Day is mentioned in Hannibal records. Two of Mark Twain's notes nevertheless suggest that he had known a printer with that last name: his notebook for 1900 mentions "Old printer Day & the spirits" (NB 43, CU-MARK†, TS p. 3), and an undated page of autobiographical notes mentions "Poor old Mr. Day" (Anderson Auction Company, lot 363). A character named "old Mr. Day" is a journeyman printer in "Tom Sawyer's Conspiracy" (148–49, 159–61).

30.27   the Sny]   A wooded island and channel across the river from Hannibal, mainly in Pike County, Illinois.

31.27   Palmyra]   The seat of Marion County, approximately twelve miles northwest of Hannibal.

Huck Finn and Tom Sawyer among the Indians
(1884)

When Mark Twain began writing "Indians" in July 1884, he was reading galley proofs of *Huckleberry Finn*, then scheduled to appear in December. That book concluded with Huck and Tom promising to "go for howling adventures amongst the Injuns, over in the Territory." Mark Twain planned to publish his sequel while that promise was still fresh in the minds of his readers. But he neither completed nor published "Indians," abandoning his effort in mid-sentence after only nine chapters.

Mark Twain's nephew and publishing partner, Charles L. Webster, enthusiastically approved the new literary project. He provided practical assistance by filling Clemens's requests for books about the West, particularly for "PERSONAL NARRATIVES of life & adventure out yonder on the Plains & in the Mountains . . . especially life *among the Indians*" (SLC to Charles L. Webster, 6 July 84, NPV, in *MTBus*, 265). Mark Twain was especially eager to find narratives that would help him refute the romantic portrayals of the Indian popularized by James Fenimore Cooper and others. He had become skeptical of Cooper's "noble savage" by 1861, when he journeyed overland from Missouri to Nevada Territory, observing Indians along the way and after his arrival. In *Roughing It* (1872) he wrote that it was the poverty and squalor of the Gosiutes (or Goshutes), natives of the inhospitable Nevada-Utah border region, that prompted him, "a disciple of Cooper and a worshipper of the Red Man," to wonder if he "had been over-estimating the Red Man while viewing him through the mellow moonshine of romance." His disenchantment left him disgusted with Cooper's romantic portrayals and unsympathetic toward the American Indian: "It was curious to see how quickly the paint and tinsel fell away from him and left him treacherous, filthy and repulsive—and how quickly the evidences accumulated that wherever one finds an Indian tribe he has only found Goshoots more or less modified by circumstances and surroundings—but Goshoots, after all. They deserve pity, poor creatures; and they can have mine—at this distance. Nearer by, they never get anybody's" (*Roughing It*, chapter 19).

In writing "Indians," Mark Twain's primary source of information about Indian character and culture was *Our Wild Indians* (1883), by army officer Richard Irving Dodge, a book full of biased generalizations, but highly commended for accuracy in its day. Dodge hoped to dispel the romantic image of the "noble Red Man" and at the same time to educate those who saw only an "ignoble savage." He regarded the Indian as a partially civilized primitive who would become a useful citizen once instilled with a sense of morality: "If our good missionaries would let him alone in his religion . . . and simply strive to supply him with a code of morals, his subsequent conversion might be easy and his future improvement assured." While he forcefully condemned the government's policy of "debasing, pauperizing, and exterminating" Indians, he saw "no future for the Indian as Indian." He advocated the gradual breakup of the tribal system so that Indians could be "individually absorbed in the great family of American citizens" (Dodge 1883, 41, 56–58, 641, 645–46). "*There's* a man who knows all about Indians, & yet has some humanity in him," Mark Twain wrote of Dodge, adding that "knowledge of Indians, & humanity, are seldom found in the same individual" (SLC to William Dean Howells, 22 Feb 77, OFH, in *MTHL*, 1:172).

Mark Twain supplemented *Our Wild Indians* with several other books: *The Plains of the Great West and Their Inhabitants* (1877), also by Dodge; *Sheridan's Troopers on the Borders* (1870) by De Benneville Randolph Keim; *The Oregon Trail* (1849) by Francis Parkman; *My Life on the Plains* (1874) by George Armstrong Custer; and William F. Cody's autobiography, *The Life of the Hon. William F. Cody, Known as Buffalo Bill, the Famous Hunter, Scout and Guide* (1879). His indebtedness to his sources is traced in the explanatory notes that follow (see also *HH&T*, 81–91).

Mark Twain's dependence on these "authorities" helps account for his inability to complete his story. Striving for an unsparingly realistic depiction of the brutality he believed to be characteristic of the Great Plains Indians, Mark Twain made their abduction of his heroine the keystone of his plot—even though his sources asserted that rape was the inevitable fate of such captives. Unable to write frankly about rape, yet convinced that realism demanded he do so, Mark Twain abandoned the story, probably around the middle of August 1884. Although his normal practice with recalcitrant material was to pigeonhole it and return to it at a later date, there is no evidence that he ever resumed work on "Indians." There are, however, two indications that he was interested in continuing the tale: in 1889 or 1890, he had the incomplete manuscript printed on the Paige typesetter, the mechanical composing machine whose development he financed for a decade; and in November 1890, he made a notebook entry reminding himself to have Tom Sawyer play the role of a medicine man (*N&J3*, 594).

33.4–5   Me and Tom Sawyer and the nigger Jim]   In the preface to *Tom Sawyer* (1876), Mark Twain stated that Huck and Tom were both "drawn from life." He modeled Huck after TOM BLANKENSHIP, and Tom after a number of boys, including himself, JOHN B. BRIGGS, and WILLIAM BOWEN. He based Jim on DANIEL, a slave owned by his uncle JOHN ADAMS QUARLES.

33.5   old Miss Watson]   MARY ANN NEWCOMB.

33.6–7   away down in Arkansaw at Tom's aunt Sally's and uncle Silas's]   The home of Sally and Silas Phelps was a fictional re-creation of JOHN ADAMS QUARLES's Missouri farm.

33.13   aunt Polly]   JANE LAMPTON CLEMENS.

33.17   Sid and Mary]   Tom Sawyer's half-brother and his cousin, loosely modeled after HENRY and PAMELA ANN CLEMENS, respectively.

35.1   widow Douglas]   MELICENT S. HOLLIDAY.

35.9   Gin'l Gaines]   The Hannibal drunkard, "General" GAINES.

41.28   out on the Great Plains]   Mark Twain's setting is the Oregon Trail, which, beginning in the early 1840s, became the great emigrant route to the Pacific Northwest. It ran for about two thousand miles from towns on the Missouri River (Independence, Missouri, was a favorite starting point) to the Columbia River region of Oregon. Most of the action of "Indians" takes place along the section of the trail that followed the Platte and North Platte Rivers through present-day Nebraska and Wyoming toward Fort Laramie.

43.31   one named Hog Face]   In *Our Wild Indians*, Dodge stated that among Indians "any personal defect, deformity of character, or casual incident furnishing ground for a good story, is eagerly seized upon as a fit name. 'Powder Face,' the war chief of the Arrapahoes . . . is known . . . by the title which was given him from having his face badly burned by an explosion of powder when he was a young man" (Dodge 1883, 228). Long before he read Dodge, however, Mark Twain had enjoyed burlesquing Indian names. In an 1862 letter to his mother written from Nevada Territory, he drew a comically repellent portrait of a Washo Indian family and gave them such names as "head-chief Hoop-de-doodle-doo," "Timid-Rat," "Bottled Thunder," and "Princess Invisible Rainbow." "You see," he wrote, "like all Indians, they glory in high-sounding names" (SLC to Jane Lampton Clemens, 20 Mar 62, *L1*, 177).

45.22–23   Man-afraid-of-his-Mother-in-law]   Mark Twain was probably burlesquing the name of a famous Oglala Sioux chief, Man-Afraid-of-His-Horse (or "Man-afraid-of-his-horses," according to Dodge 1883, 228). The name, handed down from father to son for generations, originated "around 1760 when the Sioux were obtaining their first horses and were having difficulty in learning to ride these strange animals" (Hyde, 68).

48.23–25   how else they had served the bodies . . . but it would not do to put it in a book]   In his 1870 sketch, "The Noble Red Man," Mark Twain had bitterly condemned Indian atrocities, citing Keim's *Sheridan's Troopers on the Borders* as authority for his facts. He commented then that the Indians' "favorite mutilations cannot be put into print" (SLC 1870b, 428).

50.3–7   "Tom, where did you learn about Injuns . . . . Cooper's novels] James Fenimore Cooper had presented an idealized picture of the Indian in his "Leather-Stocking Tales": *The Pioneers* (1823), *The Last of the Mohicans* (1826), *The Prairie* (1827), *The Pathfinder* (1840), and *The Deerslayer* (1841). In 1862 Clemens offered his mother an unflattering portrait of members of the Washo tribe, calling it a "full and correct account of these lovely Indians—not gleaned from Cooper's novels, Madam, but the result of personal observation" (SLC to Jane Lampton Clemens, 20 Mar 62, *L1*, 176). He continued his rebuttal of Cooper in "A Day at Niagara" (SLC 1869b), "The Noble Red Man" (SLC 1870b), chapter 19 of *Roughing It* (1872), and in passing elsewhere, presenting a harsh and unsympathetic view of Indians with which the present story is consistent.

50.36   hived]   Captured (*Lex*, 111).

56.4–5   an Injun don't kill a whole gang . . . unless he is mighty mad or in a desperate hurry]   In *Our Wild Indians* Dodge claimed: "In a close contest, or if the Indians have cause to be exceptionally angry, the wounded man is promptly dispatched. If there be plenty of time and no danger apprehended, the unfortunate prisoner will have full experience of the ingenuity in torture of these fiends" (Dodge 1883, 529).

56.16–17　they didn't kill the nigger . . . and ain't going to]　"An Indian will never take the scalp of a colored soldier, nor does he give any reason for it; all to be got out of him by way of explanation is, 'Buffalo soldier no good, heap bad medicine'" (Dodge 1883, 517).

57.2　hunted up some whites to retaliate on]　"Indians believe that the manes or shades of the departed slain in battle require to be appeased by the death of the slayer, if possible; or, failing his, by that of some one of the slayer's nation or tribe" (Dodge 1883, 182).

58.2–3　They're fond of children]　In *Our Wild Indians*, Dodge remarked on the Indians' "very great fondness" for children:

> In their raids on each other and on the whites, those children who are large enough to help themselves a little, and yet not old enough to be likely to have strong affection or memory, are carried off to the tribe, and adopted into it. These are sometimes adopted by men who have lost children, otherwise they are brought up in the families of their captors. In either case they are treated exactly as are the other children. (Dodge 1883, 532)

60.25　Brace Johnson was a beautiful man]　Brace Johnson resembles James Butler (Wild Bill) Hickok (1837–76), George Armstrong Custer (1839–76), and other historical figures who appear in the works Mark Twain consulted before writing "Indians." By 1884, the year of the story's composition, the plainsman and Indian fighter was a national type made familiar by pulp fiction, and the resemblances probably are generic and not indicative of any specific borrowing (Hart, 153–55).

61.21　he had their religion]　Dodge asserted that "nine-tenths" of the white men who lived among the Indians "sooner or later" adopted their religion, believing in "two gods, equals in wisdom and power." The "Good God" endeavors

> to aid the Indian in all his undertakings. . . . He provides all the good and pleasurable things of life. Warmth, food, joy, success in love, distinction in war, all come from him. The . . . Bad God . . . is always the enemy of each individual red man. . . . From him proceed all the disasters, misfortunes, privations, and discomforts of life. . . . The Good God is not an exacting or jealous god. For his unremitting labors, his devoted services . . . he demands nothing in return. . . . No thanks are necessary. . . . Of the Bad God they [the Indians] stand in most abject fear, and are constantly devising expedients by which they hope to evade or turn aside some portion of his wrathful power. (Dodge 1883, 100–101, 108–9)

70.28　these Sioux was Ogillalahs]　The Oglala were a division of the Teton, the largest of the seven tribes of the Sioux Indians.

71.34–72.1　Vaskiss the trader . . . Roubidou the blacksmith]　Mark Twain gleaned these names from Francis Parkman's *Oregon Trail*. Louis Vasquez (1798–1868) was a famous mountain man and fur trader, and several members of the Robidoux family (spelling of the name varied) were renowned as frontiersmen (Parkman 1880, 95, 99, 103, 113, 130; Parkman 1969, 526–28, 563).

75.13　water-spout]　A torrential burst of rain. Mark Twain apparently witnessed the effects of such a cloudburst while on a mining expedition in Nevada Territory in early January 1861 (*L1*, 150 n. 3). His description of the experience in chapters

30–31 of *Roughing It* has details in common with Huck's account here: the Indians' uncanny prophetic ability (76.26–77.3) and the eight-day entrapment by floodwaters (77.15). Nevertheless, Huck's description of the waterspout itself derives from Dodge's recollection of an occurrence on the Great Plains. Alerted to a "distant roaring, rushing sound," Dodge watched from the bank of a dry stream:

> In a few moments a long creamy wave, beaten into foam, crept swiftly with a hissing sound across the sand. This appeared to be only a few inches in depth. Following with equal speed, and at a distance of about sixty feet behind the advance of this sheet, was a straight, unbroken mass of water of at least four feet in height. The front of this mass was not rounded into a wave, but rose sheer and straight, a perfect wall of water. From this front wall the mass rose gradually to the rear, and was covered with logs and *débris* of all kinds, rolling and plunging in the tremendous current. In ten minutes from the passage of the advance wave, the water at my feet was at least fifteen feet deep, and the stream nearly half a mile wide. . . . The rain which furnished all this water was a waterspout of probably an hour's duration. (Dodge 1877, 84–85)

77.27 Sioux . . . Brulé's, mostly] Like the Oglala (see the note at 70.28), the Brulé were one of the principal tribes of the Teton Sioux.

78.24 four stakes drove in the ground] In *The Plains of the Great West and Their Inhabitants*, Dodge wrote:

> Either the character and customs of the Indians have greatly changed, or Cooper and some other novelists knew nothing of Indians when they placed their heroines as captives in the hands of these savages. . . . No words can express the horror of the situation of that most unhappy woman who falls into the hands of these savage fiends. The husband or other male protectors killed or dispersed, she is borne off in triumph to where the Indians make their first camp. Here, if she makes no resistance, she is laid upon a buffalo robe, and each in turn violates her person, the others dancing, singing, and yelling around her. If she resists at all her clothing is torn off from her person, four pegs are driven into the ground, and her arms and legs, stretched to the utmost, are tied fast to them by thongs. Here, with the howling band dancing and singing around her, she is subjected to violation after violation, outrage after outrage, to every abuse and indignity, until not unfrequently death releases her from suffering. (Dodge 1877, 395)

80.18–19 Injuns . . . are afraid to hurt a crazy man] Dodge claimed that the Indians avoided "madmen or idiots," believing them to be "directly under the malevolent influence of the Bad God." As evidence he cited the case of "a prominent scientist":

> In a country full of hostile Sioux, without a blanket or mouthful to eat, he started alone, armed only with his butterfly net and loaded only with his pack for carrying specimens. One day, when busily occupied, he suddenly found himself surrounded by Indians. He showed no fear, and was carried to the village. His pack was found loaded with insects, bugs, and loathsome reptiles. The Indians decided that a white man who would come alone into that country unarmed, without food or bedding, for the accumulation of such things, must be crazy; so, the pack having been destroyed as "bad medicine," the doctor was carefully led out of camp and turned loose. (Dodge 1883, 220–23)

Mark Twain may also have been influenced by Robert Montgomery Bird's *Nick of the Woods* (1837). In that novel Nathan Slaughter paints lizards, snakes, and skulls on his skin and feigns an epileptic fit to frighten Indians.

Jane Lampton Clemens
(1890)

In early November 1890, in response to a proposal from a newspaper syndicate "that furnishes all the western newspapers with patent insides," Orion Clemens wrote a biographical sketch of Jane Lampton Clemens, who had died on 27 October (Orion Clemens to SLC, 1 Nov 90, CU-MARK). The surviving pages of his sketch show it to have been anecdotal but conventional (*HH&T*, 381–82). After reading it in manuscript, Mark Twain sent Orion a "dispatch to halt." He was, however, evidently inspired by Orion's sketch and decided to write a memorial "magazine article" himself (Orion Clemens to SLC, 13 Nov 1890, CU-MARK). The result was "Jane Lampton Clemens," a warm and unconventional tribute, richly revealing of its author as well as its subject, although there is no indication that Mark Twain ever attempted to publish it. It was probably written in November or December 1890.

82.16–19   It dates back forty-seven years; she was forty years old, then, and I was eight . . . . my brother, two years older than I . . . lay dead]   The dating in this passage is imprecise. BENJAMIN L. CLEMENS died on 12 May 1842, at the age of nine, forty-eight years before Mark Twain wrote this sketch. JANE LAMPTON CLEMENS then was thirty-eight and Samuel Clemens was six-and-a-half.

84.18–21   I saw a vicious devil of a Corsican . . . chasing his grown daughter. . . . My mother spread her door wide to the refugee]   The brutal father, Hannibal taverner JESSE H. PAVEY, is identified in a page of autobiographical notes Mark Twain made about 1897: "The Paveys. Aunt P. protects a daughter" (SLC 1897c†). "Aunt P." was Aunt Polly, JANE LAMPTON CLEMENS's fictional counterpart.

86.7–10   the Lambtons, now Earls of Durham . . . ancestors of hers]   The Lambton family had been owners of Lambton Castle, in Durham County, England, since shortly after the Norman Conquest (1066). John George Lambton (1792–1840) had been created first Earl of Durham in 1833. His grandson, also John George Lambton (1855–1928), was third earl in 1890, the year Mark Twain wrote this sketch. Jane Clemens's paternal grandfather, William Lampton (1724–90), who evidently belonged to a collateral branch of the family, emigrated to Virginia about 1740 (Burke, 528–29; Debrett, P409; Selby, 112; Keith, 3–4, 7).

86.21   an ancestor—one Clement—who *did* something]   Gregory Clement, a London merchant and member of Parliament. In January 1649 Clement was a member of the high court of justice that tried Charles I and signed the king's death warrant. In 1660, when the monarchy was restored under Charles II, Clement went into hiding, but was found and executed that October.

86.32   "Col. Sellers" was a Lampton]   Colonel Sellers, the irrepressible speculator and visionary based on JAMES J. LAMPTON, first appeared in Mark Twain and Charles Dudley Warner's *The Gilded Age* (1874).

87.2–14   the Lampton heir came to this country . . . breeding ancestors of future American Claimants. . . . "The Earl" . . . was a Kentuckian]   Lampton family tradition held that Samuel Lampton, who emigrated to Virginia with his brother William about 1740, was the legitimate heir to the ancient Lambton estate in Durham County, England, but had been displaced by a usurping younger brother who became the Earl of Durham. Peerage records fail to support any American claim to the Lambton lands or title, making no mention of either Samuel or William Lampton, both of whom died long before the earldom was created in 1833. Nevertheless, JESSE MADISON LEATHERS, of Kentucky, great-grandson of Samuel Lampton, professed himself the rightful earl throughout an impecunious, vagrant lifetime, occasionally appealing to Mark Twain for financial assistance. In *The American Claimant* (1892), Mark Twain mocked the Lampton pretensions, portraying Colonel Sellers as successor to one Simon Lathers in attempting to appropriate the title and estate of the "Earl of Rossmore" ("Mark Twain's Blue Blood," unidentified clipping, reprinting the Louisville [Ky.] *Ledger* of unknown date, CU-MARK; Keith, 3, 4; Selby, 112; Burke, 528–29).

87.26–27   a letter from some red-hot Virginian son of my other branch]   Mark Twain had in mind a letter in which his third cousin Sherrard Clemens (1820–80)—lawyer, duelist, and Democratic congressman from Virginia (1852–53, 1857–61)—attacked his support of a Republican candidate for president: "I regret, very deeply, to see, that you have announced, your adhesion, to that inflated bladder, . . . Rutherford Burchard Hayes. You come, with myself, from Gregory Clemens, the regicide, who voted for the death of Charles, and who was beheaded, disembolled, and drawn in a hurdle. It is good, for us, to have an ancestor, who escaped, the ignominy of being hung. But, I would rather have, such an ancestor, than adhere, to . . . Hayes, who, is the mere, representative, of Wall street brokers, three ball men, Lombardy Jews, European Sioux, class legislation, special priviledges to the few, and denial of equality of taxation, to the many" (Sherrard Clemens to SLC, 2 Sept 76, CU-MARK; *BDAC*, 706; "Sherrard Clemens," New York *Times*, 3 June 80, 5; Bell, 34, 36).

89.17–20   A woman . . . sold to a Mr. B.]   JENNY, the slave sold to WILLIAM B. BEEBE.

90.1–13   My father . . . consented to take his note . . . for $250 and let him off at that]   In late 1844—nearly three years after agreeing to accept this payment (reduced from $470)— JOHN MARSHALL CLEMENS was still trying to collect from William Lester of Vicksburg, Mississippi (John Marshall Clemens to Messrs. Coleman and Johnson, 2 Nov 44, NPV; Wecter 1952, 75–76). It is not known if Lester ever paid the debt.

90.19–32   my father . . . writes this: "I still have Charley. . . . I expect to sell him for whatever he will bring. . . ." It makes a body homesick for Charley, even after fifty years. Thank God I have no recollection of him as house servant of ours]   Although Samuel Clemens assumed Charley was a slave, a close reading of John Marshall Clemens's letter of 5 January 1842 suggests that Charley may have been a horse. John Clemens originally had planned to return home after his stop in Vicksburg, Mississippi, but changed his plans and decided to continue on horseback through "Tennessee & Kentucky & try to effect a sale of my Tennessee lands." He purchased "an old saddle & a new bridle & blanket" and explained to his wife that after his journey to Tennessee he would sell Charley and then "take water again," although "steamboat travelling does not agree with me—my health is improved though by riding—and I think I shall stand the travelling cold as it will be over land, better than I do on a boat" (John Marshall Clemens to Jane Lampton Clemens and children, 5 Jan 42, CU-MARK). A promissory note given to Clemens by Abner Phillips of Tennessee "for value received this 24th day of January 1842" suggests Clemens may have sold Charley for ten barrels of tar to be delivered in Missouri within the year (Phillips 1842). If the value of this transaction was forty or fifty dollars (the amount Clemens was offered for Charley in New Orleans and Vicksburg), the price seems appropriate for a horse, but uncommonly low for a male slave, unless very old or in very poor health (Trexler, 38–41).

Villagers of 1840–3
(1897)

Mark Twain made these notes about the people of Hannibal, Missouri, in late July or early August 1897, during a summer stay in Weggis, Switzerland. Hannibal, on the Mississippi River, had barely a thousand inhabitants when Clemens's family settled there in November 1839, a few weeks before his fourth birthday. By June of 1853, however, when seventeen-year-old Clemens left to seek employment as a printer in St. Louis, the town's population had more than tripled. Although his family's connection to Hannibal ended just a few months later—with Jane, Orion, and Henry Clemens moving to Muscatine, Iowa—Clemens himself never lost touch with his boyhood home. He maintained lifelong friendships with a few of its residents and kept informed about others through correspondence and also through occasional reunions. He visited Hannibal at least seven times between his initial departure and the writing of "Villagers": in 1855 to attend to family property; in 1858 to bury his brother Henry; in 1861 before serving for a few weeks in a company of Confederate irregulars; in 1867 to lecture; in 1882 while he was traveling on the Mississippi River in preparation for the writing of *Life on the Mississippi*; in 1885 to lecture again; and in 1890 to bury his mother. Moreover, he supplemented his own store of information by purchasing a copy of Return Ira Holcombe's *History of Marion County, Missouri* upon its publication in 1884; the volume contained sketches of Hannibal's prominent citizens, including one of John Marshall Clemens that Orion Clemens had helped to prepare.

Clemens was keenly aware that his boyhood impressions had a strength and vividness unrivaled in his store of memories. In 1886, having depicted antebellum Hannibal as St. Petersburg in both *Tom Sawyer* and *Huckleberry Finn* during the preceding ten years, he acknowledged that "recent names & things take no hold on my bald-headed memory; they slip-up & slide off: but when you come to the names

& things of thirty-five years ago, you are uttering music, & my memory is alert" (SLC to George H. Himes, 17 Jan 86, MoPeS†). "Villagers," with its wealth of arresting, highly accurate detail about the people, events, and social customs of Clemens's youth, proves that Hannibal's "hold" on him remained consistently strong.

Although writing for himself only, Clemens superficially disguised his immediate family, a stratagem that perhaps facilitated his particularly candid portraits of his stern and undemonstrative father (Judge Carpenter), his feisty, good-hearted, and eloquent mother (Joanna Carpenter), and his feckless older brother Orion (Oscar Carpenter), as well as his passing remarks about his sister Pamela (Priscella Carpenter), his younger brother Henry (Hartley Carpenter), and himself (Simon Carpenter). He attempted no disguise for other relatives, however, not even when his memories included unpleasant details: his cousin James Quarles's alcoholism and dissipation, for example, and his aunt Ella Lampton's affair with the young doctor who boarded with her and her husband. And he used the real names of other Hannibal residents, with only two exceptions: Dr. Richard F. Barret (called Dr. Ray), an early suitor of Jane Clemens's, and the "unbeliever" Blennerhasset, whose identity remains unknown. Hannibal is referred to as "St P"—an abbreviation for St. Petersburg—but the names of other towns and cities appear without disguise. Although Clemens's title assigned the dates "1840–3" to this compendium of recollections, only a few actually belong to that period, when he was between the ages of four and eight. Possibly "1840–3" was merely an inadvertence, since his recollections actually span the years 1840–53, the length of his residence in Hannibal.

In an 1895 interview, Clemens remarked: "I don't believe an author, good, bad or indifferent, ever lived, who created a character. It was always drawn from his recollection of someone he had known. Sometimes, like a composite photograph, an author's presentation of a character may possibly be from the blending of . . . two or more real characters in his recollection. But, even when he is making no attempt to draw his character from life . . . he is yet unconsciously drawing from memory" (Budd, 52–53). In compiling "Villagers," Clemens had at least one literary project in mind—a book, which he tentatively called his "New Huck Finn." In July 1897, with an eye to shaping that story, he had filled thirteen pages of his notebook with random recollections of Hannibal (NB 41, CU-MARK, TS pp. 56–62). "Villagers" clearly was to serve the same function as the notebook, but in a more comprehensive and orderly fashion. Before the summer of 1897 was over Clemens began two new stories based on his memories of Hannibal: "Hellfire Hotchkiss" and "Tom Sawyer's Conspiracy." The latter apparently was intended to be the "New Huck Finn."

It was probably when he was writing "Hellfire Hotchkiss," in mid-August 1897, that Clemens separated the final nine pages of "Villagers"—"to persuade the other . . . of her tongue." (105.21–108.12 in the present text)—from the rest of the manuscript. The discussion of Oscar Carpenter (Orion Clemens) in the opening chapter of "Hellfire Hotchkiss" grew directly out of the characterization of him in the concluding pages of "Villagers," and Clemens may have hoped to utilize the earlier description in his new story. When he discontinued work on "Hellfire Hotchkiss," he stored the manuscript in an envelope together with the final pages of "Villagers," labeling the "Villagers" segment "rejected MS that may come good." The separated pages were mistakenly published as part of "The Hellfire Hotchkiss Sequence" in 1967 (*S&B*, 200–203). Two years later, when "Villagers" was first published, it was reported to be "a fragment inasmuch as the last entry breaks off in the middle of a sentence at the bottom of a page" (*HH&T*, 23). Not until August 1981 did Sam Howard, then an undergraduate at Claremont College, point out that the fragment included in "The Hellfire Hotchkiss Sequence" was in fact the proper ending of "Villagers," which is here published in its entirety for the first time. Almost all of the individuals mentioned in it are now identified, from contemporary documents and other sources, in the Biographical Directory.

96.15 "Last Link is Broken"] A sentimental song by William Clifton, written about 1840:

> The last link is broken that bound me to thee,
> And the words thou hast spoken have render'd me free;
> That bright glance misleading, on others may shine,
> Those eyes smil'd unheeding when tears burst from mine.
>
> (Clifton 1840)

In chapter 38 of *Life on the Mississippi* (1883), Mark Twain reported that this was among the songs found on the piano in the "finest dwelling" of every river town "between Baton Rouge and St. Louis." It is sung in such a dwelling by the Grangerford girls in chapter 17 of *Huckleberry Finn* (1885), but in chapter 38 is characterized by Tom Sawyer as "painful music" attractive to rats (Gribben, 1:148).

97.10–11 Put cards in minister's baptising robe. Trouble in consequence] In an 1871 lecture Clemens had attributed this prank to his fellow humorist Artemus Ward:

> Once when a schoolboy, a friend and he got hold of a pack of cards and indulged heavily in euchre. A Baptist minister was stopping at the house, and to secrete the cards they placed them in his black gown, which hung in a closet. But what was his horror to see the minister one day, in the river baptising his converts, and presently the cards commenced to float upon the water, the first cards being a couple of bowers and three aces. Well, he got walloped for this, and his aunt pictured to him the humiliation of the minister. Said she: "I don't see how he got out of it." Artemus replied: "I don't see how he could help going out on a hand like that." (Lorch 1968, 298)

In some autobiographical notes that may have been written in the same year as "Villagers," Clemens confessed: "It was Will Bowen & me. I put it on Artemus Ward" (SLC 1897c†). The embarrassed minister was WILLIAM BOWEN's grandfather, the Reverend BARTON WARREN STONE.

97.27–28 "Oh, on Long Island's Sea-girt Shore."] The opening line of "Rockaway," lyrics by Henry John Sharpe, music by Henry Russell:

> On old Long Island's sea-girt shore
> Many an hour I've whil'd away,
> In list'ning to the breaker's roar,
> That wash the beach at Rockaway.
> Transfix'd I've stood while nature's lyre
> In one harmonious concert broke,

> And catching its promethean fire,
> My inmost soul to rapture woke. Oh!
> (J.C.H., 1:106)

98.6   Kate Field]   Mary Katherine Keemle (Kate) Field (1838–96), a journalist, author, and lecturer who gained considerable popularity as a New York *Tribune* correspondent from Boston, London, and elsewhere. Clemens, who had met her in 1871, had a low opinion of her journalism and called her lecture technique "repellently artificial" (SLC 1898a, 9†).

98.23   *The two young sailors*—Irish]   The sailors have not been identified, but an entry in one of Clemens's notebooks for 1900 provides some information about them: "Huck tells of those heros the 2 Irish youths who painted ships on Goodwin's walls & ran away. They told sea-adventures which made all the boys sick with envy & resolve to run away & go to sea—then later a man comes hunting for them for a small crime—laughs at their sailor-talk" (NB 43, CU-MARK†, TS p. 6). Goodwin's was the name of a tavern in Palmyra, about twelve miles from Hannibal (Holcombe, 200).

99.6–7   The "long dog."]   The anecdote apparently alluded to, one of Clemens's favorites, has not been recovered, although the punchline recurs in his notebooks, for example in 1879: "If all one dog, mighty long dog" (N&J2, 279; see also N&J3, 359, 644). The gist of the story is suggested by an illustrated postcard that author and editor George Iles sent Clemens in 1907, showing a barn containing several cows. Upon seeing the head of a cow in one window, the hind portion of a second cow in another window, and the torso of a third cow in the doorway between the two windows, a startled observer, mistaking the three cows for one, says "Wal, if that ain't the darnedest longest cow I ever see." "This recalls your St. Louis dog story," Iles wrote on the postcard (20 July 1907, CU-MARK). In chapter 45 of *Following the Equator* (1897), Clemens had told of "a long, low dog" he had seen on a train—perhaps a version of the same anecdote, although the notebook punchline is not included. No association of the anecdote with REBECCA PAVEY can be documented, however, and it remains conceivable that Clemens was here thinking of a minstrel routine known as "the long dog scratch" (DeVoto 1932, 34; Wecter 1952, 190).

99.24   Byron, Scott, Cooper, Marryatt, Boz]   George Gordon Byron (1788–1824); Walter Scott (1771–1832); James Fenimore Cooper (1789–1851); Frederick Marryat (1792–1848); and Charles Dickens (1812–70), who used the pseudonym Boz. Mark Twain was favorably disposed toward Byron's poetry and Marryat's fiction and travel writings. His responses to the other writers were more complex—evolving, in varying degrees, from early enthusiasm to mature dislike. In chapter 46 of *Life on the Mississippi* (1883) he blamed Scott's novels for the "jejune romanticism" prevalent in the antebellum South, later dismissing them as "so juvenile! so artificial, so shoddy" (SLC to Brander Matthews, 4 May 1903, NNC, in *MTL*, 2:738). He condemned Cooper for a prose style he called "a crime against the language" (SLC 1895a, 12) and for the romanticized depiction of the American Indian he attempted to counter in "Huck Finn and Tom Sawyer among the Indians." And of Dickens he remarked: "I must fain confess that with the years I have lost much of my youthful admiration. . . . I cannot laugh and cry with him as I was wont. I seem to see all the machinery of the business too clearly, the effort is too patent. . . . How I used to laugh at Simon Tapper[t]it, and the Wellers, and a host more! But I can't do it now somehow; and time, it seems to me, is the true test of humour" ("Visit of Mark Twain," Sydney [Australia] *Morning Herald*, 17 Sept 95, 5). For an overview of Mark Twain's opinion of all these authors, see Gribben, 1:120–22, 159–60, 186–92, 452, and 2:612–18.

99.26   Oft in the Stilly Night]   A song dating from 1818, with lyrics by Thomas Moore set to a Scottish air arranged by Sir John Stevenson:

> Oft in the stilly night,
> Ere slumber's chain has bound me,
> Fond mem'ry brings the light
> Of other days around me,
> The smiles, the tears, of boyhoods years,
> The words of Love then spoken,
> The eyes that shone now dimm'd and gone,
> The cheerful hearts now broken!
>   (Ogilvie, 26)

In his 1896–97 notebook, among a series of entries about his recently deceased daughter Susy, Clemens jotted the final four of these lines from memory; in his 1902 notebook he reminded himself to use this song in a story he was planning about Huck and Tom (NB 39, TS p. 58, and NB 45, TS p. 15, CU-MARK; Gribben, 1:483).

99.26–27   Last Rose of Summer]   Thomas Moore's lyrics (1813) were sung to an old Irish melody:

> 'Tis the last rose of summer
> Left blooming alone;
> All her lovely companions
> Are faded and gone;
> No flow'r of her kindred,
> No rosebud is nigh,
> To reflect back her blushes,
> Or give sigh for sigh!
>   (Ogilvie, 118)

This song, which Mark Twain called "exquisite" in 1865, was a lifelong favorite. In his 1902 notebook, among notes for a new Huck and Tom story, he reminded himself to "Get in Last Rose" (*ET&S2*, 180; NB 45, CU-MARK†, TS p. 15; Gribben, 1:483).

99.27   The Last Link]   See the note at 96.15.

99.27   Bonny Doon]   "The Banks o' Doon" (1792), written by Robert Burns and sung to an old melody of disputed origin:

> Ye banks and braes of bonny Doon,
> How can ye bloom sae fresh and fair?
> How can ye chaunt, ye little birds,
> While I'm so wae, and full of care?
> Ye'll break my heart, ye little birds,
> That wander thro' that flow'ring thorn,
> Ye mind me of departing joys,
> Departed, never to return.
> (Ogilvie, 156–57)

Another of Mark Twain's longtime favorites, this song is given passing mention in "Schoolhouse Hill" (218.36–219.1; see also Gribben, 1:115).

99.27   Old Dog Tray]   By Stephen Foster (1853):

> Old dog Tray's ever faithful,
> Grief cannot drive him away,
> He's gentle, he is kind,
> I shall never, never find
> A better friend than old dog Tray.
> (*Heart Songs*, 156–57)

In 1866 Mark Twain called this one of the "d—dest, oldest, vilest songs" (*N&J1*, 262; see also Gribben, 1:238).

99.27–28   for the lady I love will soon be a bride]   This song has not been identified.

99.28   Gaily the Troubadour]   A song by Thomas Haynes Bayly, written in the early nineteenth century:

> Gaily the Troubadour
> Touch'd his guitar,
> When he was hastening
> Home from the war.
> Singing "From Palestine
> Hither I come,
> Lady Love! Lady Love!
> Welcome me home."
> (Bayly, 1:192)

99.28–29   Bright Alfarata]   "The Blue Juniata" (1844), by Marion Dix Sullivan, celebrates Alfarata, an Indian girl who lived with her "warrior good" on the banks of Pennsylvania's Juniata River. In his autobiography Clemens mentioned this as one of the "sentimental songs" popular with minstrel troupes (AD, 30 Nov 1906, CU-MARK, in *MTE*, 114; J.C.H., 1:93; Gribben, 2:678).

99.30–32   Old Kentucky Home . . . Massa's in de Cold Ground; Swanee River]   All by Stephen Foster: "My Old Kentucky Home" (1853), the source of the lyric Clemens recalls; "Massa's in de Cold, Cold Ground" (1852); and "Swanee River" (1851), more properly known as "The Old Folks at Home" (Gribben, 1:238).

99.33   The gushing Crusaders admired]   Probably Sir Walter Scott's *Tales of the Crusaders*, two novels (*The Betrothed, The Talisman*) first published in 1825.

100.18   the three "rich" men]   Mark Twain may be referring to Judge ZACHARIAH
G. DRAPER , who in 1850 owned real estate valued at $45,164; pork packer RUS-
SELL W. MOSS , who in the same year reported property holdings worth $23,500;
and Captain ARCHIBALD SAMPSON ROBARDS, whose real estate holdings, while
not reported in the 1850 census, were valued at $89,000 in 1860 (*Marion Census*
1850, 312, 315, 317; *Marion Census* 1860, 761).

101.7   *The Hanged Nigger*]   BEN.

101.11   *The Stabbed Cal. Emigrant.* Saw him]   Clemens is referring to a stabbing that occurred in the mid-1840s, when travelers regularly passed through
Hannibal en route to California. The body of the murdered man was taken to
Justice of the Peace JOHN MARSHALL CLEMENS's office, where young Sam, hiding
to avoid punishment for truancy, saw it ("Annapolis Laughs," Baltimore *Sun*, 11
May 1907, 10). Clemens recalled the incident repeatedly, in lectures as well as
writings (see, for example, Lorch 1968, 275, 288). Perhaps the most vivid account
appears in chapter 18 of *The Innocents Abroad* (1869), where he tells how "lagging
moonlight" gradually revealed the body with its "ghastly stab." A page of autobiographical notes he made about 1897 includes this terse summary: "All emigrant's
went through there. One stabbed to death—saw him. . . . Saw the corpse in my
father's office" (SLC 1897b†). Dixon Wecter supposed that Clemens was recalling
Hannibal's first homicide, the stabbing of James McFarland in September 1843,
but the conjecture seems unlikely for two reasons: McFarland was a local farmer,
not a transient, and Hannibal's justice of the peace in 1843 was Campbell Meredith, not John Clemens (Wecter 1952, 103–4, 291 n. 7). In 1900, while working
on his autobiography, Clemens again recalled "the young Californian emigrant
who was stabbed with a bowie knife by a drunken comrade: I saw the red life gush
from his breast" (SLC 1900, 7). Wecter, however, conjectured that this last reminiscence was of another incident entirely—an 1850 stabbing that occurred in a
Hannibal saloon (Wecter 1952, 219).

101.27   *Daily Packet Service*]   Daily steamer service between Keokuk, Iowa (60
miles north of Hannibal), and St. Louis, Missouri (135 miles south of Hannibal),
was initiated in 1843 (Scharf, 2:1115).

101.29   Planters House]   St. Louis's most elegant hotel, which opened in 1841.
It catered not only to travelers and other short-term guests, but to plantation families and their personal servants who came to spend the whole winter—the social
"season"—in the city (Kirschten, 23).

101.31–32   the modest spire of the little Cath Cathedral]   St. Louis's Catholic
Cathedral, completed in 1834, is described in the *History of Saint Louis City and
County* (1883) as "a noble and imposing structure." Its spire—resting on "a stone
tower, forty feet in height above the pediment and twenty feet square"—is "an
octagon in shape, surmounted by a gilt ball five feet in diameter, from which rises
a cross of brass ten feet high" (Scharf, 2:1652).

102.8–9   Temperance Society, Cadets of Temperance]   The Hannibal chapter of Sons of Temperance, a fraternal order that promoted abstinence from alcohol, was organized in the spring of 1847. A junior adjunct called the Cadets of Temperance, pledged to uproot the tobacco habit, was formed three years later (Wecter 1952, 152). In 1906, claiming to have been "a smoker from my ninth year," Mark Twain remembered that he joined the Cadets for the privilege of wearing a red merino sash on holidays, but withdrew after only three months. He explained that the "organization was weak and impermanent because there were not enough holidays to support it. . . . you can't keep a juvenile moral institution alive on two displays of its sash per year" (AD, 13 Feb 1906, CU-MARK , in *MTA*, 2:100).

102.9   the Co of St P Greys]   That is, the St. Petersburg Greys, presumably a militia company. No information has been discovered about its probable Hannibal prototype.

102.9–10   the Fantastics]   The Southern term for mummers, who dressed in fantastic costume and paraded on holidays (*Lex*, 78–79).

102.15   *Mesmerizer*]   In an autobiographical dictation of 1 December 1906, Mark Twain recalled the mesmerizer's show, which he believed came to Hannibal about 1850. After three nights of volunteering to be a subject and failing to fall into a trance, young Clemens simply pretended to be hypnotized: "Upon suggestion I fled from snakes, passed buckets at a fire, became excited over hot steamboat-races, made love to imaginary girls and kissed them, fished from the platform and landed mud-cats that outweighed me" (CU-MARK, in *MTE*, 120). As a result of his facility, he became the star of the show during the balance of its two-week stay in Hannibal.

102.16   *Nigger Show*]   See the note at 15.12.

102.17   *Bell-Ringers* (Swiss)]   The "Campanalogians, or Swiss Bell Ringers" gave one of their "chaste, select and novel Musical Entertainments" at Hannibal's Second Presbyterian Church on the Fourth of July in 1850 ("Grand Musical Entertainment!" Hannibal *Missouri Courier*, 4 July 50).

102.18   *Debating Society*]   Popular in pre–Civil War Missouri, these societies sought both to edify and to amuse. The Down East Debating Society of Hannibal, established in 1853, entertained by arguing such questions as "Where does fire go when it goes out?" and "When a house is on fire, does it burn up or burn down?" (Elbert R. Bowen 1959, 3).

102.30   *The Mock Duel*]   Mark Twain may be alluding to the "Glover-Buckner Tragedy" of 1846 in Palmyra, near Hannibal, which in effect made a mockery of the code duello. John Taylor, challenged by Henry Broaddus, proposed a fight "with doublebarrel shot guns, the parties two feet from the muzzles. The guns are to be presented with a rest upon a stretched cord, cocked, and discharged at the word 'fire.'" Broaddus's second, George W. Buckner, regarded these terms as a bluff and accepted on behalf of his friend, but subsequently asked Taylor's second,

Joseph W. Glover, for new terms that would not "outrage all rules of propriety." Before matters went further, however, all four men had to go into hiding from the sheriff. A few weeks later, after an exchange of insults between the opposing camps, Buckner waylaid and fatally wounded Glover and was himself killed in their ensuing struggle for his pistol. The entire affair received widespread attention throughout northeast Missouri and may have made a particular impression upon ten-year-old Clemens, since Glover's brother, SAMUEL TAYLOR GLOVER, was an acquaintance of the Clemens family (Holcombe, 276–82).

104.2   The stray calf]   When JANE and JOHN MARSHALL CLEMENS arrived in Jamestown, Tennessee, early in 1827, their temporary home was a cabin in the woods. During one of John Clemens's absences to replenish the stock for his store, a severe downpour threatened to flood the cabin. "I put a chair across the door to keep Orion in," Jane Clemens later recalled, "& I waided. The water was k[n]ee deep & rising the cow was lowing round the fense the calf inside blating the water rising round it I waided to the gate & threw it open & the calf ran out the cow took it off in the woods or it would have been washed clear away. Two of the boys that kept me in wood & attended to the cow & horse came & said their mother said I must come up there one carried Orion I went not one dry thread on me" (Jane Lampton Clemens to Orion and Mary E. (Mollie) Clemens, 6? May 80, CU-MARK).

104.18–19   Had but one slave . . . sold her down the river]   JENNY.

105.6   the Pres. preacher]   LEMUEL GROSVENOR.

105.11   *The autopsy*]   One of Samuel Clemens's most disturbing memories was of surreptitiously observing, at the age of eleven, the autopsy performed on his father by physician HUGH MEREDITH. In a notebook entry of 1903 Clemens recalled the incident, but made the dead man a fictitious uncle: "*1847*. Witnessed post mortem of my uncle through the keyhole" (NB 46, CU-MARK, TS p. 25, in Wecter 1952, 116).

Hellfire Hotchkiss
(1897)

"Began ~~Hellfire~~ Hotchkiss" Mark Twain wrote in his notebook on 4 August 1897, in Weggis, Switzerland (NB 42, CU-MARK†, TS p. 24). On the envelope in which he kept the manuscript he affirmed his choice of title, while recording a potential alternative: "Hellfire Hotchkiss, or Sugar-Rag ditto."

The setting here, Dawson's Landing, is, like St. Petersburg, a re-creation of Hannibal. Mark Twain had previously used this name for the town in *Pudd'nhead Wilson* (1894), but "Hellfire Hotchkiss" was not a sequel to that novel, even though Wilson is mentioned in passing (121.3, 8–9). Rather it is a continuation of the narrative about Oscar Carpenter (Orion Clemens) which Mark Twain began to develop as he came to the end of "Villagers of 1840–3."

Mark Twain had long seen literary possibilities in his erratic and capricious brother. In the burlesque "Autobiography of a Damned Fool," begun in 1877 but never completed, he had depicted Orion "at 18, printer's apprentice, soft & sappy, full of fine intentions & shifting religions & not aware that he is a shining ass" (SLC to William Dean Howells, 23 Mar 77, MH-H, in *MTHL*, 1:173). In 1878 he and Howells began collaborating on a play about Orion, which they soon agreed to abandon. Repenting that decision, the following year Clemens urged Howells to

keep that MS & tackle it again. It will work out all right, you will see. I don't believe that that character exists in literature in so well developed a condition as it exists in Orion's person. Now won't you put Orion in a *story*? Then he will go handsomely into a play afterwards. How deliciously you could paint him—it would make fascinating reading,—the sort that makes a reader laugh & cry at the same time, for Orion is as good & ridiculous a soul as ever was. (SLC to Howells, 21 Jan 79, NN-B, in *MTHL*, 1:246)

And again:

don't you think you & I can get together & grind out a play . . . ? Orion is a field which grows richer & richer the more he manures it with each new top-dressing of religion or other guano. Drop me an immediate line about this, won't you? I imagine I see Orion on the stage, always gentle, always melancholy, always changing his politics & religion, & trying to reform the world, always inventing something, & losing a limb by a new kind of explosion at the end of each of the four acts. Poor old chap, he is good material. (SLC to Howells, 15 Sept 79, NN-B, in *MTHL*, 1:269)

Nothing came of these proposals, however, and the depictions of Orion as Bolivar in "Autobiography of a Damned Fool," as Albert in an 1892 fragment called "Affeland (Snivelization)," as Oscar Carpenter in "Hellfire Hotchkiss," and as Oliver Hotchkiss in "Schoolhouse Hill," are the only known direct portrayals of him in Mark Twain's fiction (for the text of the "Autobiography" and a partial text of "Affeland," see *S&B*, 136–61, 170–71).

Two other figures prominent in "Hellfire Hotchkiss" had their genesis in "Villagers." James Carpenter, Oscar's intolerant, irascible father, obviously is a version of Judge Carpenter (John Marshall Clemens). His wife, Sarah, parallels Joanna Carpenter (Jane Lampton Clemens) in her devotion to Oscar, although Sarah's conventional personality and uncomplicated piety do not comport with Clemens's characterizations of his mother either in "Villagers" or in "Jane Lampton Clemens." The Carpenters' conversation in the opening chapter of "Hellfire Hotchkiss"—humorous, but embittered by James's sarcasm and his contempt for both wife and son—leaves one wondering how closely Clemens modeled their relationship on actual relations within his family.

The title character, Rachel "Hellfire" Hotchkiss, may have been inspired by Mary Nash, the older sister of a boyhood friend of Clemens's. In 1897–98 working notes for "Tom Sawyer's Conspiracy" and "Schoolhouse Hill," Clemens characterized Mary Nash as "wild" and "bad" (*HH&T*, 383; *MSM*, 431). In his autobiography—momentarily confusing her with Mary Lacy, another schoolmate—he described her as "pretty wild and determined and independent" (AD, 16 Mar 1906, CU-MARK, in *MTA*, 2:213). Rachel, just as independent, and a paragon of beauty and intelligence as well, is a unique figure in Mark Twain's fiction: an emancipated woman. And "Hellfire Hotchkiss" touches, although tentatively, on the subject of sexual identity. As Rachel notes, she and Oscar (ironically nicknamed "Thug") are hampered by their "misplaced sexes" (133.14). Or, as Pudd'nhead Wilson is reported to have put it, "Hellfire Hotchkiss is the only genuwyne male man in this town and Thug Carpenter's the only genuwyne female girl, if you leave out sex and just consider the business facts" (121.3–5).

But Mark Twain clearly was uncomfortable with unconventional female behavior of any sort. In recalling Mary Nash, he reported approvingly that, far from being "incorrigible," as all Hannibal believed, "she married, and at once settled down and became in all ways a model matron and was as highly respected as any matron in the town" (AD, 16 Mar 1906, CU-MARK, in *MTA*, 2:213). Rachel Hotchkiss likewise resolves to reform and become a respectable member of her community, but her story breaks off at just that point. Mark Twain had reached an impasse. His impulse was to champion Rachel's independence of thought and feeling, thereby criticizing society's narrow-minded efforts to "sivilize"—much as he had done in writing about Huck Finn. But he could not wholeheartedly endorse rebelliousness in a heroine. Nor, on the other hand, could he produce a tame domestic novel about a "purified" Rachel. Consequently, only three chapters into "Hellfire Hotchkiss," he set the story aside. There is no evidence that he ever returned to it. Nevertheless, late in 1898 he did plan a further appearance for Hellfire herself. His working notes for "Schoolhouse Hill" show that he considered having Forty-four fall in love with her (*MSM*, 438).

109.9   Mr. Rucker]   Evidently Joshua Thomas Tucker.

111.24   Cadets of Temperance]   See the note at 102.8–9.

112.3   Campbellite Sunday school]   The Campbellites, more properly known as the Disciples of Christ, originated in early nineteenth-century America under the leadership of Thomas Campbell (1763–1854) and his son Alexander (1788–1866). Advocating individual interpretation of the Bible as the basis of faith, the Disciples drew adherents from several Protestant denominations. Pamela Ann Clemens was a Campbellite in her early teens, and John Marshall Clemens, although never a church member, "inclined to the Campbellites" (Holcombe, 915).

113.15–16   Underwood. . . . The printer]   Presumably Thomas Watt Ustick.

115.9   the peerage]   An allusion to the frustrated ambitions of some members of Jane Lampton Clemens's family. See the notes at 86.7–10 and 87.2–14.

127.4   Shad Stover]   Shad and Hal (introduced at 130.7) were modeled after the Hyde brothers.

129.10–16   The firemen conferred an honorary membership upon her. . . . Whenever there was a fire she and her official belt and helmet were a part of the spectacle]   The characterization of Rachel Hotchkiss as an enthusiastic fire buff probably reflects Mark Twain's acquaintance with Lillie Hitchcock (1843–1929), who was devoted to San Francisco's volunteer fire companies, regularly appeared at city fires, and in 1863 was made an honorary member of the Knickerbocker Engine Company, No. 5. Mark Twain met her in 1864 when he stayed at San Francisco's Occidental Hotel, where Lillie resided with her mother. Lillie Hitchcock's spirited and unconventional behavior led to her being regarded as an eccentric, but Mark Twain thought her "lovely" and "a splendid girl" (SLC to Frank Fuller, 7 Aug 67, transcript in CtY-BR†; Floride Green, 1, 18–19; *LLMT*, 50–52).

130.36 Aunt Betsy Davis] ELIZABETH W. SMITH.

131.16–17 the town drunkard's girls] The BLANKENSHIP sisters.

Tom Sawyer's Conspiracy
(1897–?1902)

Mark Twain here tried to write another sequel to *Huckleberry Finn* (1885). Tom, Huck, Jim, Aunt Polly, Widow Douglas, Miss Watson, and Judge Thatcher all appear in this story, and the plot turns on the machinations of those scoundrels, the king and the duke of Bilgewater.

As early as 1883 Mark Twain had planned to include, in a Hannibal story, an antebellum Missouri phenomenon that was to figure significantly in "Tom Sawyer's Conspiracy." "Pater-rollers & slavery," he jotted in his notebook then, recalling the vigilante patrols that endeavored to prevent abolitionists from helping slaves escape (*N&J3*, 30). Not until 1896, however, did he make the notebook entry that is the true germ of "Conspiracy": "Have Huck tell how one white brother shaved his head, put on a wool wig & was blackened & sold as a negro. Escaped that night, washed himself, & helped hunt *for himself* under pay" (NB 39, CU-MARK†, TS p. 22). The following year he noted "Tom sells Huck for a slave" and, among ideas for a "New Huck Finn" book, sketched this scenario: "Tom is disguised as a negro & sold in Ark[ansas] for $10, then he & Huck help hunt for him after the disguise is removed" (NB 41, CU-MARK†, TS pp. 34, 57, 58). In Weggis, Switzerland, during the summer and early fall of 1897, Mark Twain developed the story on the "Tom is disguised" plan.

Although primarily a sequel to *Huckleberry Finn*, "Tom Sawyer's Conspiracy" derives some of its energy from Mark Twain's long-time fascination with detectives and detective fiction. In San Francisco in the mid-1860s he had genuinely admired the exploits of police detective George Rose, who, he nevertheless joked, followed suspects "by the foot-prints they make on the brick pavements" (*CofC*, 178). By the late 1870s he had read the sensational stories by renowned detective Allan Pinkerton, whose accounts of his agency's activities often strained credulity. (In "Tom Sawyer's Conspiracy" the insignia of the Sons of Freedom is based on the Pinkerton emblem: a vigilant eye over the motto "We Never Sleep.") And by the mid-1890s he was familiar with some of Arthur Conan Doyle's Sherlock Holmes adventures.

For years Mark Twain had attempted to capitalize on the popularity of such tales. In 1877 he wrote his "light tragedy," "Cap'ⁿ Simon Wheeler; The Amateur Detective," which the following year he tried to turn into a comic novel, "Simon Wheeler,

Detective" (for texts of both the play and the unfinished novel, see *S&B*, 220–89, 312–444). He burlesqued detective work in "The Stolen White Elephant" (1882), treated it more seriously in *Pudd'nhead Wilson* (1894), and satirized it again in "Tom Sawyer, Detective" (1896).

As these works indicate, Mark Twain's predominant impulse was to poke fun at the improbable and pretentious behavior of fictional sleuths—even as he devised a plot that depended on the application of their techniques. "Tom Sawyer's Conspiracy" is another such contradictory work. Detective Jake Flacker bears the brunt of Mark Twain's scorn, while Tom Sawyer's application, and misapplication, of the detective arts advances the story. Mark Twain was not, however, satisfied with the result. After working on "Conspiracy" intermittently over several years, possibly until 1902, he abandoned it, just a few pages short of completion.

134.1–2   we was back home and I was at the Widow Douglas's]   "Tom Sawyer, Detective" (1896) had been set in Arkansas, where Tom solved a mysterious murder. In "Tom Sawyer's Conspiracy," the boys are "back home" in St. Petersburg. The Widow Douglas was modeled after MELICENT S. HOLLIDAY.

134.3–4   Miss Watson . . . Jim]   The death of Miss Watson, whose will freed Jim, was announced in chapter 42 of *Huckleberry Finn*. Nevertheless, she anachronistically appears throughout the present story. Miss Watson was modeled after MARY ANN NEWCOMB and Jim was based on DANIEL.

135.1   Jackson's island]   Glasscock's Island, about three miles downriver from Hannibal and close to the Illinois shore (*HF*, 365–66, 384).

136.18   old Jimmy Grimes]   Possibly based on JIMMY FINN. The character, who receives only passing mention in this story, is referred to as "Admiral Grimes Keelboatman" in Mark Twain's working notes (*HH&T*, 383).

138.4–5   Harriet Beacher Stow . . . gets all the credit of starting that war]   Harriet Beecher Stowe's influential novel *Uncle Tom's Cabin*, serialized in 1851–52 and a bestseller, won countless adherents to the antislavery cause. When Stowe visited President Lincoln in the White House, he reportedly said "So this is the little woman who wrote the book that made this big war!" (Stowe, 205).

139.27   Miss Mary en de Hair-lip]   In *Huckleberry Finn*, chapters 24–29, the King and the Duke attempt to rob the Wilks girls, Mary Jane and her harelipped sister, Joanna.

141.14–15   Georges Cadoudal got up a conspiracy]   Cadoudal (1771–1804), a leader in a royalist uprising against the French revolutionary government, was guillotined for conspiring to assassinate Napoleon.

141.19   Bartholomew's Day]   In 1572, a massacre of French Protestants, or Huguenots, began in Paris on St. Bartholomew's Day, 24 August, and spread throughout France, touching off civil war.

142.22–23   get the people in a sweat about the ablitionists]   In the early 1840s abolitionist "liberators" from Illinois sharply increased their activity in eastern

Missouri and sometimes helped slaves escape to freedom. According to the *History of Marion County, Missouri*, "there was a constant state of apprehension and uneasiness among most slave owners—a fear not alone of an exodus, but of an insurrection on the part of the negroes" (Holcombe, 263).

143.7 paterollers] Patrollers: bands of vigilantes organized to prevent abolitionist activity and the escape of slaves. In Hannibal and surrounding Marion County, they were authorized to question all strangers and banish anyone who could not satisfactorily account for his presence (Mathews, 2:1208; Holcombe, 262–64).

143.21–26 our old hanted house . . . mine and Jim's little cave . . . Injun Joe's cave] Allusions to *Tom Sawyer* (chapters 25–26, 29, 31–33) and *Huckleberry Finn* (chapters 9–11).

144.3 Guy Fawkes] Fawkes (1570–1606) was a principal conspirator in England's "Gunpowder Plot" to blow up King James I and the Houses of Parliament on 5 November 1605. The conspirators increased their number until secrecy became impossible; Fawkes was caught redhanded in the cellar under the Parliament houses and was later hanged.

144.4 Titus Oates] An English conspirator (1649–1705) who fabricated a plot in which Catholics were supposedly pledged to massacre Protestants, assassinate the king, and burn London. Oates "exposed" the plot to authorities in June 1678 and many Catholics were imprisoned or executed on his testimony. In 1685 he was imprisoned for his perjury.

144.13 a Council of Ten and a Council of Three] Councils established in fourteenth- and fifteenth-century Venice to guard the state against conspiracies. Mark Twain learned about them when visiting Venice in 1867 and described them in chapter 22 of *The Innocents Abroad* (1869).

144.24–25 a resolution of oblivion] That is, a decree granting a general pardon for political offenses.

146.6 old Bradish] Modeled in part after WILLIAM B. BEEBE.

148.17 Tom's aunt Polly's] Aunt Polly was based on JANE LAMPTON CLEMENS.

150.2 Sid and Mary] Tom Sawyer's half-brother and his cousin, modeled after HENRY and PAMELA ANN CLEMENS.

151.6 Hookerville] Mark Twain's working notes identify Hookerville as Saverton, Missouri, a river town seven miles below Hannibal (*HH&T*, 383, 384).

154.9 uncle Fletcher's farm] The farm owned by JOHN ADAMS QUARLES.

156.2–5 to Captain Harper's . . . where Joe was laying sick] Captain SAMUEL ADAMS BOWEN, SR., and his son WILLIAM.

161.22 Guttingburg and Fowst] German printer Johann Gutenberg (c. 1397–1468), believed to have been the first European to print with movable type, and his partner Johann Fust or Faust (1400?–?1466).

165.26–27   the little Webster spelling book]   Either *The American Spelling Book* (1783) or its successor, *The Elementary Spelling Book* (1829). Editions of these works by Noah Webster continued to be used into the twentieth century.

166.4–5   Oliver Benton . . . and Plunket]   ABNER O. NASH and ORION CLEMENS.

166.29   Colonel Elder]   Colonel WILLIAM C. ELGIN.

167.31   Captain Haskins and Captain Sam Rumford]   BENJAMIN M. HAWKINS and SAMUEL R. RAYMOND.

168.10–11   I've got a ruputation, on account of beating the Dunlaps]   Tom is referring to his exploits on his Uncle Silas's Arkansas farm in "Tom Sawyer, Detective" (1896).

173.9   down the banks]   A scolding or reprimand (*Lex*, 14).

180.22   Cap. Haines's]   "General" GAINES.

184.18   Higgins's Bill]   Modeled after HIGGINS , a Hannibal slave. In calling him "Higgins's Bill," Mark Twain was following the prevailing usage, as he had explained it in chapter 10 of *Tom Sawyer*: "If Mr. Harbison had owned a slave named Bull, Tom would have spoken of him as 'Harbison's Bull;' but a son or a dog of that name was 'Bull Harbison.'"

189.9–11   He wanted to get the men into the court . . . and then make the grand pow-wow, the way he done in Arkansaw]   An allusion to Tom Sawyer's spectacular courtroom revelations in the concluding chapter of "Tom Sawyer, Detective" (1896).

191.25   Burrell's Gang]   A veiled reference to the infamous gang headed by John A. Murrell (1806–44). Nearly one thousand strong and operating in eight states, the gang included horsethieves, counterfeiters, and robbers who specialized in stealing slaves for sale to new owners. Mark Twain included a history of the gang in chapter 29 of *Life on the Mississippi* (1883).

193.8–10   The time I let Jim get away . . . it took a pile of money out of him and the King's pocket]   This reference to chapter 31 of *Huckleberry Finn* contains two errors: Huck did not allow Jim to escape, and the king and duke made forty dollars by turning Jim over to Silas Phelps.

197.33–35   The time Tom saw them down in Arkansaw . . . they was tarred and feathered]   The allusion is to chapter 33 of *Huckleberry Finn*.

198.23   the Queen]   Victoria (1819–1901) succeeded to the English throne in 1837 and reigned until her death.

203.18   it would a been hark from the tomb for them]   That is, the consequences would have been distressing, or even fatal. The phrase "hark from the tomb" probably derives from Isaac Watts's "A Funeral Thought":

> Hark! from the tombs a doleful sound;
> My ears, attend the cry—
> "Ye living men, come, view the ground
> Where you must shortly lie."
> (Watts, 145)

In chapter 26 of *Huckleberry Finn*, Mark Twain had used this phrase to mean a sharp reproof (*HF*, 428).

204.5–6   when we get to Cairo we're in a free state]   Cairo, Illinois, was situated at the confluence of the Mississippi and Ohio rivers. Although the state prohibited slavery, it would not have provided a safe haven for Jim. In compliance with the Fugitive Slave Act of 1793, Illinois authorities arrested blacks who were unable to produce a certificate of freedom, holding them as indentured laborers for up to a year. Even free or "unattached" blacks faced the threat of being kidnapped and sold into slavery. In communities bordering on the southern states, it was a "common practice . . . to arrest a man on some false pretense, and then, when he appeared in court without opportunity to secure papers or witnesses, to claim him as a fugitive slave" (McDougall, 36, 105–6; Hurd, 2:135; Gara, 50–52). Jim's surest route to safety was to travel (as Huck plans at 204.20–25) down the Mississippi to Cairo, then northeast, up the Ohio River.

204.16–17   "How did I come to hog half of the robber's money and get so rotten flush?]   In *Tom Sawyer* Huck had received half of the twelve thousand dollars he and Tom recovered from thieves. Widow Douglas invested Huck's half "at six per cent., and Judge Thatcher did the same with Tom's" (chapters 34 and 35).

205.20   the Burning Shame]   The King's nude stage performance before the townspeople of Bricksville in chapter 23 of *Huckleberry Finn*. Mark Twain had called the caper "The Burning Shame" in his manuscript, but changed it before publication to the "Thrilling Tragedy of the King's Camelopard or The Royal Nonesuch."

205.21–22   a nigger breakdown]   A "boisterous, rapid, shuffling dance" done on wide wooden planks, often performed competitively by dancers in succession. It had been observed among slaves as early as 1700 (*HF*, 395–96).

206.30–31   some said it had sixty thousand people in it, prob'ly a lie]   The population of St. Louis, which grew from about 10,000 in 1836 to about 40,000 in 1846, did not reach the level reported by Huck's informants until early in 1849 (Scharf, 2:1015–19). As Mark Twain repeatedly indicates, "Conspiracy" takes place about a year after *Huckleberry Finn*, that is, sometime between 1836 and 1846.

Schoolhouse Hill
(1898)

In the fall of 1897, Mark Twain began work on a tale about a mysterious stranger's visit to earth. The story was to occupy him for nearly eleven years, during which he attempted at least four versions of it: two set in nineteenth-century Missouri (the "St. Petersburg Fragment," 1897, and "Schoolhouse Hill," 1898), one in eighteenth-century Austria ("The Chronicle of Young Satan," 1897–1900), and one in medieval Austria ("No. 44, The Mysterious Stranger," 1902–8). For texts of all three surviving versions (what survives of the "St. Petersburg Fragment" was incorporated into "The Chronicle of Young Satan"), see *Mark Twain's Mysterious Stranger Manuscripts* (*MSM*, 4–11, 35–405, 487–92).

Mark Twain drafted his initial plan for "Schoolhouse Hill" in a notebook entry of mid-November 1898, which read in part:

> Story of little Satan, jr, who came to ~~Petersburg (Hannibal)~~ went to school, was popular & greatly liked by ~~Huck & Tom~~ who knew his secret. The others were jealous, & the girls didn't like him because he smelt of brimstone. *This* is the Admirable Crichton [Scottish prodigy James Crichton (1560–?85), famous for his linguistic ability and his extraordinary memory]. He was always doing miracles—his pals knew they were miracles, the others thought them mysteries. He is a good little devil; but swears, & breaks the Sabbath. By & by he is converted, & becomes a Methodist. & quits miracling. In class meeting he confesses who he is—is not believed; his new co-religionists turn against him as a ribald humbug. . . . When his fortunes & his miseries are at the worst, his papa arrives in state in a glory of hellfire & attended by a multitude of old-fashioned & showy fiends—& *then* everybody is at the boy-devil's feet at once & want to curry favor. (NB 40, CU-MARK, TS pp. 51–52; published in full in *MSM*, 428–29)

Shortly after making this entry, Mark Twain began writing "Schoolhouse Hill." He worked on it through the latter half of November and December 1898, completing only 139 pages before putting the manuscript aside. Thirty-three pages of working notes establish his commitment to the story, however, and indicate the direction it was to have taken: Little Satan, or Forty-four, was to fall in love ("the kind that sex arouses") with Hellfire Hotchkiss (or with Annie Fleming, daughter of Petersburg's Presbyterian pastor) and find that the purely intellectual happiness of Hell was tame compared to earthly love. Meanwhile, dismayed by mankind's pettiness, ignorance, and lack of freedom, he would help humans recover their original innocence by ridding them of their vanity and by founding a church to abolish their diseased "Moral Sense." He would preach against hypocrisy and, with the help of an army of little red devils summoned from Hell, print his own Bible—which Mark Twain planned to publish as an appendix, together with Forty-four's sermons and dialogues. And Forty-four was to work his wonders in a world Mark Twain populated with Hannibal residents—including John, Jane, Orion, and Pamela Clemens—in new as well as familiar fictional guises (*MSM*, 430–49).

Given this well elaborated scheme, it is difficult to say exactly why Mark Twain abandoned "Schoolhouse Hill" after only six chapters. Perhaps as his philosophical purpose continued to evolve, the story's humor came to seem inappropriate. In a letter of 12 and 13 May 1899 to William Dean Howells, Mark Twain reported that he had embarked anew on a work in "tale-form" that he had not started "right" before: "I believe I can make it tell what I think of Man, & how he is constructed, & what a shabby poor ridiculous thing he is, & how mistaken he is in his estimate of his character & powers & qualities & his place among the animals" (NN-B, in *MTHL*, 2:698–99). "Schoolhouse Hill" had been, in this estimation, just a false start. Even so, it remains an entertaining, even illuminating, fantasy, brisk in its humor and language, caustic in its commentary upon human nature, and sharply evocative of small town life.

214.20–215.1   Henry Bascom]   HENRY BEEBE.

216.22–23   Archibald Ferguson, the old Scotch schoolmaster]   JOHN D. DAWSON. The setting, however, was SAMUEL CROSS's wooden schoolhouse.

218.25   Scots wha hae wi' Wallace bled]   Robert Burns's ode (1794) commemorating the battle of Bannockburn in 1314, in which Robert Bruce's Scottish army defeated a superior English force under Edward II, establishing Scotland's independence. William Wallace had been the leader of the Scottish struggle for independence until he was captured by the English and executed in 1305. His example inspired Bruce.

218.27   *Sally Fitch*]   SARAH H. ROBARDS.

218.32   Becky Thatcher]   ANNA LAURA HAWKINS.

218.36–219.1   ye banks and braes o' bonny Doon]   The opening line of Robert Burns's song, "The Banks o' Doon" (1792); see the note at 99.27.

219.2   Jack Stillson]   JOHN H. GARTH.

219.8–9   Oh, here's a hand, my trusty fere, and gie's a hand o' thine, and we'll]   From Robert Burns's song, "Auld Lang Syne" (1799).

221.36   Margaret Stover]   Working notes suggest this character was to be modeled after one of WILLIAM PERRY OWSLEY's children, possibly Elizabeth (*MSM*, 431).

222.20   "The New Short-Hand Method, called Phonography"]   Mark Twain probably had in mind *A Manual of Phonography, or, Writing by Sound*, by Isaac Pitman, the Englishman who invented this form of shorthand. The first of many American editions of Pitman's manual was published in 1844. His system is still in use today.

223.33   "Quarante-quatre, sir. Forty-four."]   Working notes for this story indicate that Young Satan was only one of the devil's "myriads" of offspring and that Mark Twain thought of calling him "404" or "94" or "No. 45 in New series 986,000,000" before settling on Forty-four. The significance, if any, which these numbers had for Mark Twain has not been satisfactorily explained (see *MSM*, 435–36, 443, 444, 472–73).

225.30   held the age]   Had the advantage; originally, the advantage held by the player to the left of the dealer in poker (Cassidy, 1:21).

225.32–33   he went in a procession all by himself, like Parker's hog]   Mark Twain frequently used this expression (changing Parker to Baxter, Smith, or Jackson) to characterize a person with no group affiliation or loyalty (see, for example, SLC 1863; SLC 1865; *N&J2*, 136; *FM*, 207).

228.17–18   Henry's father, the nigger-trader]   WILLIAM B. BEEBE.

229.3–4   the Hotchkisses]   ORION and PAMELA ANN CLEMENS.

230.12–13   the Fox-girl Rochester rappings]   In early 1848 Margaret and Kate
    Fox, two teenaged sisters residing near Rochester, New York, alleged they had
    received messages from spirits who communicated by means of rapping noises.
    The incident marked the beginning of a spiritualist movement in America, and
    over the next few years sensational stories of rappings, trance-writing, and other
    "spirit manifestations" were reported throughout the country. In 1888 the sisters,
    who had become famous as professional mediums, denounced the movement as
    a fraud and confessed they produced the raps by cracking the joints of their big
    toes (Kerr and Crow, 80–83, 104; McCabe, 50–62).

230.22–23   widow Dawson]   ELIZABETH W. SMITH.

232.24   widow Guthrie]   MELICENT S. HOLLIDAY.

235.2   Dr. Wheelright]   WILLIAM HUMPHREY PEAKE.

237.29   Miss Pomeroy]   MARY ANN NEWCOMB.

237.33   Judge Taylor]   ZACHARIAH G. DRAPER.

239.5–6   It was in reality a Blizzard, but that expressive word had not then been
    invented]   Uses of "blizzard" to mean "a sharp blow" and a verbal "blast" have
    been documented as early as 1829 and 1834, respectively. By 1859, about ten
    years after the time of "Schoolhouse Hill," the word had acquired at least a limited
    currency for "snowstorm." American newspapers brought that meaning into gen-
    eral use during the severe winter of 1880–81 (*OED* 1933, 1:925; *OED* 1972–86,
    1:292).

243.20–21   Crazy Meadows]   Mark Twain planned to draw on his recollections
    of the JAMES RATCLIFFE family for the unhappy incidents of Crazy Meadows's
    life.

254.34–35   *man is prone to evil as the sparks to fly upward*]   Job 5:7: "Yet man is
    born unto trouble, as the sparks to fly upward."

Huck Finn
(1902)

This anecdote—which Mark Twain titled, probably tentatively, for its narrator—is
based on an incident that occurred in Hannibal. Mark Twain had included a version
of the story in chapter 53 of *Life on the Mississippi* (1883), in his account of his 1882
return to the town. During a conversation with an "old gentleman" he met on the
street:

> I asked about Miss ——.
> "Died in the insane asylum three or four years ago—never was out of it from the time she

went in; and was always suffering, too; never got a shred of her mind back."

If he spoke the truth, here was a heavy tragedy, indeed. Thirty-six years in a madhouse, that some young fools might have some fun! I was a small boy, at the time; and I saw those giddy young ladies come tiptoeing into the room where Miss —— sat reading at midnight by a lamp. The girl at the head of the file wore a shroud and a doughface; she crept behind the victim, touched her on the shoulder, and she looked up and screamed, and then fell into convulsions. She did not recover from the fright, but went mad. In these days it seems incredible that people believed in ghosts so short a time ago. But they did.

In 1897 Mark Twain recalled this same incident in "Villagers of 1840–3," identifying the prankster as Roberta Jones (97). That year, amid ideas for lectures and for new stories about Huck and Tom, he made three notebook entries which indicate that he planned to reprise and rework this episode: "Tale of scaring the woman into insanity by skull & dough face"; "Scaring woman with doughface"; and "Scaring poor Miss * * to madness—Roberta Jones" (NB 41, CU-MARK†, TS pp. 36, 45, 58). And in his notebook for 1902, which contained numerous notes for a story about Huck and Tom "50 Years Later," he wrote: "Dough-face—old lady now, still in asylum—a bride then. What went with *him*? Shall we visit her? And shall she be expecting him in her faded bridal robes & flowers?" and "doughface, but scare no one mad" (NB 45, CU-MARK†, TS pp. 12, 21).

Mark Twain probably wrote this story in 1902, when he was contemplating writing a novel in which Tom and Huck return to St. Petersburg as old men.

Biographical Directory

This directory provides biographical information about some one hundred and sixty Missourians, principally residents of Hannibal and St. Louis in the 1840s and 1850s—among them the members of Samuel L. Clemens's own family. Clemens recalled most of these individuals in the nonfiction pieces published in this volume, "Letter to William Bowen," "Jane Lampton Clemens," and "Villagers of 1840–3." He fictionalized some of them in the eight stories included here and in such works as *The Adventures of Tom Sawyer* (1876) and *Adventures of Huckleberry Finn* (1885).

Each directory entry reports all of its subject's appearances in the texts published here, as well as significant appearances in other works. Entries are ordered alphabetically by last name (or first name when the last is not known). Individuals Mark Twain alludes to by initial are so listed, with a cross reference to the full name and biography ("H., Mrs. See ELIZABETH HORR."). In family entries ("BLANKENSHIP family," "BOWEN family," etc.) a brief genealogical or historical overview may precede the biographies of specific family members, which are arranged, in census fashion, in order of birth. Within entries, names printed in SMALL CAPITALS direct the reader to an independent entry for the person named ("Bowen married SARAH H. RO-BARDS" indicates an entry for Robards).

Much of the detail in the Biographical Directory was recorded by Clemens himself—in his autobiographical dictations, letters, notebooks, working notes for stories planned or in progress, and in his published works containing direct personal reminiscence, such as *Life on the Mississippi* (1883). In order to verify and supplement the information Clemens preserved in those sources—and in "Villagers of 1840–3," the richest source of all—independent documentation has been sought wherever possible. Documents consulted include Hannibal newspapers of the 1840s and 1850s; memoirs and letters by Mark Twain's contemporaries; census, court, and genealogical records; city directories; and city and county histories. Sources cited by abbreviation or by author's last name are fully defined in References.

ARMSTRONG, JESSE M. (b. 1827?), was a clerk in a Hannibal store as a young man. In the late 1850s he opened a dry-goods firm with his brother-in-law George A. Hawes, a distant relative of Clemens's, and in 1870 he became a director and assistant cashier of the newly formed Farmers' and Merchants' Bank. In "Villagers" (95), Clemens apparently confused Armstrong with Amos J. Stillwell (1828–88), who worked in a Hannibal mill from 1848 to 1851, ran a St. Louis commission business from 1851 to 1855 with Clemens's brother-in-law, WILLIAM ANDERSON MOFFETT, then returned to Hannibal and became a prosperous pork-packer and bank president. It was Stillwell, not Armstrong, who was murdered in 1888 in the manner described in "Villagers." Both the New York *Times* and the New York *Tribune* for 31 December 1888 gave the event front-page coverage. In an account of the murder published in 1908 (a decade after Clemens wrote "Villagers"), Minnie T. Dawson reported that Stillwell's second wife, Fannie, fell in love with Joseph Carter Hearne, a prominent surgeon about three years younger than herself and twenty-three years younger than her husband. Stillwell was murdered in his bed with an axe taken from his barn, but investigators failed to find an indictable suspect. The widow inherited a substantial estate, and she married the doctor a year later. When the couple left Hannibal, they were followed to the train station by a jeering crowd. In 1895 they were formally charged with the murder. After Hearne was acquitted, charges against his wife were dropped (*Marion Census* 1850, 310, 312; Fotheringham, 10, 29, 30; "The Farmers & Merchants Bank," Hannibal *Courier-Post*, 22 Apr 1905, 1; *Portrait*, 198, 578–79; Holcombe, 604, 614–15, 953; Greene, 329; *MTBus*, 72; "Murdered by a Burglar," New York *Times*, 31 Dec 88, 1; "Murdered in His Bed," New York *Tribune*, 31 Dec 88, 1; Dawson, 12, 34, 40–42, 118, 152).

B. See BENJAMIN L. CLEMENS.

BARRET, RICHARD F. (1804–60), called Dr. Ray in "Villagers" (103), was a former suitor of Jane Clemens's whom she had hoped to marry. Clemens learned of this early romance in the spring of 1886—evidently from his sister, Pamela—a few months after his mother had revealed it to Orion Clemens. In a letter of 19 May 1886 to William Dean Howells, Clemens re-created his mother's account:

> "I will tell you a secret. When I was eighteen, a young medical student named Barrett lived in Columbia (Ky.) eighteen miles away; & he used to ride over & see me. This continued for some time. I loved him with all my whole heart, & I knew that he felt the same toward me, though no words had been spoken. He was too bashful to speak—he could not do it. Everybody supposed we were engaged—took it for granted we were—but we were not. By & by there was to be a party in a neighboring town, & he wrote my uncle telling him his feelings, & asking him to drive me over in his buggy & let him (Barrett) drive me back, so that he might have that opportunity to propose. My uncle should have done as he was asked, without explaining any-thing to me; but instead, he read me the letter; & then, of course, I could not go—& did not. He (Barrett) left the country presently; & I, to stop the clacking tongues, & to show him that I did not care, *married*, in a pet. In all these sixty-four years I have never seen him since." (NN-B, in *MTHL*, 2:567)

After studying medicine at Transylvania University, Barret established a lucrative practice in Green County, Kentucky. In 1832 he married Maria Buckner, daughter of a Kentucky lawyer and congressman. He moved to St. Louis in 1840 and assisted Dr. Joseph N. McDowell (father of JOHN MCDOWELL) and others in founding Missouri Medical College. A "pioneer in various important business enterprises," he was regarded as "one of the most active men of his generation . . . in developing the resources of the States of Illinois, Iowa and Missouri" (Conard, 1:160, 161). In his later years, Barret was described as "eminently noble and engaging,—a figure tall, graceful, and courtly, and a countenance of the Roman model," and although "at times irascible, his disposition was usually gentle and amiable. . . . His pride of race and scholarly habits made him appear exclusive and aristocratic, but his impulses were ardent, and his manners polite and engaging" (Scharf, 1:677). Mark Twain's list of potential characters for "Hellfire Hotchkiss" (*S&B*, 173) includes a Dr. Rayley, possibly to be based on Barret, but the character does not appear in the story (Conard, 1:160–62; Scharf, 1:676–77, 2:1544; Barret, 1).

BEEBE family.

WILLIAM B. BEEBE was a forwarding and commission agent who kept a store near the Hannibal steamboat landing. He is mentioned in "Jane Lampton Clemens" and in "Villagers" (89, 104) as the man who bought JENNY, the Clemens family's slave. He appears as Bat Bradish, the slave trader, in "Tom Sawyer's Conspiracy" (146–213 passim) and is alluded to as "the nigger-trader" in "Schoolhouse Hill" (215, 228). Between 1843 and 1847, John Marshall Clemens twice battled Beebe in court over financial disagreements (Henry Beebe to SLC, 14 Nov 1908, CU-MARK; Wecter 1952, 111–13).

HENRY BEEBE (b. 1836) was WILLIAM's son. In "Letter to William Bowen" (20,21), Clemens recalled details about Henry that he later used in "Schoolhouse Hill," where he portrayed him as the bully Henry Bascom (214–28 passim). A working note for that story refers to both father and son: "*Henry Bascom* (Beebe) the bully new rich man & slave trader" (*MSM*, 432). In 1908 Beebe asked Clemens whether he recalled him as a schoolmate "64 years ago," adding "I have not visited Hannibal since 1852 and have lost track of all but you." He said that he took "great pleasure" in reading Mark Twain's books, "and oftimes thought I recognized the characters mentioned in them" (Beebe to SLC, 14 Nov 1908, CU-MARK).

BEN, "*The Hanged Nigger*," mentioned in "Villagers" (101), was a young slave who belonged to Thomas Glascock of Shelby County. He was accused in October 1849 of killing a ten-year-old white boy, then raping the boy's twelve-year-old sister and slitting her throat. The Palmyra jail had to be guarded to prevent his being lynched. Although he reportedly claimed the law would not hang him because he was worth a thousand dollars, he was convicted and, after a full confession, hanged on 11 January 1850. Clemens was then fourteen and a printer's apprentice for the *Missouri Courier*, which reported the crime at length. The *Courier* office also published a twenty-five cent pamphlet giving Ben's "detailed confession" of "the manner in which he did the atrocious deed and his villainous transactions and adventures through life" ("Confession of Ben," Hannibal *Missouri Courier*, 21 Feb 50). Clemens wrote in his 1897 notebook: "Negro smuggled from Va in featherbed when lynchers were after him. In Mo he raped a girl of 13 & killed her & her brother in the woods & before being hanged confessed to many rapes of white married women who kept it quiet partly from fear of him & partly to escape the scandal" (NB 41, CU-MARK†, TS p. 57). In 1901, contemplating a book on the history of lynching, Clemens wrote to his publisher, summarizing Ben's crimes and requesting help in obtaining an account of his punishment to "be found in the St Louis Republican, no doubt—date, along about 1849" (SLC to Francis E. (Frank) Bliss, 26 Aug 1901, TxU, in Wecter 1952, 215; Holcombe, 298–99; Haines, 42–43; *Missouri v. Ben*; Hannibal *Missouri Courier*: "Atrocious Murder and Rape," 8 Nov 49; "Trial at Palmyra," 6 Dec 49; "Execution at Palmyra," 17 Jan 50; "Confession of Ben," 21 and 28 Feb 50).

BLANKENSHIP family. The father, Woodson (b. 1799?), a laborer from South Carolina, was one of Hannibal's drunkards. The 1850 census lists him and his wife, Mahala (b. 1813?), with eight children, all born in Missouri: BENSON, 21; TOM, 19; Martha, 18 or 19; Nancy, 16; Sarah, 14; Elizabeth, 12; Mary, 6; and Catherine, 3. In "Villagers" and "Hellfire Hotchkiss" (96, 131), Clemens recalls the unproven charge that the Blankenship girls were prostitutes (*Marion Census* 1850, 308, 309; AD, 8 Mar 1906, CU-MARK, in *MTA*, 2:174).

BENSON (BENCE, or BEN) BLANKENSHIP (b. 1829?) is called "the boys' friend & loafer" in Clemens's 1897 notebook (NB 42, CU-MARK†, TS p. 24). In 1847 he helped a runaway slave hiding on Sny Island (across the river from Hannibal, near the Illinois shore) by carrying provisions to him for several weeks, spurning a fifty-dollar reward for his capture—a source for an incident in chapters 8 through 11 of *Huckleberry Finn* (*MTB*, 1:63–64; Wecter 1952, 148). He is mentioned in "Villagers" (96).

TOM BLANKENSHIP (b. 1831?) was the model for Huckleberry Finn, who first appears in chapter 6 of *Tom Sawyer*. When Clemens's sister, Pamela, heard that chapter read aloud, she exclaimed, "Why, that's Tom Blankenship!" (*MTBus*, 265). Clemens himself remarked in 1906:

> In "Huckleberry Finn" I have drawn Tom Blankenship exactly as he was. He was ignorant, unwashed, insufficiently fed; but he had as good a heart as ever any boy had. His liberties were totally unrestricted. He was the only really independent person—boy or man—in the community, and by consequence he was tranquilly and continuously happy, and was envied by all the rest of us. We liked him; we enjoyed his society. And as his society was forbidden us by our parents, the prohibition trebled and quadrupled its value, and therefore we sought and got more of his society than of any other boy's. (AD, 8 Mar 1906, CU-MARK, in *MTA*, 2:174–75)

And in a letter of the same date to a former Hannibal acquaintance, Clemens commented: "You may remember that Tom was a good boy, notwithstanding his circumstances. To my mind he was a better boy than Henry Beebe & John Reagan put together, those swells of the ancient days" (8 Mar 1906 to Alexander C. Toncray, NN-B†). In April 1861 Blankenship was given a thirty-day sentence for stealing turkeys, and in June 1861 he was reported "at his old business" again, having allegedly stolen some onions from a Hannibal garden (Hannibal *Messenger*, 21 Apr and 4 June 1861, reprinted in Lorch 1940, 352). One of his sisters, when asked in 1899 if he had been the model for Huck, said: "Yes, I reckon it was him. Sam and our boys run together considerable them days, and I reckon it was Tom or Ben, one; it don't matter which, for both of 'em's dead" (Fielder, 10). In 1889 WILLIAM BENTON COONTZ sent Clemens a clipping from the Hannibal *Journal* which reported that Tom had died years earlier of cholera (Smith 1889). Nevertheless, Clemens claimed to have heard in 1902 (presumably in the spring of that year, during his last visit to Hannibal) that Tom "was Justice of the Peace in a remote village in Montana, and was a good citizen and greatly respected" (AD, 8 Mar 1906, CU-MARK, in *MTA*, 2:175). Blankenship appears as Huck in *Tom Sawyer Abroad* (1894), "Tom Sawyer, Detective" (1896), and, in the present volume, in "Huck Finn and Tom Sawyer among the Indians" (33–81), "Tom Sawyer's Conspiracy" (134–213), "Schoolhouse Hill" (214, 227), and "Huck Finn" (260–61).

BLENNERHASSET, whom Clemens describes as Hannibal's only "unbeliever," a Kentucky lawyer and freethinker, appears in "Villagers" (100, 103). No one named Blennerhasset is known to have lived in Hannibal in the 1840s and 1850s.

BOWEN family. Clemens was closely acquainted with this large family for almost two decades—during his Hannibal years (1839–53) and while he was a Mississippi River cub pilot and pilot (1857–61). He recurrently alluded to members of the family in private as well as public writings. In an 1882 notebook, for example, he observed that the "histories" of brothers "Will Bowen, [and] Sam . . . make human life appear a grisly & hideous sarcasm" (N&J2, 474–75). A year later, in chapter 4 of *Life on the Mississippi*, he wrote that "four sons of the chief merchant" were among the Hannibal boys who became steamboat pilots. And in an 1899 letter he recalled steering "a trip for Bart Bowen" and being "partner with Will Bowen on the A. B. Chambers (one trip), and with Sam Bowen a whole summer on a small Memphis packet" (26 Feb 99 to John B. Downing, *MTL*, 2:675).

SAMUEL ADAMS BOWEN, SR. (1790–1853), of Tennessee, in 1821 married his cousin, Amanda Warren Stone (1802–81), the daughter of BARTON WARREN STONE. The Bowens settled in Hannibal by 1836 and were the parents of seven children: JOHN, MARY, BARTON, ELIZABETH, WILLIAM, SAMUEL, and Amanda. By 1839 Captain Bowen was operating a Hannibal tobacco warehouse and was the county's first tobacco inspector. He and his wife are mentioned in "Villagers" (97). Mark Twain's working notes for "Tom Sawyer's Conspiracy" (*HH&T*, 383, 384) indicate that Bowen was the model for Captain Harper in that story (156). He was cast as Captain Wright in the working notes for "Schoolhouse Hill" (*MSM*, 431), although that character does not appear in the story (des Cognets, 65–66, 93; Pilcher, 259; *Lewis Census*, 371; *St. Louis Census* 1850, 416:336; *Marion Census* 1860, 761; "Died," Canton (Mo.) *Northeast Reporter*, 10 Nov 53, 2; genealogical record, MoSHi; Holcombe, 899).

JOHN HENLEY BOWEN (1822–91), mentioned in "Villagers" (97), was a steamboat clerk in the late 1840s and then a St. Louis forwarding and commission merchant. By 1860 he was a steamboat agent and a representative of the Hannibal and St. Joseph

Railroad. He was river editor of the St. Louis *Globe* in the mid-1870s and, a decade later, engaged in mining in Mexico (des Cognets, 65; genealogical record, MoSHi; chart of John H. Bowen family plot, Bellefontaine Cemetery Association, St. Louis; Hagood and Hagood 1986, 137; Morrison, 29; Kennedy 1860, 12, 64; Scharf, 1:927; Gould 1873, 119; Gould 1875, 139).

MARY RUSSELL BOWEN (b. 1827?), mentioned in "Villagers" (97), married MOSES P. GREEN in the late 1840s. The Greens were strong supporters of the Union during the Civil War. During the winter of 1861/62 Mary Bowen Green was president of the Soldier's Relief Society of Hannibal, which supplied Union troops with clothes and medicines (*Marion Census* 1850, 305; des Cognets, 65; Holcombe, 428).

BARTON W. STONE (BART) BOWEN (1830?–68) married SARAH H. ROBARDS, with whom he had one daughter. He was both a pilot and a captain, as Clemens states in "Villagers" (94, 97). In 1858 he piloted the *Alfred T. Lacey* when it conveyed Clemens to Memphis, where Henry Clemens lay dying from injuries suffered in the *Pennsylvania* explosion. A year later, when Clemens was Bowen's co-pilot on the *Alfred T. Lacey*, Bowen encouraged him to write his burlesque of Captain Isaiah Sellers and arranged for the New Orleans *Crescent* to publish the sketch in its "River Intelligence" column on 17 May 1859. A steamboat clerk who worked on the *Gladiator* in 1864 recalled that Bowen had a quarter interest in the boat and "was the captain, a most courteous and efficient commander, and deservedly recognized as being the best dark-night pilot on the river" (Rowland 1907). In 1907 Clemens remarked that Bowen had "stepped down a grade" from pilot when he became a captain, but added: "I never lost any part of my respect & affection for him on account of that retrogression; no, he was a high-minded, large-hearted man, & I hold him in undiminished honor to this day" (SLC to John B. Downing, 25–28 Feb 1907, CU-MARK†, *L1*, 340 n. 4). Bowen died from steam burns suffered in a boat wreck (*Marion Census* 1860, 761; "Death of a Steamboat Captain," San Francisco *Times*, 23 Jun 68, 1; *MTB*, 1:139; Way, 176, 188; summaries of "A Card," New Orleans *True Delta*, 11 Oct 57, 1, and "River Intelligence," St. Louis *Missouri Democrat*, 7 Dec 58, 4, provided by Edgar M. Branch; *ET&S1*, 126–33; Branch 1982b, 505; Morris Anderson, 91; *MTLBowen*, 16, 17; des Cognets, 66).

ELIZABETH CAMPBELL (ELIZA) BOWEN (1834?–?76) evidently was retarded, as Clemens noted in "Villagers" (97). On 25 August 1876 William Bowen wrote Clemens that Eliza had died "in the Asylum" (CU-MARK; des Cognets, 66; *Lewis Census*, 371; *Marion Census* 1860, 854).

WILLIAM (WILL, or BILL) BOWEN (1836–93), a schoolmate, was probably young Clemens's closest friend. During an outbreak of measles in 1844, to end the suspense of waiting to catch the disease, Clemens crawled into Bowen's sickbed, was infected, and nearly died. He and Bowen were among the boys who pried loose a boulder atop Holliday's Hill and watched it crash down the hillside, narrowly missing a black drayman, and making "infinitesimal mince-meat" of a cooper-shop (*The Innocents Abroad*, chapter 58). By the spring of 1857 Bowen was a licensed pilot. After Clemens received his license in 1859, he twice was Bowen's co-pilot—on the steamers *A. B. Chambers* and *Alonzo Child*—during the ensuing two years. From 1861 to 1866

Bowen and Clemens were estranged. Their falling-out resulted from a misunderstanding about repayment of a two-hundred-dollar loan Clemens had made to Bowen and from political differences; Jane Clemens reported that "when Sam and W B were on the Alonzo Chi they quarreled and Sam let go the wheel to whip Will for talking secesh and made Will hush" (Jane Lampton Clemens to "all in the Teritory," 12 and 14 Oct 62, NPV, in *MTBus*, 73). Despite his early Southern sympathies, Bowen piloted a transport for the North during the Civil War. He left the river in 1868 to sell fire and marine insurance in St. Louis, and moved to Austin, Texas, about 1880. In 1888 he visited the Clemens family in Hartford. Bowen was married twice: in 1857 to Mary Cunningham ("Mollie" in Clemens's "Letter to William Bowen," 23), who died in 1873; and in 1876 to Dora Goff of St. Louis. His illness, mentioned in "Villagers" (97), remains unidentified, but evidently his health had deteriorated by the time he was thirty. Clemens recorded some of his and Bowen's adventures in "Letter to William Bowen" and "Villagers" (20–21, 97) and used Bowen in several fictional works. He was one of the models for Tom Sawyer, who is a composite of several boys. He figures as Joe Harper in both *Tom Sawyer* and *Huckleberry Finn*, and in the present volume appears as himself in "Boy's Manuscript" (12–13) and as Joe Harper in "Tom Sawyer's Conspiracy" (156). (Mark Twain's working notes for "Tom Sawyer's Conspiracy" explicitly identify Bowen as the model for Harper; see *HH&T*, 383–84.) In the working notes for "Schoolhouse Hill" (*MSM*, 431), Bowen was cast as Hank Fitch, but that character does not appear in the story (AD, 16 Mar 1906, CU-MARK, in *MTA*, 2:219–21; Wecter 1952, 140; *L1*, 211, 213 n. 22, 338, 340 n. 1, 357, 359 n. 1, 389; *MTLBowen*, 7, 15, 25–26; *MTB*, 1:54, 118; Ferris, 19).

Samuel Adams (Sam) Bowen, Jr. (1838?–78), was another of Clemens's schoolmates who became a river pilot. In the summer of 1858 he and Clemens co-piloted the *John H. Dickey*. In 1861 they joined the Marion Rangers, a volunteer Confederate company which disbanded after a few weeks—an experience recounted by Mark Twain twenty-four years later in "The Private History of a Campaign That Failed" (1885). Bowen later was arrested by Union soldiers and confined to the stockade in Hannibal. He was allowed to resume piloting after swearing allegiance to the Union, but he continued to assist the Southern cause by secretly carrying Confederate army mail between St. Louis and Memphis. In 1878, while piloting the *Molly Moore*, Bowen contracted yellow fever, died, and was buried at the head of an island in the Mississippi River. When floodwaters later exposed the gravesite, Clemens reportedly made arrangements to have the coffin reinterred. Bowen is included in "Villagers" (97), with emphasis on the details of his irregular marriage. Clemens had previously given an account of that marriage in chapter 49 of *Life on the Mississippi* (1883), calling Bowen "George Johnson" and characterizing him as a "shiftless young spendthrift, boisterous, good-hearted, full of careless generosities, and pretty conspicuously promising to fool his possibilities away early, and come to nothing." In his autobiography he again discussed Bowen's marriage, describing it as a "curious adventure" (AD, 9 Mar 1906, CU-MARK, in *MTA*, 2:185–86). Clemens's working notes show that he considered casting Bowen in "Tom Sawyer's Conspiracy" as Joe

Harper's brother Jack and in "Schoolhouse Hill" as Hank Fitch's brother Sam (*HH&T*, 384; *MSM*, 431), but neither character appears in the stories (*Lewis Census*, 371; Branch 1982a, 195–96; Grimes, 18–19; *N&J2*, 527, 561–62).

BRADY, VIRGINIA (JENNY) (b. 1837?), mentioned as Clemens's classmate in "Villagers" (95), was the daughter of carpenter James Brady, Hannibal's first mayor. Her brother Norval (b. 1839) was an occasional playmate of Clemens's. Mark Twain's working notes show that he considered portraying her as Jenny Mason in "Schoolhouse Hill" (*MSM*, 431), but that character does not appear in the story (*Marion Census* 1850, 308; Holcombe, 941; Wecter 1952, 141; Sweets 1986–87, 1).

BREED, DANA F. (1823–92), left New England in 1842 to settle in Hannibal. He worked as a store clerk until November 1849, when he opened a dry goods store with THOMAS K. COLLINS. He did not, despite what Clemens says in "Villagers" (94), marry LETITITIA RICHMOND. In 1851 he married Elizabeth Foreman; after her death in 1874, he married Mrs. Faustina Williams. In 1890, when Clemens came to Hannibal for his mother's funeral, Breed met him at the train station and served as a pallbearer ("New Store!" Hannibal *Missouri Courier*, 29 Nov 49; Holcombe, 910; Hagood and Hagood 1985, 8; "The Funeral of Mrs. Clemens," unidentified Hannibal newspaper, 30 Oct 90, clipping in Scrapbook 20: 126–27, CU-MARK).

BRIGGS family. William (b. 1799?) and Rhoda Briggs (b. 1811?) of Kentucky were listed in the 1850 Hannibal census with eight children, ranging in age from nine months to nineteen years (*Marion Census* 1850, 315–16). Clemens mentions three of the children in "Villagers."

WILLIAM (BILL) BRIGGS, JR. (b. 1831?), in 1849 joined the gold rush to California ("Letter from California," Hannibal *Missouri Courier*, 17 Jan 50). Clemens encountered him in San Francisco in 1863, and wrote home: "The man whom I have heard people call the 'handsomest & finest-looking man in California,' is Bill Briggs. I meet him on Montgomery street every day. He keeps a somewhat extensive gambling hell opposite the Russ House. I went up with him once to see it" (SLC to Jane Lampton Clemens and Pamela A. Moffett, 18? May 63, *L1*, 252). Amelia Ransome Neville, in her memoir of San Francisco, provides a description of Briggs in his later years:

> In the eighties it happened that we knew Bill Briggs, successful professional gambler of that later time who came to Shasta Springs for summer visits. Conservative guests avoided him, but others found him an engaging person, devoted to his small son and talking of everything but cards. His profession he left at home, and nothing could persuade him into a game while he sojourned among us. But he wore his mustache and wide-awake hat and the largest solitaire diamond I have ever seen in a ring. When he died, he left a fortune to the little son, then at a military school, and a reputation for square dealing. (Neville, 41)

Clemens recalls Briggs in "Villagers" (95).

ARTEMISSA BRIGGS (b. 1833?) was an early infatuation of Clemens's who kindly but firmly rejected his attentions. Both in "Villagers" (95) and his autobiography, Clemens indicates that she married stonemason JOSHUA RICHMOND, but the Hannibal *Journal* of 16 March 1853 records her marriage to bricklayer William J. Marsh. Working notes for "Schoolhouse Hill" (*MSM*, 431) show that Clemens planned to introduce her as Cassy Gray, but that character does not appear in the story (AD, 16 Mar 1906, CU-MARK, in *MTA*, 2:212, 214; Wecter 1952, 183, 305 n. 15; Fotheringham, 39).

JOHN B. BRIGGS (1837–1907) was one of Clemens's "special mates" (AD, 16 Mar 1906, CU-MARK, in *MTA*, 2:219). In 1850 both joined the Hannibal chapter of the Cadets of Temperance, nearly sixty boys pledged not to smoke or chew tobacco. Briggs worked in DAVID J. GARTH's tobacco factory, married Mary Miller, another Clemens classmate, and later became a farmer. In some autobiographical notes Clemens recalled an early misadventure that may have involved Briggs: "Burglaries (with John Briggs?) of potatoes &c which we could have got at home. *Caught nearly*—family back—hear them from under bed" (SLC 1898b, 1†). When he visited Hannibal in 1902, he spent an afternoon with Briggs and remarked "We were like brothers once" ("Friendship of Boyhood Pals Never Waned," Hannibal *Evening Courier-Post*, 6 Mar 1935, 5C, partially paraphrased in *MTB*, 3:1170–71). In his notebook for 1902, Clemens reminded himself to "draw a fine character of John Briggs. Good & true & brave, & robbed orchards tore down the stable stole the skiff" (NB 45, CU-MARK†, TS p. 13). That same year, he considered using an event from his friend's youth in a story:

The time John Briggs's nigger-boy woke his anger & got a cuffing (which wounded the lad's heart, because of his love & animal-like devotion to John (it is two or 3 years gone by—a lifetime to a boy, yet John still grieves & speaks to Huck & Tom about it & they even meditate a flight south to find him)—John went, hearing his father coming, for he had done something so shameful that he could never bring himself to confess to the boys what it was; no one knew but the negro lad. John's father is in a fury, & accuses the lad, who doesn't deny it; ~~Beebe comes along~~ no corporeal punishment is half severe enough—he sells him down the river. John aghast when he sneaks home next day & learns it. "What did you sell him for, father?" Tells him. John is speechless,—can't confess. (SLC 1902†)

Clemens's description is not entirely clear, but apparently the father believed the slave had struck or threatened John when, in fact, it was John who had committed the "shameful" act of striking the slave. Clemens recalls John Briggs in "Villagers" (95). His working notes for "Tom Sawyer's Conspiracy" (*HH&T*, 383) indicate that he considered including Briggs as Ben Rogers, although he ultimately did not do so. (Presumably Clemens had had Briggs in mind when he depicted Ben Rogers in chapter 2 of *Tom Sawyer* and chapter 2 of *Huckleberry Finn*.) In working notes for "Schoolhouse Hill" (*MSM*, 432), Briggs was cast as David Gray, but Gray is not among the characters in the story (Cadets of Temperance 1850; AD, 13 Feb 1906, CU-MARK, in *MTA*, 2:99–100; Greene, 96d; "Good-Bye to Mark Twain," Hannibal *Courier-Post*, 3 June 1902, 1; "Not Funny This Time," St. Louis *Globe-Democrat*, 2 June 1902, 1).

BRIGGS, CAREY, mentioned in "Villagers" (105), has not been identified.

BRITTINGHAM family. A large family, originally from Maryland, that settled in Hannibal by 1840. Thomas E. Brittingham (b. 1798?) ran a drugstore on North Main Street with his two sons. Clemens worked directly over Brittingham's drugstore in 1848–49 when he was a printer's apprentice on the *Missouri Courier*. And he may have been briefly employed by the druggist: in chapter 42 of *Roughing It* (1872) he recalled that one of his boyhood jobs was as a clerk "in a drug store a part of a summer." Clemens probably was remembering Thomas when he alluded to a Brittingham in "Clairvoyant" (32). Possibly, however, he was thinking of James S. Brittingham (b. 1816?), a clerk in TILDEN RUSSELL SELMES's store from 1844 to 1858. The exact family relationship of the two men is unknown (*Marion Census* 1840, 89; *Marion Census* 1850, 308, 310; Holcombe, 909; T. P. McMurry to SLC, 16 July 72, CU-MARK; Hagood and Hagood 1986, 56).

BROWN, WILLIAM LEE (BILL) (1831?–1903), is mentioned in "Letter to William Bowen" (21). In an autobiographical dictation of 21 May 1908, Clemens called this classmate W. B. "Buck" Brown and identified him as the oldest and largest student in JOHN D. DAWSON's one-room schoolhouse:

his age was twenty-five, and to the most of us he seemed not of our world, but a patriarch stricken with age, a relic of a hoary antiquity. He was very studious, very grave, even solemn; he had a kindly smile and a disposition in harmony with it. . . . At the noon recess he always remained at the school-house to study his lessons while he ate his dinner, and Will Bowen and John Briggs and I always remained also, and sacrificed our dinner for the higher profit of pestering him and playing pranks upon him, but he never lost his temper. (CU-MARK†)

Clemens perhaps confused William with his brother, James Burkett (Buck) Brown (1827–1915), who later became mayor of Hannibal. The 1850 Hannibal census (compiled in October) lists William as a cooper who attended school "within the year," as had Clemens (*Marion Census* 1850, 320; Holcombe, 910; Hagood and Hagood 1986, 97; Wecter 1952, 305 n. 16).

BUCHANAN family included the households of brothers ROBERT and JOSEPH SYLVESTER BUCHANAN.

ROBERT BUCHANAN (1802–75) came from St. Louis to Hannibal in 1832, acquired 300 acres of land, and established the first tannery in Marion County. Twice married, he had eight children, and Clemens was well acquainted with the three eldest: Henry Charles (b. 1830), a tinner and tinware manufacturer who became a wealthy real estate investor; Edwin or Edward (1834?–?80), an apprentice blacksmith whom Mark Twain called a "dull-witted lout" in chapter 51 of *Life on the Mississippi*; and JOSEPH ELIJA. In "Villagers" (96), Clemens calls Robert Buchanan the proprietor of the Hannibal *Journal*, although other sources say his brother JOSEPH was the owner. Both were involved in running the paper. Orion Clemens learned the trade of printing in the *Journal* office in the early 1840s. When the Buchanan brothers joined the California gold rush in 1850, Pamela Clemens wrote Orion that "Robt. Buchanan has taken the Journal Office and put it into the hands of young Bob and Sam Raymond," meaning Buchanan's nephew ROBERT SYLVESTER BUCHANAN and SAMUEL R. RAYMOND (29 Jan 50, NPV, in *MTBus*, 15). In an 1874 letter to Orion, Clemens recalled how "old Robert Buchanan . . . used to set up articles at the case without previously putting them in the form of manuscript. I was lost in admiration of such marvelous intellectual capacity" (9 Dec 74, NPV, in *MTB*, 1:facing 536). And in some autobiographical notes made about 1898, Clemens wrote: "The printing office—that was the darling place—Buchanan Journal (2 offices) then Courier"

(SLC 1898b, 6†). Mark Twain's working notes for "Schoolhouse Hill" (*MSM*, 431) suggest that he planned to introduce Robert Buchanan as Big Bob Turner, but the story does not include him (*Marion Census* 1850, 319; Holcombe, 899, 911; Greene, 579; "Interesting Letter from California," Hannibal *Western Union*, 9 Jan 51; "The equilibrium of California emigration . . . ," Hannibal *Missouri Courier*, 29 Apr 52; Ellsberry 1965a, 21–22; Kennedy 1859, 76; *Marion Census* 1860, 866; Hallock, 46).

JOSEPH SYLVESTER (BIG JOE) BUCHANAN (b. 1806?), a native of Missouri, is mentioned in "Villagers" (96). He was a steamboat engineer before turning to journalism. He helped to found Hannibal's first newspaper, the short-lived *Commercial Advertiser*, in 1837. In 1840, together with MATTHEW S. FIFE, he began publishing a newspaper that went through several name changes before becoming the Hannibal *Journal* in March 1842. In January 1850 Big Joe turned the *Journal* over to his son, ROBERT SYLVESTER BUCHANAN, and joined the gold rush. His name appears in Clemens's 1897 notebook amid plans for "Tom Sawyer's Conspiracy," but no character based on him figures in the story (*Marion Census* 1850, 325; Holcombe, 898, 899, 987; *MTB*, 1:27; *MTBus*, 15; "The 'Journal' . . . ," Hannibal *Missouri Courier*, 31 Jan 50; Wecter 1952, 223; NB 41, CU-MARK, TS p. 60).

ARGYLE ('GYLE) BUCHANAN (b. 1806?), mentioned in "Villagers" (96), was a farmer near Hannibal. His exact relation to ROBERT and JOSEPH SYLVESTER BUCHANAN is not known (*Marion Census* 1850, 305).

ROBERT SYLVESTER (YOUNG BOB) BUCHANAN (b. 1829), mentioned in "Villagers" (96), was the son of JOSEPH SYLVESTER BUCHANAN. He became a printer and, in 1850, co-proprietor of the Hannibal *Journal* with SAMUEL R. RAYMOND. They dissolved their partnership in 1851 and sold the newspaper office to Orion Clemens. Young Bob and URBAN E. HICKS, a *Journal* printer, were expelled from the Methodist church for "going to see Dan. Rice's Circus" (Hicks to SLC, 30 Mar 86, CU-MARK). Working notes for "Schoolhouse Hill" (*MSM*, 431) suggest that Mark Twain planned to portray him as Little Bob Turner, but the character does not appear in the story (*Marion Census* 1850, 318; *Marion Census* 1860, 208; "Dissolution," Hannibal *Missouri Courier*, 6 Mar 51; Wecter 1952, 239).

JOSEPH ELIJA (LITTLE JOE) BUCHANAN (b. 1830), mentioned in "Villagers" (96), was the son of ROBERT BUCHANAN. He worked as a printer's devil on the Hannibal *Journal* in 1850 and later became a steamboat engineer. In 1897 Mark Twain included Buchanan's name in a notebook list of Hannibal people and incidents he planned to use in writing "Tom Sawyer's Conspiracy." He did not use Buchanan in the story, however (Greene, 579; Ellsberry 1965a, 21–22; Wecter 1952, 223; Honeyman, 6; Stone, Davidson, and McIntosh, 62; NB 41, CU-MARK, TS p. 60).

BURTON. See BENJAMIN L. CLEMENS.

CARPENTER family. See CLEMENS family.

CLEMENS family. Called the Carpenters in "Villagers," the writer's family provided models for several characters in his stories about Huck Finn and Tom Sawyer.

JOHN MARSHALL CLEMENS (1798–1847), born in Virginia, studied law in Columbia, Kentucky, and in 1822 was licensed to practice. After he married Jane Lampton in 1823, they lived for approximately two years in Columbia before moving to Gainesboro, Tennessee, where their first child, Orion, was born. In 1827 the family settled in Jamestown, Tennessee, where John Clemens became a county commissioner, then a county court clerk, and opened a store. With an eye to the family's future, he began his purchase of thousands of acres of land, most of it just south of Jamestown. His total acquisition—which Samuel Clemens estimated at "seventy-five thousand acres," costing "somewhere in the neighborhood of four hundred dollars" (SLC 1870a, 3)—brought John Clemens's heirs years of frustration, but none of the wealth he envisioned. In the spring of 1835, the family and their one slave, Jenny, moved to Florida, Missouri, where Samuel Langhorne Clemens was born. In Florida, John Clemens practiced law, kept store, and did some farming. He was appointed judge of Monroe County Court in 1837; it was this appointment that earned him the honorific "Judge," which he bore the rest of his life. In November 1839 John Clemens moved his family to Hannibal, where he promoted the construction of the Hannibal and St. Joseph Railroad and helped found and govern the Hannibal Library Institute. He kept a store on Main Street until the early 1840s, when he was forced into poverty by Ira Stout, a dishonest land speculator. It was probably in 1844 that John Clemens was elected justice of the peace; the earliest evidence placing him in that position is a court record dated 17 September 1844. Albert Bigelow Paine's statement that he was elected in 1840 is disproved by newspaper accounts of the election, and Dixon Wecter's conjecture that he was elected in 1842 is inconsistent with an 1843 court record showing the position was held by another man (*Clemens v. Townsend; MTB*, 1:41; Wecter 1952, 103, 291 nn. 5, 7). Samuel Clemens's recollection that his father "was elected County Judge by a great majority in '49" ("Villagers," 104) also is incorrect. John Clemens declared his candidacy for clerk of the circuit court in November 1846 but died of pneumonia in March 1847, more than four months before the election. "My father may have hastened the ending of his life by the use of too much medicine," Orion Clemens observed in 1880. "He doctored himself from my earliest remembrance. During the latter part of his life he bought Cook's pills by the box and took one or more daily" (notes on SLC to Orion Clemens, 6 Feb 61, *L1*, 116 n. 11). Presbyterian pastor Joshua Thomas Tucker called John Clemens "a grave, taciturn man, a foremost citizen in intelligence and wholesome influence" (Wecter 1952, 86). He was more fully characterized in *The History of Marion County, Missouri*, in a biographical sketch prepared with Orion's assistance:

He never laughed aloud, and seldom smiled. He was sternly and irreproachably moral. He had a gray eye of wonderful keenness, that seemed to pierce through you. He wore his hair short and combed back. He could wield a vigorous and scathing pen, reminding one of the style of "Junius," when he chose to write for the papers. He never joined any church, though he inclined to the Campbellites. His shattered nerves made him irritable, but he never swore except once, and then he was very, very angry. His honesty no man questioned, and he carried scruples further than common in that direction. . . . He was a Whig, believed strongly in Henry Clay, and took an interest in politics. He seldom indulged in joking. If he did, the subject was pure and clean, and accompanied with a little twinkle at the corner of the eye, and only a perceptible smile. (Holcombe, 915)

Samuel Clemens confirmed these descriptions, remembering his father as "exceedingly dignified in his carriage and speech" and "austere" in manner; "pleasant with his friends, but never familiar" (AD, 29 Dec 1906, CU-MARK†). John Clemens is mentioned in "Jane Lampton Clemens" (90); he is Judge Carpenter in "Villagers" (93, 101, 103–5, 106), and James Carpenter in "Hellfire Hotchkiss" (109–19, 125) (Wecter 1952, 6–7, 14, 15, 28–57 passim, 69–70, 103, 110–11, 114–15; Tompkins and Eve; Gregory 1965, 30; Brashear 1934, 95; Pamela A. Moffett to Samuel E. Moffett, 15 Oct 99, CU-MARK; Return Ira Holcombe to SLC, 24 Sept 83, CU-MARK; SLC to Orion Clemens, 4 Sept 83, CU-MARK).

JANE LAMPTON CLEMENS (1803–90), born in Adair County, Kentucky, married John Marshall Clemens in part to spite a former suitor, RICHARD F. BARRET (Wecter 1952, 17–18, 23). Mark Twain characterized his mother in "Jane Lampton Clemens" (82–92). In an autobiographical sketch he commented that she had "come handy to me several times in my books, where she figures as Tom Sawyer's 'Aunt Polly.' I fitted her out with a dialect, & tried to think up other improvements for her, but did not find any" (SLC 1897–98, 49, in MTA, 1:102). Jane Clemens's Hannibal pastor, JOSHUA THOMAS TUCKER, called her "a woman of the sunniest temperament, lively, affable, a general favorite" (Wecter 1952, 86). She is Joanna Carpenter in "Villagers" (93, 103–8) and Sarah Carpenter in "Hellfire Hotchkiss" (109–19). She is Aunt Polly in "Tom Sawyer's Conspiracy" (134–209 passim), as she had previously been in *Tom Sawyer* (1876), *Huckleberry Finn* (1885), *Tom Sawyer Abroad* (1894), and "Tom Sawyer, Detective" (1896).

ORION CLEMENS (1825–97), pronounced O'-ree-ən, clerked in a store after the family moved to Hannibal in 1839. When he reported that he was taught to "adjust the scales one way for buying and another way for selling," his father placed him in the Hannibal *Journal* office, where he began his printer's apprenticeship under ROBERT and JOSEPH SYLVESTER BUCHANAN (Pamela A. Moffett to Orion Clemens, 27 Apr 80, CU-MARK). About 1842 he moved to St. Louis to work in the printing house of THOMAS WATT USTICK, returning to Hannibal in mid-1850 to start a weekly called the *Western Union*. Within a year he purchased the Hannibal *Journal* and on 4 September 1851 published the first issue of the consolidated Hannibal *Journal and Western Union*, shortening the name to Hannibal *Journal* after six months. He sold the paper and its printing establishment to WILLIAM T. LEAGUE in September 1853 and moved with his mother and brother Henry to Muscatine, Iowa, where he bought an interest in the Muscatine *Journal*. On 19 December 1854 he married Mary Eleanor (Mollie) Stotts (1834–1904), with whom he had one child, Jennie (1855–64). The following June, Orion sold the Muscatine *Journal* and moved to Keokuk, Iowa, his wife's home town, purchasing the Ben Franklin Book and Job Office. In June of 1857 he sold the unprofitable print shop and in the fall of the year moved to Jamestown, Tennessee, where he studied law and was admitted to the bar. He returned to Keokuk in July 1858, evidently remaining until May 1860, when he moved to Memphis, Missouri, to attempt to set up a law practice. On 27 March 1861, Orion was appointed secretary of the newly formed Nevada Territory, a position secured for him by Edward Bates, an old acquaintance from St. Louis, who was Lincoln's first attorney general. Accompanied by Samuel Clemens, Orion arrived in Carson City on 14 August 1861. Until late 1864, when Nevada became a state, Orion was comparatively prosperous since, despite his failure to become wealthy by speculating in mining stock, he enjoyed a government salary. Unable to secure a state office comparable to his territorial post, he attempted, unsuccessfully, to practice law in Carson City, then in California, where he also prospected and tried his hand at writing correspondence for the Meadow Lake *Morning Sun* and the San Francisco *American Flag*. Finally, however, Orion was forced to leave the West. He returned to St. Louis in September 1866, while his wife, Mollie, went to live with her parents in Keokuk. He was an occasional correspondent for the San Francisco *Times* in late 1866 through early 1867. He lived chiefly in St. Louis (Mollie joined him there in 1869) for about three years, supporting himself by working as a newspaper compositor. In late 1870 Orion and Mollie moved to Hartford, Connecticut. There, until 1872, Orion edited the *American Publisher*, the house paper of the American Publishing Company, Mark Twain's publishers. In the fall of 1873, after trying unsuccessfully to find work elsewhere, Orion moved to New York City, where he worked as a newspaper proof-reader. Mollie joined him a few months later, and they remained in New York until mid-1874, when, with Samuel Clemens's help, they returned to Keokuk to purchase a chicken farm. Over the next two decades Orion tried, in vain, to earn a living as a chicken farmer, lawyer, lecturer, and author. From the mid-1870s until his death in 1897, Orion was dependent on quarterly checks sent him by his brother. Meanwhile he compiled, often in public, a record of spectacular vacillation on political and religious matters. In a letter of 9 February 1879, Mark Twain regaled William Dean Howells with some of Orion's exploits:

> He has belonged to as many as five different religious denominations; last March he withdrew from deaconship in a Congregational Church & the superintendency of its Sunday School, in a speech in which he said that for many months (it runs in my mind that he said 13 years,) he had been a confirmed *infidel*, & so felt it to be his duty to retire from the flock.
>
> . . . After being a republican for years, he wanted me to buy him a democratic newspaper merely because his prophetic mind told him Tilden would be President—in which case he would be able to get an office for his services.
>
> A few days before the Presidential election, he came out in a speech & publicly went over to the democrats; but at the last moment, while voting for Tilden & 6 State democrats, he prudently "hedged" by voting for 6 State republicans, also. He said it might make him safe, no matter who won.
>
> The new convert was made one of the secretaries of a democratic meeting, & placed in the list of speakers. He wrote me jubilantly of what a ten-strike he was going to make with that speech. All right—but think of his innocent & pathetic candor in writing me something like this, a week later: "I was more diffident than I had expected to be, & this was increased by the silence with which I was received when I came forward; so I seemed unable to get the fire into my speech which I had calculated upon, & presently they began to get up & go out; & in a few minutes they all rose up & went away."
>
> How *could* a man uncover such a sore as that & show it to another? Not a word of complaint, you see—only a patient, sad surprise.
>
> . . . His next project was to write a burlesque upon Paradise Lost. . . .
>
> . . . Afterward he took a rabid part in a prayer meeting epidemic; dropped that to travesty Jules Verne; dropped that, in the middle of the last chapter, last March, to digest the matter of an infidel book which he proposed to write; & now he comes to the surface to rescue our "noble & beautiful religion" from the sacrilegious talons of Bob Ingersoll [the prominent agnostic lecturer and writer]. (NN-B, in *MTHL*, 1:253–55)

Orion's impulsive, impractical nature proved a source of anxiety and exasperation to the entire family, as did his sudden and severe shifts in mood. As Mark Twain recalled in his autobiography, Orion's "day was divided—no, not divided, mottled—from sunrise to midnight with alternating brilliant sunshine and black cloud. Every day he was the most joyous and hopeful man that ever was, I think, and also every day he was the most miserable man that ever was. . . . He was always truthful; he was always sincere; he was always honest and honorable," but "he was always dreaming; he was a dreamer from birth" (AD, 28 Mar 1906, CU-MARK, in *MTA*, 2:269, 272). Mark Twain considered Orion an author's "treasure" and urged Howells to "put him in a book or a play right away. . . . One can let his imagination run riot in portraying Orion, for there is nothing so extravagant as to be out of character with him" (SLC to Howells, 9 Feb 79, NN-B, in *MTHL*, 1:253, 256). Orion influenced the characterization of Washington Hawkins in *The Gilded Age* (1874). He appears as Oscar Carpenter in "Villagers" and "Hellfire Hotchkiss" (93, 105–8, 109–24). Mark Twain's working notes for "Tom Sawyer's Conspiracy" and "Schoolhouse Hill" (*HH&T*, 384; *MSM*, 432) reveal that Plunket the editor and Oliver Hotchkiss (166, 167, 224, 229–59) were based on Orion (Wecter 1952, 78, 225, 239; *MTB*, 1:27, 100; *MTA*, 2:268–74; *Bible* 1862; Mary E. (Mollie) Clemens, 3, 5–11, 15, 21; Orion Clemens to SLC, 7 Jan 61, CU-MARK; Lorch 1929b; *L1*, 58, 79 n. 11, 114 n. 9, 115, 121, 325 n. 5, 342 n. 1, 375 n. 5; correspondence between Orion Clemens, Mary E. (Mollie) Clemens, and other family members, 1867–74, CU-MARK; Pamela A. Moffett to Samuel E. Moffett, 23 Feb 80, CU-MARK).

PAMELA ANN (also PAMELIA or MELA) CLEMENS (1827–1904), pronounced Pə-mee'-la, was born in Jamestown, Tennessee. She attended ELIZABETH HORR's Hannibal school and in November 1840 was commended by her teacher for her "amiable deportment and faithful application to her various studies" (Horr 1840). In 1839 she joined the Campbellites after having been introduced to the movement by the daughters of its founder, Alexander Campbell (see the note at 112.3). In February 1841 she and her mother joined the Presbyterian Church. Pamela played piano and guitar and helped to support the family by giving music lessons. In September 1851, she married WILLIAM ANDERSON MOFFETT and moved to St. Louis. "Her character was without blemish, & she was of a most kindly & gentle disposition," Samuel Clemens wrote after her death (AD, 28 Mar 1906, CU-MARK†). Pamela is Priscella Carpenter in "Villagers" (93, 105) and—as Mark Twain's working notes indicate (*MSM*, 432)—Hannah Hotchkiss in "Schoolhouse Hill" (224, 229–38, 244). She was probably the model for Tom's cousin Mary in *Tom Sawyer, Huckleberry Finn*, "Huck Finn and Tom Sawyer among the Indians" (33), and "Tom Sawyer's Conspiracy" (150, 155, 156, 162, 168) (*Bible* 1817; Moffett 1881; *MTBus*, 5, 19, 24; Sweets 1984, 17; Pamela A. Moffett to Orion Clemens, 27 Apr 80, CU-MARK; Wecter 1952, 109).

PLEASANT HANNIBAL CLEMENS lived for only three months after his birth in 1828 or 1829. In "Villagers" (104) he is Han Carpenter (Orion Clemens to SLC, 18 May 85, CU-MARK; *MTBus*, 44).

MARGARET L. CLEMENS (1830–39) was born in Jamestown, Tennessee, and died in Florida, Missouri. "Margaret was in disposition & manner like Sam full of life," Jane Clemens later wrote, recalling the morning that Margaret left for school with Pamela, reciting lines from her lesson: "God is a spirit & they that worship him must worship him in spirit & in truth. When they came from school M. was sick & never was in her right mind 3 minuts at a time. She died in about a week" (Jane Lampton

Clemens to Orion Clemens, 25 Apr 80?, CU-MARK). In "Villagers" (104) she is M. Carpenter (*Bible* 1817).

BENJAMIN L. (BEN) CLEMENS (1832–42) was born in Three Forks of Wolf, Fentress County, Tennessee. One of Clemens's early memories was of kneeling with his mother at Benjamin's deathbed. He recalls this incident in "Jane Lampton Clemens" (82–83) and alludes to it and to his unexplained "case of memorable treachery" toward Benjamin in "Villagers," where his brother figures as Burton and B. Carpenter (93, 104). Among some fragmentary autobiographical notes probably made within a year of writing "Villagers," Clemens commented: "Dead brother Ben. My treachery to him" (SLC 1898b, 7†). And in his 1902 notebook he noted: "I saw Ben in shroud" (NB 45, CU-MARK†, TS p. 21; *Bible* 1817; Wecter 1952, 33–34).

SAMUEL LANGHORNE (SAM) CLEMENS (1835–1910) was born in Florida, Missouri, on 30 November 1835, six months after his family settled there. He calls himself Simon Carpenter in "Villagers" (93, 99, 101). In his autobiography he claimed that after his father's death in March 1847 he was taken from school "at once" and made a printer's devil in Joseph P. Ament's *Missouri Courier* newspaper office (AD, 29 Mar 1906, CU-MARK, in *MTA*, 2:276). Apparently, though, he was a part-time assistant to Henry La Cossitt of the Hannibal *Gazette* for one year before he began his apprenticeship to Ament in the spring of 1848. And he received at least some schooling after his father's death, since the 1850 Hannibal census (compiled in October) reports his attendance "within the year" (*Marion Census* 1850, 307). By January 1851 Clemens had left Ament's newspaper office and was setting type for Orion on the Hannibal *Western Union*. On 16 January 1851 the paper printed a sketch by him, "A Gallant Fireman," his earliest known publication (see *ET&S1*, 62). He remained with Orion on the Hannibal *Journal*, contributing several sketches, until he moved to St. Louis in 1853, probably in the first two weeks of June. Although Mark Twain gave to Tom Sawyer many of his own Hannibal experiences, he acknowledged that Tom was "a combination of the characteristics of three boys whom I knew, and therefore belongs to the composite order of architecture" ("Preface," *The Adventures of Tom Sawyer*). According to Albert Bigelow Paine the three boys were Clemens himself, "chiefly, and in a lesser degree John Briggs and Will Bowen" (*MTB*, 1:54). During his 1902 visit to Hannibal, Clemens commented: "Sometimes it was Will Bowen, John Garth, Ed Stevens, Jim Holmes, Meredith, or myself, just as the occasion was fit" ("Good-bye to Mark Twain," Hannibal *Courier-Post*, 3 June 1902, 1; Wecter 1952, 131, 200–202, 236, 263; *L1*, 1; *Marion Census* 1850, 307, 318).

HENRY CLEMENS (1838–58) was a family favorite. "Do you remember Henry's studious habits when he was only three years old? His bright face & lovable ways?" Pamela reminisced in a letter to Orion (Pamela A. Moffett to Orion Clemens, 27 Apr 80, CU-MARK). Like his brother Samuel, Henry belonged to the Cadets of Temperance and worked on the Hannibal *Journal*. After Samuel left for St. Louis, Henry continued to assist Orion on the Muscatine (Iowa) *Journal* and in the Ben Franklin Book and Job Office. In the spring of 1858, he became a "mud clerk" (purser's assistant) on the steamer *Pennsylvania*, employment which Samuel Clemens, then a cub pilot, helped him to obtain. Henry died on 20 June 1858 from injuries suffered in the explosion of the *Pennsylvania*, as Mark Twain recounted in a moving letter written at the time (see *L1*, 80–82) and in 1883 in chapter 20 of *Life on the Mississippi*. Shortly after Henry's death, Orion contrasted his brothers: "Sam a rugged, brave, quick tempered, generous hearted fellow—Henry quiet, observing, thoughtful, leaning on Sam for protection,—Sam & I too leaning on him for knowledge picked up from conversation or books, for Henry seemed never to forget any thing, and devoted much of his leisure hours to reading" (Orion Clemens to Miss Wood, 3 Oct 58, NPV, in *MTB*, 3:1591–92). In his autobiography, Mark Twain recalled:

> My mother had a good deal of trouble with me, but I think she enjoyed it. She had none at all with my brother Henry, who was two years younger than I, and I think that the unbroken monotony of his goodness and truthfulness and obedience would have been a burden to her but for the relief and variety which I furnished in the other direction. . . . I never knew Henry to do a vicious thing toward me, or toward anyone else—but he frequently did righteous ones that cost me as heavily. It was his duty to report me, when I needed reporting and neglected to do it myself, and he was very faithful in discharging that duty. He is Sid in *Tom Sawyer*. But Sid was not Henry. Henry was a very much finer and better boy than ever Sid was. (AD, 12 Feb 1906, CU-MARK, in *MTA*, 2:92–93)

Sid Sawyer (Tom's half-brother) is mentioned in "Huck Finn and Tom Sawyer among the Indians" (33) and appears in "Tom Sawyer's Conspiracy" (150, 153–56, 162, 168) and "Schoolhouse Hill" (214), as he had in both *Tom Sawyer* and *Huckleberry Finn*. In "Villagers" (93, 99) Henry Clemens is Hartley Carpenter (Cadets of Temperance 1850; *MTB*, 1:85, 100; Lorch 1929a, 418).

COLLINS, THOMAS K. (1822–85), mentioned in "Villagers" (94, 102), was born in Maryland and came to Hannibal in 1840 to clerk in his brother's store. In 1849, with DANA F. BREED as partner, he opened a dry goods store and became one of Hannibal's leading merchants. He was elected mayor in 1874 (Holcombe, 917–18, 941; Thomas S. Nash to SLC, 23 Apr 85, CU-MARK).

COONTZ, WILLIAM BENTON (BEN) (1838–92), was an occasional playmate of Clemens's and a Cadet of Temperance. After graduating from Bacon College (Ohio) in 1856, he was a riverboat pilot, grocer, leather dealer, steamboat agent, and salesman. He was a member of the Hannibal city council from 1871 to 1874, and mayor in 1877. In "Villagers" (102) Clemens notes that Coontz's son, Robert, attended West Point. In fact, Robert Coontz (1864–1935) graduated from the United States Naval Academy in 1885 and became a high-ranking naval officer. When Clemens returned to Hannibal in 1890 for Jane Clemens's funeral, William Coontz greeted him at the train station. Coontz perhaps was the model for Pete Kruger in "Tom Sawyer's Conspiracy" (167), since early working notes for that story call the character Pete Koontz (HH&T, 383). In his notes for "Schoolhouse Hill" (*MSM*, 431), Mark Twain considered portraying Coontz as a "fool—½ idiot" named Flip Coonrod, but the character does not appear in the story (Holcombe, 918–19; *Portrait*, 506; Hagood and Hagood 1986, 252 n. 7; Cadets of Temperance 1850; "The Funeral of Mrs. Clemens," unidentified Hannibal newspaper, 30 Oct 90, clipping in Scrapbook 20:126–27, CU-MARK).

CRAIG, JOE, a schoolmate recalled in "Letter to William Bowen" (20), probably was the son of Joseph Craig, who settled in Hannibal by 1833 and owned the tanyard where town drunkard JIMMY FINN slept (Holcombe, 895, 900; Henry Beebe to SLC, 14 Nov 1908, CU-MARK; Marion County 1845).

CROSS, SAMUEL (1812–86), was seven years old when his family immigrated to Pennsylvania from Ireland. He moved to Missouri in 1837 and by 1840 was a teacher in Hannibal. With John Marshall Clemens, ZACHARIAH G. DRAPER, and HUGH MEREDITH, Cross helped found the Hannibal Library Institute. A member of the First Presbyterian Church—like Jane and Pamela Clemens—he was also one of the church's elders. In the spring of 1849 he led a party of Hannibal citizens to California and settled in Sacramento, where he practiced law and eventually became a judge. Cross ran the school Clemens attended in the mid-1840s, after instruction by ELIZABETH HORR and MARY ANN NEWCOMB. (Cross's older brother, William, was also a Hannibal schoolteacher, though not one of Clemens's instructors, as previously thought; see Wecter 1952, 131.) In an autobiographical dictation of 15 August 1906, Clemens recalled the "early days" when Hannibal had only two schools, both of them private: "Mrs. Horr taught the children, in a small log house at the southern end of Main Street; Mr. Sam Cross taught the young people of larger growth in a frame school-house on the hill" (CU-MARK, in *MTE*, 107). Clemens mentions Cross only in passing in "Villagers" (97). His working notes for "Schoolhouse Hill" (*MSM*, 436) show that he re-created the physical setting of Cross's school—a frame house on the public square facing Center Street, a "coasting hill"—in the opening chapter of that story, although he based the schoolmaster there on JOHN D. DAWSON (*Marion Census* 1840, 89; Greene, 257; Wecter 1952, 111, 131, 217–18; "Hannibal Academy . . . ," Hannibal *Western Union*, 19 June 51; Sweets 1984, 63; "The Emigration," clipping from unidentified Hannibal newspaper, ca. May 49, facsimile in Meltzer, 15; "We received . . . ," Hannibal *Missouri Courier*, 3 Jan 50; Wright, 282; "Death of Judge Samuel Cross," Sacramento *Bee*, 14 June 86, 3; "Death of Judge Cross," Sacramento *Record-Union*, 14 June 86, 3; *MSM*, 436; *Marion Census* 1850, 311).

DANIEL (b. 1805?) was a slave owned by Clemens's uncle, JOHN ADAMS QUARLES, who had a farm of several hundred acres near Florida, Missouri. In 1897, Clemens recalled that during his summers there:

> All the negroes were friends of ours, & with those of our own age we were in effect comrades. . . . We had a faithful & affectionate good friend, ally & adviser in "Uncle Dan'l," a middle-aged slave whose head was the best one in the negro-quarter, whose sympathies were wide & warm, & whose heart was honest & simple & knew no guile. He has served me well, these many, many years. I have not seen him for half a century, & yet spiritually I have had his welcome company a good part of that time, & have staged him in books under his own name & as "Jim," & carted him all around—to Hannibal, down the Mississippi on a raft, & even across the Desert of Sahara in a balloon—& he has endured it all with the patience & friendliness & loyalty which were his birthright. It was on the farm that I got my strong liking for his race & my appreciation of certain of its fine qualities. This feeling & this estimate have stood the test of fifty years & have suffered no impairment. The black face is as welcome to me now as it was then. (SLC 1897–98, 44–46, in *MTA*, 1:100–101)

On 14 November 1855 Quarles emancipated his "old and faithful servant Dann who is now in the fiftieth year of his age about Six feet high complexion black" (Quarles, 240). Daniel appears as Uncle Dan'l in *The Gilded Age* (1874). He is Jim in *Huckle-*

berry Finn (1885), *Tom Sawyer Abroad* (1894), "Huck Finn and Tom Sawyer among the Indians" (33–76 passim), and "Tom Sawyer's Conspiracy" (134–212 passim).

DAVIS, FRANCIS (b. 1812), mentioned briefly in "Villagers" (99), was co-owner with WILLIAM SHOOT of Hannibal's Shoot and Davis Livery Stable. He married JOSE-PHINE PAVEY, and his son by a previous marriage, George Davis, married her younger sister REBECCA PAVEY (*Marion Census* 1850, 312; *Marion Census* 1860, 762; Holcombe, 903).

DAVIS (or DAVIES), JOHN (1810?–85), a Welshman mentioned in "Villagers" (95), married Clemens's schoolteacher, MARY ANN NEWCOMB, in the late 1840s. He was employed as a teamster in 1850, but by 1859 had changed the spelling of his name to Davies and was selling "books and fancy goods" from his store on Main Street (*Marion Census* 1850, 320–21; Fotheringham, 20; Hagood and Hagood 1985, 19; Ellsberry 1965a, 41; "Former Florida Neighbor of Clemens Family Head of School Attended Here by Mark Twain," Hannibal *Evening Courier-Post*, 6 Mar 1935, 12B).

DAVIS, LUCY, is mentioned in "Villagers" (95) as a Hannibal "schoolmarm." In a letter to Clemens on 31 March 1870, WILLIAM BOWEN reported meeting "Old Lucy Davis" on the St. Louis wharf: "Old *Luce*' asked for you instanter! Said you were the worst Boy, 'and *I declare in my heart* he's the funniest man in my acquaintance' Wants to know if you still climb out on the roof of the house and jump from 3^d story windows" (CU-MARK).

DAWSON family.
    JOHN D. DAWSON (b. 1812?), from Scotland, had fourteen years' teaching experience when he opened his school in Hannibal in April 1847. In 1849 he went to California, where he was a miner in Tuolumne County by 1850. Dawson's was the last school attended by Clemens, who remarked in 1906: "I remember Dawson's schoolhouse perfectly. If I wanted to describe it I could save myself the trouble by conveying the description of it to these pages from *Tom Sawyer*" (AD, 8 Mar 1906, CU-MARK, in *MTA*, 2:179). The school described in *Tom Sawyer* (chapters 6–7, 20–21) is reprised in the opening chapter of "Schoolhouse Hill" (214–24), with the schoolmaster modeled after Dawson. The school's location, however, as described in "Schoolhouse Hill," reflects Clemens's recollection of SAMUEL CROSS's schoolhouse. In "Villagers" (93, 94) Clemens mentions Dawson's school four times (Wecter 1952, 132–33; "Letter from California," Hannibal *Missouri Courier*, 17 Jan 50; *Tuolumne Census*, 135).
    THEODORE DAWSON was the schoolmaster's son. Clemens recalled him as "inordinately good, extravagantly good, offensively good, detestably good—and he had pop-eyes—and I would have drowned him if I had had a chance" (AD, 8 Mar 1906, CU-MARK, in *MTA*, 2:179). Mark Twain's working notes for "Schoolhouse Hill" (*MSM*, 432) show that he planned to introduce "pop-eyed" Theodore as Gill Ferguson, but he did not do so.

DRAPER, ZACHARIAH G. (1798–1856), born in South Carolina, was one of the leading citizens of Hannibal, where he settled in 1827 and held several political offices,

including those of postmaster, city councilman, county court judge, and state representative. He was one of John Marshall Clemens's few intimate friends. In 1841
both were jurymen in the trial of three Illinois abolitionists sentenced to twelve years
in the penitentiary for trying to induce slaves to escape to Canada. Both helped found
the Hannibal Library Institute in 1844, and in 1846 they initiated plans to construct
a railroad from Hannibal to St. Joseph. Draper heads the list of "Villagers" (93), and
he probably was one of the "three 'rich' men" Mark Twain alludes to later in that work
(see the note at 100.18). He did not die "without issue," as Clemens states, but fa-
thered five children, three of whom died at an early age. Working notes for "Schoolhouse Hill" (*MSM*, 432) reveal that Judge Taylor (237–38) was based on Judge
Draper (*Marion Census* 1850, 315; Holcombe, 253, 256–58, 894, 895, 900, 901,
942, 959; Greene, 92; Hagood and Hagood 1986, 9 n. 1, 161; Wecter 1952, 72–73,
110, 111; Brashear 1934, 200, n. 11; eulogy, Hannibal *Journal*, 27 May 52, excerpted
in Wecter 1950, 1).

ELGIN, WILLIAM C. (1802?–51), born in Virginia, moved to Hannibal in 1836. He
worked for several years as a merchant, and by 1847 was proprietor of the City Hotel.
A contemporary of Clemens's called "Col. Elgin . . . a prominent figure in Hannibal
society. . . . He had a great gift of Mesmerism which he practiced greatly to the
entertainment of some and the annoyance of others, among the latter his wife. . . .
he used to claim that he could mesmerize her hand or leg without her knowledge and
render either member 'paralized' temporarily" (Ayres 1917). In June 1851, Colonel
Elgin and twenty-three other residents died when cholera struck Hannibal. Mark
Twain's working notes for "Tom Sawyer's Conspiracy" (*HH&T*, 383, 385) identify
Elgin as the model for Colonel Elder (166–68, 170, 178, 203, 210). For clarification
of the reference to him in "Villagers" (101), see ALLEN B. MCDONALD (*Marion
Census* 1850, 306; "City Hotel," Hannibal *Missouri Courier*, 13 Jan 49; Wecter 1952,
120, 214; "Obituary," Hannibal *Western Union*, 26 June 51).

FIFE, MATTHEW S. (b. 1810?), mentioned in "Villagers" (93), was editor of several
Hannibal newspapers in the early 1840s, including the Hannibal *Journal*, where
Orion Clemens served his printer's apprenticeship before moving to St. Louis about
1842. Fife also was Jane Clemens's dentist. In his 1897 notebook Clemens recalled
him in conjunction with Dr. HUGH MEREDITH and Mrs. Utterback, a faith healer
who twice cured his mother of a toothache: "Mrs. Utterback cured Ma. D^r· Fife
pulled her teeth Dr Meredith—hoarse deep voice" (NB 41, CU-MARK⸙, TS p.
61). By the mid-1850s Fife had settled in St. Louis, where he worked as a wholesale
shoe dealer (Holcombe, 899, 987; SLC 1897–98, 63–64, in *MTA*, 1:108; *St. Louis
Census* 1860, 651:184; Knox, 58; Kennedy 1859, 160; Edwards 1867, 333).

FINN, JAMES (JIMMY) (d. 1845), as Clemens notes in his autobiography, was "Town
Drunkard, an exceedingly well defined and unofficial office" in Hannibal in the
1840s. The position was first held by "General" GAINES, then by Woodson BLANKEN-
SHIP, who for a time was the "sole and only incumbent of the office; but afterward
Jimmy Finn proved competency and disputed the place with him, so we had two
town drunkards at one time" (AD, 8 Mar 1906, CU-MARK, in *MTA*, 2:174). In

1867 Mark Twain recalled that the temperance people tried to reform Finn, but "in an evil hour temptation came upon him, and he sold his body to a doctor for a quart of whiskey, and that ended all his earthly troubles. He drank it all at one sitting, and his soul went to its long account and his body went to Dr. Grant" (SLC 1867a, 1). Chapter 23 of *A Tramp Abroad* (1880) contains a similar story in which Finn, lying sick in the tanyard, agrees to sell his skeleton to the doctor. In *Life on the Mississippi* (1883) Mark Twain wrote that he died "a natural death in a tan vat, of a combination of delirium tremens and spontaneous combustion" (chapter 56). James McDaniel, a Hannibal contemporary of Clemens's, confirmed that Finn "was found dead in Jim Craig's tan-yard" (Abbott, 16). Court records of 6 November 1845 show that Marion County reimbursed Joseph Craig (father of Clemens's schoolmate JOE CRAIG) for boarding and nursing Finn when he was ill, and assumed the cost of "making a coffin, furnishing shroud and burying James Finn a pauper" (Marion County 1845). Finn was the primary model for Huck's father ("pap Finn") in *Tom Sawyer* (1876) and *Huckleberry Finn* (1885), although Blankenship (father of TOM BLANKENSHIP, the acknowledged model for Huck) and Gaines may have contributed to his characterization. Finn also may have influenced the characterization of Jimmy Grimes in "Tom Sawyer's Conspiracy" (136). He is mentioned in "Letter to William Bowen" (20).

FOREMAN (or FORMAN), JAMES A. (JIM) (1835?–1903), was a Hannibal clerk who in 1850, like Clemens, joined the Cadets of Temperance. By 1854 he was clerking in a St. Louis dry goods store. Clemens and Foreman met again in May 1902 in St. Louis, where Foreman was a cashier in a printing firm. That summer Clemens wrote ANNA LAURA HAWKINS Frazer: "Guess again! Jim Foreman is in one of the books, but you have not spotted him" ("Laura Hawkins Frazer Always Remembered as Idol of His Boyhood," Hannibal *Evening Courier-Post*, 6 Mar 1935, 3C). A page of Clemens's Hannibal notes includes the phrase "Jim Foreman the model boy" and identifies Foreman's fictional counterpart—the "Model Boy, Willie Mufferson," who appears in chapter 5 of *Tom Sawyer* (SLC 1897b[†]). The allusion to Foreman's "Handkerchief" in "Villagers" (99) is explained by a passage in *Tom Sawyer:* "His [Willie Mufferson's] white handkerchief was hanging out of his pocket behind, as usual on Sundays—accidentally. Tom had no handkerchief, and he looked upon boys who had, as snobs" (*ATS*, 38; *Marion Census* 1850, 306; Hagood and Hagood 1985, 27; Cadets of Temperance 1850; Knox, 52, 61; Gould 1902, 674, 2620).

FUQUA, ARCHIBALD (ARCH) (b. 1833?), Clemens's classmate in DAWSON's school, was one of six children of Mary Ann and Nathaniel Fuqua, a tobacco merchant. In his autobiography Clemens remembered envying young Arch's "great gift"—his ability to crack his big toe with a snap audible at thirty yards (AD, 8 Mar 1906, CU-MARK, in *MTA*, 2:180). In "Boy's Manuscript" (12–13) Arch is Archy Thompson, the boy who sells a louse to WILLIAM BOWEN (*Marion Census* 1850, 318; *Marion Census* 1860, 750–51; Wecter 1952, 142).

GAINES. In his autobiography Clemens remembered "General" Gaines as "our first town-drunkard" (SLC 1897–98, 54, in *MTA*, 1:105). He recorded Gaines's boast—

"Whoop! Bow your neck & spread!"—in his "Letter to William Bowen" (20) and in 1876 used the phrase in the speech of a tall-talking raftsman in the manuscript of *Huckleberry Finn* (1885), a passage he published in *Life on the Mississippi* (1883) and later removed, at his publisher's suggestion, from *Huckleberry Finn* (*HF*, 110). Jim's remarks about "ole Gin'l Gaines" in "Huck Finn and Tom Sawyer among the Indians" (35) led Dixon Wecter to speculate that Gaines was an "ancient and disreputable relic of the Indian Wars" (Wecter 1952, 150). Working notes for "Tom Sawyer's Conspiracy" mention "Genl. Gaines (new town drunkard)" and suggest that he was to be the model for a "Gen¹ Haines" (*HH&T*, 383); the character who appears in the story is called Cap. Haines (180–81, 186, 188, 193, 209).

GARTH family. Clemens knew two sons of tobacco and grain merchant John Garth (1784–?1857) and his wife, Emily (d. 1844?) (*Portrait*, 776–77; Hagood and Hagood 1985, 29).

DAVID J. GARTH (1822–1912) in the 1850s became Hannibal's leading manufacturer of tobacco. Clemens recalled in his autobiography that Garth sold one extremely cheap brand of cigar known as "Garth's damndest": "He had had these in stock a good many years, and although they looked well enough on the outside, their insides had decayed to dust and would fly out like a puff of vapor when they were broken in two" (AD, 13 Feb 1906, CU-MARK, in *MTA*, 2:101). Garth was Clemens's Sunday school teacher at the First Presbyterian Church. By 1862 he had moved to New York City, where he established Garth, Son & Company, a nationwide chain of tobacco warehouses and wholesale houses. Garth is mentioned in "Letter to William Bowen" and "Villagers" (21, 95, 101). Mark Twain's working notes for "Schoolhouse Hill" (*MSM*, 432) include "Kaspar Helder (poor little German cigar   (Garth's d—dest)," but the story mentions neither the character nor the cigar (*Marion Census* 1850, 317; Greene, 96d; *Portrait*, 776; "David J. Garth Dead at 90 Years," New York *Times*, 19 July 1912, 9).

JOHN H. GARTH (1837–99), Clemens's close friend, attended Missouri State University, then worked in the family's Hannibal tobacco company. He married another childhood friend of Clemens's, HELEN V. KERCHEVAL, and in 1862 moved to New York City, where he worked with his brother in the tobacco business. Nine years later he returned to Hannibal and was active in various enterprises—banking, the lumber business, and manufacturing. When Clemens visited Hannibal in May 1882, he was the Garths' guest at "Woodside," their 600-acre estate just outside of town. Although Clemens says in "Villagers" (101) that the Garths raised three children, Hannibal histories mention only two, Anna and John David. Working notes for "Schoolhouse Hill" (*MSM*, 432) show that Jack Stillson (219) was modeled after John Garth (*Portrait*, 776–77; Greene, 271; *MTB*, 3:1332; John H. Garth to SLC, 7 July 83, CU-MARK; Hagood and Hagood 1986, 246).

GLOVER, SAMUEL TAYLOR (1813–84), practiced law in his native Kentucky before moving to Palmyra, Missouri. He was well known in Hannibal as the defense counsel in three highly publicized trials of the 1840s. In 1841 he helped defend three Illinois abolitionists accused of urging slaves to escape to Canada; John Marshall Clemens and other jurymen found them guilty—a verdict applauded in the courtroom—and they were sentenced to twelve years in the penitentiary. In 1846 Glover successfully defended Hannibal merchant WILLIAM PERRY OWSLEY when he was tried for the murder of SAM SMARR. He also was one of two lawyers appointed to defend BEN, a slave, who in October 1849 was accused of murdering a young white girl and her brother. Glover served as John Marshall Clemens's lawyer in 1843, when Clemens successfully sued WILLIAM B. BEEBE to recover a debt of $484.41. Glover was active in the Whig party, and in the early 1850s he became acquainted with Orion Clemens, who, as editor of the Hannibal *Journal*, was an ardent Whig supporter. Although Glover stammered, he was praised as a masterful courtroom advocate and an accomplished public speaker. After moving to St. Louis in 1849, and particularly after the Civil War, he was considered to be the West's most brilliant constitutional lawyer, but as Clemens indicates in "Villagers" (102), Hannibal residents were unimpressed. During Clemens's 1882 visit to Hannibal an old resident of the town informed him that a "perfect chucklehead," evidently Glover, had become the "first lawyer in the State of Missouri" (*Life on the Mississippi*, chapter 53). Glover's history somewhat resembles that of the protagonist of *Pudd'nhead Wilson* (1894), who struggles for nearly twenty years against the public's misperception of him as a fool (Holcombe, 251, 258, 276, 299; *Clemens v. Beebe*; NCAB, 25:370–71; Scharf, 2:1494; Conard, 3:66; Orion Clemens to SLC, 7 Jan 61, CU-MARK; Orion Clemens to Samuel T. Glover, 9 Oct 78, CU-MARK).

GREEN, MOSES P. (b. 1820?), was Hannibal city attorney from 1852 to 1856, mayor in 1864, and a delegate to the Missouri State Convention in 1865. As "Villagers" (97) notes, Green was a "Union man," who in 1862 headed a committee to secure emancipation of the slaves. He married MARY RUSSELL BOWEN (Fotheringham, 27; Holcombe, 519, 551, 941).

GROSVENOR, LEMUEL (1814–70), a native of Boston who was educated at Andover Theological Seminary, came to Hannibal in August 1846 to serve as temporary pastor of the First Presbyterian Church. He offered to spend an hour a day giving "young gentlemen" free instruction in either Latin or Spanish (Hannibal *Gazette*, 10 June 47, quoted in Welsh, 39). Grosvenor was almost certainly the Presbyterian clergyman who in "Villagers" (105) ministers to John Marshall Clemens on his deathbed. In May 1848 he moved to Illinois (Clarence W. Bowen, 1:260–61, 6:304; Sweets 1984, 44; Fotheringham, 104–5).

H., Mrs. See ELIZABETH HORR.

HANNICKS, JOHN (b. 1810?), from Virginia, is mentioned in "Villagers" (102). He and his wife, Ellen (b. 1816?), and their three children were among the forty-three free blacks living in Hannibal in 1850. Mark Twain described him in the first installment of "Old Times on the Mississippi" (1875), later chapter 4 of *Life on the Mississippi* (1883), as "a negro drayman, famous for his quick eye and prodigious voice," who reports the first sign of dark smoke above one of the river's points by shouting, "S-t-e-a-m-boat a-comin'!" In 1851 a local newspaper praised the "exertions of good-humored 'JOHN,' the Drayman, in turning out with his dray and hauling water" to the scene of a fire ("Fire," Hannibal *Missouri Courier*, 15 May 51). In a list of anecdotes in his 1887–88 notebook, Mark Twain included "John Hanicks' laugh" and his "Giving his 'experience'" (*N&J*3, 355; *Marion Census* 1850, 310; DeBow, 660).

HARDY, RICHARD (DICK), an artist and sign painter, is mentioned in "Letter to William Bowen" and "Villagers" (20, 96) ("Behold the Sign!!!" Hannibal *Missouri Courier*, 16 Dec 52; Thomas S. Nash to SLC, 23 Apr 85, CU-MARK).

HAN. See PLEASANT HANNIBAL CLEMENS.

HARTLEY. See HENRY CLEMENS.

HAWKINS family. Six members of the family are mentioned in "Villagers," and Mark Twain used two Hawkins children in his books.

SOPHIA BRADFORD HAWKINS (b. 1795?) and her husband, Elijah, a farmer, moved to Missouri from their native Kentucky in 1839 with their children and slaves. They bought a large tract of land in Ralls County, but resided chiefly in Hannibal, in Marion County. They had ten children, eight of whom can be identified: Eleanor, Jameson F., BENJAMIN M., ELIJAH ('LIGE, or 'LIJE), Catherine (Kitty), George William (Buck), ANNA LAURA, and JEFFERSON. According to "Villagers" (95), Mrs. Hawkins was widowed by about 1840 (*Portrait*, 248–49; Jackson 1976b, 51; *Marion Census* 1840, 90; *Marion Census* 1850, 305; "A 'green one,' . . . ," Hannibal *Missouri Courier*, 25 Mar 52; Frazer, 73; William Bowen to SLC, 31 Mar 70, CU-MARK).

BENJAMIN M. (BEN) HAWKINS (b. 1822?) went to California in the 1849 gold rush and returned to Hannibal in 1851. He served as a second lieutenant in the Mexican War and was Hannibal city marshal in 1852, 1853, and 1855. In 1856 he was elected county sheriff on the Know Nothing ticket, and he later became a lieutenant colonel in the Confederate Army. Clemens mentions him in "Letter to William Bowen" and "Villagers" (21, 95). Working notes for "Tom Sawyer's Conspiracy" (*HH&T*, 383–84) indicate that Captain Haskins, the militia captain and sheriff (167, 185, 188, 208, 213), is modeled after him (*Marion Census* 1860, 768; "The Emigration," clipping from unidentified Hannibal newspaper, ca. May 49, facsimile in Meltzer, 15; "Late from California," Hannibal *Missouri Courier*, 29 Nov 49; "Local Items," Hannibal *Western Union*, 16 Jan 51; Holcombe, 284, 331–32, 428, 941; *Portrait*, 248, 249).

ELIJAH ('LIGE, or 'LIJE) HAWKINS (b. 1828?) opened a Hannibal dry goods store in January 1849. In "Villagers" (95), Clemens writes that he became a "rich merchant in St Louis and New York," but Hawkins was still a resident of Hannibal in 1870. The marginal note "'Lige" on the final manuscript page of "Tupperville-Dobbsville" (CU-MARK) suggests that Clemens planned to use Hawkins in that story (*Marion Census* 1850, 305; "O! For California! New Firm," Hannibal *Missouri Courier*, 31 June 49; Caroline Schroter to Jane Lampton Clemens, 29 May 70, CU-MARK).

SOPHIA F. C. HAWKINS (b. 1833?), a native of Kentucky, is said in "Villagers" to have married a "prosperous tinner" (95). In 1850 she was living with the widowed SOPHIA BRADFORD HAWKINS, ELIJAH, and ANNA LAURA, but her exact relation to them has not been determined (*Marion Census* 1850, 306).

ANNA LAURA HAWKINS (1837–1928), born in Georgetown, Kentucky, on 1 December 1837, was only a few years old when her family moved to Hannibal. Laura, as she was called, at one time lived in a two-story frame house on Hill Street, almost directly across from the Clemenses. She and Samuel Clemens were childhood playmates, sweethearts, and classmates. "I remember very well when we moved into the house opposite where Mr. John M. Clemens lived," she said in an 1899 interview. "I remember also the first time I ever saw Mark Twain. He was then a barefooted boy, and he came out in the street before our house and turned hand-springs, and stood on his head, and cut just such capers as he describes in Tom's 'showing off' before Becky. We were good friends from the first" (Fielder, 11). In 1913 she recalled that she "liked to play with him every day and all day long. Sam and I used to play together like two girls. He had fuzzy light curls all over his head that really ought to have belonged to a girl." She remembered him as "a gentle boy, and kind of quiet, and he always did have that drawl. He was long-spoken, like his mother" (Abbott, 17). In 1918 Laura said:

The first school I went to was taught by Mr. Cross, who had canvassed the town and obtained perhaps twenty-five private pupils. . . . Mr. Cross did not belie his name . . . Sam Clemens wrote a bit of doggerel about him. . . .

Cross by name and Cross by nature,
Cross hopped out of an Irish potato.

. . . After a year together in that school Sam and I went to the school taught by Mrs. Horr. It was then he used to write notes to me and bring apples to school and put them on my desk. . . . We hadn't reached the dancing age then, but we went to many "play parties" together and romped through "Going to Jerusalem" [also called musical chairs], "King William was King George's Son," and "Green Grow the Rushes—O." (Frazer, 73)

She also recalled: "He took me out when I was first learning to skate, and I fell on the ice with such force as to make me unconscious; but he did not forsake me" (Wharton, 676). Laura Hawkins attended Van Rensselaer Presbyterial Academy in Rensselaer, Missouri, and in 1858 married James W. Frazer (1833–75), a Ralls County physician, with whom she had two sons. Although Clemens mistakenly believed her dead when he wrote "Villagers" in 1897, she had returned to Hannibal in 1895 and become matron of the Home for the Friendless. Clemens dined with her in Hannibal in 1902 and in October 1908 had Laura and her granddaughter as guests at his home in Redding, Connecticut, when he gave her his photograph inscribed "To Laura Fraser, with the love of her earliest sweetheart" (MoFlM). Laura Hawkins is mentioned in "Letter to William Bowen" and in "Villagers" (21, 95). She probably influenced the characterization of Amy Johnson in "Boy's Manuscript" (1–18). Mark Twain portrayed her as Becky Thatcher in *Tom Sawyer, Huckleberry Finn*, and "Schoolhouse Hill" (218), and used her name for one of the principal characters in *The Gilded Age* (Wecter 1952, 181–83; "Mrs. Fraser Dies; Chum of Twain," New York *Times*, 27 Dec 1928, 23; "Laura Hawkins Frazer Always Remembered as Idol of His Boyhood," Hannibal *Evening Courier-Post*, 6 Mar 1935, 3C; Holcombe, 647; photograph of the Frazers' gravestone in Rensselaer, Missouri, courtesy MoFuWC).

JEFFERSON HAWKINS, Laura's brother, is mentioned in "Villagers" (95). He died when very young and was buried in Hannibal (*Portrait*, 248).

HAYWARD, Mrs. See MILDRED CATHERINE SHOOT.

HICKS, URBAN EAST (1828–1905), a journeyman printer, came to Hannibal in the mid-1840s and apparently worked for the Hannibal *Gazette* until May 1848, then for the Hannibal *Journal*. Probably beginning in the fall of 1850 he worked on Orion Clemens's Hannibal *Western Union* where, by January 1851, Samuel Clemens and JIM WOLF were apprentices. Hicks was a member of the Sons of Temperance. He appears to have been fond of public entertainments and was expelled from the Methodist Episcopal Church South for going to a circus. As Clemens notes in "Villagers" (98), Hicks "saw Jenny Lind," suggesting that he was the unnamed Hannibal villager who declared, in a letter published by Orion, that seeing Jenny Lind perform in St. Louis had been worth every cent of the ten-dollar cost (see Wecter 1952, 193–94). In his autobiography Clemens wrote that it might have been in May 1850 (he was sure of the month, but not the year) that he and Hicks attended performances by an itinerant mesmerist, at which Hicks won brief local celebrity by proving to be an apt subject. Spurred by envy, Clemens pretended that he, too, was mesmerized and outdid Hicks with faked feats of telepathy (AD, 1 Dec 1906, CU-MARK, in *MTE*, 118–25). In the spring of 1851 Hicks emigrated to the Pacific Northwest, where he worked on newspapers and served as a volunteer in the Yakima and Klikitat Indian wars. He remained in the region for the rest of his life, working as a newspaper editor, publisher, and compositor in Oregon and Washington. In 1886, upon receiving news of Hicks's whereabouts, Clemens wrote: "I remember Urban E. vividly & pleasantly; & also the fencing-matches with column-rules & quack-medicine stereotypes. . . . if I could see Hicks here I would receive him with a barbecue & a torchlight procession, & put the entire house at his disposal" (SLC to George H. Himes, 17 Jan 86, MoPeS†). An entry in Clemens's notebook for 1897 shows that he considered using his and Hicks's experience with the hypnotist in "Tom Sawyer's Conspiracy": "The mesmerizer—Tom gets no pay, yet was superior to Hicks, who got $3 a week" (NB 41, CU-MARK†, TS p. 58). The incident was not included, however ("Remarks of Mr. U. E. Hicks . . . ," Hannibal *Missouri Courier*, 13 Jan 49; Hicks, 20; Hicks to SLC, 30 Mar 86, CU-MARK; George H. Himes to SLC, 30 Jan 86, 23 Jan 1907, CU-MARK; Wecter 1952, 205).

HIGGINS was "the one legged mulatto, who belonged to Mr. Garth," according to Hedrick Smith, a Hannibal contemporary of Clemens's (Smith 1889). An 1851 article in Orion Clemens's newspaper, possibly written by Samuel Clemens (see Wecter 1952, 238–39), reported Higgins's reaction when a Miss Jemima walked through town in the first bloomer costume seen there:

Higgins (everybody knows HIGGINS,) plied his single leg with amazing industry and perseverance, keeping up a running fire of comment not calculated to initiate him in the good graces of the person addressed. When the leg became tired, its owner would seat himself and recover a little breath, after which, the indomitable leg would drag off the persevering Higgins at an accelerated pace. ("The New Costume," Hannibal *Western Union*, 10 July 51)

Higgins is mentioned in "Letter to William Bowen" (21). In chapter 8 of *Huckleberry Finn*, Jim tells a story about "dat one-laigged nigger dat b'longs to ole Misto Bradish" (*HF*, 55). Mark Twain's working notes for "Tom Sawyer's Conspiracy" (*HH&T*, 384) list "One-legged Higgins (Bradish's nigger)," but in the story itself he has become "Higgins's Bill, the one-legged nigger" (184).

HOLLIDAY, MELICENT S. (b. 1800?), a native of Virginia, was considered the grand lady of Hannibal. She lived just north of town on Holliday's Hill (called Cardiff Hill in Mark Twain's fiction) in a mansion built for her by a brother. ANNA LAURA HAWK-INS Frazer recalled that when she and Samuel Clemens were young, "our favorite walk" was up Holliday's Hill:

Mrs. Holiday liked children, and her house, I remember, had a special attraction for us. She owned a piano, and it was not merely a piano; it was a piano with a drum attachment. Oh, 'The Battle of Prague,' executed with that marvelous drum attachment! It was our favorite selection, because it had so much drum in it. I must have been about ten at that time, and Sam was two years older. (Abbott, 17)

In "Villagers" Clemens mistakenly says Mrs. Holliday's father was "a British General in the Revolution" (95–96); in fact, her grandfather, Angus McDonald, fought in the Continental army and in 1777 was commissioned lieutenant-colonel by George Washington. Mrs. Holliday was married twice. Nothing is known about her first husband. Her second husband, Captain Richard T. Holliday, went bankrupt in 1844. He served as justice of the peace in 1844–45, concurrently with Judge John Marshall Clemens, and was elected city recorder for the years 1846 through 1848. He joined the 1849 gold rush, but died shortly after arriving in California. Having been told by a fortune-teller that she would meet a future husband on the river, Mrs. Holliday frequently traveled on the Mississippi. After the Civil War she lost her property and lived with friends, spending a few days with one, then moving on to another. On several occasions she annoyed the Clemenses in St. Louis by appearing uninvited and remaining for lengthy visits. Pamela Clemens's daughter remembered the elderly Mrs. Holliday as a "pathetic character" who "finally died in an insane asylum" (*MTBus*, 50). Mark Twain portrayed her as the widow Douglas in *Tom Sawyer*, where she is described as "fair, smart and forty, a generous, good-hearted soul and well-to-do, her hill mansion the only palace in the town, and the most hospitable and much the most lavish in the matter of festivities that St. Petersburg could boast" (chapter 5). She reappears as widow Douglas in *Huckleberry Finn* and in "'Tom Sawyer's Conspiracy" (134, 153, 156, 165, 208). Mark Twain's working notes for "Schoolhouse Hill" (*MSM*, 432) indicate that widow Guthrie (232, 236) was modeled after Mrs. Holliday (*Marion Census* 1850, 326; Wecter 1952, 157–58; Greene, 96g; NCAB, 15:235–36; *Clemens v. Townsend; Missouri v. Owsley;* Holcombe, 941; *MTBus*, 26, 49–50; Morris Anderson, 89–90).

HONEYMAN family. Robert D. Honeyman, a carpenter and contractor, and his wife, Amanda, are listed in the 1850 census together with five children between the ages of two and fourteen. Clemens recalled the three eldest children in "Villagers" (*Marion Census* 1840, 90, and 1850, 310; Greene, 259; Wecter 1950, 8; Honeyman, 27).

LAVINIA HONEYMAN (b. 1835?) was probably a classmate of Clemens's, though her schooling continued beyond his; in 1853 her grandiloquent valedictory oration at Misses Smith & Patrick's School was published in Orion Clemens's Hannibal *Journal* (Wecter 1952, 184). She is mentioned in "Villagers" (102).

SAMUEL H. (SAM) HONEYMAN (b. 1837?), mentioned in "Villagers" (98), was an occasional playmate of Clemens's and a member of the Cadets of Temperance. In 1866 he published Hannibal's city directory, advertising his services as an agent for the Missouri State Horse Insurance and Detective Company. A contemporary, Norval Brady, recalled that Honeyman lost an arm in the Civil War and died shortly after the hostilities ended (*Marion Census* 1850, 310; Cadets of Temperance 1850; Honeyman, 27, 64; "'Gull' Brady Was Last Survivor," Hannibal *Evening Courier-Post*, 6 Mar 1935, 6C).

LETITIA HONEYMAN (b. 1840), mentioned in "Villagers" (98), was a schoolmate of Clemens's (*Marion Census* 1850, 310).

HORR, ELIZABETH (1790?–1873), born in New York, was Clemens's first schoolteacher. Her husband, Benjamin W. Horr (1789?–1870), was a cooper and an elder in the Presbyterian Church to which Jane and Pamela Clemens belonged. Samuel Clemens never forgot Elizabeth Horr. Early in 1870, he wrote to her about his marriage and sent her a copy of *The Innocents Abroad*. She thanked her "kind Pupil" for his "generous expression of remembrance" (Horr to SLC, 16 May 70, CU-MARK). In an 1897 notebook entry for "Tom Sawyer's Conspiracy," Clemens recalled "Mrs. Horr, with the little colored pictures as rewards of merit" (NB 41, CU-MARK†, TS p. 59). In 1906 he remembered:

> My school days began when I was four years and a half old. . . . There were no public schools in Missouri in those early days, but there were two private schools in Hannibal—terms twenty-five cents per week per pupil, and collect it if you can. Mrs. Horr taught the children, in a small log house at the southern end of Main Street; Mr. Sam Cross taught the young people of larger growth in a frame school-house on the hill. I was sent to Mrs. Horr's school, and I remember my first day in that little log house with perfect clearness. . . . Mrs. Horr was a New England lady of middle-age with New England ways and principles, and she always opened school with prayer and a chapter from the New Testament. (AD, 15 Aug 1906, CU-MARK, in *MTE*, 107, 108)

He also recalled being disciplined with a switch on the first day of school, as well as Mrs. Horr's later prediction that he would one day be "*President of the United States, and would stand in the presence of kings unabashed*" (AD, 10 Sept 1906, CU-MARK†). In "Villagers" (95, 97, 101) Clemens alludes to Mrs. Horr or "Mrs. H." four times (*Marion Census* 1850, 314; Ellsberry 1965a, 17; Sweets 1984, 17, 63).

HUNTER, ELLA. See ELLA EVELINA (HUNTER) LAMPTON.

HURST family. Clemens mistakenly writes in "Villagers" (94) that his boyhood friend JOHN LEWIS ROBARDS "married a Hurst—new family." In fact, in 1861 Robards married Sara Helm, whose family was relatively "new" to Hannibal, having arrived from Kentucky in 1852 (Holcombe, 608, 992). No Hurst family has been identified among the town's residents.

HYDE family. Clemens mentions ELIZA HYDE and her "tough and dissipated" brothers, ED and DICK, in "Villagers" (96). They were the children of Edmund Hyde, who died in the late 1840s, and his wife, Mary (*Marion Census* 1850, 315; "Final Settlement," Hannibal *Missouri Courier*, 11 Oct 49).

ELIZA HYDE, on 27 April 1848, married Robert Graham, the "stranger" Clemens mentions in "Villagers" (96). See the note at 96.15 for a discussion of "The Last Link is Broken," the song Clemens associated with her (Hannibal *Journal*, 4 May 48, cited in Wecter 1950, 5).

ED HYDE appears to have left Hannibal by October 1850, since his name is not listed in the census.

RICHARD E. (DICK) HYDE (b. 1830?), a native of Missouri, had no occupation in 1850 and resided with his wife in his mother's home. In his autobiography Clemens recalled the "rowdy young Hyde brothers" who tried to murder their "harmless old uncle: one of them held the old man down with his knees on his breast while the other one tried repeatedly to kill him with an Allen revolver which wouldn't go off" (SLC 1900, 7, in *MTA*, 1:132). An entry in Clemens's 1897 notebook suggests that Shad and Hal Stover in "Hellfire Hotchkiss" (127, 130, 132, 133) were modeled after Ed and a Henry Hyde (NB 40, CU-MARK, TS p. 24, in *S&B*, 173). Henry might be another brother not listed in the census, but Clemens may have meant Richard (*Marion Census* 1850, 315; Hannibal *Journal*, 17 May 49, cited in Wecter 1950, 4).

JACKSON, referred to in "Villagers" (97) as the man who married ROBERTA JONES, has not been identified.

JENNY, a slave, was a young girl when Jane's grandmother gave her to Jane and John Marshall Clemens, possibly in the spring of 1825. She accompanied the Clemenses in their move that year from Columbia, Kentucky, to Gainesboro, Tennessee. When the family moved to Jamestown, Tennessee, in 1827, Jenny was hired out to PATSY and JOHN ADAMS QUARLES, Jane's sister and brother-in-law in Overton County, Tennessee. By the spring of 1835, having rejoined the Clemenses, Jenny traveled with them to Florida, Missouri. Annie Moffett Webster recalled hearing Jane Clemens tell stories in a "soft drawling voice" about "the long ride" from Jamestown to Florida: Jane Clemens "could not be reconciled to the fact that Jenny always secured the pacing horse leaving the trotting horse for Orion." Jane also "told many stories of Jenny who could only be managed by threats to 'Rent her to the Yankees.' The Northern people demanded so much more than Southerners did, that that was a threat that frightened her" (Webster 1918, 13, 14). Probably in late 1842 or early 1843 the Clemenses sold Jenny to WILLIAM B. BEEBE of Hannibal. Clemens recalled Jenny's sale in "Jane Lampton Clemens" (89) and in "Villagers" (104), where he noted her subsequent employment as a steamboat chambermaid. In his 1905–8 notebook, Clemens wrote: "We sold slave to Beebe & he sold her down the river. We saw her several times afterward. She was the only slave we ever owned in my time" (NB 38, CU-MARK†, TS p. 10; *Marion Census* 1840, 90; Varble, 99, 104, 115–16; Pamela A. Moffett to Orion Clemens, 27 Apr 80, CU-MARK; Wecter 1952, 72).

JONES, ROBERTA, is identified in "Villagers" (97) as the perpetrator of a practical joke that misfired with a tragic consequence. The incident is the subject of the brief sketch "Huck Finn," where Roberta Jones is called Rowena Fuller (260–61). Although Clemens notes in "Villagers" that Roberta married a man named Jackson, the Hannibal *Journal* of 23 November 1848 records her marriage to William B. Hall of Ohio (cited in Wecter 1950, 7). See the note at 97.27–28 for the opening lines of "Rockaway," a song that Clemens associated with her.

KERCHEVAL family.

WILLIAM F. KERCHEVAL (1813?–97) was a trader, according to the 1850 Hannibal census. Clemens identifies him in "Villagers" (101) as a tailor. In 1849–50 Kercheval was co-owner of a dry goods firm, and in the fall of 1851 he became manager of the "People's Store," which also sold dry goods. Clemens claimed in his autobiography that of the nine times he almost drowned as a boy, he was saved once by Kercheval's "good slave woman" and once by the tailor's "good apprentice boy" (AD, 9 Mar 1906, CU-MARK, in *MTA*, 2:184; *Marion Census* 1850, 305; Hagood and Hagood 1985, 44; "Fall of 1849. Kercheval & Green . . . ," Hannibal *Missouri Courier*, 18 Oct 49; "Dissolution of Copartnership," Hannibal *Western Union*, 12 Dec 50; "W. F. Kercheval . . . ," Hannibal *Missouri Courier*, 1 Jan 52).

HELEN V. KERCHEVAL (1838–1923), WILLIAM's daughter, married Clemens's friend JOHN H. GARTH on 18 October 1860. In his autobiography Clemens called her "one of the prettiest of the schoolgirls" (AD, 9 Mar 1906, CU-MARK, in *MTA*, 2:184). She is mentioned twice in "Villagers" (101). In working notes for "Schoolhouse Hill" (*MSM*, 431), Clemens cast her as Fanny Brewster, but the character does not appear in the story (*Marion Census* 1850, 305; *Portrait*, 776; Hagood and Hagood 1986, 246).

KRIBBEN, WILLIAM J. (BILL) (d. 1878), of St. Louis, was a Mississippi steamboat pilot. In 1863 he was arrested by Union soldiers on the charge of disloyalty, but was released on bond pending a trial, the outcome of which is not known. During the Civil War he was secretary and treasurer of the Western Boatmen's Benevolent Association and contributed to the organization's decline by embezzling its "ample fund" (*Life on the Mississippi*, chapter 15). He died of yellow fever when co-piloting the *Molly Moore* with SAMUEL ADAMS BOWEN, JR. Clemens's notebook entries during his 1882 visit to the Mississippi River indicate that Kribben was buried at the head of Island 68 in Arkansas (*N&J2*, 527, 562). "Villagers" (97) calls him "the defaulting secretary" (Kennedy 1857, 302, where his name is entered as W. S. Kibben; "Paroled," clipping from unidentified newspaper, ca. Apr 63, CU-MARK; McNeil 1861; M. Clabaugh to SLC, 19 July 90, CU-MARK).

LAKENAN, ROBERT F. (1820–83), born in Winchester, Virginia, was admitted to the bar in 1845 and shortly afterward moved to Hannibal. As Mark Twain recalled in his autobiography, he "took an important position in the little town at once, and maintained it. He brought with him a distinguished reputation as a lawyer. He was educated, cultured . . . grave even to austerity" and "was contemplated with considerable awe by the community" (AD, 9 Mar 1906, CU-MARK, in *MTA*, 2:181–82).

In the late 1840s he helped to found the Hannibal and St. Joseph Railroad and became its director, then its general attorney. Except for the years 1861 to 1866, when he retired to his farm in Shelby County, he lived in Hannibal. In 1876 he was elected state senator and in 1882 state representative. He was married twice: in January 1850 to Lizzie Ayres, who died the following December, and in 1854 to a reluctant MARY JANE MOSS. In "Villagers" (93, 94) Lakenan is mentioned three times (*Marion Census* 1850, 314; Holcombe, 608–10; Ellsberry 1965a, 37; "Married," Hannibal *Missouri Courier*, 10 Jan 50; "Died," Hannibal *Western Union*, 19 Dec 50).

LAMPTON family.

   JAMES J. LAMPTON (1817–87) was Jane Lampton Clemens's "favorite cousin" (SLC 1897–98, 19, in *MTA*, 1:89). Born in Kentucky to Jennie and Lewis Lampton (the brother of Jane's father), he studied both law and medicine and was a major in the Kentucky militia. He lived for a time in Louisiana, Missouri (about twenty-five miles southeast of Hannibal), but by the late 1850s had moved to St. Louis with his wife, four daughters, and a son. One daughter, Katharine, remembered Samuel Clemens's frequent visits to the Lampton home when he was a Mississippi River pilot: "He and father were great cronies; both were keenly intellectual men, deeply interested in politics and all the great questions of the day" (Paxson, 4). Although a lawyer by profession, in the 1860s Lampton worked as a salesman and bill collector, then went into business for himself as a cotton and tobacco agent. His eldest daughter, Julia, regarded as the beauty of the family, went insane after learning of President Lincoln's assassination; she tried to hang herself, claiming she was Judas Iscariot, and was placed in the St. Louis County Asylum. A relative who met Lampton in 1863 described him as "a man of tall, erect figure, with a military bearing. . . . a very pleasant gentleman; affable, cultured and well educated" (Keith, 9, 15). Mark Twain portrayed his cousin in *The Gilded Age* (1874) as Colonel Sellers, the incorrigible optimist who believes each new speculative venture will yield him a fortune. In his autobiography Clemens described Lampton as "a man with a big, foolish, unselfish heart in his bosom, a man born to be loved"; and he recalled seeing him in St. Louis in 1885: "He was become old & white-headed, but . . . the happy light in his eye, the abounding hope in his heart, the persuasive tongue, the miracle-breeding imagination—they were all there; & before I could turn around he was polishing up his Aladdin's lamp & flashing the secret riches of the world before me" (SLC 1897–98, 21–22, 25–26, in *MTA*, 1:90, 91–92). "Jane Lampton Clemens" (86–87) includes a brief discussion of Lampton (*St. Louis Census* 1860, 649:353; Kennedy 1860, 303; Edwards 1867, 505; Varble, 29; Paxson, 4; Keith, 9, 15, 51; Turner, 593–94; *MTBus*, 121; James J. Lampton to SLC, 24 Dec 79, CU-MARK; Katharine Lampton Paxson to SLC, 13 Dec 1904, CU-MARK; "Died," St. Louis *Globe-Democrat*, 3 Mar 87, 7).

   JAMES ANDREW HAYS (JIM) LAMPTON (1824–79), described in "Villagers" (98), was the son of Benjamin Lampton and his second wife, Polly Hays. He was the half brother of Jane Lampton Clemens, but as he was twenty-one years her junior, Jim generally kept company with her older children, Orion and Pamela. Born in Columbia, Kentucky, Lampton was about ten when his family moved to Florida, Missouri.

He was orphaned by the age of eighteen, and the following year, in December 1843, married Margaret Glascock. She died in early 1845, leaving a baby who survived only a few months. Lampton inherited property through this infant, including a slave named Lavinia. He settled briefly in Hannibal, where he rented the dwelling next to the Clemenses' Hill Street home, then attended McDowell Medical College in St. Louis. In November 1849 he married Ella Evelina Hunter and moved to New London, about 10 miles south of Hannibal, evidently intending to practice medicine there. He soon retired from the profession, however, because he couldn't bear the sight of blood. In New London he served as an agent for Orion Clemens's Hannibal *Western Union*. By the fall of 1853 the Lamptons had returned to St. Louis, where Jim worked as a clerk in the surveyor general's office until he became a steamboat agent in the mid-1860s. An active Mason, Lampton was described by a fellow lodge member as "a cultured gentleman, of large worldly experience and bright intelligence. . . . His genial disposition made him friends, and his frank and honest nature held them to him. He was a transparent man, and carried his whole true character in full view of the world" (Garrett, 7–8; *Bible* 1862; Woodruff, 24; Colonial Dames, 39; *MTBus*, 17–18; Varble, 161–63, 209–10; Hannibal *Journal*, 22 Nov 49, cited in Wecter 1950, 7; "Agents for the Western Union," Hannibal *Western Union*, 10 Oct 50; SLC to Pamela A. Moffett, 3? Sept 53, 8 Oct 53, *L1*, 13, 17; Knox, 110; Edwards 1866, 533; "Death of A. J. H. Lampton," St. Louis *Missouri Republican*, 4 Feb 79).

ELLA EVELINA (HUNTER) LAMPTON (1834?–1904), the wife of JAMES ANDREW HAYS LAMPTON, was born in Virginia. Her birthdate is uncertain, in part because she may have deliberately reduced her age by as much as ten years. A notation in Jane Clemens's Bible records Ella's birth in May 1834 (*Bible* 1817), making her fifteen years old when she married James Lampton, even though one history of the Lampton family reports her earlier marriage to a man named Plunkett (Keith, 9). Other documents give 1837 as Ella's birthdate. Her work as a newspaper correspondent, disparaged in "Villagers," remains unidentified. James and Ella Lampton took young Dr. JOHN J. MCDOWELL into their home as a boarder probably in the late 1850s; in 1860 he lived with them in Carondelet, a St. Louis suburb. Ella and John McDowell's intimacy, as "Villagers" (98) notes, was "an arrant scandal to everybody with eyes." Although Clemens and his aunt cared little for one another, he assisted her when his uncle's death left her in straitened circumstances. In 1881 he wrote his sister, Pamela: "I have no feeling toward Ella (*now*) but compassion for her bereavements & hard fortune, & admiration of her courage & spirit in facing disaster with a brave front" (4 Feb 81, NPV, in *MTBus*, 136). During the 1880s he sent her money and tried to find secretarial work for her daughter, CATHERINE, but was increasingly irritated by requests for assistance. On the envelope to one of her letters, he wrote: "Neither read nor answered—a woman who has been all her life a coarse, vain, rude, exacting idiot" (Ella Lampton to SLC, 2 Aug 85, CU-MARK†; *St. Louis Census* 1860, 656:637; *St. Louis Census* 1900, 893:15; Pamela A. Moffett to SLC, 7 Feb 81, CU-MARK; SLC to Charles L. Webster, 31 Mar 83, 17 May 83, NPV, in *MTBus*, 212–14; SLC to Annie Moffett Webster, 18 Oct 86, NPV, in *MTBus*, 366; "Funerals," St. Louis *Star*, 23 Aug 1904, 8).

CATHERINE C. (KATE) LAMPTON (b. 1856), mentioned briefly in "Villagers" (98), was the only child of ELLA and JAMES ANDREW HAYS LAMPTON. Born in St. Louis, she had the red hair that was considered a Lampton family trait (*Bible* 1817; *MTBus*, 136; Gould 1882, 683).

LEAGUE, WILLIAM T. (BILL) (1832–70), was a printer's apprentice in the *Missouri Courier* office, which opened in Hannibal in the spring of 1848. Clemens recalled him in a 1907 letter to the editor of the Hannibal *Courier-Post*: "Next spring it will be 59 years since I became an apprentice in the Courier office under Joseph P. Ament, along with William T. League, Wales McCormick & a Palmyra lad named Dick Rutter. Two of the group still survive: viz, the Courier & the undersigned" (3? Dec 1907 to W. H. Powell, MoHM†). In the fall of 1851 League helped to establish the weekly Hannibal *Whig Messenger* and in 1852 became its sole proprietor. It was League who bought out Orion Clemens's Hannibal *Journal* in September 1853. Clemens mentions League in "Letter to William Bowen" (21). In noting in "Villagers" (98) that League became proprietor of the "'Courier'" and "made it a daily and prosperous," Clemens was thinking of the daily Hannibal *Messenger*, established by League in 1858 and renamed the Hannibal *Courier* in the mid-1860s. League, however, had sold the paper in 1860 (*Marion Census* 1850, 319; Shoemaker, 254; Orion Clemens 1853; Holcombe, 988; Ellsberry 1965a, 10).

LEATHERS, JESSE MADISON (1846?–87), a distant cousin of Clemens's from Kentucky, wrote the author on 27 September 1875 and introduced himself as the great-grandson of Samuel Lampton, of Culpepper County, Virginia, whose brother William was Samuel Clemens's great-grandfather. He believed he had legitimate claim to the earldom of Durham and expressed his hope of recovering the title and estate from the Lambton family in England. Clemens thought his relative's chances "inconceivably slender" and said as much in a cordial letter of 5 October 1875 ("Mark Twain's Blue Blood," unidentified clipping, reprinting the Louisville [Ky.] *Ledger* of unknown date, CU-MARK). Leathers soon wrote that he was "out of business, and money, (a thing that has often happened with me)" and made the first of several requests for financial assistance (24 Jan 76, CU-MARK). Although Clemens sent Leathers small sums of money over the years, supplementing his meager and intermittent income as a newspaper advertising solicitor and a collections agent, he avoided meeting him and did nothing to further his claim to the earldom. He did, however, encourage Leathers to write and publish his autobiography as a means of earning money, a project begun but abandoned. Leathers died in a New York City charity hospital of tuberculosis complicated by alcoholism. Clemens used his story as the basis for *The American Claimant*, published in 1892 (Leathers to SLC, sixteen letters between 1875 and 1886; Leathers to Olivia L. Clemens, 6 Apr 81; G. E. Hutchinson to "Gentlemen," 23 Oct 79; John W. Chapman to SLC, 7 and 14 Feb 87, all documents in CU-MARK; Chapman, 721).

LEVERING family. Alice and Franklin Levering came to Hannibal in 1841 (*Marion Census* 1850, 307; Holcombe, 962). Clemens knew their two oldest children.
CLINT LEVERING (1837?–47), a playmate of Clemens's, died at the age of ten. While "bathing with a number of his playmates, [he] was carried beyond his depth,

and in spite of the exertions of those who were with him, was drowned" (Hannibal *Gazette*, 20 Aug 47, in Wecter 1952, 169). In chapter 54 of *Life on the Mississippi* (1883), where he called Clint "Lem Hackett," Mark Twain described the terrified reaction of the village boys, who were encouraged to view Clint's death as divine retribution for sinfulness. In his 1897 notebook, he wrote that the drowning was regarded as "a judgment" on Clint and his parents because Clint's great-grandmother had given protection to two Jewish boys "when they were being chased & stoned" (NB 41, CU-MARK†, TS p. 59); in the notebook entry, however, he mistakenly calls the drowned boy "Writer" (i.e., "Righter"), the name of Clint's younger brother. Clint Levering's drowning is mentioned in "Letter to William Bowen" and in "Villagers" (20, 101).

AARON RIGHTER LEVERING (1839–1912), referred to in "Villagers" (101), was a Cadet of Temperance with Clemens. At thirteen he began work in a hardware store and at twenty started his own hardware business. In 1870 he helped to organize the Farmers' and Merchants' Bank of Hannibal, and became the cashier. A deacon in the Fifth Street Baptist Church, he was for many years a Sunday school superintendent and public school director. When Clemens visited Hannibal in 1902, he attended a reception at the Farmers' and Merchants' Bank where he was greeted by Levering and fellow bank officers JOHN LEWIS ROBARDS and WILLIAM R. PITTS (Holcombe, 962, 1064; Hagood and Hagood 1986, 252 n. 7; Cadets of Temperance 1850; "The Farmers & Merchants Bank," Hannibal *Courier-Post*, 22 Apr 1905, 1; "Mark Twain Sees the Home of His Boyhood," St. Louis *Post-Dispatch*, 30 May 1902, 1).

LOCKWOOD, LUCY. No information. Though Clemens says in "Villagers" (95) that she married LOT SOUTHARD, the Hannibal *Missouri Courier* of 8 November 1849 records Southard's marriage to Emma Beecham.

M. See MARGARET L. CLEMENS.

McCORMICK, WALES R., mentioned in "Villagers" (98), was a printer's apprentice with Clemens on Joseph P. Ament's Hannibal *Missouri Courier*. In his autobiography, Clemens recalled that he and McCormick boarded with Ament's family. Although paid no wages, they were promised two suits a year, but instead received their employer's old clothes. Cast-off shirts gave Clemens "the uncomfortable sense of living in a circus-tent" and were so snug on the "giant" McCormick as to nearly suffocate him, "particularly in the summertime." Clemens characterized Wales as "a reckless, hilarious, admirable creature; he had no principles, and was delightful company" (AD, 29 Mar 1906, CU-MARK, in *MTA*, 2:276). In his notebook for 1887–88, Clemens remembered that McCormick had been reprimanded several times by the itinerant preacher Alexander Campbell for saying "Great God! when Great Scott would have done as well. . . . Weeks afterward, that inveterate lighthead had his turn, & corrected the Reverend. In correcting the pamphlet-proof of one of Campbell's great sermons, Wales changed 'Great God!' to 'Great Scott,' & changed Father, Son & Holy Ghost to Father, Son & Caesar's Ghost. In overrunning, he reduced it to Father, Son & Co., to keep *from* overrunning" (*N&J3*, 305). Mc-

Cormick also abbreviated Jesus Christ to J. C., and when told by Campbell never to diminish the Savior's name, "enlarged the offending J. C. into Jesus H. Christ" (AD, 29 Mar 1906, CU-MARK, in *MTA*, 2:279–82). In another reminiscence, Clemens wrote that "Wales inserted five names between the Savior's first & last names—said he reckoned Rev. Campbell will be satisfied now" (SLC 1898b, 5–6†). By 1850 McCormick had left Hannibal, eventually settling in Quincy, Illinois, where Clemens saw him while on a lecture tour in 1885. McCormick was the inspiration for the handsome and flirtatious printer named Doangivadam in "No. 44, The Mysterious Stranger": "Hamper him as you might, obstruct him as you might, make things as desperate for him as you pleased, he didn't give a damn, and said so. He was always gay and breezy and cheerful, always kind and good and generous and friendly and careless and wasteful, and couldn't keep a copper, and never tried" (*MSM*, 268). Letters from McCormick indicate that Clemens regularly gave him financial assistance in the middle and late 1880s (SLC to Olivia L. Clemens, 23 Jan 85; Wales R. McCormick to SLC, 3 Feb 85, 23 Jan 88, 12 Nov 88, all in CU-MARK; Jackson and Teeples, 239).

McDERMID (or McDAVID), DENNIS (d. 1853), was "that poor fellow in the calaboose" recalled in "Letter to William Bowen" (21). He died in the fire that destroyed Hannibal's small jail in the early hours of 23 January 1853. Writing in the Hannibal *Journal* on 27 January, Orion Clemens reported that Dennis McDermid (called McDavid in the Hannibal *Tri-Weekly Messenger* of 25 January) had been made "insane by liquor" and was imprisoned for "breaking down the door of a negro cabin with an ax, and chasing out the inmates." He had started the blaze when he "set his bed clothes on fire with matches, as he usually carried them in his pocket to light his pipe" (Wecter 1952, 254–55). In 1883, in chapter 56 of *Life on the Mississippi*, Clemens remembered giving the matches to the "whiskey-sodden tramp." Claiming to have been only ten years old at the time (in fact, he was seventeen), he confessed to having felt "as guilty of the man's death as if I had given him the matches purposely that he might burn himself up with them." In an autobiographical sketch written in 1900, he explained that it was his "trained Presbyterian conscience" that made him feel guilty even though he had meant the tramp "no harm, but only good, when I let him have the matches" (SLC 1900, 6, in *MTA*, 1:131).

McDONALD, ALLEN B. (b. 1805?), "the desperado" mentioned in "Villagers" (95), was a plasterer from Kentucky (*Marion Census* 1850, 323). The story of McDonald's fight with CHARLEY SCHNEIDER (or SCHNIETER) is given in the *History of Marion County, Missouri* much as it is in "Villagers" (101). When John Marshall Clemens was justice of the peace,

Charlie Schnieter and a carpenter named McDonald got into a scuffle on the sidewalk in front of Mr. Clemens' office. They were litigants in his court, and he stepped out to see what was going on. McDonald was trying to make Schnieter shoot himself with his own pistol. Mr. Clemens commanded the peace, and not being obeyed he struck McDonald on the forehead with a stonemason's mallet. The plan succeeded, though McDonald expressed doubts of its legality. McDonald was so frequently in difficulties, and so desperately reckless, that he was regarded by most people as half insane and very dangerous. He afterward leveled a shot-gun at Col. Elgin from behind, but the Colonel turned his head, revealing part of his face. McDonald said he believed he was attacking John M. Clemens, but nobody else believed him. (Holcombe, 914)

McDowell, John J. (b. 1834?), a native of Kentucky and a physician, was the son of Joseph Nash McDowell (1805–68), a brilliant, but eccentric, surgeon who in 1840 helped to found the first medical college in St. Louis. (A discussion of the father can be found in Wecter 1952, 160–61, where, however, he is confused with his uncle, Ephraim D. McDowell, "the originator of ovariotomy.") John McDowell started living with Clemens's aunt and uncle, Ella and James Andrew Hays Lampton, by the summer of 1860, and Clemens comments in "Villagers" (98) on the "arrant scandal" of McDowell's affair with Ella. In 1870 McDowell described his relationship with the Lamptons in more innocent terms: "When I was a youth, I determined to leave home to find some one who would be kind to me. My mother was dead, and my father . . . had a second time entered the marriage relation. My stepmother and I could not agree. Mr. and Mrs. Lampton met me, took me to their home and were so kind to me that I never left them. I have felt as one of the family ever since that day" (Keith, 10; *St. Louis Census* 1850, 415:258; *St. Louis Census* 1860, 656:637; Scharf, 2:1526–27; Varble, 252–53).

McManus, Jimmy, mentioned in "Villagers" (97), was a boatman who robbed Clemens in June 1858 after the explosion of the steamboat *Pennsylvania*, in which Henry Clemens died. In an 1882 notebook, Clemens recalled: "McManus (Jimmy) robbed me of brass watch chain, & $20—& robbed old Calhoun of underclothes" (*N&J2*, 454; Kennedy 1860, 333).

McMurry, T. P. (Pet) (d. 1886), mentioned in "Villagers" (98), was the journeyman printer for the Hannibal *Missouri Courier* office in the late 1840s, when Clemens and Wales McCormick were apprentices there. He married in 1853 and became a merchant, eventually settling in Knox County, Missouri. In a letter to Clemens of 16 July 1872, McMurry recalled him as "a little sandy-headed, curly-headed boy . . . mounted upon a little box at the case, pulling away at a huge Cigar, or a diminutive pipe," who loved to sing "the poor drunken man's expression, who was supposed to have fallen in the rut by the wayside: 'If ever I *git up agin, I'll stay up,—if I kin!*' " (CU-MARK). When Clemens lectured at Quincy, Illinois, in 1885, he was visited by McMurry, "an old man with bushy gray whiskers down to his breast, & farmer-like clothes on":

When I saw him last, 35 years ago, he was a dandy, with plug hat tipped far forward & resting almost on his very nose; dark red, greasy hair, long, & rolled under at the bottom, down on his neck; red goatee; a most mincing, self-conceited gait—the most astonishing gait that ever I saw—a gait possible nowhere on earth but in our South & in that old day; & when his hat was off, a red roll of hair, a recumbent curl, was exposed (between two exact partings) which extended from his forehead rearward over the curve of his skull, & you could look into it as you would into a tunnel. But now—well, see O W Holmes's "The Last Leaf" for what he is now. (SLC to Olivia Clemens, 23 Jan 85, CU-MARK, in *LLMT*, 233)

McMurry was probably the model for the title character of "Jul'us Caesar," a sketch Clemens wrote in 1855 or 1856 but never published (see *ET&S1*, 111–17). In an

1897 notebook, Clemens alluded to a prank he had played on McMurry: "Drinking Pet's bottle of medicine & re-filling it" (NB 41, CU-MARK†, TS p. 60; Hannibal *Journal*, 15 Aug 53, cited in Wecter 1950, 7; Mrs. T. P. McMurry to SLC, 18 Aug 89, CU-MARK).

MEREDITH family.

HUGH MEREDITH (1806–64), recalled in "Villagers" (93), was born in Pennsylvania. He was the Clemens family's physician in Florida and Hannibal, Missouri. Meredith and John Marshall Clemens were active in planning improvements for both towns, and in 1844 both helped found the Hannibal Library Institute. Dr. Meredith joined the Gold Rush in 1849, but returned home early in 1851. He took charge of Orion Clemens's Hannibal *Journal* for several weeks during the winter of 1851/52, while Orion was in Tennessee attending to the Clemens family's property there. In his autobiography Clemens recalled the occasion when Orion—making a surprise visit to Hannibal, but unaware that Meredith's family was living in the Clemenses' former house—unwittingly climbed into bed with the doctor's "two ripe old-maid sisters" (AD, 28 Mar 1906, CU-MARK, in *MTA*, 2:272–74; *Marion Census* 1850, 326; Gregory 1965, 31; Wecter 1952, 55, 111, 116–17, 241–42; Brashear 1934, 200 n. 11; "We received . . . ," Hannibal *Missouri Courier*, 3 Jan 50; "Returned Californians," Hannibal *Western Union*, 9 Jan 51; "Dr. Hugh Meredith . . . ," Hannibal *Western Union*, 3 Apr 51).

CHARLES MEREDITH (b. 1833?), mentioned in "Villagers" (93), was born in Pennsylvania and was the oldest of the doctor's five children. He once saved Clemens from drowning in Bear Creek. In 1849–51 he traveled to the California gold fields with his father, and in the spring of 1852 made a second trip west (*Marion Census* 1850, 326; SLC 1903, 3; Hagood and Hagood 1986, 91; "From the Plains," Hannibal *Missouri Courier*, 24 June 52).

JOHN D. MEREDITH (1837–70), mentioned twice in "Villagers" (93, 96), was born in Missouri. He was a Cadet of Temperance with Clemens. Orion Clemens taught the trade of printing to one of Dr. Meredith's sons—probably John, who made printing his profession and in the late 1850s worked for the Hannibal *Messenger*. In his autobiography Samuel Clemens recalled Meredith as "a boy of a quite uncommonly sweet and gentle disposition. He grew up, and when the Civil War broke out he became a sort of guerrilla chief on the Confederate side, and I was told that in his raids upon Union families in the country parts of Monroe County—in earlier times the friends and familiars of his father—he was remorseless in his devastations and sheddings of blood" (AD, 9 Mar 1906, CU-MARK, in *MTA*, 2:185; *Marion Census* 1850, 326; Hagood and Hagood 1986, 128; Cadets of Temperance 1850; Orion Clemens 1880–82, 4; Fotheringham, 41).

MOFFETT, WILLIAM ANDERSON (WILL) (1816–65), was Clemens's brother-in-law. In 1835 or 1836 William and his brother Erasmus moved from their native Virginia to Florida, Missouri, where they found jobs in a grocery. In the early 1840s the brothers moved to Hannibal and with partner George Schroter opened a general store. William moved to St. Louis in the spring of 1851 and established Moffett,

Stillwell and Company, a firm of commission merchants; after that partnership dissolved in 1855, he formed a commission business with his old partner, Schroter. On 20 September 1851 he married Pamela Ann Clemens, with whom he had two children: Annie E. (1852–1950) and Samuel Erasmus (1860–1908). In the spring of 1857, Moffett loaned Clemens the $100 initial payment for his apprenticeship as a river pilot, and Clemens often stayed with the Moffetts in St. Louis during his piloting years. Moffett died in St. Louis, leaving Pamela a widow at age thirty-seven. In his autobiography, Clemens recalled Moffett as "a merchant, a Virginian—a fine man in every way" (AD, 29 Mar 1906, CU-MARK, in *MTA*, 2:289). "Villagers" (105) includes a less flattering description (*Bible* 1862; *Marion Census* 1850, 306; Webster 1918, 1–2; "We direct attention . . . ," Hannibal *Missouri Courier*, 3 Apr 51; *MTBus*, 19, 26, 33, 36, 38; *Portrait*, 579).

Moss family.
RUSSELL W. MOSS (b. 1810?), a native of Kentucky, entered the meat packing business in 1850 with William Samuel, and their firm, situated on Hannibal's levee, reputedly was the second largest pork and beef packing house in the United States. Moss is described as "rich" in "Villagers" (94; see also the note at 100.18). He and his wife, Mary (b. 1816), also from Kentucky, had six children; the two oldest are mentioned in "Villagers" (*Marion Census* 1850, 312; "Mammoth Packing House," Hannibal *Western Union*, 14 Nov 50; Holcombe, 903).

MARY JANE MOSS (b. 1832?) was "the '*belle* of Hannibal'" (Anna Laura Hawkins Frazer to SLC, 16 Mar 1909, CU-MARK). She was friendly with Pamela Clemens and frequently visited the Clemens home. "It was not deemed proper in Hannibal in the 40's for a young woman to go down Main street unaccompanied by an older person," and Mary Moss used "to stop at the Clemens house at the head of the street to beg Jane Clemens, always good company for both old and young, to go along with her shopping" (Brashear 1935). In 1854 she married lawyer ROBERT F. LAKENAN — "to please her parents, not herself," Mark Twain recalled in his autobiography (AD, 9 Mar 1906, CU-MARK, in *MTA*, 2:182). In "Villagers" (93, 94) Clemens also comments on Mary Moss's unhappy marriage (*Marion Census* 1850, 312; Holcombe, 609, 610).

CORNELIUS (NEIL) MOSS (b. 1836) attended Sunday School with Clemens at the Old Ship of Zion Methodist Church and later was a classmate at DAWSON's school. According to "Villagers" (94), by age thirty, after studying at Yale, Moss was "a graceless tramp in Nevada." He evidently was the destitute schoolmate whom Clemens met in Virginia City and wrote about in chapter 55 of *Roughing It* (1872):

[He] came tramping in on foot from Reese River, a very allegory of Poverty. The son of wealthy parents, here he was, in a strange land, hungry, bootless, mantled in an ancient horse-blanket, roofed with a brimless hat, and so generally and so extravagantly dilapidated that he could have "taken the shine out of the Prodigal Son himself," as he pleasantly remarked. He wanted to borrow forty-six dollars—twenty-six to take him to San Francisco, and twenty for something else; to buy some soap with, maybe, for he needed it.

In an 1863 letter to his family, Clemens wrote that Moss had recently left San Francisco to work a mining claim in Coso, California: "He says he has had a very hard time ever since he has been in California—has done pretty much all kinds of work to make a living—keeping school in the country among other things" (18? May 63, *L1*, 252). In chapter 5 of *The Tragedy of Pudd'nhead Wilson* (1894), Mark Twain assigned some of Neil Moss's experiences to Tom Driscoll, who is ridiculed when he returns home from Yale flaunting Eastern fashions (*Marion Census* 1850, 312).

N., Miss. See MARY ANN NEWCOMB.

NASH family.
ABNER O. NASH (1804?–59) opened one of Hannibal's first general stores in 1831, when there were fewer than a dozen families living in the area. He was elected to the town's first Board of Trustees, later was its president, and was a founding member of the Presbyterian Church. He declared bankruptcy in 1844, and in 1849 accepted the low-paying postmastership. *The Adventures of Tom Sawyer* (1876) alludes to him as "the aged and needy postmaster, who had seen better days" (chapter 5). Twice married, Nash and his second wife, Andosia, had six children residing with them in 1850. Nash is mentioned in "Villagers" (96). Mark Twain's working notes for "Tom Sawyer's Conspiracy" (*HH&T*, 383) indicate that postmaster Oliver Benton (166) was modeled after him (*Marion Census* 1850, 318; Greene, 281; Wecter 1952, 298 n. 15).
MARY NASH (b. 1832?) was the postmaster's daughter by his first marriage. In his autobiography, mistakenly calling her Mary Lacy (the name of another schoolmate), Clemens claimed she was one of his early infatuations but was "out of my class because of her advanced age. She was pretty wild and determined and independent. She was ungovernable, and was considered incorrigible. But that was all a mistake. She married, and at once settled down and became in all ways a model matron and was as highly respected as any matron in the town. Four years ago she was still living, and had been married fifty years" (AD, 16 Mar 1906, CU-MARK, in *MTA*, 2:213). In "Villagers" (96) Clemens wonders if Mary Nash had married SAMUEL R. RAYMOND; she actually married John Hubbard of Frytown in 1851. On her fiftieth wedding anniversary she sent Clemens a greeting and he responded with congratulations. Working notes show that he considered portraying her as "wild" Mary Benton, the daughter of postmaster Oliver Benton, in "Tom Sawyer's Conspiracy" and as "*bad*" Louisa Robbins in "Schoolhouse Hill," but the characters do not appear in the stories (*HH&T*, 383; *MSM*, 431). In his characterization of Rachel ("Hellfire") Hotchkiss (119–33), Mark Twain may have drawn on his recollection of Mary Nash (*Marion Census* 1850, 318, 319; "Married," Hannibal *Western Union*, 23 Jan 51; SLC to Mary Nash Hubbard, 13 Jan 1901, MoHM).
THOMAS S. (TOM) NASH (b. 1835?), Mary's half brother, was one of Clemens's playmates, a Cadet of Temperance, and a fellow pupil in SAMUEL CROSS's school. In his autobiography Clemens recalled the winter night when he and Tom skated on the Mississippi, with Tom falling through the ice; the accident led to "a procession of diseases" culminating in scarlet fever, which left Tom deaf (AD, 12 Feb 1906, CU-MARK, in *MTA*, 2:97–98). In working notes for the "St. Petersburg Fragment," an early version of his "Mysterious Stranger" tale, Mark Twain wrote that "Tom Nash's mother took in a deserted child; it gave scarlet-fever death to 3 of her children &

deaf[ness] to 2" (*MSM*, 416). In the Jacksonville, Illinois, asylum for the deaf and dumb, Tom learned to talk in a loud unmodulated voice. He returned to Hannibal in 1849, worked in the post office for four years, was apprenticed to WILLIAM T. LEAGUE of the Hannibal *Messenger*, and in later years was a house and sign painter. When Clemens returned to Hannibal in 1902, "old and white headed" Tom Nash greeted him at the train station, made a trumpet of his hands at Clemens's ear, nodded toward the crowd, "and said, confidentially—in a yell like a fog horn—'Same damned fools, Sam'" (AD, 12 Feb 1906, CU-MARK, in *MTA*, 2:98–99). Clemens recalls Nash in "Villagers" (96). His working notes show that he considered portraying Nash as Jack Benton in "Tom Sawyer's Conspiracy" and as Frank Robbins in "School-house Hill" (*HH&T*, 383; *MSM*, 431), but the characters do not appear in the stories (*Marion Census* 1850, 318; Cadets of Temperance 1850; Thomas S. Nash to SLC, 23 Apr 85, CU-MARK; Fotheringham, 44; Stone, Davidson, and McIntosh, 163).

NEWCOMB, MARY ANN (1809–94), was one of Clemens's schoolteachers. Born in Vermont and educated in the East, she traveled west to join the faculty of Marion College, near Palmyra, Missouri, but settled in Florida instead. She ran a school there and became acquainted with the Clemens family. In 1839 she moved to Hannibal. Apparently Mary Newcomb's Select School was Clemens's second school, after ELIZABETH HORR's. Class was conducted in the basement of the Presbyterian church on Fourth Street, between Bird and Hill streets. Advanced students were taught in half of the room by Miss Newcomb, younger students in the other half by Miss TORREY. Miss Newcomb became a boarder in the Clemens house, taking her noon meal and sometimes her evening meal there. Her two granddaughters claimed that when Clemens visited Hannibal in 1902 he said "I owe a great deal to Mary Newcomb, she compelled me to learn to read." Their grandmother "often commented on Mark Twain's drawl" and recalled the Clemens family as "delightful":

> Mark Twain's mother, Mrs. Jane Clemens, was an intellectual woman, blessed with abounding good humor and a ready wit which her son Sam, inherited. His father, John M. Clemens, was a courteous, well-educated gentleman, Miss Newcomb said. Never a practical man, but an energetic dreamer, he was a good conversationalist. Although the family was usually in less than moderate circumstances, she never heard any grumbling when she visited them. ("Former Florida Neighbor of Clemens Family Head of School Attended Here by Mark Twain," Hannibal *Evening Courier-Post*, 6 Mar 1935, 12B)

In the late 1840s Miss Newcomb married widower JOHN DAVIS. Mark Twain's working notes for "Autobiography of a Damned Fool," an unfinished story written in 1877, indicate she was the model for Mrs. Bangs, "a very thin, tall, Yankee person, who came west when she was thirty, taught school nine years in our town, and then married Mr. Bangs. . . . She had ringlets, and a long sharp nose, and thin, colorless lips, and you could not tell her breast from her back if she had her head up a stove-pipe hole looking for something in the attic" (*S&B*, 140, 163). Miss Newcomb was the prototype for Miss Watson, the widow Douglas's stern spinster sister, who is characterized in chapter one of *Huckleberry Finn* and mentioned in "Huck Finn and Tom Sawyer among the Indians" (33) and "Tom Sawyer's Conspiracy" (134, 187, 201, 208). Working notes for "Schoolhouse Hill" (*MSM*, 432) indicate that she was the model for Miss Pomeroy (237). In "Letter to William Bowen" and "Villagers"

(21, 95, 96), Clemens refers to her by name and as "Miss N." (*Marion Census* 1850, 320–21; Gregory 1965, 31).

OSCAR. See ORION CLEMENS.

OUSELEY. See OWSLEY.

OWSLEY, WILLIAM PERRY (b. 1813), was the Hannibal merchant who shot SAM SMARR. He was a member of an extensive and well-to-do Kentucky family; a distant cousin, also named William Owsley, was governor of Kentucky from 1844 to 1848. He married Almira Roberts and by the mid-1830s had settled in Marion County. Owsley was the father of six children, two of whom, Elizabeth (Bettie) and Anna (Nannie), were classmates of Clemens's in JOHN D. DAWSON's school. He shot Smarr in 1845, at the corner of Hill and Main streets, just a few yards from the Clemens home. Nine-year-old Samuel Clemens saw Smarr die, and justice of the peace John Marshall Clemens took depositions of twenty-nine witnesses. Smarr, a farmer, believed Owsley had stolen two thousand dollars from a friend, and in the weeks prior to the shooting denounced Owsley as "a damned pick pocket" and "the damnedest rascal that ever lived in the county." Reportedly Smarr said, "I dont like him, and dont want him to put himself in my way, if he does ever cross my path I will kill him." About a week before the shooting, Smarr walked up and down the street past Owsley's store, calling out "O yes! O yes, here is Bill Owsley, has got a big stock of goods here, and stole two thousand dollars from Thompson in Palmyra." His companion, Tom Davis, joined in the abuse of Owsley and fired his pistol once or twice in the street. When Owsley learned the cause of the commotion, it "appeared to affect him a good deal, he had a kind of twitching and turned white around the mouth, and said it was insufferable, and he could not stand it." Several other townsmen warned Owsley that his life had been threatened and in the week that followed observed him grow increasingly moody and absent-minded. On the afternoon of 22 January 1845, Smarr, who had come into town to sell some beef, was walking down Main Street with Joseph Brown. In Brown's own words:

Mr. Owsley came up behind us and approaching Mr. Smar said to the best of my recollection "You Sam Smar." Mr. Smar turned round, seeing Mr. Owsley in the act of drawing a pistol from his pocket, said Mr. Owsley dont fire, or something to that effect. Mr. Owsley was within about four paces of Mr. Smar when he drew the pistol and fired twice in succession, after the second fire, Mr. Smarr fell, when Mr. Owsley turned on his heel and walked off. (*Missouri v. Owsley*)

Smarr was carried into Orville R. Grant's drugstore and laid on the floor, his opened shirt exposing a bullet hole. He died in about half an hour. When the case was brought to trial a year later, Owsley was successfully defended by SAMUEL TAYLOR GLOVER. Although Clemens says in "Villagers" (101) that "he presently moved away," Owsley kept his shop on Main Street until June 1849, when he sold the business and left for California. In 1853 he was back in Hannibal, working as a dry goods clerk. When Clemens visited Hannibal in 1902, "he dined and spent a few hours very pleasantly" at the home of Owsley's daughter Elizabeth ("Mark Twain Going Home," Hannibal *Morning Journal*, 3 June 1902). Clemens fictionalized the murder of Smarr in chapter 21 of *Huckleberry Finn*, where Colonel Sherburn kills "old Boggs," and later recalled Smarr's death in an autobiographical sketch (SLC 1900, 7, in *MTA*, 1:131). He mentions the incident in his "Letter to William Bowen" and "Villagers" (21, 101). Working notes for "Schoolhouse Hill" (*MSM*, 431) indicate that schoolgirl Margaret Stover (221) was modeled after one of the Owsley children— probably Elizabeth (*Marion Census* 1850, 323; Owsley, 28, 29, 133; AD, 8 Mar 1906, CU-MARK, in *MTA*, 2:179; *Missouri v. Owsley* for all details and witness testimony regarding the shooting; Holcombe, 276, 901; Wecter 1952, 106–9; "O! For California! New Firm," Hannibal *Missouri Courier*, 31 June 49; Hagood and Hagood 1986, 101; advertisement for Rayburn's dry goods store, Hannibal *Journal*, 5 May 53; John and Elizabeth Owsley Hatch to SLC, 15 Oct 1909, CU-MARK; SLC to Elizabeth Owsley Hatch, 23 Oct 1909, CtHMTH).

PAVEY family.

JESSE H. PAVEY (1798?–?1853), a native of Kentucky, was the proprietor of Pavey's Tavern, near the corner of Main and Hill streets in Hannibal. He and his wife, Catharine (b. 1800?), had at least eight children: MARY J. (see MARY J. SHOOT), Julia, JOSEPHINE, Sarah, NAPOLEON W. (POLE), REBECCA (BECKY), Fanny, and Susan. By the summer of 1850 Pavey had resettled his family in St. Louis, where he worked as a carpenter. In 1855, when Clemens worked in St. Louis as a journeyman printer, he boarded at the widowed Mrs. Pavey's home. In an August 1897 notebook entry, which tentatively lists characters for "Hellfire Hotchkiss," Clemens included "The tavern gang—at Pavey's," and in a 1902 notebook he recalled, "Becky Pavey & Pole 'Pig-tail done' tavern   Bladder-time. Weeds" (NB 42, CU-MARK, TS p. 24, in *S&B*, 173; NB 45, CU-MARK†, TS p. 21). (Pigtail and bladder, two types of prepared tobacco, were evidently manufactured at the tavern.) Clemens describes a confrontation between his mother and Jesse Pavey in "Jane Lampton Clemens" (84), and in "Villagers" (98) he condemns Pavey's laziness and bad temper (Hannibal *Journal*, 7 Jan 47, locating Pavey's Tavern on Second (i.e., Main) near Hill, cited by Dixon Wecter in his annotated copy of *MTB*, 1:27, CU-MARK; *St. Louis Census* 1850, 416:291; James Green 1850, 270; Morrison, 197; SLC to Laura Hawkins Frazer, ca. Feb 1909, Hannibal *Evening Courier-Post*, 6 Mar 1935, 3C; Varble, 219, 221; SLC to Frank E. Burrough, 15 Dec 1900, MoCgS; *N&J1*, 37).

JOSEPHINE PAVEY (b. 1828?), mentioned in "Villagers" (99), married FRANCIS DAVIS, the partner of livery keeper WILLIAM SHOOT (*Marion Census* 1850, 312; Holcombe, 903).

NAPOLEON W. (POLE) PAVEY (b. 1833?), characterized in "Villagers" (98–99), was the "notoriously worldly" boy described at length in the first installment of "Old Times on the Mississippi" (1875), later chapter 4 of *Life on the Mississippi* (1883): he left Hannibal for a long time, then "turned up as apprentice engineer or 'striker' on a steamboat" and swaggered around town "in his blackest and greasiest clothes, so that nobody could help remembering that he was a steamboatman. . . . This fellow had money, too, and hair oil. . . . No girl could withstand his charms. He 'cut out' every boy in the village." Pavey is listed as a steamboat engineer, "Second Class," in the 1857 St. Louis city directory (*St. Louis Census* 1850, 416:291; Kennedy 1857, 171, 304).

REBECCA (BECKY) PAVEY (b. 1835?) is recalled in "Villagers" (99) as a heartbreaker (see also the note at 99.6–7). She married George Davis, the stepson of her sister JOSEPHINE (*St. Louis Census* 1850, 416:291; *Marion Census* 1850, 312).

PEAKE, WILLIAM HUMPHREY (b. 1775?), was one of John Marshall Clemens's few intimates. When Mark Twain visited Hannibal in 1902, he told a reporter that "he remembered old Dr. Peake better than almost any of the Hannibal citizens of fifty years ago. He described Dr. Peake as a Virginian, who, on state occasions, wore knee breeches and large silver buckles on his low cut shoes, and wore a wig. He, Judge Draper and the elder Clemens, Sam's father, were subscribers for the Weekly National Intelligencer, published at Washington, D.C., and it was their custom to discuss the speeches made in Congress from the time the paper was received until the next copy came to hand" ("Good-bye to Mark Twain," Hannibal *Courier-Post*, 3 June 1902, 1). In his autobiography, Mark Twain similarly recalled Peake, who "had great influence and his opinion upon any matter was worth much more than that of any other person in the community." He remembered the time he made the skeptical doctor a believer in mesmerism: when pretending to be hypnotized, he recited details of Peake's past which the old man did not remember revealing to him (AD, 1 Dec, 2 Dec 1906, CU-MARK, in *MTE*, 124–28). Peake is mentioned three times in "Villagers" (93, 102, 104). Working notes for "Schoolhouse Hill" (*MSM*, 432) indicate that the oracular Dr. Wheelright (235, 238) was based on him (*Marion Census* 1850, 326; Hannibal *Gazette*, 1 July 47, cited in Wecter 1950, 1).

PITTS family.

JAMES P. PITTS (b. 1807?), a harness maker, moved to Hannibal in 1836. In "Villagers" (102) Clemens recalls how Pitts greeted every steamboat even though he had no business to conduct at the landing. In chapter 55 of *Life on the Mississippi* (1883), written fifteen years before "Villagers," Clemens attributed this behavior to John Stavely, another Hannibal saddler. Evidently *Life on the Mississippi* was correct: one history of Hannibal comments on "John W. Stavely, who came here in 1842" and whose regular and conspicuous appearance at the wharf led neighboring towns to call Hannibal "Stavely's Landing" (Greene, 71; Holcombe, 971; *Marion Census* 1850, 307, 314; *N&J2*, 478 n. 160).

WILLIAM R. (BILL) PITTS (b. 1832?), JAMES's son, at fourteen began a six-year apprenticeship in the harness-maker and saddler's trade, which he completed in four years by working overtime. From the age of twenty, he ran his own business, retiring in 1890. He served twice on the city council and helped to found the Farmers' and Merchants' Bank in 1870. Clemens met him on two return visits to Hannibal, in April 1867 and in May 1902. He mentions Bill Pitts in his "Letter to William Bowen" and in "Villagers" (21, 102). Mark Twain's working notes indicate that he planned to portray Pitts as Jake Fitch in "Tom Sawyer's Conspiracy" and as George Pratt in "Schoolhouse Hill" (*HH&T*, 383; *MSM*, 431), but neither character appears in the stories (*Marion Census* 1850, 314; Holcombe, 971; Greene, 398, 407; "Mark Twain Sees the Home of His Boyhood," St. Louis *Post-Dispatch*, 30 May 1902, 1).

PRENDERGAST, THOMAS B. (1830?–69), recalled in "Villagers" (102), was a white minstrel performer famous as a tenor and a female impersonator (Rice, 66, 217; Wittke, 68–69, 236, 237; Brown, 297).

PRISCELLA. See PAMELA ANN CLEMENS.

QUARLES family.

JOHN ADAMS QUARLES (1802–76) was Clemens's uncle. Clemens was particularly fond of him and stated in his autobiography, "I have not come across a better man than he was" (SLC 1897–98, 36–37, in *MTA*, 1:96). Quarles married Jane Lampton Clemens's younger sister, Martha Ann (Patsy) Lampton (1807–50), with whom he had ten children. In the mid-1830s the family moved from Tennessee to Florida, Missouri, where John Quarles built a general store and became a prosperous shopkeeper and farmer, active in the town's development. He purchased over 230 acres of farm land near Florida and by Clemens's recollection owned some fifteen or twenty slaves. Until Clemens was about twelve, he spent two to three months every year on the Quarles farm, which some fifty years later he recalled as "a heavenly place for a boy." Clemens acknowledged that while he "never consciously used" Quarles in a book, "his farm has come very handy to me in literature, once or twice. In 'Huck Finn' and in 'Tom Sawyer Detective' I moved it down to Arkansas. It was all of six hundred miles, but it was no trouble" (SLC 1897–98, 37, in *MTA*, 1:96). Mark Twain's working notes for "Tom Sawyer's Conspiracy" (*HH&T*, 384) identify Quarles as the model for Uncle Fletcher; in the story, mention is made of Uncle Fletcher's farm, thirty miles from St. Petersburg (154, 155, 156), but the character himself does not appear (Selby, chart 23, 134; Wecter 1952, 36, 40, 50; Gregory 1969, 230–33).

JAMES A. (JIM) QUARLES (1827–66), JOHN ADAMS QUARLES's son, was born in Tennessee and brought to Florida, Missouri, as a child. In 1848 he moved to Hannibal and opened a copper, tin, and sheet iron manufactory in partnership with George W. Webb. In 1851 James married sixteen-year-old Sophronia (Fronnie) Reno, with whom he had two sons. By the fall of 1852 he had entered into two additional business partnerships to sell stoves, but both of these enterprises failed. Clemens records Quarles's "dissipation" and neglect of business and family in "Villagers" (97). In an August 1897 notebook entry Clemens included James Quarles in a list of characters for "Hellfire Hotchkiss" (NB 42, CU-MARK, TS p. 24, in *S&B*, 173), but no one based on him figures in the story (*Bible* 1817; *Marion Census* 1850, 310; Selby, 133; marriage notice, Hannibal *Journal and Western Union*, 2 Oct 51, cited in Wecter 1950, 7; "Dissolution," Hannibal *Western Union*, 7 Aug 51; "Dissolution," Hannibal *Missouri Courier*, 2 Sept 52).

R., SAM. See SAMUEL R. RAYMOND.

RALLS, JOHN (1807–82), mentioned in "Villagers" (96), was a Mexican War veteran and lawyer who lived in New London, Missouri. In 1861, when Clemens and a few friends flirted with the Confederacy by forming the Marion Rangers, they had Colonel Ralls swear them in as private soldiers. In "The Private History of a Campaign That Failed" (1885), Clemens recalled Ralls's "old-fashioned speech . . . full of gunpowder and glory, full of that adjective-piling, mixed metaphor, and windy declamation which was regarded as eloquence in that ancient time and that remote region" (Conard, 5:292; Ellsberry 1965b, 2:29–30).

RATCLIFFE (or RATCLIFF) family. The father, James (1795?–1860), a pioneer physician in Hannibal, had an affluent practice, sat on the first municipal board of health, and owned one of the best houses in town. (In historical records of Marion County his surname also appears as Ratliff and Rackliff.) Will records show that Ratcliffe was survived by his second wife and five sons. Aside from the account given in "Villagers" (102–3), little is known of this family. In the 1880s Mark Twain wrote about the homicidal Ratcliffe son in "Clairvoyant" (29), and in his 1905–8 notebook he recalled the "Ratcliffe family—crazy. One, confined, chopped his hand off; chased stepmother with knife" (NB 48, CU-MARK†, TS p. 10). Mark Twain apparently drew on one of the Ratcliffe men in creating Crazy Meadows, the village lunatic with the "wild mad laugh" in "Schoolhouse Hill" (242–46); a marginal note on the manuscript reads: "Crazy's history and misfortunes and his family and lost boy—Ratcliff" (*MSM*, 411; Holcombe, 897; Wecter 1952, 198; *Marion Census* 1850, 309; Ellsberry 1965a, 5).

RAY, DR. See RICHARD F. BARRET.

RAYMOND, SAMUEL R. (SAM), had settled in Hannibal by 1849. He helped organize the Liberty Fire Company and dressed in fireman's uniform for the company's fundraising parties. In 1850 he became editor and co-proprietor with ROBERT SYLVESTER BUCHANAN of the Hannibal *Journal*. In 1851 Raymond and his partner sold the *Journal* to Orion Clemens, and Raymond moved to Pike County, Missouri. Back in Hannibal by 1853, Raymond edited the *Messenger* and by 1859 was proprietor of the *Gazette*. Mark Twain mentions him twice in "Villagers" (96, 102), in the first instance wondering if he had married MARY NASH. In fact, in 1850 Raymond married Helen Holmes, who died a year later of cholera. An entry in Mark Twain's 1897 notebook hints that Raymond was the illegitimate son of either ROBERT, ARGYLE, or JOSEPH SYLVESTER BUCHANAN: "The new fire Co—Raymond, whose real name was Buchanan" (NB 41, CU-MARK†, TS p. 58). Working notes for "Tom Sawyer's Conspiracy" indicate that he planned to introduce Raymond as "Fire Marshal Sam . . . Rumford," who was "envied because said to be illegitimate" (*HH&T*, 383, 384), but Rumford instead appears in the story as captain of a militia company, with no illegitimacy mentioned (167–68, 178, 210). Raymond is also included in the working notes for "Schoolhouse Hill" (*MSM*, 436) as the model for Joe Buckner of the Big 6 Fire Company, but that character does not appear in the story (Hannibal *Missouri Courier*: "Liberty Fire Company," 4 Oct 49; "The New Fire Engine," 29 Nov 49; "Grand Levee & Tea-Party!" 20 Dec 49; "The 'Journal,' of this city . . . ," 31 Jan 50; "Married," 9 May 50; "New Paper," 3 Feb 53; "Mr. S. R. Raymond . . . ," Hannibal *Western Union*, 29 May 51; Fotheringham, 48).

REAGAN, JIM (JIMMY). In a 1902 letter Clemens told ANNA LAURA HAWKINS Frazer that the "'new boy'" in one of his books "was Jim Reagan—just from St. Louis" ("Laura Hawkins Frazer Always Remembered as Idol of His Boyhood," Hannibal *Evening Courier-Post*, 6 Mar 1935, 3C). The book was *Tom Sawyer* (1876), in chapter one of which Tom challenges a newcomer to a fight. In "Boy's Manuscript" (2, 8–10, 14), Reagan possibly was the model for Billy Rogers's rival, Jim Riley. Reagan is mentioned in "Villagers" (105).

RICE, SAMUEL D., a Methodist minister according to one history of Hannibal, probably was the "*Rev. Mr. Rice*," recalled in "Villagers" (97) as a Presbyterian. In 1838 Rice purchased the Hannibal *Commercial Advertiser* from JOSEPH SYLVESTER BUCHANAN. When the paper failed in 1839, some Hannibal citizens formed a stock company and purchased the newspaper office for Rice's benefit. In 1843 Rice officiated at the marriage of Clemens's uncle, JAMES ANDREW HAYS LAMPTON. He was elected city recorder in 1845, and afterward started a newspaper in Louisiana, Missouri, where he died (Holcombe, 898, 941, 987; Woodruff, 24).

RICHMOND, JOSHUA (b. 1816?), a mason, was Clemens's first Sunday school teacher at the Old Ship of Zion, a small brick Methodist church situated on Hannibal's public square. Clemens remembered him as "a very kindly and considerate Sunday-school teacher, and patient and compassionate, so he was the favorite teacher with us little chaps. . . . I was under Mr. Richmond's spiritual care every now and then for two or three years, and he was never hard upon me" (AD, 16 Mar 1906, CU-MARK, in *MTA*, 2:214). Clemens mistakenly recalled in his autobiography and in "Villagers" (95) that Richmond married ARTEMISSA BRIGGS; in 1849 he married Angelina Cook (*Marion Census* 1850, 310, 322; "Married," Hannibal *Missouri Courier*, 18 Jan 49; Wecter 1952, 86, 183).

RICHMOND, LETITITIA. No information. In "Villagers" (94), Clemens mistakenly writes that she married DANA F. BREED.

ROBARDS family.
    ARCHIBALD SAMPSON ROBARDS (1797–1862), formerly a plantation owner in his native Kentucky and an officer in the Fifth Kentucky Regiment, moved to Hannibal with family and slaves in 1843. He became wealthy in the milling business, and in 1853 his flour won the highest prize at New York's Crystal Palace Exhibition. In 1849 he took a company of fifteen to the California gold fields, furnishing the necessary vehicles, provisions and stock. Robards did much to advance Hannibal's agricultural, manufacturing, and commercial interests. He was mayor in 1846 and 1854 and an elder in the Christian Church. He married Amanda Carpenter (1807–65), with whom he had six children. Clemens recalls Robards and five of his children in "Villagers" (93–94; see also the note at 100.18). He included the same five—"George, Clay, John Robards   Jane & Sally Robards"—among other old Hannibal acquaintances he listed in his 1902 notebook, after his final visit to the town (NB 45, CU-MARK†, TS p. 21; *Marion Census* 1850, 317, where the name is entered as Roberts,

as it was then pronounced; *Marion Census* 1860, 761; *Portrait*, 143–44; Holcombe, 945, 991–92; "Flour! Flour! Flour!" Hannibal *Journal*, 2 May 53).

GEORGE C. ROBARDS (1833?–78) is described in Clemens's autobiography as a "slender, pale, studious" youth with long black hair who was the "only pupil who studied Latin" at DAWSON's school (AD, 8 Mar, 9 Mar 1906, CU-MARK, in *MTA*, 2:179, 181). In "Villagers" (93, 94), Clemens alludes to Robards's unhappy romance with MARY JANE MOSS and reports his abandonment of Hannibal. Robards returned by 1860, however, for he is listed in the census that year as a Hannibal farmer. He served as a major in the Confederate Army, was a Hannibal real estate and insurance agent in the mid-1870s, and was elected county assessor in 1876 (*Marion Census* 1850, 317; *Marion Census* 1860, 761; Holcombe, 992; *Portrait*, 144; Hallock, 120).

SARAH H. (SALLY or SALLIE) ROBARDS (1836–1918), Samuel Clemens's classmate in DAWSON's school, took piano lessons from Pamela Clemens. She married riverboat pilot and captain BARTON STONE BOWEN and, after Bowen's death, the Reverend H. H. Haley, a pastor of Hannibal's Christian Church. In an autobiographical sketch, Clemens recalled that while in Calcutta in 1896, he met Sally Robards—one of Hannibal's "dearest and prettiest girls"—and learned that when they were teenagers she had seen him prancing around nude rehearsing for his role as a bear in a play (SLC 1900, 1–6, where Robards is called Mary Wilson, in *MTA*, 1:125–30). He recalled her in his 1902 notebook: "Sally Robards—pret[t]y. Describe her now in her youth & again in 50 ys   After when she reveals herself" (NB 45, CU-MARK†, TS p. 21). She is mentioned in "Villagers" (94). Mark Twain's working notes for "Schoolhouse Hill" (*MSM*, 431) indicate that Sally Fitch (218, 221) was based on her (*Marion Census* 1850, 317; *Marion Census* 1860, 761; *Portrait*, 144; Holcombe, 981; RoBards 1915; "Mrs. Haley Is Laid to Rest," Hannibal *Courier-Post*, 8 Aug 1918, clipping in RoBards Scrapbooks, vol. 2).

JOHN LEWIS ROBARDS (1838–1925), characterized in "Villagers" (93–94), attended Methodist Sunday school with Clemens. At DAWSON's school, where the pair were classmates, Robards always won the silver medal for "Amiability" and Clemens the medal for "Good Spelling" (AD, 7 Feb 1906, CU-MARK, in *MTA*, 2:67). "I was alway[s] trading Good Spelling for Amiability—for advantage at home," Clemens recalled (SLC 1898b, 7†). When he was twelve years old, Robards accompanied his father on the expedition to California. He reportedly "loved to read history and the classics, and early chose to be a soldier, and applied himself diligently for examination at West Point. While thus engaged, being a capital shot, his right eye was impaired by a fragment of a cap of the pistol, and this destroyed his prospects for a successful career" (Holcombe, 992). After attending the University of Missouri and studying law in Louisville, Kentucky, Robards returned to Hannibal in 1861 to practice. Clemens mistakenly notes in "Villagers" that he married "a Hurst—new family." In April 1861 Robards married Sara (Sallie) Crump Helm, whose family had settled in Hannibal in 1852; the couple had seven children, three of whom lived to adulthood. In 1861 John Robards, Samuel Clemens, and others formed the Marion Rangers, whose misadventures as Confederate irregulars Mark Twain described in "The Private History of a Campaign That Failed" (1885). In that sketch Clemens poked fun at his friend's practice of spelling his name "RoBards" by portraying him as a Dunlap who changed his name to "d'Un Lap." He later regretted the attack: "I think John Robards deserved a lashing, but it should have come from an enemy, not a friend" (SLC to the Reverend John Davis, 19? Apr 87, ViU, excerpted in Wecter 1952, 298 n. 13). Robards was a leading member of Park Methodist Episcopal Church, South, and the founder of Mount Olivet Cemetery. When the bodies of Henry and John Marshall Clemens were transferred from Hannibal's old Baptist cemetery to Mount Olivet in 1876, Robards oversaw the transfer, and in 1890 he attended the burial service for Jane Lampton Clemens (*Portrait*, 143–45; Holcombe, 608, 992; RoBards 1915; "RoBards—Sarah Crump Helm . . . ," St. Louis *Christian Advocate*, 13 Feb 1908, clipping in RoBards Scrapbooks, vol. 1; "The Death of Mrs. J. L. RoBards," Hannibal *Journal*, 4 Jan 1918, clipping in RoBards Scrapbooks, vol. 1; "RoBards Rites to Be Friday," unidentified Hannibal newspaper, 1925 clipping in RoBards Scrapbooks, vol. 3; AD, 9 Mar 1906, CU-MARK, in *MTA*, 2:182–83; Wecter 1952, 118–19; "The Funeral of Mrs. Clemens," unidentified Hannibal newspaper, 30 Oct 90, clipping in Scrapbook 20:126–27, CU-MARK).

HENRY CLAY ROBARDS (1841?–85), mentioned in "Villagers" (94), was a captain in the Confederate Army. He died in Columbia, Missouri (*Marion Census* 1850, 317; *Portrait*, 144).

RUTTER, RICHARD H. (DICK) (b. 1835?), whose name appears in "Villagers" (98), worked alongside Samuel Clemens, WILLIAM T. LEAGUE, and WALES R. MC-CORMICK in the late 1840s as a printer's apprentice on the Hannibal *Missouri Courier*. He was the son of John P. Rutter, a former clerk of the Marion County Circuit Court in Palmyra. In August 1850 Dick Rutter was living on the outskirts of Palmyra with three siblings and his unemployed father (*Marion Census* 1850, 281; *Marion Census* 1860, 1016; SLC to W. H. Powell, 3? Dec 1907, MoHM; Frank Daulton to SLC, 5 Mar 83, CU-MARK; Holcombe, 842–43).

SANDY was a young slave who worked for the Clemenses in Hannibal. Mark Twain reported in his autobiography: "I used Sandy once . . . it was in 'Tom Sawyer;' tried to get him to whitewash the fence, but it did not work" (SLC 1897–98, 49, in *MTA*, 1:102). Sandy appears in chapters 1 and 2 of *Tom Sawyer* as Jim, "the small colored boy" (not to be confused with Jim in *Huckleberry Finn*, who is modeled after DAN-IEL). Clemens recalls Sandy in "Jane Lampton Clemens" (89).

SCHNEIDER (or SCHNIETER), CHARLEY, in "Villagers" (101), was the man whom John Marshall Clemens saved from an attempted assault by ALLEN B. MCDONALD.

SELMES family.

TILDEN RUSSELL SELMES (1808?–70) was originally from England. One of Hannibal's leading merchants, he was proprietor of the Wildcat store at the corner of Main and Hill streets and in the early 1850s was one of four owners of the ferry line crossing the river at Hannibal. He was elected mayor in 1852 and 1853, and by 1860 had established the Hannibal City Bank. His wife, Mary, died in 1849, and he married Sarah P. Benton in 1850. Clemens mentions Selmes twice in "Villagers" (94, 96) and refers to him in "Clairvoyant" (32). While the working notes to "Tom Sawyer's

Conspiracy" (*HH&T*, 384) mention "Old Selmes (English)," he does not appear in the story (*Marion Census* 1850, 310; *Marion Census* 1860, 770; Caroline Schroter to Jane Lampton Clemens, 29 May 70, CU-MARK; Greene, 51, 52, 257; Fotheringham, 51, 73; Holcombe, 941; "Obituary," Hannibal *Missouri Courier*, 12 July 49; "Married," Hannibal *Western Union*, 14 Nov 50; Conard, 2:534).

SARAH JOHNSON SELMES, the merchant's beautiful daughter, is mentioned in "Villagers" (96). In 1848 she married Robert M. Funkhouser, who became one of St. Louis's most prominent merchants (Davis, 3; Conard, 2:534; Edwards and Hopewell, 143).

SEXTON family. Louisa Sexton (b. 1812? in Kentucky) and her daughter, Margaret (b. 1836? in Missouri), are both described in "Villagers" (99). They boarded with the Clemens family in the mid-1840s, and young Samuel and Henry Clemens were rivals for Margaret's attention. In January 1850 Margaret evidently was taking music lessons from Pamela, for Jane Clemens wrote of her as one of the "music scollars" who played "dewets" at the house (Jane Lampton Clemens to Orion Clemens, 30 Jan 50, NPV, in *MTBus*, 16). By the summer of 1850 Mrs. Sexton and Margaret had moved to St. Louis. Writing his family from Virginia City on 16 February 1863, Clemens enclosed his photograph for Margaret, commenting: "Had your letter arrived a little sooner, I could have sent it to her myself, as a Valentine" (*L1*, 245; *St. Louis Census* 1850, 418:361).

SHOOT family.

WILLIAM SHOOT (1809–92) was co-owner with FRANCIS DAVIS of the livery stable mentioned by Clemens in "Villagers" (98). In 1852 the stable and twenty-eight horses were consumed in a fire. A third partner was added to operate the rebuilt Shoot, Jordan & Davis Livery Stable, advertised as "the largest and most splendid Stable, outside of St. Louis, in the State" ("Monroe House," Hannibal *Journal*, 19 May 1853). In May 1853 Shoot became proprietor of Hannibal's finest hotel, the Brady House, which he renamed the Monroe House (*Marion Census* 1850, 312; *Marion Census* 1860, 776; Hagood and Hagood 1985, 74; "Another Destructive Fire!" Hannibal *Missouri Courier*, 1 Apr 52; "The New Hotel," Hannibal *Journal*, 11 May 53).

MARY J. SHOOT (b. 1822?), the eldest daughter of JESSE H. PAVEY, was thirteen years old when she married WILLIAM SHOOT, as Clemens notes in "Villagers" (99). The couple had at least four children: John A., MILDRED CATHERINE (KITTY), Julia F. and MARY B. (MOLLIE). Mary J. Shoot is listed in the 1866 Hannibal city directory as a dealer in millinery items; by the mid-1870s she had moved to New York with her daughter Mary (*Marion Census* 1850, 312; *Marion Census* 1860, 776; Honeyman, 52; SLC to unidentified correspondent, 19 Oct 76, TS in CU-MARK).

MILDRED CATHERINE (KITTY) SHOOT (b. 1840?) married Charles P. Heywood in 1858, four years after he arrived in Hannibal from Massachusetts to become paymaster of the Hannibal and St. Joseph Railroad. In 1871 she introduced herself to Clemens after he gave a lecture in Homer, New York. Clemens wrote his wife of the meeting and described Shoot as one of the "little-girl friends of my early boyhood" (4 Dec 71, CU-MARK†). In "Villagers" (99) he mistakenly calls her "Mrs. Hayward"

(*Marion Census* 1850, 312; Holcombe, 954–55; Mildred C. Heywood to SLC, 15 Jan 1910, CU-MARK).

MARY B. (MOLLIE) SHOOT (1863?–1954) is incorrectly identified in "Villagers" (99) as "Mrs. Hayward's daughter." In fact, she was the much younger sister of MILDRED CATHERINE SHOOT (Mrs. Charles P. Heywood). Mary B. Shoot was born in Hannibal, but by the mid-1870s had moved with her mother to New York. Using the stage name Florence Wood, she made her debut in Augustin Daly's stock company and had modest success as an actress. In noting that she later became a "troublesome" London newspaper correspondent, Clemens was confusing her with Florence Hayward (1865–1925) of St. Louis, a journalist who had annoyed him during his 1896–97 stay in London by pressing him for an interview ("Mrs. Felix Morris, a Former Actress," New York *Times*, 19 Apr 1954, 23; Odell, 10:184, 208, 570, 604; 12:242, 251;13:592; 15:6, 217, 503, 792; NCAB, 11:160–61; SLC to Florence Hayward, 29 Oct 96, 29 Jan 97 and 3 July 97, MoHi).

SIMON. See SAMUEL LANGHORNE CLEMENS.

SIMON was the black drayman who was almost killed when young Samuel Clemens and WILLIAM BOWEN rolled a huge rock down the side of Holliday's Hill. Clemens relates that boyhood misadventure in chapter 58 of *The Innocents Abroad* (1869). He mentions Simon in "Villagers" (97).

SMARR, SAM (1788?–1845), a beef farmer, was shot to death in January 1845 by merchant WILLIAM PERRY OWSLEY. Witnesses said Smarr was generally a peaceful man and "in good circumstances as to property." He was "as honest a man as any in the state," said one Hannibal resident, but "when drinking . . . was a little turbulent and made a good deal of noise." A second witness agreed that Smarr was a kind and good neighbor when sober, but when drinking "he was very abusive, and did not care much what he said." Another regarded him as "dangerous . . . though some think not." The murder is mentioned in "Letter to William Bowen" and "Villagers" (21, 101), and is re-created in chapter 21 of *Huckleberry Finn* (1885), where Colonel Sherburn shoots "old Boggs." In 1900 Clemens wrote: "I can't ever forget Boggs, because I saw him die, with a family Bible spread open on his breast. . . . Boggs represents Smarr in the book" (SLC to Miss Goodrich-Freer, 11 Jan 1900, ViU†; *Missouri v. Owsley*).

SMITH, ELIZABETH W. (BETSY, or BETSEY) (b. 1795?), a native of Virginia, was a good friend of Jane Lampton Clemens's. Mark Twain described "Aunt Betsy" in his autobiography: "She wasn't anybody's aunt, in particular; she was aunt to the whole town of Hannibal; this was because of her sweet and generous and benevolent nature, and the winning simplicity of her character." He remembered taking his mother, aged sixty or so, and Aunt Betsy to their first minstrel show in St. Louis: the two women "were very much alive; their age counted for nothing; they were fond of excitement, fond of novelties, fond of anything going that was of a sort proper for members of the church to indulge in" (AD, 30 Nov 1906, CU-MARK, in *MTE*, 115). Betsy Smith was evidently the model for Aunt Betsy Davis in "Hellfire Hotchkiss" (130–33); working notes for "Schoolhouse Hill" (*MSM*, 432) indicate that Widow Dawson (230, 231, 235, 237) was modeled after her (*Marion Census* 1850, 318; *Marion Census* 1860, 762).

SOUTHARD, LOT (b. 1825?), a clerk, boarded at the Clemens home until late in 1846 or January 1847. In 1860 he clerked for TILDEN RUSSELL SELMES and by the mid-1860s was a partner in a boot and shoe manufacturing firm. In "Villagers" (95) Clemens says that he married LUCY LOCKWOOD, but the Hannibal *Missouri Courier* records his marriage on 7 November 1849 to Emma Beecham (*Marion Census* 1850, 308; Henry Clemens to unidentified correspondent, 4 Feb 47, CU-MARK; Fotheringham, 54; Honeyman, 47; "Married," Hannibal *Missouri Courier*, 8 Nov 49).

STEVENS family.
    THOMAS B. STEVENS (b. 1791?), mentioned in "Clairvoyant" and "Villagers" (27, 96), was a Hannibal jeweler and watchmaker. He had four children whom Clemens knew: John, RICHARD C., EDMUND C., and Jenny (*Marion Census* 1850, 306; SLC to Pamela A. Moffett, 2 Apr 87, NPV, in *MTBus*, 379).
    RICHARD C. (DICK) STEVENS, as Clemens notes in "Villagers" (96), became a pilot on the upper Mississippi (Kennedy 1857, 302).
    EDMUND C. (ED) STEVENS (b. 1834?), Clemens's friend and classmate, became a watchmaker. In 1861 he was a corporal in the Marion Rangers, the inept band of Confederate volunteers Clemens described in "The Private History of a Campaign That Failed" (1885). Stevens, he recalled, was "trim-built, handsome, graceful, neat as a cat; bright, educated, but given over entirely to fun. . . . As far as he was concerned, this military expedition of ours was simply a holiday." In 1901 Clemens wrote: "I had a good deal of correspondence with Ed a year or two before he died. . . . We were great friends, warm friends, he & I. He was of a killingly entertaining spirit; he had the light heart, the care-free ways, the bright word, the easy laugh, the unquenchable genius of fun, he was a friendly light in a frowning world—he should not have died out of it" (SLC to John Stevens, 28 Aug 1901, CU-MARK†). Clemens recalls Stevens in his "Letter to William Bowen" and in "Villagers" (21, 96). Working notes show that he considered portraying him as Jimmy Steel in "Tom Sawyer's Conspiracy" and as watchmaker Ed Sanders in "Schoolhouse Hill" (*HH&T*, 383; *MSM*, 432), but those characters do not appear in the stories (*Marion Census* 1850, 306).

STONE, BARTON WARREN (1772–1844), is alluded to in "Villagers" (97); see also the note at 97. 10–11. He was an eminent frontier evangelist born in Port Tobacco, Maryland, and reared there and in Virginia. Early in the nineteenth century, he became a leader in the Christian Church. In the 1830s he guided most of his group into union with the Disciples of Christ, led by Thomas and Alexander Campbell (see the note at 112. 3). The grandfather of Clemens's best friend, WILLIAM BOWEN, Stone died at the Bowen home in November 1844 (Hill, 734; *MTBus*, 24).

STOUT, IRA, a land speculator, was involved in several real estate transactions with John Marshall Clemens. On 13 November 1839, Stout sold Clemens a quarter of a city block in the heart of Hannibal (the northwest corner of Hill and Main streets) for

$7,000. That same day Clemens sold Stout 160 acres of Florida farm land for $3,000, and a week later sold him an additional 326 acres in Monroe County for $2,000. In his autobiography Mark Twain remembered "several years of grinding poverty and privation which had been inflicted upon us by the dishonest act of one Ira Stout, to whom my father had lent several thousand dollars" (AD, 28 Mar 1906, CU-MARK, in *MTA*, 2:274). The transaction by which John Marshall Clemens became responsible for Stout's debts, alluded to in "Villagers" (104), has not been identified, but when the quarter-block in Hannibal was sold in 1843 for the benefit of Clemens's creditors, the price amounted to less than $4,000—"a difference so striking," wrote Dixon Wecter, "as to lend color to the Clemenses' later bitter prejudice against Stout as a sharp customer." Wecter's research of Marion County records led him to characterize Stout as a "dead beat" who became involved "in a web of litigation" with various Hannibal residents, some of whom successfully sued him for nonpayment of debts. By 1850 Stout had moved from Hannibal to Quincy, Illinois (Wecter 1952, 51–52, 56, 69–70; Jackson 1976a, 499; "Correction," Hannibal *Western Union*, 16 Jan 51).

STRIKER family. The father, a blacksmith, appears to have moved to Hannibal about 1842 and to have died by 1850. "Villagers" (95) includes mention of him and Margaret (b. 1840?), a daughter (*Marion Census* 1850, 307).

STRONG, Mrs., was a daughter of Hannibal taverner JESSE H. PAVEY. According to "Villagers" (99), she settled in Peoria, Illinois. In 1869 Clemens wrote his sister after a lecture there: "One of Mrs. Pavey's daughters (she married a doctor & is living in an Illinois town & has sons larger than I am,) was in the audience at Peoria. Had a long talk with her. She came many miles to be there" (SLC to Pamela A. Moffett, 14 Jan 69, NPV, in *MTBus*, 103).

TORREY (or TORRY), Miss, evidently was a teacher at MARY ANN NEWCOMB's school. Clemens mentions her in "Letter to William Bowen" (21) and refers to her three times in "Villagers" (95). In the working notes for "Schoolhouse Hill" (*MSM*, 432), Mark Twain cast her as a character named Foster, but she does not appear in the story.

TUCKER, JOSHUA THOMAS (1812–97), from 1840 to 1846 the pastor of Hannibal's First Presbyterian Church, was born in Massachusetts and educated at Yale College and Lane Theological Seminary (Walnut Hills, Ohio). Jane and Pamela Clemens joined the church in February 1841, at which time Samuel Clemens probably left the Methodist Sunday school and began attending the Presbyterian Sunday school instead. In 1847 Tucker moved to St. Louis, where he worked as an editor. He was pastor of Congregational churches in Holliston, Massachusetts, from 1849 to 1867, and Chicopee Falls, Massachusetts, from 1867 to 1877. Clemens mentions Tucker in "Villagers" (97), and in "Hellfire Hotchkiss" (109–10, 112) evidently modeled Mr. Rucker after him ("Recent Deaths," Boston *Evening Transcript*, 12 June 97, 7; "The Rev. Dr. Joshua T. Tucker," New York *Times*, 12 June 97, 7; Tucker, 211–12; Fotheringham, 104–6; Sweets 1984, 4, 6, 17, 51).

USTICK, THOMAS WATT (b. 1801?), was a prominent St. Louis book and job printer. Orion Clemens was hired by Ustick as a typesetter about 1842, and Samuel Clemens worked in Ustick's printing house in the summer of 1853. Ustick is mentioned in "Villagers" (105). Presumably he was the model for Underwood, the St. Louis printer mentioned in "Hellfire Hotchkiss" (113), although no evidence has been found that he was John Marshall Clemens's (James Carpenter's) "old and trusty friend" (*St. Louis Census* 1850, 416:331; James Green 1849, 129; SLC to Jane Lampton Clemens, 31 Aug 53, *L1*, 9, 11 n. 5).

WOLF (or WOLFE), JIM (b. 1833?), mentioned in "Villagers" (98), was an apprentice printer who lodged with the Clemens family in the early 1850s and worked with Samuel Clemens on the Hannibal *Western Union*, the newspaper Orion Clemens started in September 1850. Mark Twain remembered Wolf as a tall slim boy some two to three years his senior, who came from a country hamlet and "brought all his native sweetnesses and gentlenesses and simplicities with him" (SLC 1900, 10, in *MTA*, 1:135). He was "always tongue-tied in the presence of my sister, and when even my gentle mother spoke to him he could not answer save in frightened mono-syllables" (AD, 16 Oct 1906, CU-MARK, in *MTE*, 137). Endlessly amused by Wolf's bashfulness, Clemens delighted in making him the butt of practical jokes. "A Gallant Fireman," Clemens's first known venture into print, published in the Han-nibal *Western Union* on 16 January 1851, humorously described Jim Wolf's slow response to the threat of a fire at the newspaper office (see *ET&S1*, 62). In "Jim Wolf and the Tom-Cats," published in 1867 and retold in 1900 in an autobiographical sketch, Clemens recounted how Wolf crawled in his nightshirt onto a slippery roof to silence noisy cats, lost his footing, and landed in the middle of a candy pull hosted by Pamela Clemens (SLC 1867b; SLC 1900, 11–13, in *MTA*, 1:135–38). In 1897, Wolf traveled from his Illinois home to attend Orion Clemens's funeral in Keokuk, Iowa, and introduced himself to Pamela's daughter as the "Hero of the candy pull" (Webster n.d., 5). In chapter 23 of *A Tramp Abroad* (1880), Clemens portrayed Wolf as bumpkin Nicodemus Dodge (SLC to Pamela A. Moffett, 8 Oct 53, *L1*, 17; *MTBus*, 265).

References

This list defines the abbreviations used in citations and provides full bibliographic information for works cited by author's last name or by short title. Any document or edition of a book owned by Clemens or his family is identified with an asterisk (*), excepting Clemens's own writings.

Abbott, Keene.
    1913.   "Tom Sawyer's Town." *Harper's Weekly* 57 (9 August): 16–17.

AD   Autobiographical Dictation.

American Publishing Company.
    1866–79.   "Books received from the Binderies, Dec 1st 1866 to Dec 31. *1879*," the company's stock ledger, NN-B.

AMT
    1959.   *The Autobiography of Mark Twain*. Edited by Charles Neider. New York: Harper and Brothers.

Anderson, Morris.
    1943.   "Red-Letter Books Relating to Missouri." *Missouri Historical Review* 38 (October): 85–93.

Anderson Auction Company.
    1911.   "The Library and Manuscripts of Samuel L. Clemens [Mark Twain]. Part I." Sale no. 892 (7 and 8 February). New York: Anderson Auction Company.

ATS
    1982.   *The Adventures of Tom Sawyer*. Foreword and notes by John C. Gerber; text established by Paul Baender. Mark Twain Library. Berkeley, Los Angeles, London: University of California Press.

Ayres, John W.
    1917.   "Recollections of Hannibal." Letter dated 22 August. Undated clipping from the Palmyra (Mo.) *Spectator*, Morris Anderson scrapbook, MoHM. Reprinted in part by Wecter 1952, 149.

Barret, Richard F.
    1826.   "An Inaugural Dissertation, on the Modus Operandi of Narcotics and
    Sedatives." M.D. diss., Transylvania University, Kentucky.

Barrett, William Fletcher.
    1884.   "Mark Twain on Thought-Transference." *Journal of Society for Psychical
    Research* 1 (October): 166–67.

Bayly, Thomas Haynes.
    1844.   *Songs, Ballads and Other Poems.* 2 vols. London: Richard Bentley.

BDAC
    1961.   *Biographical Directory of the American Congress, 1774–1961.* Washing-
    ton, D.C.: Government Printing Office.

Bell, Raymond Martin.
    1984.   "The Ancestry of Samuel Clemens, Grandfather of Mark Twain." 413
    Burton Avenue, Washington, Pa.: Raymond Martin Bell. Mimeograph.

Bellamy, Gladys Carmen.
    1950.   *Mark Twain as a Literary Artist.* Norman: University of Oklahoma
    Press.

Bible
  * 1817.   "Family Record. Births, Marriages, Deaths." In *The Holy Bible: Con-
    taining the Old and New Testaments, Together with the Apocrypha: Translated
    Out of the Original Tongues . . . by the Special Command of His Majesty King
    James I. of England.* Philadelphia: M. Carey. CU-MARK; owned originally by
    Jane and John Marshall Clemens.

  * 1862.   "Family Record. Births. Marriages. Deaths." In *The Holy Bible, Con-
    taining the Old and New Testaments, Translated Out of the Original Tongues;
    and with the Former Translations Diligently Compared and Revised.* New York:
    American Bible Society. PH in CU-MARK, courtesy of Rachel M. Varble; loca-
    tion of original is not known. Owned originally by Orion and Mollie E. Clemens.

Bowen, Clarence W.
    1926–43.   *The History of Woodstock, Connecticut.* 8 vols. Norwood, Mass.:
    Plimpton Press.

Bowen, Elbert R.
    [1959].   *Theatrical Entertainments in Rural Missouri before the Civil War.* Uni-
    versity of Missouri Studies, vol. 32. Columbia: University of Missouri Press.

Branch, Edgar Marquess.
    1982a.   "Sam Clemens, Steersman on the *John H. Dickey.*" *American Literary
    Realism* 15 (Autumn): 195–208.

    1982b.   "A New Clemens Footprint: Soleather Steps Forward." *American Lit-
    erature* 54 (December): 497–510.

Brashear, Minnie M.
    1934.   *Mark Twain, Son of Missouri.* Chapel Hill: University of North Carolina
    Press.

1935. "Mark Twain's Niece, Daughter of His Sister, Pamela, Taking Keen Interest in Centennial." Hannibal *Evening Courier-Post*, 6 March, 11.

Brown, T. Allston.
1870. *History of the American Stage*. New York: Dick and Fitzgerald.

Budd, Louis J., ed.
1977. "A Listing of and Selection from Newspaper and Magazine Interviews with Samuel L. Clemens, 1874–1910." *American Literary Realism* 10 (Winter): iii–100.

Burke, Sir Bernard.
1904. *A Genealogical and Heraldic Dictionary of the Peerage and Baronetage, the Privy Council, Knightage and Companionage*. Edited by Ashworth P. Burke. London: Harrison and Sons.

Cadets of Temperance.
[1850]. "The Property of Cadets of Temperance Hannibal Mo." MS of two pages containing the membership roster, MoHM.

Campbell, R. A., ed.
1875. *Campbell's Gazetteer of Missouri*. Rev. ed. St. Louis: R. A. Campbell.

Cassidy, Frederic G., ed.
1985–. *Dictionary of American Regional English*. 1 vol. to date. Cambridge: Harvard University Press, Belknap Press.

Cayleff, Susan E.
1987. *Wash and Be Healed: The Water-Cure Movement and Women's Health*. Philadelphia: Temple University Press.

Chapman, John W.
1932. "The Germ of a Book: A Footnote on Mark Twain." *Atlantic Monthly* 150 (December): 720–21.

Clemens, Mary E. (Mollie).
* 1862–66. "Mrs. Orion Clemens. 'Journal.' For 1862." PH of MS of fifty-five pages in CU-MARK, courtesy of Franklin J. Meine; location of original is not known. Published in part by Lorch 1929b, 357–59.

Clemens, Orion.
1853. "Notice to the Public." Hannibal *Tri-Weekly Messenger*, 29 September, 3, reprinting the Hannibal *Journal* of 22 September. Reprinted in *L1*, 18 n. 3.

* 1880–82. Autobiography. MS fragment of four pages, transcribing pages 696–705 of the original text, excerpted in Wecter 1952, 240–42.

Clemens, Samuel L. See SLC.

Clemens v. Beebe
1843. *John M. Clemens v. William B. Beebe*. File 3347, Marion County Circuit Court, Palmyra, Missouri.

Clemens v. Townsend
1844–47. *John M. Clemens v. Eurotus H. Townsend*. File 3612, Marion County Circuit Court, Palmyra, Missouri.

Clifton, William.
[1840?]. "The Last Link Is Broken. A duet composed and arranged for the piano forte, by Wm. Clifton." New York: Firth and Hall. The Lester S. Levy Sheet Music Collection, Johns Hopkins University.

CLjC
Copley Newspapers Incorporated, James S. Copley Library, La Jolla, California.

CoC
1969. *Clemens of the "Call": Mark Twain in San Francisco.* Edited by Edgar M. Branch. Berkeley and Los Angeles: University of California Press.

Cody, William F.
1879. *The Life of the Hon. William F. Cody, Known as Buffalo Bill, the Famous Hunter, Scout and Guide: An Autobiography.* Hartford: F. E. Bliss.

Colonial Dames.
n.d. "Ralls County Records." Compiled by The National Society of the Colonial Dames of America in the State of Missouri. TS, MoSHi.

Conard, Howard L., ed.
1901. *Encyclopedia of the History of Missouri.* 6 vols. New York: Southern History Co.

CSmH   Henry E. Huntington Library, San Marino, California.

CtHMTH   Mark Twain Memorial, Hartford, Connecticut.

CtY-BR   Beinecke Rare Book and Manuscript Library, Yale University, New Haven, Connecticut.

CU-MARK   Mark Twain Papers, The Bancroft Library, University of California, Berkeley.

Custer, George Armstrong.
1874. *My Life on the Plains.* New York: Sheldon and Co.

Davis, Chester L.
1971. "Letters from Laura Frazer (Becky Thatcher) to Paine 1907–1912." *Twainian* 30 (July–August): 1–4.

Dawson, Minnie T.
1908. *The Stillwell Murder, or a Society Crime.* Hannibal.

DeBow, J. D. B.
1853. *The Seventh Census of the United States: 1850. Embracing a Statistical View of Each of the States and Territories.* Washington, D.C.: Robert Armstrong.

Debrett, John.
1980. *Debrett's Peerage and Baronetage.* Edited by Patrick Montague-Smith. London: Debrett's Peerage. Detroit: Gale Research Company.

des Cognets, Anna Russell.
1884. *William Russell and His Descendants.* Lexington, Ky.: Samuel F. Wilson.

DeVoto, Bernard.
1932. *Mark Twain's America.* Boston: Little, Brown, and Co.

1942. *Mark Twain at Work*. Cambridge: Harvard University Press.

Dodge, Richard Irving.
* 1877. *The Plains of the Great West and Their Inhabitants, Being a Description of the Plains, Game, Indians, &c. of the Great North American Desert*. New York: G. P. Putnam's Sons.

* 1883. *Our Wild Indians: Thirty-three Years' Personal Experience among the Red Men of the Great West*. Hartford: A. D. Worthington and Co.

Edwards, Richard.
1866. *Edwards' Annual Director to the Inhabitants, Institutions, Incorporated Companies, Manufacturing Establishments, Business, Business Firms, etc., etc., in the City of St. Louis, for 1866*. St. Louis: Edwards, Greenough and Deved.

1867. *Edwards' Annual Director to the Inhabitants, Institutions, Incorporated Companies, Manufacturing Establishments, Business, Business Firms, etc., etc., in the City of St. Louis, for 1867*. St. Louis: Edwards, Greenough and Deved.

Edwards, Richard, and M. Hopewell.
1860. *Edwards's Great West and Her Commercial Metropolis, Embracing a General View of the West, and a Complete History of St. Louis*. St. Louis: Edwards's Monthly.

Ellsberry, Elizabeth Prather, comp.
[1965a]. "Will Records of Marion County, Missouri, 1853–1887." Box 206, Chillicothe, Mo.: Elizabeth Ellsberry. Mimeograph.

[1965b]. "Will Records of Ralls County, Missouri." 2 vols. Box 206, Chillicothe, Mo.: Elizabeth Prather Ellsberry. Mimeograph.

ET&S1
1979. *Early Tales & Sketches, Volume 1 (1851–1864)*. Edited by Edgar Marquess Branch and Robert H. Hirst, with the assistance of Harriet Elinor Smith. The Works of Mark Twain. Berkeley, Los Angeles, London: University of California Press.

Fatout, Paul, ed.
1976. *Mark Twain Speaking*. Iowa City: University of Iowa Press.

Ferris, Ruth, ed.
1965. "Captain Jolly in the Civil War." *Missouri Historical Society Bulletin* 22 (October): 14–31.

Fielder, Elizabeth Davis.
1899. "Familiar Haunts of Mark Twain." *Harper's Weekly* 43 (16 December): 10–11.

FM
1972. *Mark Twain's Fables of Man*. Edited by John S. Tuckey. Text established by Kenneth M. Sanderson and Bernard L. Stein. Berkeley, Los Angeles, London: University of California Press.

Fotheringham, H.
1859. *Hannibal City Directory, for 1859–60*. Hannibal: H. Fotheringham.

Frazer, Laura Hawkins.
    1918.   "Mark Twain's Childhood Sweetheart Recalls Their Romance." *The Literary Digest* 56 (23 March): 70, 73–75.

Gara, Larry.
    1961.   *The Liberty Line; The Legend of the Underground Railroad.* Lexington: University of Kentucky Press.

Garrett, Thomas E.
    1879.   *A Memorial of James Andrew Hayes Lampton, Past Master of George Washington Lodge, No. 9, A. F. & A. M.* St. Louis: Woodward, Tiernan, and Hale.

Gosse, Philip.
    1924.   *The Pirates' Who's Who.* Boston: Charles E. Lauriat Co.

Gould, David B., comp.
    1873.   *Gould's St. Louis City Directory for 1873.* St. Louis: David B. Gould and Co.

    1875.   *Gould's St. Louis Directory for 1875.* St. Louis: David B. Gould.

    1882.   *Gould's St. Louis Directory, for 1882.* St. Louis: David B. Gould.

    1902.   *Gould's St. Louis Directory for 1902, for the Year Ending April 1st, 1903.* St. Louis: Gould Directory Co.

Green, Floride.
    1935.   *Some Personal Recollections of Lillie Hitchcock Coit.* San Francisco: The Grabhorn Press.

Green, James, comp.
    [1849].   *The Saint Louis Business Directory, for the Year of Our Lord 1850.* St. Louis: James Green.

    1850.   *Green's St. Louis Directory, for 1851.* St. Louis: Charles and Hammond.

Greene, C. P., ed.
    1905.   *A Mirror of Hannibal.* Hannibal: C. P. Greene.

Gregory, Ralph.
    1965.   *Mark Twain's First America: Florida, Missouri, 1835–1840.* Florida, Mo.: Friends of Florida.

    1969.   "John A. Quarles: Mark Twain's Ideal Man." *Bulletin of the Missouri Historical Society* 25 (April): 229–35.

Gribben, Alan.
    1980.   *Mark Twain's Library: A Reconstruction.* 2 vols. Boston: G. K. Hall and Co.

Grimes, Absalom.
    1926.   *Absalom Grimes: Confederate Mail Runner.* Edited by M. M. Quaife. New Haven, Conn.: Yale University Press.

Hagood, J. Hurley, and Roberta (Roland) Hagood.
    1985.   "A List of Deaths in Hannibal, Missouri, 1880–1910, from City of Hannibal Records. Also a Partial List of Burials from Other Years in the Old Baptist

Cemetery and Other Miscellaneous Related Materials." 5100 Wyaconda St., Hannibal: J. Hurley and Roberta Hagood. Mimeograph.

1986.   *Hannibal, Too: Historic Sketches of Hannibal and Its Neighbors*. Marceline, Mo.: Walsworth Publishing Co.

Haines, Harold H.
1944.   *The Callaghan Mail, 1821–1859*. Hannibal: Harold H. Haines.

Hallock, W. S.
1877.   *Hallock's Hannibal Directory for 1877–78*. Hannibal: W. S. Hallock.

Hart, James D.
1950.   *The Popular Book. A History of America's Literary Taste*. New York: Oxford University Press.

Hearn, Michael Patrick, ed.
1981.   *The Annotated Huckleberry Finn*. New York: Clarkson N. Potter.

Heart Songs
1909.   *Heart Songs Dear to the American People*. Boston: Chapple Publishing Co.

HF
1988.   *Adventures of Huckleberry Finn*. Edited by Walter Blair and Victor Fischer, with the assistance of Dahlia Armon and Harriet Elinor Smith. The Works of Mark Twain. Berkeley, Los Angeles, London: University of California Press.

HH&T
1969.   *Mark Twain's Hannibal, Huck & Tom*. Edited by Walter Blair. The Mark Twain Papers. Berkeley and Los Angeles: University of California Press.

Hicks, Urban E.
1886.   *Yakima and Clickitat Indian Wars, 1855 and 1856: Personal Recollections of Capt. U. E. Hicks*. Portland, Oreg.: Himes the Printer.

Hill, Samuel S., ed.
1984.   *Encyclopedia of Religion in the South*. [Macon, Ga.]: Mercer University Press.

Hirst, Robert H.
1975.   "The Making of *The Innocents Abroad*: 1867–1872." Ph.D. diss., University of California, Berkeley.

Holcombe, Return I.
* 1884.   *History of Marion County, Missouri*. St. Louis: E. F. Perkins. Citations are to the 1979 reprint edition. Hannibal: Marion County Historical Society.

Honeyman, Samuel H., comp.
1866.   *Hannibal City Directory for 1866*. Hannibal: S. H. Honeyman.

Horr, Elizabeth.
* 1840.   MS of one page, a school certificate commending "Miss Pamelia Clemens," 27 November, CU-MARK. Published in *MTB*, 1:39.

Howard, Oliver N., and Goldena Howard.
  1985.   *The Mark Twain Book*. Marceline, Mo.: Walsworth Co.

Hurd, John Codman.
  1858–62.   *The Law of Freedom and Bondage in the United States*. 2 vols. Boston: Little, Brown, and Co.

Hyde, George E.
  1937.   *Red Cloud's Folk: A History of the Oglala Sioux Indians*. Norman: University of Oklahoma Press.

Jackson, Ronald Vern, ed.
  1976a.   *Illinois 1850 Census Index*. Bountiful, Utah: Accelerated Indexing Systems.
  1976b.   *Missouri 1840 Census Index*. Bountiful, Utah: Accelerated Indexing Systems.

Jackson, Ronald Vern, and Gary Ronald Teeples, eds.
  1976.   *Missouri 1850 Census Index*. Bountiful, Utah: Accelerated Indexing Systems.

J.C.H., comp.
  1887.   *The Good Old Songs We Used to Sing*. 2 vols. Boston: Oliver Ditson Co.

Keim, De Benneville Randolph.
  1870.   *Sheridan's Troopers on the Borders: A Winter Campaign on the Plains*. Philadelphia: Claxton, Remsen, and Haffelfinger.

Keith, Clayton.
  1914.   *Sketch of the Lampton Family in America, 1740–1914*. N.p.

Kennedy, Robert V., comp.
  1857.   *Kennedy's Saint Louis City Directory for the Year 1857*. St. Louis: R. V. Kennedy.
  1859.   *St. Louis Directory, 1859*. St. Louis: R. V. Kennedy.
  1860.   *St. Louis Directory, 1860*. St. Louis: R. V. Kennedy and Co.

Kerr, Howard, and Charles L. Crow, eds.
  1983.   *The Occult in America: New Historical Perspectives*. Urbana: University of Illinois Press.

Kirschten, Ernest.
  1960.   *Catfish and Crystal*. Garden City, N.Y.: Doubleday and Co.

Knox, T. H., comp.
  1854.   *The St. Louis Directory, for the Years 1854/55*. St. Louis: Chambers and Knapp.

KyLoU   University of Louisville, Louisville, Kentucky.

L1
  1988.   *Mark Twain's Letters, Volume 1 (1853–1866)*. Edited by Edgar Marquess Branch, Michael B. Frank, Kenneth M. Sanderson, Harriet Elinor Smith, Lin Salamo, and Richard Bucci. The Mark Twain Papers. Berkeley, Los Angeles, London: University of California Press.

References   361

Lewis Census
   1850.   *Population Schedules of the Seventh Census of the United States, 1850. Roll 404. Missouri: Lawrence, Lewis, and Lincoln Counties.* National Archives Microfilm Publications, microcopy no. 432. Washington, D.C.: General Services Administration.

Lex
   1963.   *A Mark Twain Lexicon.* By Robert L. Ramsay and Frances G. Emberson. New York: Russell and Russell.

LLMT
   1949.   *The Love Letters of Mark Twain.* Edited by Dixon Wecter. New York: Harper and Brothers.

Lorch, Fred W.
   1929a.   "Mark Twain in Iowa." *Iowa Journal of History and Politics* 27 (July): 408–56.
   1929b.   "Orion Clemens." *Palimpsest* 10 (October): 353–88.
   1940.   "A Note on Tom Blankenship (Huckleberry Finn)." *American Literature* 12 (November): 351–53.
   1968.   *The Trouble Begins at Eight: Mark Twain's Lecture Tours.* Ames: Iowa State University Press.

McCabe, Joseph.
   1920.   *Spiritualism: A Popular History from 1847.* London: T. Fisher Unwin.

McDougall, Marion Gleason.
   1891.   *Fugitive Slaves (1619–1865).* Publications of the Society for the Collegiate Instruction of Women, Fay House Monographs, no. 3. Boston: Ginn and Co.

McNeil, John.
   1861.   Col. John McNeil to Maj. Gen. Justus McKinstry, 13 September, with enclosures. "Union Provost Marshal's File of Papers Relating to Two or More Civilians," record group 109, item 215. National Archives and Records Service, Washington, D.C.

Marion Census
   1840.   *Population Schedules of the Sixth Census of the United States, 1840. Roll 226. Missouri: Macon, Madison, Marion, Miller, and Monroe Counties.* National Archives Microfilm Publications, microcopy no. 704. Washington, D.C.: General Services Administration.
   1850.   *Population Schedules of the Seventh Census of the United States, 1850. Roll 406. Missouri: Marion, Mercer, Miller, and Mississippi Counties.* National Archives Microfilm Publications, microcopy no. 432. Washington, D.C.: General Services Administration.
   1860.   *Population Schedules of the Eighth Census of the United States, 1860. Roll 632. Missouri: Maries and Marion Counties.* National Archives Microfilm Publications, microcopy no. 653. Washington, D.C.: General Services Administration.

Marion County.
   1845.   Marion County Court Records, Book C, 400, entry for 6 November. Marion County Circuit Court, Palmyra, Missouri.

Mathews, Mitford M., ed.
   1951.   *A Dictionary of Americanisms on Historical Principles*. 2 vols. Chicago: University of Chicago Press.

Meltzer, Milton.
   1960.   *Mark Twain Himself: A Pictorial Biography*. New York: Bonanza Books.

MH-H   Houghton Library, Harvard University, Cambridge, Massachusetts.

MiD   Detroit Public Library, Detroit, Michigan.

Missouri v. Ben
   1849.   *State of Missouri v. Ben, a slave*. File 5800, Marion County Circuit Court, Palmyra, Missouri.

Missouri v. Owsley
   1845.   *State of Missouri v. William P. Owsley*. File 3873, Marion County Circuit Court, Palmyra, Missouri.

MoCgS   Southeast Missouri State College, Cape Girardeau.

Moffett, Pamelia (or Pamela) A.
 * 1881.   "Deed. Quit-Claim," recorded on 17 October, transferring title of Moffett's Dunkirk, New York, property to Charles L. Webster, NPV.

MoFlM   Mark Twain Shrine, Mark Twain State Park, Florida, Missouri.

MoFuWC   Westminster College, Fulton, Missouri.

MoHi   Missouri State Historical Society, Columbia.

MoHM   Mark Twain Museum, Hannibal, Missouri.

MoPeS   St. Mary's Seminary, Perryville, Missouri.

Morrison.
   1852.   *Morrison's St. Louis Directory, for 1852*. St. Louis: Missouri *Republican*.

MoSHi   Missouri Historical Society, St. Louis.

MS   Manuscript.

MSM
   1969.   *Mark Twain's Mysterious Stranger Manuscripts*. Edited by William M. Gibson. The Mark Twain Papers. Berkeley and Los Angeles: University of California Press.

MTA
   1924.   *Mark Twain's Autobiography*. Edited by Albert Bigelow Paine. 2 vols. New York: Harper and Brothers.

MTB
   1912.   *Mark Twain: A Biography*. Edited by Albert Bigelow Paine. 3 vols. New York: Harper and Brothers. Volume numbers in citations are to this edition; page numbers are the same in all editions.

MTBus
1946. *Mark Twain, Business Man.* Edited by Samuel Charles Webster. Boston: Little, Brown, and Co.

MTE
1940. *Mark Twain in Eruption.* Edited by Bernard DeVoto. New York: Harper and Brothers.

MTEnt
1957. *Mark Twain of the "Enterprise."* Edited by Henry Nash Smith, with the assistance of Frederick Anderson. Berkeley and Los Angeles: University of California Press.

MTHL
1960. *Mark Twain-Howells Letters.* Edited by Henry Nash Smith and William M. Gibson, with the assistance of Frederick Anderson. 2 vols. Cambridge: Harvard University Press, Belknap Press.

MTL
1917. *Mark Twain's Letters.* Edited by Albert Bigelow Paine. 2 vols. New York: Harper and Brothers.

MTLBowen
1941. *Mark Twain's Letters to Will Bowen.* Edited by Theodore Hornberger. Austin: University of Texas.

MTMF
1949. *Mark Twain to Mrs. Fairbanks.* Edited by Dixon Wecter. San Marino, Calif.: Huntington Library.

MTTB
1940. *Mark Twain's Travels with Mr. Brown.* Edited by Franklin Walker and G. Ezra Dane. New York: Alfred A. Knopf.

N&J1
1975. *Mark Twain's Notebooks & Journals, Volume I (1855–1873).* Edited by Frederick Anderson, Michael B. Frank, and Kenneth M. Sanderson. The Mark Twain Papers. Berkeley, Los Angeles, London: University of California Press.

N&J2
1975. *Mark Twain's Notebooks & Journals, Volume II (1877–1883).* Edited by Frederick Anderson, Lin Salamo, and Bernard L. Stein. The Mark Twain Papers. Berkeley, Los Angeles, London: University of California Press.

N&J3
1979. *Mark Twain's Notebooks & Journals, Volume III (1883–1891).* Edited by Robert Pack Browning, Michael B. Frank, and Lin Salamo. The Mark Twain Papers. Berkeley, Los Angeles, London: University of California Press.

NB   Notebook.

NBolS   Marcella Sembrich Memorial Studio, Bolton Landing, New York.

NCAB
1898–1984. *The National Cyclopedia of American Biography.* Vols. 1–62, A–M, and Index. New York: James T. White and Co.

n.d.   No date.

Neville, Amelia Ransome.
    1932.   *The Fantastic City: Memoirs of the Social and Romantic Life of Old San Francisco.* Edited and revised by Virginia Brastow. Boston: Houghton Mifflin Co.

NN-B   Henry W. and Albert A. Berg Collection, The New York Public Library, Astor, Lenox, and Tilden Foundations, New York City.

NNC   Columbia University, New York City.

NNU-F   Fales Collection, New York University, New York City.

NPV   Jean Webster McKinney Family Papers, Francis Fitz Randolph Rare Book Room, Vassar College Library, Poughkeepsie, New York.

Odell, George C. D.
    1927–49.   *Annals of the New York Stage.* 15 vols. New York: Columbia University Press.

OED
    1933.   *The Oxford English Dictionary: Being a Corrected Re-issue, with an Introduction, Supplement, and Bibliography, of A New English Dictionary on Historical Principles.* Edited by James A. H. Murray, Henry Bradley, W. A. Craigie, and C. T. Onions. 13 vols. Oxford: Oxford University Press, Clarendon Press.

    1972–86.   *A Supplement to the Oxford English Dictionary.* Edited by R. W. Burchfield. 4 vols. Oxford: Oxford University Press, Clarendon Press.

OFH   Rutherford B. Hayes Library, Fremont, Ohio.

Ogilvie, Frank B., comp.
    * 1896. *Two Hundred Old-Time Songs.* New York: J. S. Ogilvie Publishing Co.

Owsley, Harry Bryan.
    1890.   "Genealogical Facts of the Owsley Family in England and America from the Time of the 'Restoration' to the Present." Typescript, Daughters of the American Revolution, National Society Library, Washington, D.C.

Parkman, Francis.
    1880.   *The Oregon Trail: Sketches of Prairie and Rocky-Mountain Life.* 7th ed., rev. Boston: Little, Brown, and Co.

    1969.   *The Oregon Trail.* Edited by E. N. Feltskog. Madison: University of Wisconsin Press.

Paxson, Katharine Lampton.
    1974.   "A Cousin's Recollections of Mark Twain." *Twainian* 33 (November–December): 4.

PH   Photocopy.

Phillips, Abner.
    * 1842.   MS of one page, a promissory note, dated 24 January, undertaking to deliver ten barrels of tar to John Marshall Clemens on or before 25 December, or to pay him the value thereof, CU-MARK.

Pilcher, Margaret Campbell.
[1911]. *Historical Sketches of the Campbell, Pilcher and Kindred Families.* Nashville, Tenn.: [Marshall and Bruce Co.].

Portrait
1895. *Portrait and Biographical Record of Marion, Ralls and Pike Counties, with a Few From Macon, Adair, and Lewis Counties, Missouri.* Chicago: C. O. Owen and Co. Citations are to the 1982 revised reprint edition. New London, Mo.: Ralls County Book Co.

Quarles, John A.
1855. Deed of emancipation, recorded on 14 November by George Glenn, clerk. Monroe County Deed Records, Book O, 240, Monroe County Circuit Court, Paris, Missouri.

Rice, Edward Le Roy.
1911. *Monarchs of Minstrelsy, from "Daddy" Rice to Date.* New York: Kenny Publishing Co.

RoBards, John Lewis.
1915. "Mark Twain As a Boy and a Man Who Made the World Laugh." Hannibal *Morning Journal*, 27 June. Clipping in RoBards Scrapbooks, vol. 3.

RoBards Scrapbooks
n.d. Scrapbooks compiled by John Lewis RoBards, 3 vols., Joint Collection, Western Historical Manuscript Collection and the State Historical Society of Missouri Manuscripts, University of Missouri, Columbia.

Routledge, Edmund, ed.
1869. *Every Boy's Book: A Complete Encyclopaedia of Sports and Amusements.* London: George Routledge and Sons.

Rowland, John E.
* 1907. "Londoner Remembers Old Times on the River. John E. Rowland Writes of Early Steamboating on the Mississippi," clipping from unidentified newspaper, enclosed in John B. Downing to SLC, 3 June 1907, CU-MARK.

St. Louis Census
1850. *Population Schedules of the Seventh Census of the United States, 1850. Rolls 414–418. Missouri: City and County of St. Louis.* National Archives Microfilm Publications, microcopy no. 432. Washington, D.C.: General Services Administration.

1860. *Population Schedules of the Eighth Census of the United States, 1860. Rolls 647–656. Missouri: City and County of St. Louis.* National Archives Microfilm Publications, microcopy no. 653. Washington, D.C.: General Services Administration.

1900. *Population Schedules of the Twelfth Census of the United States, 1900. Rolls 889–901. Missouri: City of St. Louis.* National Archives Microfilm Publications, microcopy no. T623. Washington, D.C.: General Services Administration.

S&B

1967.   *Mark Twain's Satires & Burlesques.* Edited by Franklin R. Rogers. The Mark Twain Papers. Berkeley and Los Angeles: University of California Press.

Scharf, J. Thomas.

1883.   *History of Saint Louis City and County, from the Earliest Periods to the Present Day.* 2 vols. Philadelphia: Louis H. Everts and Co.

Selby, P. O., comp.

1973.   *Mark Twain's Kinfolks.* Kirksville, Mo.: Missouriana Library, Northeast Missouri State University.

Shoemaker, Floyd C.

1927.   "A Valuable and Historic Donation as a Memorial to Her Father." *Missouri Historical Review* 21 (January): 254–55.

SLC (Samuel Langhorne Clemens).

1863.   "Letter from Mark Twain." Letter dated 12 December. Virginia City *Territorial Enterprise,* 15 December, clipping in Scrapbook 3:42–43, CU-MARK. Reprinted in *MTEnt,* 95–100.

1865.   "San Francisco Letter." Letter dated 20 December. Virginia City *Territorial Enterprise,* 22 or 23 December, undated clipping in Yale Scrapbook, 47, CtY-BR. Reprinted in part by Smith and Anderson, 80–81.

1867a.   "Letter from 'Mark Twain.'" Letter dated 16 April. San Francisco *Alta California,* 26 May, 1. Reprinted in *MTTB,* 141–48.

1867b.   "Jim Wolf and the Tom-Cats." New York *Sunday Mercury,* 14 July, 3.

1869a.   *The Innocents Abroad; or, The New Pilgrims' Progress.* Hartford: American Publishing Co.

1869b.   "A Day at Niagara." Buffalo *Express,* 21 August, 1–2.

1870a.   Autobiography. MS of thirteen pages, CU-MARK. Published in *AMT,* 22–25, and, with omissions, as "The Tennessee Land" in *MTA,* 1:3–7.

1870b.   "The Noble Red Man." *Galaxy* 10 (September): 426–29.

1872.   *Roughing It.* Hartford: American Publishing Co.

1874.   *The Gilded Age: A Tale of Today.* Charles Dudley Warner, coauthor. Hartford: American Publishing Co.

1875.   "Old Times on the Mississippi." Articles 1–7. *Atlantic Monthly* 35 (January–June): 69–73, 217–24, 283–89, 446–52, 567–74, 721–30; *Atlantic Monthly* 36 (August): 190–96.

1876.   *The Adventures of Tom Sawyer.* Hartford: American Publishing Co. See *ATS.*

1880.   *A Tramp Abroad.* Hartford: American Publishing Co.

1882.   "The Stolen White Elephant." In *The Stolen White Elephant, Etc.,* 7–35. Boston: James R. Osgood and Co.

1883.   *Life on the Mississippi.* Boston: James R. Osgood and Co.

1885a.   *Adventures of Huckleberry Finn.* New York: Charles L. Webster and Co. See *HF.*

1885b.   "The Private History of a Campaign That Failed." *Century Magazine* 31 (December): 193–204.

1891.   "Mental Telegraphy." *Harper's New Monthly Magazine* 84 (December): 95–104.

1892.   *The American Claimant.* New York: Charles L. Webster and Co.

1894.   *The Tragedy of Pudd'nhead Wilson and the Comedy Those Extraordinary Twins.* Hartford: American Publishing Co.

1895a.   "Fenimore Cooper's Literary Offences." *North American Review* 161 (July): 1–12.

1895b.   "Mental Telegraphy Again." *Harper's New Monthly Magazine* 91 (September): 521–24.

1896.   "Tom Sawyer, Detective." *Harper's New Monthly Magazine* 93 (August, September): 344–61, 519–37. See *TSA,* 107–77.

1897a.   *Following the Equator: A Journey Around the World.* Hartford: American Publishing Co.

1897b.   Autobiographical notes. MS of one page beginning "Injun Joe's death . . . ," possibly written in 1897, CU-MARK.

1897c.   Autobiographical notes. MS of one page beginning "Campmeeting . . . ," possibly written in 1897, PH in CU-MARK; location of original is not known.

1897–98.   "My Autobiography. [Random Extracts from it.]" MS of seventy-five pages, CU-MARK. Published, with omissions, as "Early Days" in *MTA,* 1:81–115.

1898a.   "Ralph Keeler." MS of twenty-four pages, CU-MARK. Published in *MTA,* 1:154–64.

1898b.   Autobiographical notes. MS of seven pages beginning "Talk about going . . . ," probably written in 1898, CU-MARK.

1900.   "Selections from My Autobiography." TS of nineteen pages, with Clemens's holograph revisions, CU-MARK. Published as "Playing 'Bear'—Herrings—Jim Wolf and the Cats" in *MTA,* 1:125–43.

1902.   "Huck." MS of one page, probably written in 1902, CU-MARK.

1903.   "Something about Doctors." MS of fourteen pages (title supplied by Albert Bigelow Paine), CU-MARK.

1938.   *Mark Twain's Letter to William Bowen, Buffalo, February Sixth, 1870.* Prefatory note by Clara Clemens Gabrilowitsch, foreword by Albert W. Gunnison. San Francisco: Book Club of California.

Smith, Hedrick.
* 1889.   "He Returns, after Thirty-Eight Years to His First Love. Hedrick Smith Talks about Hannibal and Touches upon Things That Were Once Familiar," clipping from the Hannibal *Journal* of unknown date, enclosed in Benton Coontz to SLC, 18 Apr 89, CU-MARK.

Smith, Henry Nash, and Frederick Anderson, eds.
  1957.   *Mark Twain: San Francisco Correspondent*. San Francisco: Book Club of California.

Stone, H. N., D. M. Davidson, and W. R. McIntosh.
  1885.   *Stone, Davidson & Co.'s Hannibal City Directory*. Hannibal: Stone, Davidson and Co.

Stowe, Lyman Beecher.
  1934.   *Saints, Sinners, and Beechers*. Indianapolis: Bobbs-Merrill Co.

Sweets, Henry H., III.
  1983.   "Joe Harper Drawn from Childhood Playmate." *The Fence Painter* 3 (Summer): 1–2.

  1984.   *The Hannibal, Missouri Presbyterian Church: A Sesquicentennial History*. Hannibal: Presbyterian Church of Hannibal.

  1986–87.   "Norval 'Gull' Brady Clemens Boyhood Friend." *The Fence Painter* 6 (Winter): 1.

Tompkins, Christopher, and Joseph Eve.
  * 1822.   MS of one page, the license granted John Marshall Clemens to practice law in Kentucky, signed on 29 October by two "Judges empowered by law to grant licences," CU-MARK.

Trexler, Harrison Anthony.
  1914.   *Slavery in Missouri, 1804–1865*. Baltimore: Johns Hopkins Press.

TS   Typescript.

TS
  1980.   *The Adventures of Tom Sawyer; Tom Sawyer Abroad; Tom Sawyer, Detective*. Edited by John C. Gerber, Paul Baender, and Terry Firkins. The Works of Mark Twain. Berkeley, Los Angeles, London: University of California Press. Texts reissued, with corrections and the original illustrations, in *ATS* and *TSA*.

TSA
  1982.   *Tom Sawyer Abroad; Tom Sawyer, Detective*. Foreword and notes by John C. Gerber, text established by Terry Firkins. Mark Twain Library. Berkeley, Los Angeles, London: University of California Press.

Tucker, Ephraim.
  1895.   *Genealogy of the Tucker Family*. Worcester, Mass.

Tuolumne Census
  1850.   *Population Schedules of the Seventh Census of the United States, 1850. Roll 36. California: Solano, Sonoma, Sutter, Trinity, Tuolumne, Yolo, and Yuba Counties*. National Archives Microfilm Publications, microcopy no. 432. Washington, D.C.: General Services Administration.

Turner, Arlin.
  1955.   "James Lampton, Mark Twain's Model for Colonel Sellers." *Modern Language Notes* 70 (December): 592–94.

TxU   Harry Ransom Humanities Research Center, University of Texas, Austin.

Varble, Rachel M.
1964.   *Jane Clemens: The Story of Mark Twain's Mother.* Garden City, N.Y.: Doubleday and Co.

ViU   Clifton Waller Barrett Library, Alderman Library, University of Virginia, Charlottesville.

Watts, Isaac.
1802.   *Hymns and Spiritual Songs.* Brookfield, Mass.: E. Merriam and Co.

Way, Frederick, Jr.
1983.   *Way's Packet Directory, 1848–1983.* Athens: Ohio University.

Webster, Annie Moffett.
n.d.   Reminiscence. MS of seven pages beginning "My Grandmother loved . . . ," NPV.

1918.   "Family Chronicle Written for Jean Webster McKinney by Her Grandmother." TS of forty-four pages, 26 October, NPV.

Wecter, Dixon.
[1950].   Handwritten notes made on a typed transcription of "Villagers of 1840–3," CU-MARK.

1952.   *Sam Clemens of Hannibal.* Boston: Houghton Mifflin Co., Riverside Press.

Weiss, Harry B., and Howard R. Kemble.
1967.   *The Great American Water-Cure Craze: A History of Hydropathy in the United States.* Trenton, N.J.: Past Times Press.

Welsh, Donald H.
1962.   "Sam Clemens' Hannibal, 1836–1838." *Midcontinent American Studies Journal* 3 (Spring): 28–43. The article actually covers the years 1846–48.

Wharton, Henry M.
1902.   "The Boyhood Home of Mark Twain." *Century Magazine* 64 (September): 674–77.

Wittke, Carl.
1930.   *Tambo and Bones: A History of the American Minstrel Stage.* Durham, N.C.: Duke University Press.

Wood, George B., and Franklin Bache.
1883.   *The Dispensatory of the United States of America.* 15th rev. ed. Philadelphia: J. B. Lippincott and Co.

Woodruff, Mrs. Howard W., comp.
1969.   "The Marriage Records of Ralls County, Missouri: Books 'A' and 'B,' 1821–1866." 7231 Sycamore, Kansas City, Mo.: Mrs. Howard W. Woodruff. Mimeograph.

Wright, George Frederick, ed.
1880.   *History of Sacramento County, California.* Oakland, Calif.: Thompson and West.

Note on the Text

The basic goal of this volume has been to collect the best of what Mark Twain wrote—but did not publish—about the Matter of Hannibal. That goal has occasioned some departure from the usual pattern of the Mark Twain Library. For the first time, texts have been reprinted from four separate volumes in the scholarly edition (The Mark Twain Papers and Works of Mark Twain), each prepared by a different editor, at various intervals between 1967 and 1980. It was therefore all but inevitable that these texts would require a relatively large number of corrections and adjustments. And, since much of the interest in these selections lay in their relation to the historical and biographical facts, a "sparingly annotated" reprint could scarcely justify itself, let alone satisfy the universal curiosity about that relation. Too much has been learned even in the last five years about the factual basis of Mark Twain's fiction to warrant a simple sifting of the original annotation. The editors have therefore corrected the texts wherever possible, and have included an extensive correction and enrichment of the editorial commentary first published with these several selections in The Mark Twain Papers and Works of Mark Twain.

Except for the first two selections, "Boy's Manuscript" and "Letter to William Bowen," all have been reprinted here from their typesetting in the scholarly edition—not necessarily page for page, but virtually without resetting. Where piecemeal re-setting has nevertheless been required, and where typesetting was necessarily *de novo* (as it was for the first two selections, and of course for all editorial commentary), the type has been proofread in accord with the standards of the Modern Language Association's Committee on Scholarly Editions (CSE). Whether or not any part of a selection was reset, it was carefully re-compared with the manuscript or documents on which it is based. Changes in the original typesetting have been made in order to accommodate new historical or manuscript evidence, correct errors of transcription, apply the original editorial policy more consistently, or simply to eliminate needless intrusions, such as editorial footnotes on the text page. All changes to the texts, however slight, are listed here: the reading now adopted appears to the *left* of the bullet • the reading being changed appears to the *right* of it.

Boy's Manuscript (1–19). Reprinted and emended here is the "Reading Text" published in Supplement A of *TS*, 420–35, edited by John C. Gerber and Paul Baender. MS in CU-MARK. That printing has been reset throughout, partly to make a few corrections, but chiefly to conform with the typeface used for all the other selections.

1 *title*	*Boy's Manuscript* • [*not in*]		7.29	*that's* • *that's*
1.1	[*two . . . missing*] • [*not in*]		12.4	that 'll • that'll
1.18	APPLES • APPLES		14.28	home, • home
2.32	heart, • heart		15.6	Giant-Killer • Giant Killer
5.26	*some thing* • *something*		15.15	knucks • Knucks
6.9	said: "Thanks • said:—"Thanks		17.24	baste • haste
7.7	way. But • way.—But		18.18	spool cannon • spool-cannon
7.15	*No!* • *No!*		18.27	it • [*not in*]

Letter to William Bowen (20–23). This letter has not yet been published in the Mark Twain Papers series, where it will appear in *Mark Twain's Letters, Volume 3, 1869–1870*, accompanied by a complete textual commentary. The text has been established from photographs and direct inspection of pages 1–8 and 13–14 of the original manuscript at the University of Texas (TxU). For manuscript pages 9–12 ("unto . . . father-in-law," 22.2–32), which are lost, the source of the text is necessarily SLC 1938, 8–10, and a TS at the Mark Twain Memorial (CtHMTH), each of which derives independently from a (now lost) transcript of the complete MS prepared in 1887 by William Bowen. In addition, because the manuscript was written in a violet ink, now faded, we have drawn on SLC 1938 and the TS, as well as a third transcript (prepared from the MS, minus pages 9–12), all of which were made when the MS was somewhat more legible than it is now. Authorial deletions are represented with a slash or a horizontal rule through the type; insertions are enclosed by carets. Authorial errors are not corrected, so long as they can be intelligibly transcribed. A complete record of all emendation is on deposit with, and available upon request from, the Mark Twain Project, 480 Library, University of California, Berkeley, 94720.

Tupperville-Dobbsville (24–26). Reprinted and emended here is the text published in *HH&T*, 55–57, edited by Walter Blair. MS in CU-MARK.

25.30   use. The • use.—The

Clairvoyant (27–32). Reprinted but not emended here is the text published in *HH&T*, 61–66, edited by Walter Blair. MS in CU-MARK.

Huck Finn and Tom Sawyer among the Indians (33–81). Reprinted and emended here is the text published in *HH&T*, 92–140, edited by Walter Blair. It has been recompared with photocopy of the manuscript, which is housed chiefly at the Detroit Public Library (MiD), although random pages are also owned by CtHMTH, KyLoU, CLjC, NNU-F, and NBolS. Where pages are missing from the manuscript, the omissions are necessarily supplied from galley proof of type which the author had set on the Paige typesetter directly from his manuscript when it was still intact (CU-MARK). Seven additional pages of the manuscript have been found since *HH&T*

appeared in 1969, and they provide a handful of corrections to a portion of the text previously based on galley proof.

33.13	Polly • Sally		75.17	Never • Ne'er
37.21	*Injuns* • Injuns		75.17	a cloud • clouds
39.23	while • a while		75.25	*wall* • wall
59.4	to • to do		76.26	Injun. Water-spouts • Injun.—
61.14	Injuns • Indians			Water-spouts
62.9	awhile • a while		78.13	*general* • general
62.28	had got • has got		79.33	noddle • noodle
67.36	dark, • [*damaged comma*]		80.1	woman • woman's
73.5	come! . . . by! • come . . . by!!		80.2	maybe • may be

Jane Lampton Clemens (82–92). Reprinted but not emended here is the text published in *HH&T*, 43–53, edited by Walter Blair. MS in CU-MARK.

Villagers of 1840–3 (93–108). Reprinted and emended here are the text published in *HH&T*, 28–40, edited by Walter Blair, and (as part of "The Hellfire Hotchkiss Sequence") the text published in *S&B*, 200–203, edited by Franklin R. Rogers. MSS in CU-MARK. Separately published in *HH&T* and *S&B*, they are here published together for the first time as Mark Twain wrote them (the pieces join at 105.21). For further explanation of the original confusion, see pages 279–80.

93.1	[¶] Judge • [*no* ¶] JUDGE		99.30	*melodies* • *Melodies*
93.2	Judge • *Judge*		100.1	Alfarata • Alforata
94.35–36	merchants. This • merchants.—This		100.19	exigeant • exigent
			102.34	stillhouse • still house
95.2	Married - - - - - - - • Married-----		104.32	school • School
			105.21	water, • water;
95.26	Married - - - - - • Married - - - -		105.21–108.12	trying to . . . tongue. • trying
95.33	- - - - - *Striker* • - - - - *Striker*			
97.26	Miss - - - - - - • Miss - - - - -		106.1	jugfull • jugful
98.16	J—s • J--s		106.1	dipperfull; you • dipperful. You
99.20	[Cloak • Cloak		106.2	ANYthing • *any*thing
99.25	knights • Knights		106.22	despondences • despondencies
99.29	Alfarata • Alforata		106.30	irresistably • irresistibly

Hellfire Hotchkiss (109–33). Reprinted and emended here is the text published in *S&B*, 175–203, edited by Franklin R. Rogers. MS in CU-MARK. The alternate passage originally following "you.'" (118.25) has been omitted, and the portion mistakenly included from "Villagers of 1840–3" has been moved to its proper place at the end of that selection (105.21–108.12). The editorial footnotes and the footnote superscript numbers interpolated in the *S&B* text have been silently omitted. Since *S&B* was not approved by the Center for Editions of American Authors (CEAA), predecessor to the CSE, the text of this selection has been re-edited, complete textual records prepared for it, and inspected by the CSE. The record of Mark Twain's alterations in his MS is too long to publish here, but it is available upon request from the

Mark Twain Project. Except that ampersands (&) have been silently amended to "and," the following list records all editorial emendations of the MS, the unaltered reading of which appears to the right of the bullet.

109 *title*	*Hellfire Hotchkiss*	Chapter 1 • Hellfire Hotchkiss, or Sugar-Rag ditto
110.18	pure • Pure
111.34	enthusiasms • enthusiams
112.3	Campbellite • Cambellite
113.23	the • the/this
113.27–28	slave-|holding • slave-holding
118 *title*	2 • [*not in*]
118.28	t'other • 'tother
122.18	idea • ida
122.27	somebody • Somebody

122.28–29	bosom. Uncle • bosom.— |Uncle
122.34–35	down-|stream • downstream
124.15	it's • its
124 *title*	3 • [*not in*]
127.33	she • She [*also at 128.21 and 129.8*]
130.7	twenty-one • twenty one
131.22	it all • it it all
132.17	people • People
133.11	be the • the
133.13	be • we

Tom Sawyer's Conspiracy (134–213). Reprinted and emended here is the text published in *HH&T*, 163–242, edited by Walter Blair. MS in CU-MARK.

135.20	go; • go,
136.5	that 'll • that'll
138.22	What 's • What's
138.31	lookyhere • looky here
138.35	that 'll • that'll
140.34	what's • What's
142.6	that 'll • that'll
144.3	Lookyhere • Looky here
145.28	that 'll • that'll
160.36	EDITOR. • EDITOR. [Mark Twain's own footnote.]
161.16–25	COMPOSITION . . . Printer • [*altered to follow Mark Twain's instructions in the MS*]
165.22	absent minded • absent-minded

168.23	Shoul---*der* . . . for----*word* • Shoul---*der* . . . for----*word*
174.10	look • looked
174.20	this 'll • this'll
176.33	you • You
177.9	what • What
177.16	what • What
179.36	trail, • [*damaged comma*]
184.34	what • What
185.4	you • You
186.18	want's, • want's
189.29	wasn't • was not
190.27	his • [*not in*]
198.16	a going • agoing

Schoolhouse Hill (214–59). Reprinted and emended here is the text published in *MSM*, 175–220, edited by William M. Gibson. MS in CU-MARK.

230.36	days • days [MT's note]
235.26	feelins • feelin's
237.29	schoolm'am • school m'am
238.29	kept. As • kept. [¶]As
241.22	came, • came
241.28	Oliver 'll • Oliver'll

242.5	said • said, in words broken by sobs
252.23	[*centered rule*] • [*not in*]
253.10	week?— Ah • week?—Ah
255.36	enterprize • enterprise
258.16	what • What
259.14	go • Go

Huck Finn (260–61). Reprinted and emended here is the text published in *HH&T*, 143–44, edited by Walter Blair. MS in CU-MARK.

260 *title   Huck Finn • Doughface*

Bernard L. Stein, a former associate editor with the Mark Twain Project, was the first to suggest reprinting these several Hannibal writings together, for which he has our—and we trust the reader's—thanks. On behalf of the CSE, Kay Seymour House inspected the printer's copy for this reprinting, as well as the textual apparatus prepared for "Letter to William Bowen" and "Hellfire Hotchkiss" but not published here. Our thanks to her for this careful, conscientious, and always helpful scrutiny. Thanks are also due to Sam Howard, who uncovered the editorial confusion over the ending of "Villagers of 1840–3" (now corrected), and unhesitatingly shared his discovery with the editors. Special thanks are likewise due to Michael B. Frank, an associate editor with the Mark Twain Project, whose discerning and meticulous review of the printer's copy contributed materially to the annotation. The editors are also grateful to: Coralee Paull, whose research at the Missouri Historical Society, St. Louis, made a number of important contributions to the Biographical Directory; Henry H. Sweets III, curator of the Mark Twain Museum, Hannibal; Roberta Hagood, also of Hannibal; Jerry P. Sampson, recorder of deeds for the Marion County Circuit Court, Palmyra, Missouri; Ralph Gregory, former curator of the Mark Twain Birthplace Shrine, Florida, Missouri, and of the Mark Twain Museum, Hannibal; and four editorial assistants in the Mark Twain Project, David J. Goodwin, Janice E. Braun, Daniel J. Widawsky, and Craig Stein. Fran Mitchell, our production coordinator at the University of California Press, and Wilsted & Taylor Publishing Services, Oakland, California, were again unfailingly patient and helpful with every aspect of the technical production for this volume. Editorial costs were met jointly by the Research Materials Program of the National Endowment for the Humanities, an independent federal agency, and the William Randolph Hearst Foundation.

Robert H. Hirst
June 1988   *General Editor, Mark Twain Project*